W9-ALU-600

Magnolia Wednesdays

"[Wax] writes with breezy wit and keen insight into family relations." —*The Atlanta Journal-Constitution*

"An honest, realistic story of family, love, and priorities, with genuine characters." —*Booklist*

"Bittersweet . . . Vivien [is] an easy protagonist to love; she's plucky, resourceful, and witty." —*Publishers Weekly*

"Atlanta-based novelist Wendy Wax spins yet another captivating tale of life and love in this wonderfully entertaining book." —*Southern Seasons Magazine*

"A winner—brilliant with acerbic, biting wit . . . Sweet and satisfying without ever losing that acidic edge—I loved this book and will be looking for more by this author." —*Night Owl Reviews*

"I loved how Vivi grew . . . [other] characters were great as well . . . And there was a twist with Vivi's brother-in-law's death that I didn't see coming at all . . . This was a heartwarming story and one that I truly enjoyed." —*So Many Books, So Little Time*

"I love a good girly book set in the South . . . *Magnolia Wednesdays* is a funny yet poignant novel that will take the reader into the wilds of Suburbia Atlanta . . . heartwarming . . . a wonderful way to spend an afternoon." —*Charlotte's Web of Books*

"The book is full of fun and surprises . . . If you want to get a good night's sleep, don't start reading this book, because you won't be able to put it down . . . Thrilling all the way to the end." —*Petit Fours and Hot Tamales*

continued . . .

The Accidental Bestseller

Magnolia
WEDNESDAYS

Wendy Wax

JOVE BOOKS, NEW YORK

THE BERKLEY PUBLISHING GROUP
Published by the Penguin Group
Penguin Group (USA) Inc.
375 Hudson Street, New York, New York 10014, USA
Penguin Group (Canada), 90 Eglinton Avenue East, Suite 700, Toronto, Ontario M4P 2Y3, Canada
(a division of Pearson Penguin Canada Inc.)
Penguin Books Ltd., 80 Strand, London WC2R 0RL, England
Penguin Group Ireland, 25 St. Stephen's Green, Dublin 2, Ireland (a division of Penguin Books Ltd.)
Penguin Group (Australia), 250 Camberwell Road, Camberwell, Victoria 3124, Australia
(a division of Pearson Australia Group Pty. Ltd.)
Penguin Books India Pvt. Ltd., 11 Community Centre, Panchsheel Park, New Delhi—110 017, India
Penguin Group (NZ), 67 Apollo Drive, Rosedale, Auckland 0632, New Zealand
(a division of Pearson New Zealand Ltd.)
Penguin Books (South Africa) (Pty.) Ltd., 24 Sturdee Avenue, Rosebank, Johannesburg 2196, South Africa

Penguin Books Ltd., Registered Offices: 80 Strand, London WC2R 0RL, England

This is a work of fiction. Names, characters, places, and incidents either are the product of the author's imagination or are used fictitiously, and any resemblance to actual persons, living or dead, business establishments, events, or locales is entirely coincidental. The publisher does not have control over and does not have any responsibility for author or third-party websites or their content.

MAGNOLIA WEDNESDAYS

A Jove Book / published by arrangement with the author

PRINTING HISTORY
Berkley trade edition / March 2010
Jove mass-market edition / May 2011

ISBN: 978-0-515-14984-5

JOVE®
Jove Books are published by The Berkley Publishing Group,
a division of Penguin Group (USA) Inc.,
375 Hudson Street, New York, New York 10014.
JOVE® is a registered trademark of Penguin Group (USA) Inc.
The "J" design is a trademark of Penguin Group (USA) Inc.

PRINTED IN THE UNITED STATES OF AMERICA

10 9 8 7 6 5 4 3 2

ACKNOWLEDGMENTS

It would be nice if a book sprang completely out of the imagination fully formed with all the pertinent details in place. I keep waiting for this to happen, but each time there are countless things that need to be identified and understood to make characters and their environments feel real. The Internet is a great place to start, but for me there's nothing like a live person willing to talk about what they do and know.

This time out, I'd like to thank Phyllis DeNeve, owner of Atlanta Dance, and her instructors, especially Vonnie Marie Heard, for introducing me to ballroom dance and for allowing me to observe belly dance. It took me a while to realize I was better off watching than participating. Eight years of ballet should have made me a lot more graceful than I am!

Thanks, too, to Marcia Kublanow and Rita Silverman for sharing their knowledge of New York City and for helping me find a place for Vivien to live. And to Trish Coughlin Higgins for bringing Stone Seymour, senior international correspondent, to life. I also want to thank

Rebecca Ritchie, interior designer, who is not only talented but knows how almost everything works, for her input on the interiors of Magnolia Hall and Melanie's Magnolia Ballroom.

I owe a big thank-you to Chief J. C. Mosier, precinct one constables' office, Harris County, Texas, for giving me the information I needed in a way I could understand.

And as always I'm grateful to Karen White, unflagging critique partner and friend, for not allowing me to settle for "the things in the box." I'm glad we're on this road together.

1

WELL-BRED GIRLS FROM good southern families are not supposed to get shot.

Vivien Armstrong Gray's mother had never come out and actually told her this, but Vivi had no doubt it belonged on the long list of unwritten yet critically important rules of conduct on which she'd been raised. Dictates like "Always address older women and men as ma'am and sir" and "Never ask directly for what you want if you can get it with charm, manners, or your family name." And one of Vivien's personal favorites, "Although it's perfectly fine to visit New York City on occasion in order to shop, see shows and ballets, or visit a museum, there's really no good reason to live there."

Vivien had managed to break all of those rules and quite a few others over the past forty-one years, the last fifteen of which she'd spent as an investigative reporter in that most Yankee of cities.

The night her life fell apart Vivi wasn't thinking about rules or decorum or anything much but getting the footage she needed to break a story on oil speculation and price manipulation that she'd been working on for months.

It was ten P.M. on a muggy September night when Vivien pressed herself into a doorway in a darkened corner of a Wall Street parking garage a few feet away from where a source had told her an FBI financial agent posing as a large institutional investor was going to pay off a debt-ridden commodities trader.

Crouched beside her cameraman, Marty Phelps, in the heat-soaked semidarkness, Vivien tried to ignore the flu symptoms she'd been battling all week. Eager to finally document the first in a string of long-awaited arrests, she'd just noted the time—ten fifteen P.M.—when a bullet sailed past her cheek with the force of a pointy-tipped locomotive. The part of her brain that didn't freeze up in shock realized that the bullet had come from the wrong direction.

Marty swore, but she couldn't tell if it was in pain or surprise, and his video camera clattered onto the concrete floor. Loudly. Too loudly.

Two pings followed, shattering one of the overhead lights that had illuminated the area.

Heart pounding, Vivien willed her eyes to adjust to the deeper darkness, but she couldn't see Marty, or his camera, or who was shooting at them. Before she could think what to do, more bullets buzzed by like a swarm of mosquitoes after bare flesh at a barbecue. They ricocheted off concrete, pinged off steel and metal just like they do in the movies and on TV. Except that these bullets were real, and it occurred to her then that if one of them found her, she might actually die.

Afraid to move out of the doorway in which she cowered, Vivien turned and hugged the hard metal of the door. One hand reached down to test the locked knob as she pressed her face against its pockmarked surface, sucking in everything that could be sucked, trying to become one with the door, trying to become too flat, too thin, too "not there" for a bullet to find her.

Her life did not pass before her eyes. There was no highlight reel—maybe when you were over forty a full viewing would take too long?—no snippets, no "best of Vivi," no "worst of," either, which would have taken more time.

What there was was a vague sense of regret that settled over her like a shroud, making Vivi wish deeply, urgently, that she'd done better, been more. Maybes and should-haves consumed her; little bursts of clarity that seized her and shook her up and down, back and forth like a pit bull with a rag doll clenched between its teeth.

Maybe she *should* have listened to her parents. Maybe she *would* have been happier, more fulfilled, if she hadn't rebelled so completely, hadn't done that exposé on that Democratic senator who was her father's best friend and political ally, hadn't always put work before everything else. If she'd stayed home in Atlanta. Gotten married. Raised children like her younger sister, Melanie. Or gone into family politics like her older brother, Hamilton.

If regret and dismay had been bulletproof, Vivien might have walked away unscathed. But as it turned out, would've's, should've's, and could've's were nowhere near as potent as Kevlar. The next thing Vivien knew, her regret was pierced by the sharp slap of a bullet entering her body, sucking the air straight out of her lungs and sending her crumpling to the ground.

Facedown on the concrete, grit filling her mouth, Vivien tried to absorb what had happened and what might happen next as a final hail of bullets flew above her head. Then something metal hit the ground followed by the thud of what she was afraid might be a body.

Her eyes squinched tightly shut, she tried to marshal

her thoughts, but they skittered through her brain at random and of their own accord. At first she was aware only of a general ache. Then a sharper, clearer pain drew her attention. With what clarity her befuddled brain could cling to, she realized that the bullet had struck the only body part that hadn't fit all the way into the doorway. Modesty and good breeding should have prohibited her from naming that body part, but a decade and a half in New York City compelled her to acknowledge that the bullet was lodged in the part that she usually sat on. The part on which the sun does not shine. The part that irate cab drivers and construction workers, who can't understand why a woman is not flattered by their attentions, are always shouting for that woman to kiss.

Despite the pain and the darkness into which her brain seemed determined to retreat, Vivi almost smiled at the thought.

There were shouts and the pounding of feet. The concrete shook beneath her, but she didn't have the mental capacity or the energy to worry about it. The sound of approaching sirens pierced the darkness—and her own personal fog—briefly. And then there was nothing.

Which at least protected her from knowing that Marty's camera was rolling when it fell. That it had somehow captured everything that happened to her—from the moment she tried to become one with the door to the moment she shrieked and grabbed her butt to the moment they found her and loaded her facedown onto the stretcher, her derriere pointing upward at the concrete roof above.

Vivien spent the night in the hospital apparently so that everyone in possession of a medical degree—or aspirations to one—could examine her rear end. The pain pills muted the pain in her posterior to a dull throb, but there didn't seem to be any medication that could eliminate her embarrassment.

When she woke up the next morning, exhausted and irritated from trying to sleep on her side as well as round-the-clock butt checks, she found a bouquet of butt-shaped balloons from the network news division sitting on her nightstand. A bouquet of flowers arranged in a butt-shaped vase sat beside it. No wonder there was a trade deficit. We seemed to be importing endless versions of buttocks.

Making the mistake of flipping on the television, she was forced to watch a replay of last night's shooting—the only footage in what they called a sting gone awry was of her—and discovered that she was one of the last human beings on the face of the earth to see it. Everyone from the morning anchors at her own network to the hosts of the other networks' morning talk shows seemed to be having a big yuck over it.

If she'd been one for dictates and rules, she would have added, "If a well-bred girl from a good southern family slips up and *does* somehow get shot, she should make sure the wound is fatal and not just humiliating."

If she'd died in that parking garage, they would have been hailing Vivi as a hero and replaying some of her best investigative moments. Instead she was a laughingstock.

Vivien swallowed back her indignation along with the contents of her stomach, which kept threatening to escape. She desperately wanted to take her rear end and go home where both of them could get some privacy.

The phone rang. She ignored it.

It was almost noon when Marty strolled into the room. He was tall and lanky with straight brown hair he was always pushing out of his eyes and a long pale face domi-nated by a beak of a nose. She always pictured him rolling

AV equipment into a high school classroom or caressing computer keys with his long, surprisingly delicate fingers. He was a gifted photojournalist and over the last ten years had demonstrated that he would follow her anywhere to get a story and could shoot video under the most trying circumstances as he had, unfortunately, proven yet again last night.

Marty looked relaxed and well rested. But then, he hadn't taken a bullet in his butt last night. Or had people prodding and laughing at him since.

"You don't look so good," he said by way of greeting.

"You're kidding?" Vivien feigned chagrin. "And here I thought I was all bright-eyed and bushy-tailed and ready for my close-up."

He dropped down onto the bedside chair, and she envied the fact that he could sit without discomfort or forethought. If he noted the jealousy that must have flared in her eyes, he didn't comment.

"If you've brought anything shaped like a butt or with a picture of a butt on it, or are even remotely considering using the word 'butt' in this conversation, you might as well leave now," she said.

"My, my, you certainly are touchy this morning."

"Touchy?" She snorted. "You don't know the half of it."

They regarded each other for a moment while Vivien wondered if she could talk him into breaking her out of here.

"Your mother called me on my cell this morning," Marty said. "I heard from Stone, too."

About five years ago her mother, noting that Vivien had had a longer relationship with her cameraman than she'd ever had with anyone she dated and frustrated at the slowness of Vivien's responses, had started using Marty as a middleman. Stone Seymour, who actually was her boyfriend, or, as he liked to call himself, Vivien's main squeeze, used Marty to reach her, too, especially when he was on assignment in some war-smudged part of the globe from which communication was difficult and sporadic and Vivien had forgotten to clear her voice-mail box or plug in her phone.

"How in the world did he hear about this already?" Stone was CIN's senior international correspondent and the network's terrorist expert, which meant he spent great blocks of time in places so remote that even the latest technology was rendered useless.

"He was doing live shots from outside Kabul early this morning and one of the New York producers told him. And, um, I think he might have seen the, um, video on . . ." There was a long, drawn-out bobbing of his Adam's apple. ". . . Um, YouTube."

Her gaze moved from Marty's throat to his face, which was strangely flushed. "Did you say YouTube?"

Marty shifted uncomfortably in his chair, his long frame clearly too large for the piece of furniture just like his Adam's apple seemed too large for his throat. He looked away.

"What does YouTube have to do with me?"

Marty met her gaze, swallowed slowly and painfully again. "I hit my head when I fell and missed most of what happened after that."

She waited. As an investigative reporter, silence had always been one of her best weapons.

"But apparently the target sensed something was up from the beginning. When the undercover guy approached him to complete the transaction, he got nervous and pulled out a gun. I never expected a commodities trader to show up armed. Isn't white-collar crime supposed to be nonviolent?

"Anyway, he must have been really nervous, because

the agent said the guy's hand was shaking so badly they're not even sure whether the first shot was intentional. That was the bullet that came between us and made me drop my camera."

"So how'd I get shot? What were all the rest of those bullets?"

"It just got out of control. Somebody on the FBI's side fired back—some rookie, it looks like—and then it was the shoot-out at the O.K. Corral. I don't think they even realized we were there. I sure would like to know why your contact kept that tidbit to himself."

It was Vivi's turn to look away and for her Adam's apple to feel too big for her throat. She hadn't actually notified her contact that they'd planned to be there. She'd thought they'd get better footage if no one was mugging for the camera. And she hadn't expected the commodities trader to have a gun, either.

"The target is dead," Marty continued. "And there's going to be an internal investigation. It was a real screwup. And, um, strangely enough when I dropped my camera it got wedged up against a tire, rolling. And, um, trained on you. I mean what are the odds of that happening? It's actually kind of funny, really." His voice trailed off when he saw her face. "In a bizarre sort of way."

"Yeah," Vivien said. "It's hysterical."

"So anyway, while I was out cold the FBI took my camera and watched the video to see if it would provide any clues as to what went down, who was at fault. But, um, unfortunately the only thing on the tape was . . . you."

"And?"

"And someone made a copy. And, um, posted it on YouTube."

Vivien stared at him in silence, not intentionally this time, but because she couldn't help it.

"It's been extremely popular. Phenomenally so. I think

you've already had fifty thousand views in less than twenty-four hours. You've got four and a half stars."

Now Vivien's life flashed before her eyes. In Technicolor and 3-D. She watched it in painful slo-mo. Those first years in New York, alone and friendless, a southern-fried fish out of water in a sea of self-assured northern sharks.

Then came the long grueling years spent building credibility, honing her interview techniques, building her contact base, developing her research skills. Not to mention the endless hours spent smothering her southern accent, mercilessly shortening and clipping those lazy vowels and drawn-out syllables so that she could have been from anywhere, or nowhere, under the equally merciless tutelage of New York's most expensive voice coach.

The years of working twice as hard as any man around her. Of always putting the job, the story, the next break before anything else. Before family, before friends, before lovers. She had worked with single-minded determination until the name Vivien Gray became synonymous with "inside scoop."

All of it ground to dust by a ten-minute video of her butt.

Scooting on her side, she managed to swing her legs off the bed and lower her feet to the floor and ultimately to stand. Marty jumped up from his chair, concerned. "What are you doing? Are you allowed to get out of bed?"

"I don't know and I don't care. They've poked and prodded me since I got here. And when they weren't poking or prodding they were laughing. Or trying not to. One of the doctors actually told me I should have 'turned the other cheek.'"

A snort of amusement escaped Marty's lips, and she shot him a withering look. "Don't you dare laugh. Don't you dare!"

Wincing with each step, she carried her clothes into the

bathroom and removed the hospital gown. Her body was bruised and battered. Her underwear and jeans had holes laced with blood where the bullet had passed through. Vivien pushed back the nausea she felt at the remembered feel of steel slamming into her flesh. Gingerly she stepped into the jeans, careful not to dislodge the dressing on her wound as she pulled them up, then tossed the underwear into the trash can.

She was about to slip an arm into the shirt she'd been wearing the night before when she noticed that it, too, had a hole in the same spot. Holding it up in front of her, she opened the bathroom door and reached out a bare arm. "Give me the T-shirt you have on under your long sleeves." She held her hand out until she felt the cotton cross her palm, then pulled it on over her head and down over her rear end.

As she walked back into the hospital room ready to bully Marty into helping her slip out of the hospital and into a cab, it occurred to her that the well-bred southern girls' code of conduct might be in need of an addendum. Because surely if such a girl should have the bad taste to not only get shot but *survive*, she'd better make damned sure her abject humiliation wasn't captured on camera, aired on national television, or uploaded to YouTube.

2

THE CAB DEPOSITED them in front of Vivien's apartment building on West 68th on New York's Upper West Side around two P.M. after a quick stop at Duane Reade for salve and bandages and a liter of ginger ale that she hoped would settle her stomach. Telling the cab driver to wait, Marty carried her butt planter and the drugstore bag past the day doorman, Ralph, through the lobby, and up in the elevator to her apartment on the twenty-fifth floor. Inside, he set her things on the kitchen counter and turned to face her.

"Are you sure you'll be okay?"

"Well, you can stay and dress my wound for me, if you want."

"Oh, um, sure." Marty's Adam's apple did its thing. He pushed a hank of hair out of his eyes. "If you need me to, I can . . ."

"Just yanking your chain." She went up on tiptoe and gave him a kiss on his cheek. "Thanks for coming to get me. I'm going to take it easy today, but I'll probably be in the office tomorrow. I need to salvage something from this story, though I don't know what at this point."

He paused at the door. "What do you want me to tell your mother?"

"Nothing. She is *not* your responsibility."

He shrugged, unwilling to admit that he couldn't say no to Caroline Baxter Gray, former debutante and emotional steamroller, who'd pursued his cooperation as relentlessly as she'd ever campaigned for her husband's political career.

"Just tell her I'll call her later."

He gave her a look.

"And I will. I will call her in a little bit." When she had the strength. When she didn't feel quite so . . . vulnerable. When she didn't feel like she needed to throw up.

"Okay." It was clear he didn't believe her, but there was really nothing he could do about it. He'd never been able to refuse her, either. *Not* that she was like her mother, who believed the Gray political dynasty was similar to the Kennedys'—if, Vivien thought, the Kennedys had southern drawls and a penchant for pig pulls. "Call me if you need me."

"Thanks." She walked him to the door and locked it behind him, more relieved than she'd ever admit to be home. The apartment, a corner unit in a prewar brick building, was small even by New York standards. One bedroom, one bath, and a combination galley kitchen, dining room, and living room squeezed into six hundred fifty square feet. But the location just north of Lincoln Center was incredibly convenient, and her unit had large windows facing both north and east. She'd bought it ten years ago when her salary had taken its first big hike upward and in the ensuing years had refinished the original oak floors, gutted and redone the tiny bathroom, doing the same to the kitchen several years later. And in between she'd had built-ins built in everywhere humanly possible.

Vivi loved its compactness, felt safe in her hidey-hole when she pulled the door shut behind her at night. The windows made it light and airy but forced the central air to work overtime to try to combat the heat and humidity that smote the city during the summer's final hurrah.

Her mother had compared it unfavorably to a hamster's cage and declared it could fit inside their master bathroom back at Magnolia Hall in Atlanta. On her mother's subsequent visits, which generally coincided with the opening of the New York City Ballet or an especially splashy Broadway play, they met in the lounge of the St. Regis where her parents invariably stayed or at whatever new restaurant was in vogue at the time.

In her tiny bedroom, which was just large enough to accommodate a queen-sized bed, a nightstand, and a dresser, Vivien stepped carefully out of her jeans and pulled off Marty's T-shirt. Naked, she walked toward the open door of the equally tiny bathroom to stare into the mirror that covered it. Usually she avoided doing this. She was forty-one after all, and although she'd started out with pretty good genes—the females on both the Baxter and Gray sides of the family had long aspired to and held titles like Miss Cornpone, Tobacco Leaf, and Black-Eyed Pea—nothing about her was quite as high or tight or firm as it had once been.

Like her mother and sister, she topped out around five feet ten, six feet in heels, with long limbs and a neck that had been referred to as swanlike. Her short dark hair had been cut in long layers and her brown eyes were deeply set in an angular face that Vivien had discovered early on worked better in photographs and on camera than in person.

She might have been able to believe herself beautiful

if she hadn't been inherently clumsy and completely
lacking in rhythm, despite having a mother who'd once
dreamed of being a prima ballerina and a younger sister
who'd majored in dance. And she might have felt herself
a true Baxter or Gray, if she hadn't always been such a
square peg smashed into a round family hole; hadn't been
born with the uncontrollable urge to dig for the truth
behind the simplest word or deed, which was not exactly
a welcome personality trait in a family that had made
its living in and from politics since the War of Northern
Aggression.

Her legs were still pretty good and her stomach
reasonably flat, though there was a slight swell that
she suspected was yet another one of the hallmarks of
approaching middle age. Her breasts, though lower, were
still full. Swiveling, she took in the flare of her hip, then
contemplated the source of her current problem and the
stark white bandage covering it, and wondered how a
brief and almost insignificant creasing of a fairly insignificant part of her anatomy could have garnered so much
unwelcome attention. Surely those fifty thousand people
who'd already raced to YouTube to see her take one in the
rear, needed to "get a life."

Reaching around the door, she lifted her robe from the
hook and drew it on, tying its frayed chenille belt firmly
around her waist. Her stomach heaved itself up into her
throat and she froze, staring at her whitening face, while
she willed it back down. When it seemed she'd won the
battle, she padded through the living area and into the
kitchen where she found a lone package of saltines from
some long-ago take-out meal, mangled it open, and nibbled determinedly on one of the crackers.

On the counter, the blinking red light on the base of
the phone indicated voice mail. Carrying the phone into
the living area, she lowered herself gently onto the couch,

then scrolled down to see who'd called. Resigned, she punched in her access code and brought the receiver up to her ear.

The unhurried cadence of her mother's drawl belied the urgency of her message and the degree of her irritation, but Vivi had forty-one years of experience recognizing both. "Vivien, I have just gotten off the phone with Marty and he has sworn to me that you are all right. But I am fully prepared to get on a plane this moment and come up there to take care of you, if you would like. Please call me and let me know what is happening. It is completely humiliating to have to communicate with you through a third party. I am your mother and . . ."

Vivi hit delete; she'd heard the concluding part of that particular speech before. The next voice belonged to her widowed sister, Melanie, who lived with her two teenagers, Shelby and Trip, in one of Atlanta's northeastern suburbs, close, but not too close, to their parents' home in Buckhead.

Melanie, who was younger than Vivi by three years, had always been a pleaser, unwilling to so much as rock the boat that Vivien periodically tried to take out and sink in deep water. Right up until the moment Melanie set eyes on Jordan Jackson Jr., the handsome young *Republican* with political aspirations that she'd met in college and married soon after. Vivien still wasn't sure if marrying a Republican and helping him win first a seat on the county commission and then in the Georgia House of Representatives had been Melanie's singular act of rebellion or an impulse so powerful she'd simply been unable to resist.

Once the scandal had died down and her family had reluctantly absorbed their Arnold Schwarzenegger, the Gray dynasty had soldiered on. But the sisters' relationship had never been the same.

Their mother maintained that Melanie couldn't help but resent the fact that Vivien had left her behind, but the reality was that once Melanie married and Vivien fled north, the only thing they had in common was their shared childhood. And it wasn't as if all of those memories were good enough to cling to.

On the occasions when they *were* together, Vivi stifled yawns while Melanie described the far too intimate details of pregnancy and motherhood as well as the brilliance of her children, the mind-numbing minutiae of suburban life, and the joys of campaigning for J.J., which didn't sound all that joyful to Vivi. About three years before J.J. died, Melanie, who had first taught ballroom dance while in college, bought a dance studio, which she'd remodeled and renamed after the gilt and glass ballroom at Magnolia Hall. At that point the fascinating cast of characters who took lessons there became another topic of conversation through which Vivien smiled politely while her thoughts wandered to more pressing matters like the interview subject she hadn't been able to pin down, the inadequacies of her current research assistant, and whether she was smiling and nodding in the right places.

"Vivi?" Melanie's voice and cadence in her message were identical to their mother's—and Vivien's before she'd wrestled it into submission. The thing that set it apart was its lack of recrimination. "Shelby showed me your, um, video on YouTube. I can't believe you were shot." There was a catch in Melanie's voice—most likely the whole gun thing made her think about J.J. dying on that hunting trip two years ago. "Anyway, I wasn't sure if you were home from the hospital yet, but I wanted to make sure you were okay. You know if there's anything I can do, if you'd like to come down here and recuperate, whatever. I'm here and you're, um, always welcome."

Vivien flushed with embarrassment. Her stay with

Melanie after J.J.'s death had been cut short by an emergency at work—or what had seemed like an emergency at the time. She'd seen the shock in Melanie and her children's eyes, noted the numbness of their movements, and known that she should stay and do what she could for as long as they needed her. Instead, barely three days after the funeral she'd muttered her apologies and vowed to come back soon. And then she'd practically raced to the Atlanta airport, away from their pain, back to the safety of her work and her life. Vivien felt the shame all over again, just remembering it.

On the couch, Vivi worked her way onto her side and pulled the old afghan up over her shoulder, scrunching the pillow under her cheek, too tired to bother looking for the remote in order to turn on the TV. Her body ached and her stomach still roiled, but she'd already consumed her meager stash of saltines. She could call one of her usual spots for delivery, but she didn't think anyone would make the trip for a box of crackers, which was the only thing she could imagine allowing past her lips right now.

She dozed for a while and when she woke the light was fading outside and the traffic noises were no longer gently muffled but loud and aggressive. She guessed five P.M.; the digital clock on the TV stand read six fifteen. She was debating whether to go back to sleep or forage for something else in the cracker family when the phone rang. Caller ID said simply, "Out of Area."

This time the voice was male and she was so glad to hear it tears formed behind her lids. "Vivi, are you there?" Stone's voice was smooth and warm with a soul-deep resonance that was clearly a gift from the gods. Men trusted it; women got wicked little shivers in private places from it. He was big and broad-shouldered with an even-featured face and a strong jaw that came across well on camera; all in all a very impressive package. Though she would never say so to anyone else, Vivi thought what was inside was even better.

"I'm here." She didn't normally dwell on the distance that so often separated them, but right now she wished Stone were here sitting next to her giving her that look that said both "cut the crap" and "I think you're fabulous" and not on the other side of the world in Kabul. "When the ID said 'out of area,' it wasn't joking. What time is it there?"

"Two forty-five A.M." She couldn't hear anything in the background. When he'd called while he was embedded with a battalion in Iraq, she'd sometimes heard gunfire. Once there'd been an explosion that made her heart race in her chest until he spoke, but he said it was nothing, that he wouldn't have been on the phone if he'd been under attack.

It was rare that they got to talk privately. With the eight-and-a-half-hour time difference Stone would usually lie low during his daytime, then do live "hits" during his night so that his reports were live during the network's daily newscasts here. Sometimes the control room in New York would patch her in between Stone's live shots so that they could speak, but there were often four or five other people standing by on the line.

"I haven't had a chance to call since I reached Marty this morning. Are you okay?" he asked more quietly. And after she'd reassured him that she was, he added, "You're up to sixty thousand views on YouTube." She could almost picture the smile settling on his lips. "I've ordered you a pair of Kevlar underwear for Christmas."

"I should warn you that I'm not finding anything about this at all funny," she said stiffly.

"If it had happened to someone else, you'd be laughing your ass off." There was a pause and a small chuckle. "Sorry. Couldn't help myself."

Vivien drew in a deep breath. Exhaled. Pretended to be irritated. "I don't think I'll leave reporting for stand-up comedy just yet."

He laughed and she felt her mood lighten in response. "Point taken. But I was thinking maybe I'd come home and change your bandages for a while. Maybe do a little targeted physical therapy. I make a mean can of chicken soup."

Despite her stomach, despite the ridiculousness of her situation, despite the fact that it was time to figure out how to actually apply the salve and put on a fresh bandage, she smiled. After three years together a part of her kept waiting for Stone to realize he could do better, get someone much younger or at least prettier. But when he was in the country, it was Vivien he came home to. "When he was in the country" were, of course, the salient words. As one of the network's most experienced correspondents, he was more often gone than present. Which might explain why things were still so good between them.

"Seriously, Viv," Stone said. "I could probably get back for a couple of days. I don't like the idea of you being alone right now with no one to look after you."

"I'm perfectly able to look after myself," Vivien said, completely unable to tell him how much his offer meant to her. "This was just a freak accident. And it's not like I'm mortally wounded or anything. If I haven't already expired from embarrassment, it's unlikely I'm going to." She knew she was protesting too much, but she couldn't seem to stop. Well-bred southern girls didn't whine or sound needy; she was pretty certain that was on the list somewhere. "I'm fine. More than fine really. I've been taking care of myself for a long time. I think I can do it a little bit longer."

"All right." She heard the reluctance in his voice and was glad he wasn't there to see how mightily she was pretending. "But I need to hear from you more often. I'll pick up messages whenever I can, so I expect you to email or text me regularly to let me know how you're feeling. If I don't hear from you, I'm going to be on a plane. Do you hear me?"

Vivien couldn't believe how tightly she was clinging to his words. Clearly, the whole shooting thing had completely unnerved her. She felt like a quivering mass of neediness; her emotions were churning almost as heavily as her stomach.

"Got it," she said, all plucky glibness. "Now you stop worrying about me and get back to work. Or sleep. Or something. I'm absolutely fine."

Or as fine as someone who'd been shot in the butt and humiliated on a national scale could be. As one of her well-wishers had put it, the worst was surely behind her.

3

VIVIEN GOT TO work later than usual, then spent an inordinate amount of time getting to her office because everyone from the security guard in the lobby to the director of the nightly newscast had a pithy comment or observation about her wound and/or her anatomy. On her desk, she found a plaster cast of a set of buttocks. A blonde in her midtwenties stood next to it. Vivien wasn't sure if the two were related.

"Are those yours?" Vivien nodded at the buttocks, which were clearly female and much perkier than her own. At the moment she was in no mood even for people she knew and liked, and she doubted the blonde belonged in either category.

"No." The woman had professionally arched eyebrows the exact color of her hair and knew how to use them. "I assumed they belonged to you."

Vivien sighed and walked around to sit gingerly behind her desk. Without being asked, the blonde took the seat on the opposite side. Vivien moved the buttocks to her

right so that she could see the other woman. "I'm not in
the best possible mood today. How can I help you?"

"Well, actually, I'm here to help you."

"Oh?"

The woman smiled, but it was a smile reflecting tri-
umph, not warmth. "I've been hired to help round out
the investigative department."

This was news to Vivi, who *was* the investigative
department at CIN and had never considered herself
in need of "rounding out." "So you're going to be my
assistant?"

"Well, no," the woman said. "I'm supposed to file stories. Like you do." A different kind of smile lifted her
unnaturally full lips. "Only without the gunplay."

"So you're a reporter?"

"Oh, yes." The blonde leaned forward to extend a perfectly manicured hand across the desk, narrowly missing
the buttocks. "I'm Regina Matthews. I covered politics
and government for KCAL in San Francisco, and I uncov-
ered and reported on a number of scandals in my three
years there. I've been talking to Dan Kramer for the last
few months, but I had some things I wanted to wrap up
before I moved to New York."

Her gaze didn't waver. It carried the message, "I'm here
for your job. I may not have it locked up yet, but it's only
a matter of time." Vivien recognized the certainty in the
younger woman's eyes because hers had once telegraphed
the same message to the reporter she had been brought in
to ultimately replace.

Vivien shook the proffered hand and tried not to show
her shock. Dan had been interviewing and recruiting for
months and she'd never gotten wind of it? Some investigative journalist she'd turned out to be!

"Well, how nice for you." It was impossible not to
notice that the lovely Regina was right about the same age

Vivien had been when she'd started at CIN a lifetime ago. Vivi realized she wanted to throw up, but then she always wanted to do that lately. She swallowed down the nausea, reached for the plaster buttocks, and handed them to her new colleague. "Consider these a 'welcome to the network' gift." She enjoyed the grimace that twisted the blonde's Angelina Jolie lips. "We'll have to do lunch one day. But right now you'll have to excuse me. I was out yesterday and I really need to get to work."

She held her smile until the other woman left the office, holding the buttocks out in front of her like Vivien had once held her nephew, Trip, who at the time was wearing only a sagging, poop-filled diaper.

As she watched the younger reporter leave, shards of ragged emotion jabbed at Vivien from all sides, ambushing her with their intensity. At first Vivi resisted them. She had always prided herself on her calm and logic. She did not run off half-cocked like others did; she thought and planned and then she acted. She could and had spent up to six months nailing down the details on an important story, making sure she had covered every angle, that no possibility had been left unexplored. Even when pressure had been applied from higher up, she'd never agreed to run anything until everything was in place and the story was unimpeachable and complete. This was how she'd built her reputation.

But lately these overpowering surges of emotion had become more frequent. And they'd begun to cloud her judgment, to muddy her thinking. Like two days ago when she'd decided not to tell her FBI contact that she and Marty would be in the parking garage.

Like right now when they ricocheted inside her like pinballs. When she could feel the rage and indignation simmering in her veins like a pot of water coming to a boil.

Could it be perimenopause? Vivien wondered as she tried to rein herself in. Her period had been irregular, her whole sense of herself strangely out of whack. Should she go in for a checkup? Try to figure it out?

She managed to stay seated until she was certain Regina and the buttocks were gone. But she couldn't think clearly enough to answer any of the questions she'd posed. Nor could she plot out her next move.

Instead, she got up from her desk and walked to Dan's office at the opposite end of the hall. She didn't knock as she normally would have, nor did she plan out what she wanted to say or the way in which she wanted to say it. She was a Vivien on emotional steroids, an utter basket case of conflicting urges and shocking impulses.

Dan looked up when she entered the room; a warm smile lit his face. "Are you sure you should be back so soon? I figured you'd take the rest of the week off." If he was angry at her screwup, he didn't mention it. He'd been a good boss, firm but evenhanded; generally willing to let her work in her own way as long as she delivered. But all she could see right now was the traitor who had hired a blonde behind her back.

"Where did that Regina business come from and why wasn't I told?"

Dan's expression changed from one of concern to outright shock. The transition might have been comical if Vivien had had even a shred of a sense of humor left.

"What did you say?" he asked.

She strode forward until she reached his desk. There she placed her hands on the polished wood and pressed closer. "What's going on, Dan? How could you hire someone to do what I do without even mentioning it to me?"

There was a tiny voice in her brain that murmured, "Be quiet. This is not the way to discuss this." But she shoved the voice aside even as she purposely leaned closer so that she could loom over him. "You're invading his space," the munchkin-sized voice said. "This is not the way to get what you want."

But she didn't actually know what she wanted. Or even, at the moment, who she was. She was aflame with anger and righteous indignation. She was every woman who had worked hard, pulled herself up, claimed her place. Only to have some younger, bigger-lipped woman brought in to shove her out of the way.

"I wasn't aware that I needed to run hiring decisions by you." Dan's tone and face turned cold, frigid in a way she'd seen but never experienced. "We started looking earlier this year when the focus groups began to indicate that a fresher, hipper approach would hold more appeal."

He rose so that she could no longer tower over him. They were practically nose to nose over his desk. Both of them knew that "fresher" and "hipper" were the legally acceptable terms for "younger."

"Now you've done it," the voice said. "There's no way this can end well."

And as the rage seeped out of Vivien with the speed of air escaping a balloon, she realized that the voice was right.

"Your numbers have been slipping, Vivien. Your stories just don't grab viewers like they used to." His tone turned wry and a little bit nasty. "You got quite a spike with that stunt in the parking garage, of course. But unless you're planning to get injured on a regular basis, those numbers are not sustainable."

She realized then that things were both further along and far worse than she'd realized. She was on her way out whatever she did; they'd just hoped they could get her to train Regina, acclimate her to New York, and maybe introduce her to her contacts before she left. So that their fresher, hipper, *younger* reporter would already be up to speed and familiar to the audience when she took over Vivien's job.

Her fury returned in full flame. She couldn't even imagine training someone else to take her place, couldn't stomach pretending everything was fine while everyone in the business knew that she was on her way out. She simply wouldn't stand for being a lame-duck investigative reporter. She would not do this.

"Oh, no," the little voice said. "Please be careful. Have you taken leave of your senses?"

"I am not going to train someone else to do my job," Vivien said, ignoring the voice. "I don't care what color blonde she dyes her hair or how many collagen treatments she's had on her lips."

And then, because she had apparently lost her mind and control of her faculties, she looked him in the eye and shouted, "You'll have to get someone else to train her because I quit!"

⊚

BACK IN HER office Vivien told the horrified little voice to shut up. She emptied a box of blank DVDs and began to fill it with her things. An ancient photo of her family. One of Stone and her at a recent industry awards banquet. The awards and plaques on her wall that she'd won over the years. The one plant that had managed to survive her sporadic ministrations.

Her contacts were on her PDA and her story files were already backed up on her laptop, so the whole process took her maybe ten minutes. She was ready to flounce out of her office, down the elevator, and out of the building when her phone rang. She paused.

If she was no longer employed here, was she required to answer the phone? Her secretary, Sara Spiegel, poked her head in the doorway, took in the stripped wall of fame and the box filled with Vivien's things. "Oh."

Vivien always hated it when someone felt compelled to state the obvious, but it was clear she had to say something. "I'm leaving," she said. *Obvious, obvious, obvious.* Maybe she should mention that she'd completely lost control of herself in a way she never had before and hoped never to again, and was only just now starting to grasp the ramifications of what she'd done. "I quit."

"Oh." At thirty, Sara Spiegel was not the sharpest tool in the shed. But she'd been a good and faithful worker and had spent the last seven years in front of Vivien's office. "You have a phone call. It's your doctor's office." Sara was also a world-class hypochondriac and would never take a call lightly from a person entitled to wear a white coat.

"It's probably just an appointment reminder or some bookkeeping thing. I'll call them back later." Vivien hefted her box onto one hip.

"Are you sure you want to do that?" Sara asked anxiously. "My aunt Matilda didn't return a call from her internist one time and three years later she was dead."

"Your Aunt Matilda was ninety-one when she died."

"Right. But her sister, Gertie, made it to ninety-five."

Knowing better than to follow the thread of this conversation further, Vivien hugged Sara with her free arm. "Thanks for everything. You've been great."

"Are you sure you have to quit?" Sara asked. "Couldn't you change your mind?"

Good question. Now that all the emotions that had engulfed her seemed to have retreated, she couldn't quite believe she was on her way out the door. Could she apologize and blame it on the pain pills? Post-traumatic stress syndrome? Where had all that rage come from? And where had it gone?

As frightening as the glut of emotions were, she would have preferred them to the knee-wobbling, gut-wrenching emptiness and sense of impending doom that filled her now.

As if everything had been yanked out from beneath her. As if she didn't have a friend left in the world. She drew in a sharp breath of shock as her vision blurred with tears. Tears? Good God, she hadn't cried in ten years, if you didn't count her brother-in-law J.J.'s funeral. Now the waterworks kicked in at the smallest provocation.

At the nearest Starbucks Vivien ordered a chamomile tea instead of her usual macchiato and a biscotti in place of the beckoning carrot cake, in hopes of settling her stomach. At a vacant table near the window, she sipped the warm tea and nibbled the biscotti tentatively, praying it would stay down. Between bites she tried to focus on her situation, but she couldn't seem to marshal the resources required. Each time she tried to analyze what had just happened, her brain skittered away from the subject like a mouse playing hide-and-seek with a cat. Checking voice mail, she saw that the doctor's office had tried her cell phone, too. Not really wanting to deal with it, she pressed play and listened to the nurse/receptionist's message. "Hi, this is Dr. Sorenson's office. The doctor has reviewed the lab work they did on you in the hospital and there's something there that he would like to discuss. Please call to schedule an appointment for this afternoon; he promised to fit you in."

The biscotti turned to lead in her stomach. Dr. Sorenson, her internist, actually her only regular doctor, was not a spur-of-the-moment kind of guy. She went to his office once a year for her annual well-woman checkup, which included her annual Pap and general physical, and on the rare occasions when an infection or some other small malady presented itself.

What could the hospital have found that would compel him to see her so quickly? Was it some kind of tumor? A cancer?

Just as rage had taken her in its grip earlier, now panic consumed her. She chastised herself for being so ridiculous. And silently apologized to Sara for all the times she'd poked fun at her secretary for doing this very thing. Other than the recent bullet in her butt, she had always been healthy. The fact that she'd been riding such an emotional roller coaster lately did *not* mean there was something seriously wrong with her, there was just no reason to travel down that mental road.

Vivien pressed redial and waited anxiously for someone to answer. After she gave her name she said, "I had a message to call to schedule an appointment for *today* with Dr. Sorenson." She expected the woman to laugh at her, but the woman said, "Yes, I have a note to fit you in. Can you be here at two thirty?"

Since Vivien no longer had a job, getting there at two thirty was not a problem. But everything else about this was. "Did the note say why he wanted to see me?" she asked.

"No."

"Is there someone I might talk to who could give me some idea why he wants to see me?"

"No."

Vivien was too busy trying not to hyperventilate to take the receptionist's one-word responses personally. This was New York; abrupt was a way of life.

"Look, all I'm saying is it's pretty unusual to be seen so quickly. Maybe you could help me find out whether it's something serious or not. So I can be prepared. Because frankly, one more shock could send me right over the edge. Work with me a little here. What do you think I should do?"

There was a pause, presumably while the woman searched for a sufficient one-word answer. Finally she said, "I'm going to go out on a limb on this one. But I think you should show up at two thirty like the doctor asked you to. So that he can tell you whether you need to be worrying or not." Then there was dial tone.

In New York, abrupt might be a way of life, but sarcasm was the national pastime.

And so it was that Vivien Armstrong Gray clutched her box of stuff to her chest and boarded the 57 bus to the Iris Cantor Women's Health Center, where at 2:42 P.M. Dr. Peter Sorenson blew what remained of the world as she knew it the rest of the way out of the water.

4

I'M WHAT?" VIVIEN asked, certain she'd misheard.

"You're pregnant."

"No, I'm not." She shook her head from side to side, adamant.

"Well, according to the hCG levels in your blood you are." Dr. Sorenson shrugged, equally certain there was no arguing with science. "I've scheduled you for an ultrasound next door so we can confirm how far along you are. There are several really great ob-gyns practicing here at the center. I'll be glad to refer you to one of them."

"But I can't be pregnant."

He looked at her face, which she knew was crumpled in horror and disbelief and the vain attempt to hold back tears. "Ah, so I guess those aren't tears of joy."

He handed her a tissue, which she used to try to staunch the flow. "I am way too old to have a baby."

"Apparently not," he pointed out not unkindly.

"And I'm not married."

"Not really a requirement," he said.

"And as of today I don't even have a job." The tears

started again. "And I'm a complete emotional train wreck."

He smiled. "That part will go away in about twenty years."

Vivien sniffed and blotted some more. "I don't even particularly *like* children." God, she sounded so pathetic she could hardly stand it.

"Look," he said gently. "I can see this is a shock. Let's just take it one step at a time, okay? You'll go have the ultrasound, see if it confirms how far along your blood levels indicate, and then you'll know what your options are."

Numb and weary, she stood and followed a nurse to the ultrasound department where they confirmed that she was somewhere between eight and nine weeks pregnant. An embryo the size of an orange seed was inside her womb.

On her fortieth birthday last year someone had given her a card that read, "Cheer up. You could be this old and pregnant, too!"

And now, apparently, she was.

☺

FOR THE NEXT week Vivien barely left her apartment except to pick up the odd cracker item or buy a lottery ticket at Fairway Grocery; in her current state of mind, winning millions of dollars seemed more likely than producing real income.

Alone in her hidey-hole, seeking every ounce of comfort it offered, she grappled with what to do. She was barely pregnant, the embryo so tiny she could barely imagine it as more than the seed it resembled. And yet this tiny, seed-shaped thing would alter the course of her life forever, whatever she decided to do.

Intellectually, politically, she had always believed in a woman's right to choose. Had argued vehemently that those who disapproved of abortion and birth control should be forced to adopt all the unwanted and abused children in the world, every last one of them, before they tried to force others to bear children they might not be equipped to care for physically or emotionally.

She still believed a woman should have the right to govern her own body, to choose whether or not to become a mother. But in the wee-est hours of the morning as she stared out her living room window watching the sun steal up behind the buildings to fill the cracks and spaces of the city with light, she also knew that she couldn't give up anything that she and Stone had created together. Even if she were unemployed and alone.

So she made an appointment with her new ob-gyn, a smart, no-nonsense woman named Myra Grable, who gave her a prescription for prenatal vitamins, suggested she buy a copy of *What to Expect When You're Expecting*, explained the added risks that came with a pregnancy at her age, and promised that the nausea and exhaustion would pass.

But Dr. Grable didn't tell Vivien how to tell Stone he was going to be a father. Or where she might find the energy to go out and look for a new job. Or how she was going to go back on camera, assuming she could even find a job like the one she'd left, while her body swelled and she remained unmarried. Hollywood celebrities seemed to do these things with impunity, but Vivien didn't know any television journalists who'd reported during unmarried pregnancies. So far she looked the same as always. But what would happen when her body began to change?

"Why did you quit? It's so much easier to find another job when you've already got one." Stone and pretty much every member of her family asked her that question in the following weeks, but it was almost impossible to answer. Because how could she describe the torrent of emotions that had propelled her to that scene with Dan when she wasn't ready to admit that the torrent was hormone-induced? That she was pregnant. And completely freaked out about it.

Her family would disapprove. And Stone? Stone, whom she had affectionately nicknamed Rolling Stone because of his love of rock 'n' roll and the joy with which he raced from story to story and war to war. He'd told her more than once that he loved her. It was possible he might marry her, might well offer to do "the right thing." But she wasn't even sure she believed in marriage anymore. She didn't understand how in the world her parents had stayed married for so long. And at forty-one, most of her friends' first marriages were already over. Did she want to marry someone to whom she was first and foremost a responsibility? It was the one thing that might make her feel even more pathetic than she already did.

Finally, when her cozy hidey-hole began to feel too small and her wallowing had produced no answers, she was forced to concede that no one was going to call and offer her a job. So she got up early on that Wednesday morning, took a shower, got dressed, and spent the day at the kitchen table first making a list of who to approach, then working the phone to set up appointments.

By early afternoon she wanted to crawl back into her cocoon on the couch. She'd only been granted three face-to-face interviews because "people were cutting back." "There was so much wrong out there that investigative pieces just didn't break through the public malaise as they once had." And though no one came out and said so, because she was forty-one and the first thing that sprang to mind when she said her name was no longer "inside scoop," but "bullet in butt."

Still Vivien dressed carefully for the first interview. Her clothes were already snugger in the waist and bust, but even she wouldn't have known she was pregnant if she hadn't been forced to know. When she walked into CIN's rival, CCN, she felt cautiously optimistic because, after all, who in New York had more experience at investigative reporting than she did?

But when she was seated in the news director's office, the first question wasn't "When can you start?" but "What were you thinking when that first shot whizzed by?"

At the second interview she was asked whether she was relieved to have been shot in a place so well padded. And he wasn't referring to the parking garage. At the third, there weren't even any questions. Just a twenty-something HR person who knew nothing about her and didn't seem to want to. Vivien slogged home through the late-afternoon traffic and told herself something would turn up. And for a while she thought maybe something really would.

Friends and colleagues gave her leads on openings they'd heard about. But when she followed up she was inevitably deemed overqualified for the positions, and Vivi, who hadn't yet won the lottery and was growing increasingly desperate, had too much pride to beg.

Her closest friends took her out to eat and commiserate over the arrival of Regina Matthews, who was already appearing in brief bits on the air as they prepared the audience for the woman who would take over Vivien's spot. "She'll never be you," a former colleague told Vivi over lunch at a nearby deli. "But she does have great lips."

Stone chided her for giving up so easily. She was great at what she did and she had one of the best demo reels in the business.

"All they're thinking about when they see me is whether I have a scar on my butt," she replied. "Or why they should hire me when CIN felt they needed somebody younger."

"You'll find something. And when I get back, we're going to take a vacation somewhere," he said. "Somewhere fun where nobody's shooting anybody else."

It sounded heavenly to Vivien, except that there was no telling when he might actually get back, and by the time he did she'd be noticeably pregnant or, possibly, a mother.

Yet she couldn't bring herself to tell him about the baby. Some small part of her was not only in shock and delusional but seemed to think that if she didn't mention her pregnancy, it would simply go away. In these earliest months when the chance of a miscarriage was highest, she told herself there was no need for a discussion that might end up moot. And so she kept the news to herself even though she knew that the longer she waited the harder it would be to tell him if she had to. And the harder it became to talk normally as if everything, other than her lack of employment, was just fine.

☺

BY THE TIME she completed her first trimester, September had given way to October and Vivien could no longer pretend that her condition was temporary or that she was somehow going to find a position in New York even half as good as the one she'd left. In fact, she had begun to doubt she could find anything that came anywhere close to resembling journalism as she knew it.

She'd already talked to everyone who'd agreed to see her and a few who hadn't, and had been reduced to answering newspaper and online ads like some rookie fresh out of journalism school. Today's interview was with the editor of a weekly publication that might best be described as *USA Today* meets *People* magazine with a heavy dose of the *National Enquirer*.

Vivi studied John Harcourt surreptitiously as she took

a seat in his cramped, windowless office. He might have been twelve, thirteen at the most. Which meant Vivien could have already been at CIN a full two years before he was born.

He was not, as it turned out, familiar with her work, but he thought that her name sounded somewhat familiar.

Despite an almost irresistible urge to stand up and walk out, this time Vivien listened to the little voice that reminded her of how that had worked out the last time and instead ran through the highlights of her career. As she did so she told herself that if she couldn't get this appallingly low-paying job at the *Weekly Encounter*, she deserved to be unemployed.

"Honestly," he said. "The column we're looking to start doesn't really sound like your kind of thing at all." He was shaking his head, clearly getting ready to blow her off.

"Oh, I've covered all kinds of things," she assured him. "I enjoy investigative journalism, and I've worked in the broadcast field for a long time. But I'm a writer/reporter first and foremost. I started in print and I can cover anything and make it interesting."

"I'm sure you could." His expression said, *not*. "But I seriously doubt you'd want to . . ."

"Why don't you let me be the judge of what I'd want to do." She leaned forward, her words coming from between clenched teeth.

"He's already afraid of you," the little voice cautioned. "If you scare him too badly, he won't hire you to get coffee."

Vivien knew the voice was right. But just as her emotions had pushed her beyond control with Dan, her desperation was shoving at her now. She needed a job and she needed it right away. And given the fact that she was unmarried and pregnant, print would be a better choice for her now anyway. People didn't really care about the personality behind a byline. There were no celebrity journalists on a publication like the *Weekly Encounter*.

Vivien slid back in her chair and unclenched her jaw. "I mean, I can't think of anything I'd be unable to research or unprepared to write about." There that was better, calmer. More like a normal person. "And given the salary range you advertised you're unlikely to get anyone with half my experience to do it."

"Yes," he said. "That's why it's listed as entry-level. If I'd realized who you were, I wouldn't have wasted either of our time." He started to rise.

"Wait! I mean, no. Please. Sit down." She lowered her voice as he did as she asked, then drew a deep breath and let it out in an effort to remove the panic from her voice and her eyes. Later, much later, she'd let herself think about the fact that she was begging to be considered for a job so far beneath her.

"Why don't you just tell me what the job is? And we'll decide together whether I'm right for it or not." She spoke sweetly. While smiling. It was one of the most painful things she'd ever done.

"Well." He sat back and steepled his fingers, which made him look older—at least fourteen. "Our polls show that our readers are tired of all the celebrity articles. Oh, they want to know about Brad and Angelina and their kids, but they want to read about people like themselves, too. But maybe with some kind of kick to it, you know?"

She nodded, smiling with intent interest, just as she would have for the cutaway close-up Marty always shot to cut into the interview.

"What we're envisioning is a weekly column from the suburbs. A sort of ongoing commentary on the current state of motherhood and apple pie with a few soccer moms beating the crap out of referees whose calls they don't like thrown in for good measure." He smiled, warming to his subject. "Snippets of real life as recorded in the real America."

Vivien stopped smiling and nodding, pretty much blown away that this child had managed to come up with the one topic Vivien was not even remotely qualified to or interested in writing about. She might have stood then and admitted defeat, except that she had a "bun in the oven" and she simply couldn't afford to be without an income—even one as small as the *Weekly Encounter* was offering.

So she stayed in her seat and arranged her features to telegraph abject admiration. "I think that's brilliant," she said. "We could call it Snapshots from the Suburbs. Or maybe Postcards from Suburbia."

He nodded, starting to unbend. Liking her for liking his idea.

"Maybe it could be written with an insider's knowledge but from a . . . newcomer's perspective," Vivien continued. "You know, like by someone just discovering the whole wonderful world of suburbia. As if an alien spaceship had deposited them in . . . east Cobb, Georgia . . ." She pulled the name of the area where her sister lived out of the air. ". . . and had to learn how to blend in to its surroundings. Live like the natives."

The editor leaned toward her, his head nodding faster as Vivien painted the picture.

"There could be columns about . . . finding day care . . . a babysitter . . . striving to win the best yard award . . . being a troop leader. Selling Girl Scout cookies. Taking a ballroom dance class." Again she pulled details of Melanie's daily life out of her memory, offering them up, trying to convince him even as she tried to convince herself. She could do this. She wished she didn't have to, would give anything to snap her fingers and go back to her old life, but she could research and write this column. In a way it wouldn't be all that different from the way she'd investigated the worlds of gangs, drugs, corporate espionage, and financial machinations in order to report on them.

The suburbs might seem like an alternate universe to her now, but if she went and lived there and immersed herself in the culture, she could turn the weekly column into something much larger than John Harcourt had ever imagined. Maybe aim for national syndication. Or uncover something that could propel her back into investigative journalism.

And she wouldn't even have to look for an expert to help her. Vivien might never have sat on a bleacher, driven a minivan, or idled in a car-pool line, but her sister had done all of those things and actually seemed to enjoy them.

She felt a slight stirring of . . . not exactly excitement, but a determination to accept her current reality and to do what had to be done. To take advantage of the details that seemed to be falling so neatly into place.

Hadn't Melanie practically begged her to come recuperate at her house? And weren't Melanie and her children, Vivien's niece and nephew, the walking embodiment of suburban life? They were her entrée to this brave new world, her personal tour guides to life in the hinterlands.

All she had to do was take her sister up on her invitation. While she was there she'd stick to Melanie like white on rice so she didn't miss a single nuance of suburban life.

Vivien looked the young man in the eye and knew she had him. She could never use her own name of course; it would be far too humiliating to ever let anyone know how low she'd sunk and how little she was forced to work for. She wouldn't even tell her family or Stone. The number of things she wasn't telling him gave her pause, but at the moment securing this job was her number one priority.

"I can do this for you, and I can make it first-rate," Vivien said. "But I'm going to have to go undercover in order to write about things the way I really see them. I can use an obvious sort of pseudonym to pique the readers' interest. And, of course, the *Weekly Encounter* will have to keep my identity secret."

She smiled and stuck out her hand to seal the deal. "What do you think?"

He barely hesitated, and she realized she should have asked for more money, but she would be employed and she would be reporting. What she made of it would be up to her.

"I like it. I like it a lot," he said, shaking her hand with real enthusiasm. "We'll start promoting the coming of a new column next week; that will give you a couple of weeks to get situated and start filing your stories."

He walked her to the lobby, all but rubbing his hands together in glee. "I'll set up an appointment for you with HR—they'll be the only people other than me who'll know your true identity."

Vivien felt lighter as she walked outside to hail a cab even though she'd already gained five pounds. Her mind whirled as she thought about all the things she'd need to take care of before she left the city—forwarding her mail, subletting her apartment, making up a suitable cover story. From the backseat of the cab, she punched in Melanie's cell phone number and waited impatiently for her sister to pick up.

Melanie hadn't exactly *begged* her to come down to recuperate, but despite their differences they were sisters, flesh and blood. Vivien knew that Melanie would never turn her away.

A well-bred girl from a good southern family might break an unwritten rule or two, but she'd never question a family member's intentions. Or ask how long that family member intended to stay.

5

IN HER OFFICE at the Magnolia Ballroom and Dance Studio, Melanie hung up the phone. Resting her hands on the desk, she sat for several long minutes staring through the inset glass wall to the dance floor, trying to process the fact that her sister had just invited herself for a visit and had actually claimed that spending time with Shelby and Trip was one of her prime motivations for coming.

In a corner of the studio a private rhumba lesson was under way. Melanie watched as longtime instructor Enrique Delray patiently guided a recently retired couple through the slow-slow-quick foot movements. With studied grace he demonstrated both how to lead and how to follow, talking the entire time in the vaguely Latin accent that made him wildly popular.

The threesome looked small in the large and decidedly elegant space. Originally built as a freestanding exercise facility, the dance studio was a long rectangle with two abutting mirrored walls and polished hardwood floors. When Melanie had purchased the business and building from the previous owner five years ago, it had been

called Let's Dance! and its claims to fame had been a
seventies-era disco ball and a decidedly laid-back teaching approach.

Melanie's first official act had been to change the name
of the studio to Magnolia Ballroom after her favorite room
at Magnolia Hall. Then she'd decorated the space to fit
its new name, replacing the disco ball with two carefully
placed French chandeliers she'd unearthed in the bowels
of an architectural salvage store and framing the large
plate-glass window that fronted the parking lot with a
gold brocade valance and side panels. The draperies in
turn framed a collection of white-clothed tables that she'd
paired with reproduction Louis XIV chairs. The lone solid
wall had been treated with mahogany wainscoting and an
ornately carved chair rail.

A "DJ" area where instructors took turns playing
music during their classes and for the Friday and Saturday
night practice parties had been tucked into one corner of
the ballroom. From there, a short hallway led to the rest-
rooms and kitchen. Between these, Melanie had created
a more casual conversation area with a chenille sofa and
an arrangement of club chairs and ottomans designed for
sinking into and getting a load off.

Normally, Melanie felt a great deal of satisfaction as she
surveyed her domain. Despite the intentional elegance,
she had created a warm and welcoming environment and
had made it a point to hire instructors who were not only
well trained and certified but friendly and enthusiastic.
The one thing Melanie had no patience for was "attitude."
Some of their students danced competitively, but many
had arrived with no dance experience at all after becoming fans of the hit TV show *Dancing with the Stars*. Others
came for the exercise and the opportunity to socialize and
de-stress. It was almost impossible to worry while doing

the cha-cha or the tango. Or while shimmying across the
floor to classic belly-dancing music.

Today her usual sense of accomplishment eluded her as
her thoughts circled back to Vivien's unprecedented visit
and the unstated reasons behind it.

There was a cursory knock on her open door and
then Ruth Melnick stuck her head inside. "Hi, doll. I'm
here."

Somewhere in her early seventies with beautifully
coiffed white hair, a direct manner better suited to her
New York beginnings and barely softened by her decades
in Atlanta, Ruth had been taking lessons at the Magnolia
Ballroom almost as long as Melanie had owned it. Ruth's
transition from student to friend and unpaid worker had
been gradual, but Melanie could no longer imagine the
studio without her. Ruth had warm brown eyes that
assessed people at the speed of light. Beneath her gruff
exterior beat a heart so big Melanie wasn't sure how it fit
inside her slightly barreled chest. Ruth manned the front
desk three afternoons a week and seemed happy to fill
in whenever Melanie needed her. She also continued to
take classes more, Melanie thought, to fill her days than
anything else. And possibly, Melanie suspected, to add to
the studio's financial bottom line without facing charges
of charity.

"There's been real interest in the new Wednesday
night belly-dancing class," Ruth said. "And I still have to
answer a few email queries. I'm thinking about taking it
myself." She gave an exaggerated shake of her wide hips.

"It's great exercise and a lot of fun. I've got Naranya
scheduled to teach, but I'm going to be there, too. I can
always fill in in a pinch." Over the last year Melanie
had added a number of dance-based exercise classes and
a mommy/toddler class on weekday mornings and was

constantly on the lookout for ways to increase revenue. "Let's remind the instructors to push it in their classes, and I want to make sure it's mentioned in any calls soliciting former students."

"Will do," Ruth said. "I just gave a tour and brochure to a bride-to-be. The wedding's not until April, but she signed up for belly dance. Cute—about thirty, redheaded. Said she was looking to add a less painful form of exercise to her workout schedule."

"Maybe that's how we should be marketing the class," Melanie said. "As an ancient Middle Eastern weight-loss technique."

"I like it." Ruth laughed, then looked pointedly at the clock on the wall. "Don't you need to get going?"

"Yes." Melanie glanced at her watch. "I've got to go pick up Shelby and get her to the tutor, but I'll be back to do the eight and nine P.M. classes. Diedre's out sick."

Melanie sprinted out the door. In the parking lot, she fired up the Honda Odyssey, then aimed her trusty steed east on Upper Roswell Road toward the high school where Shelby was undoubtedly already waiting and fuming.

At a red light she texted Trip to confirm that he'd made it home on the bus. She had barely hit "send" when the driver behind her laid on the horn. Startled, Melanie accelerated, almost running into the SUV in front of her. Cautioning herself to calm down, Melanie focused on the road as she covered the last miles to the school's front entrance.

"You're late," Shelby said in greeting. "If you'd let me drive to school like everybody else, I wouldn't have to stand around like a total geek waiting for you to show up."

"Hello to you, too." Melanie resisted responding to the taunt. Nor did she comment on the fact that Shelby's skirt was far too short and her makeup much too heavy. Or explain that she would gladly have let Shelby drive to school if she hadn't already demonstrated a tendency to simply drive right by the building without stopping.

These were just a few of the countless things Melanie didn't say to her daughter because anything she said was like a match to tinder. And because ever since J.J.'s abrupt and unexpected death two years ago, the three of them had lost their tether as if they were planets shot out of their orbits, ripped free of their gravitational pull.

"I'm adding a belly dancing class to the weeknight schedule," she said, looking for a non-incendiary topic of conversation.

Shelby half shrugged, the subject not even important enough to require the movement of both shoulders.

The drive to the tutor wasn't all that far; like everything in the northern suburb of east Cobb, ten to fifteen minutes would pretty much do it. But Melanie wasn't prepared to pass those minutes in silence like some hired chauffeur. She searched for another safe topic.

"Aunt Vivi called. She's going to come stay with us for a while. She said she wanted to spend some time with you and Trip."

This did, in fact, capture Shelby's attention. She turned to face Melanie. "She always acts like she can't wait to get away from here. What's the point of going somewhere that you can't wait to leave?"

This was a good question, especially since Melanie was fairly certain Vivien had shattered some land and speed records bailing out on them after J.J.'s funeral, something Melanie had been too numb to fully process at the time.

"Well, I'm sure it'll be nice to have her around." Melanie said this without any certainty whatsoever.

"Right." Shelby gave her the look she'd been perfecting for some time now. The one that said her mother was a complete and utter moron. "Like she ever cared about any of us."

As she pulled to a stop in front of the tutor's house, Melanie whipped her checkbook from her purse and began to fill it in, her efforts centered on *not* thinking about her sister's reappearance, her daughter's hostility, or the amount of money that flew out of their bank account on a weekly basis. "Here." She handed the check to Shelby, then watched her daughter climb out of the minivan with a big splash of thigh. "I'll be back in forty-five minutes." Which she sincerely hoped would be enough time to get to the grocery store, stock up, check out, and get back to the tutor's.

Inching down Johnson Ferry Road toward the Publix Super Market, she called home to make sure Trip was actually there.

"How was your day?" she asked after his mumbled greeting.

"Fine."

"Good."

There was a long pause. Melanie sighed and checked her rearview mirror before forcing her way into the other lane. She ignored the horns that blared in protest. She knew just how pissed off the woman behind her probably was at losing an entire car length, but she simply didn't have the time to poke along right now. "I'm going to pick up some groceries and a frozen pizza for dinner. Will you preheat the oven to four hundred in thirty minutes?"

"Okay."

"And set the table?"

"Yeah."

"Are you sure you're all right?"

"Yeah."

This was the extent of her conversations with Trip these days. He wasn't hostile like Shelby, didn't act out; he just didn't seem to have much to say to her. Or anyone else for that matter. Even the psychologist she'd taken him to in the months after J.J.'s death had admitted he'd been largely unable to get her son to speak.

Once inside the grocery store, Melanie raced through the aisles, tossing things into her cart, nodding to acquaintances—also mostly working moms—the full-time stay-at-homes having presumably wheeled through the aisles at a more leisurely pace earlier in the day.

In the checkout line she tried to understand why after all these years of grocery shopping she could not assess the quickest line. She'd avoided the checkout people that she knew moved too slowly, sidestepped the apparently single father who'd just started unloading a cart overflowing with microwave dinners, high-sugar cereals, and a stunning assortment of junk food, and passed by the elderly woman who was studying a debit card she apparently had no earthly idea how to use. Yet she'd ended up stuck behind an off-duty employee who'd brought in her newborn so that every other employee within a mile radius could come coo over it.

Finally she was out of there and speed-pushing the cart through the parking lot where she was almost mowed down by other women with the same grim focused looks on their faces that she knew must be on hers. She was five minutes late to the tutor's and arrived to find Shelby out on the driveway.

Shelby spent the six-minute ride home texting. Her thumbs flew over the tiny keyboard, her gaze fixed to the tiny screen that had become her lifeline to the world, or at least that part of it that mattered to her. Every few seconds there was the sound of an incoming message. This was followed by more thumb action.

"Who are you 'talking' to?" Melanie asked.

"Nobody you know."

"I don't have to know them," Melanie replied carefully, although she knew she should. Should know everyone

Shelby hung out with. Meet their parents. Be on top of things. "I just need a name. Some clue as to who you're friendly with."

"Jason and Ally." Shelby's fingers never slowed nor did she offer another iota of information. She grimaced in distaste when Melanie asked her to take a few of the grocery bags into the house. Inside, Melanie pried Trip away from the PS3 and sent him out for the rest of the bags. He didn't grimace. Or speak.

Shelby was texting again before Melanie had even unwrapped the pizza. After she slid it into the oven, she made Shelby stop long enough to mix a salad and forced Trip to turn off the TV and set the table, but even she wasn't looking forward to a meal during which she would try to pry information about their days from them and they would give her the smallest possible drips and drabs. She had to be back at the studio in thirty minutes.

Melanie helped herself to a slice of pizza. "Shelby, turn your phone off now. You know we don't bring them to the table."

Her daughter pushed the phone away from her and sent an ugly glare at her mother. Melanie didn't comment; the ugly looks had become pretty much par for the course. But she did pocket the phone, then smiled and attempted, once again, to start a conversation.

"So who do you think will be going to the World Series?" she asked her son. When J.J. had been alive, this question might have prompted a dinner-long discussion with good-natured taunting and real vested interest. Trip, who had once lived and breathed sports, baseball in particular, just shrugged.

They consumed the meal and cleared the table in silence, technically together but locked in their own little worlds. Melanie would have liked to blame their lack of communication on the fact that two out of three of them were teenagers and, therefore, horribly hormonally imbalanced while she was clearly stressed to the max. But she was afraid the real reason was J.J.'s absence; the vast emptiness he'd left between them seemed impossible to fill.

"I've got two classes tonight," she said as she prepared to leave. Without comment she returned Shelby's phone and pocketed the key to Shelby's car, which had been taken from Shelby three weeks ago when her truancy had been discovered. "I should be back by ten thirty."

She fixed her daughter with a stare. "Watch out for your brother. And please help him with his Spanish if he needs it."

Shelby didn't answer. Trip was seated at the kitchen counter and was emptying his backpack all around him in preparation for doing homework. Melanie dropped a kiss on the top of his head—she only got to be taller than him when he was seated—and strode out of the house, rushing yet again.

For the next two hours she lost herself in the music and her students' excitement as she taught the first class the intricate steps of the merengue and then the second class the bouncy shuffle of the Texas two-step.

She was beyond tired when she finally drove the van into the driveway; she could hardly wait to peel off the clothes she'd put on at six thirty that morning and crawl into bed. All thought of relaxing fled when the van's headlights illuminated a flash of white moving near the backyard fence and Melanie recognized her daughter's back retreating around the side of the house.

If she'd come home thirty seconds later, she wouldn't have known that Shelby had gone out. In the garage, Melanie turned off the car and sat longing for bed. But she couldn't pretend she hadn't seen Shelby tiptoeing around the house. Or ignore the fact that Shelby had, once again, flagrantly disobeyed her.

Melanie got out of the car. If there had been another choice, she would have taken it. But it was her job to protect her daughter whether she wanted to be protected or not. Even if the person she was protecting Shelby from was Shelby herself.

6

THE APARTMENT WAS too clean. Vivien hadn't even left yet and already it felt like it belonged to someone else. Her furniture still sat on her wool rugs, which sat on her hardwood floors. Her artwork still covered the walls. But her essence was already packed away in the oversized suitcase that held the only clothes she owned that might have enough elastic in them to see her through the next months.

She knew she was lucky to have found someone to sublet the apartment. Lucky that a friend of a friend had been temporarily reassigned to the New York bureau and didn't want to commit to anything permanent until he knew how long the assignment might last. Lucky that she didn't need board approval to have someone there to water her plants, flush the toilets, keep the apartment from sitting empty. Especially lucky given the state of the stock market, the demolition of her 401(k), and her lack of a serious job, that she had someone to pay her rent.

Lucky.

Wheeling the suitcase behind her, Vivien rode the

elevator down to the lobby and handed the envelope with a set of keys to the doorman. "You treat him right, Ralph, you hear?" she said as the cab pulled up out front. "And anything that gets delivered by mistake can be sent to that address in Atlanta I gave you."

"You got it." Ralph stepped smartly to the front door and opened it for her, then did the same with the cab. Ralph had been there every one of the ten years Vivien had owned her apartment and she had never once seen him slouch or grouse. Over her shoulder she saw him tip his hat to her and continued to watch as first Ralph and then the building dwindled and then disappeared.

At Hartsfield–Jackson Atlanta International Airport, Vivi retrieved her suitcase from the baggage carousel and wheeled it out to the curb. At home in New York she would have cued up for a cab or maybe already lined up the limo service that serviced the network. Here people actually drove to the airport and circled like the planes above them, landing only briefly to retrieve their traveler before swooping out again to the highway of their choice.

It was early November and the sky was a perfect blue, the air just shy of crisp. The leaves that would have been every shade of red and gold imaginable just a few weeks ago were now pale and faded, their grip on their branches loosened. The smallest breeze would send them spiraling to the ground.

She spotted Melanie in the driver's seat of a silvery gray minivan. Despite the exhaustion that had become her constant companion, Vivien's lips began to lift into a smile. She was always glad to see Melanie; it was just what happened after that initial burst of pleasure that was sometimes unpredictable. But the smile died before it was fully formed when she saw who sat in the passenger seat. Vivien blinked twice, hoping that she'd been mistaken, but despite their mother's disdain for minivans and the suburbs from which they were launched, Caroline Baxter Gray was, in fact, riding shotgun.

The van slid up to the curb in front of Vivi, and Melanie hopped out and ran around to greet her. They hugged quickly—the police at Hartsfield didn't allow time for major reunions—and Vivien was shocked at how thin Melanie had become. She had the sense that if she squeezed too hard something might snap. This, of course, could not be said of Vivi. Now in her fourth month, she wasn't yet showing, but had already packed on an extra six pounds.

Nonetheless, Melanie insisted on taking the suitcase from her and hefting it into the back of the van. The backseat door rolled open unaided and Vivien did a double take.

Melanie held up the key remote. "Sorry. Should have warned you."

"And not just about your automatic doors." She tilted her head toward the car where Caroline sat somewhat like the queen of Sheba, waiting for her minions to drive on.

Melanie shot her an apologetic smile, but her eyes didn't look the least bit sorry. "She asked me if I'd heard from you. What was I supposed to do, pretend you just showed up on my doorstep without warning?"

Despite an irritated signal from a nearby policeman, neither of them moved.

"You big chicken." Vivien was amazed at how unprepared she was to see her mother. Not to mention the completely irrational fear that somehow her mother would take one look at her and know all the things that Vivien was hiding.

"Look who's talking," Melanie replied and Vivien wondered how they'd reverted back to childhood so immediately. In a moment they'd be tossing their hair and sticking their tongues out at each other. "Anyway, it's just lunch. We have to drop her off for her hair appointment right afterward."

Caroline's window glided down and she leaned out expectantly. The policeman was moving their way now, so Vivien stepped forward to kiss her mother's perfectly made-up cheek. "Hello, Mother."

Caroline looked her up and down, and Vivien knew without a word being said that she had failed to measure up. As usual.

"It's, um, great to see you," Vivien said.

Caroline nodded and smiled as if to say, "Of course it is." She completely ignored the existence of the policeman, who blew his whistle and motioned for Melanie to drive on. Vivien, glad of the reprieve, climbed into the backseat and was grateful when her sister filled the drive with idle conversation and innocuous questions about the weather in New York and the details of Vivien's flight.

Caroline felt no such restraint. "You look a little peak-ed," her mother said when they had been sufficiently fawned over by the maitre d' at Caroline's restaurant du jour and then seated at a favored table.

"Peak-ed?" Vivien overpronounced as her mother had. "Is that still a word?" As always when in Caroline's company, Vivien felt as if she'd been plopped down in a reenactment of *Gone with the Wind*. Or that it might be time to ring for one of the family retainers to fetch her fan. But at least she hadn't said, "You look a little pregnant."

Melanie smothered a smile. It was one of the things that still bound them, their reaction to their mother's regal airs. How covert they were in these reactions and how hard they tried to appease her varied depending on an ever-changing array of factors. Even at the ripe old ages of thirty-eight and forty-one, neither of them was immune.

"You haven't eaten a bite. Are you feeling all right?" Caroline ignored Vivien's word challenge.

Vivien took a moment to consider her answer. The nausea had eased up over the last week, but the memory of it was still strong enough to keep all but the most insistent hunger pains at bay. She could feel herself drooping though; despite Dr. Grable's assurance that the exhaustion would ease up, she always felt in need of a nap. This had not been a problem while she was in New York and unemployed and could lie in bed for hours at a time. But if she wanted to keep her condition to herself, she could hardly admit that a two-and-a-half-hour plane ride had worn her out.

Lifting her water glass, she took a gulp, then smiled as disarmingly as she knew how. "I think I'm just a bit dehydrated from the plane. I can't seem to get enough to drink."

"Are you sure you're recovered from . . ." Her mother lowered her voice as if every woman in that place hadn't watched the three of them walk in and then discussed Vivien's humiliating wound at length.

"The wound is healed, Mother." Vivien stared into Caroline Baxter Gray's assessing gaze, the one that could make you feel like a fly pinned down by its wings. "I, um, just felt a need to take some time off to recuperate and, um, regroup before I seriously look for a new opportunity." She simply couldn't bring herself to admit that she'd only quit because they'd been planning to fire her. Or that she'd already searched for a job and discovered herself virtually unemployable.

For a brief moment Vivien allowed herself to consider all the things she was unwilling to admit or discuss. The months ahead played out in her mind, full of evasion and sidestepping. Trying to fool the people who knew her the best.

Panic filled the spot where the nausea normally resided. How was she ever going to pull this off? What had she been thinking when she'd decided to come here?

"I must say I had no idea how many people down here watched you on television until *after* the . . . incident," Caroline said. "I got so many calls of concern I had to stop answering the phone."

Vivien had no doubt these people had taken great delight in tweaking the nose of the ever-proper Caroline Baxter Gray. She could just imagine the glee with which they'd dialed their phones.

Vivi sent Melanie a silent plea for intervention, but Melanie seemed consumed with getting the cream and sweetener levels in her coffee just right.

"And, of course, it was hard to explain why I wasn't up there taking care of you." Caroline's tone signaled a massive hurt somehow surmounted. "Like a mother should."

Melanie added another sugar substitute and stirred, her attention riveted to her cup.

Vivien sighed. She was much too tired for confrontation. And not near enough to the top of her game to come close to winning. "I'm sorry I didn't ask you to come take care of me." She almost smiled, picturing Caroline attempting to clean and change the bandage on her wound. It would have been one for the memory books. "I was just . . . overwhelmed. I wasn't really thinking." This, at least, was true.

Melanie stopped stirring. She looked up from her cup.

Caroline smiled. It was not a big smile and it was not all-encompassing or all-inclusive. She still did not approve of Vivien's behavior or, for that matter, 90 percent of her life choices—and those were only the ones she knew about. But for the moment, Vivien's apology would suffice. They could move on.

As her mother paid the bill and flirted again with the

maitre d' on the way out, Vivien didn't allow herself to think about her mother's reaction when her pregnancy became obvious. Like Scarlett O'Hara, she would simply think about that "tomorrow."

◯

NOT TOO FAR from where the Gray women lunched, Ruth Melnick sat on a gray tweed couch in the office of Myron Guttman, PhD. Her husband, Ira, sat unhappily beside her. She knew he was unhappy because of the woe-is-me expression on his normally ruddy face and because he'd told her so. "How many cockamamie marriage counselors are you planning to drag me to?" he'd complained when they met in front of the tall glass building on Peachtree Dunwoody Road. "The rent in this building is astronomical. And now I'm going to pay part of it to hear what a crummy husband I am. Why do we have to pay these people to hear it? You've told me plenty of times already."

"We're going to see as many counselors as it takes," Ruth replied unperturbed. "Until we find one you actually listen to. You stopped listening to me a long time ago." About twenty-five years ago to be exact, right when they'd hit the halfway mark in their marriage and the only thing he'd seemed to care about anymore was his business.

Now she and Ira sat side by side but worlds apart while Myron Guttman, PhD, tried to get to the crux of their problem. "Let's try to figure out what you each want from your relationship. Then we'll look at what it might take to satisfy you both."

Ira snorted.

"All right, Mr. Melnick," the therapist said in response. "Let's start with you. What is it you want that you're not getting from your wife?"

"Respect."

It was Ruth's turn to snort.

"And a little understanding of why I put so much of my time into the business."

The therapist opened his mouth to pursue the subject. Ruth raised a hand to stop him. This was their sixth marriage therapist in as many years—Miriam Youngblood, half Jewish, half Native American, and former goodwill ambassador of both the Temple Sisterhood and the Cherokee Nation, had been her personal favorite. She knew what was coming better than the therapist did.

"Perhaps," Ruth said smoothly, striving for the professional nonjudgmental tone all six of their counselors had used, "you could tell us why you feel so compelled to work eighty-hour weeks when you no longer *need* to?" She smiled and cupped her chin in the palm of one hand like Miriam Youngblood, the Jewish Medicine Woman, used to do.

Ira looked down at his watch. He sighed a long-suffering sigh. "We're paying this guy a fortune," he said. "Let *him* talk."

"All right, Mr. Melnick," the psychologist said in the same tone as Ruth had. "Why *do* you feel compelled to work eighty-hour weeks now that you don't have to? Wouldn't it make sense to take it a little easier, spend a little more time with your wife? Enjoy the fruits of your labor?"

Ruth shot Ira a "take that" look. They rarely achieved anything substantial in counseling, but there was the occasional validation. And she'd always been afraid of what might happen if they just gave up and stopped going.

"Look, I love my wife," Ira said. "I wouldn't have stuck around for fifty years if I didn't."

Ruth's mouth gaped open at the left-handed compliment. "Lucky me," she said. "I feel so honored."

"I don't run around. I'm not looking for some little chickadee on the side." Ira continued addressing his comments to the counselor as if Ruth hadn't spoken. "I work because that's what men do. And because there is no such thing as too much financial security, especially in today's environment."

He turned to Ruth now. "And I've never heard my wife complain because there's too much money in the bank. Or because she can buy too many clothes or tchotchkes for the house. Or give too much money to charity or to the grandkids."

He paused and Ruth knew exactly what was coming next just as she knew how he liked his oatmeal in the morning and what he preferred in bed.

"I built and run a successful bagel company. I *am* the Bagel Baron. And I'm tired of hearing her complain about it. What am I going to do on some cruise ship out in the middle of the ocean? Or on some tour of drafty old castles in England, for chrissakes? I'm only seventy-five, which I hear is the new forty. Am I really supposed to move to Florida with all the old *altakakas*. Or sit around the house all day making chitchat with a woman I've been talking to every day for the last fifty years?"

"Poor you!" Ruth said. "Your horrible, demanding wife expects you to spend some time with her when you've been generous enough to stay with her all these years. Where do you want me to pin the medal?"

"Now, let's just calm down and try to . . ." Dr. Guttman's tone was both reasonable and conciliatory as he began to lay out how they might proceed. Ira was looking at his watch again, impatient to get back to the thing he cared about most. And that thing wasn't her.

For the first time Ruth saw the futility of expecting someone else to solve their problems. What were the chances that someone else, even a trained someone else, could convince Ira to notice her again? They'd been having this same conversation for years and it had gotten them nowhere. She was tired of being reasonable. She'd had it with understanding.

"You know what," she said to the two of them. "I'm done with this." She scooted away from Ira's familiar bulk. "You're a nice boy," she said to Dr. Guttman. "I'm sure your mother's very proud. But for once my husband is right. This is a waste of time and money."

One of Ira's bushy gray eyebrows sketched upward. She absolutely hated it when he did that.

"Mrs. Melnick," the psychologist said. "What exactly do you want from your husband? Maybe if you offer a specific thing you want him to do we could start from there."

"What do I want?" she asked. "I want some attention and some of his time. I want him to at least pretend that he wants to be with me. Not act as if I'm the lucky winner in the stayed-married sweepstakes."

"But specifically, what can he do to demonstrate these things to you?"

Ruth thought about this one. There was no one thing she wanted. How did you quantify an amount of attention, a level of interest? She had filled her days with volunteer work, mah-jongg, and ballroom-dance classes, which she loved and which made her feel almost like a young girl again. Next week she'd start belly dancing! She'd spent so much time at the Magnolia Ballroom that she'd come to think of Melanie Jackson as another daughter; it broke her heart how hard the poor thing was trying to put on a brave front.

Ruth looked at the psychologist and then turned to really look at her husband. Ira didn't look bad for seventy-five. He'd thickened through the middle like she had, and had lost several inches from his once-towering frame. His shoulders were no longer quite so massive, and his hair, which had once been a thick, wavy black, was now a much sparser iron gray. But he had a vitality about him still; the air of confidence that had initially attracted Ruth to him was still intact.

"He can come to some sessions at the Magnolia Ballroom with me. They have practice parties every Friday and Saturday night and there's a lesson for the first hour. He could at least try one of them."

The doctor's eyes widened in surprise. Ira's closed in exasperation.

"Do you see what I'm dealing with here?" he said to Dr. Guttman. He turned to her. "When have you ever seen me dance, Ruth? You knew from the day you met me I wasn't a dancer. And I don't see any reason to start now."

Ruth was tired of begging for scraps of attention, tired of being made to feel that everything else in his world was more important than her. "I'm the reason, Ira," she said. "Me. And I don't see why this should be a problem now that you're forty again. Are you too old to learn a new trick?"

"You see?" Ira railed, looking for backup from the other male in the room. "You see how unreasonable she is. What does the fox-trot have to do with love? How will learning to . . . cha-cha improve our marriage?"

"Well, it's obviously . . ." Dr. Guttman began.

"It's a symbol of your interest in me, you schmo," Ruth interrupted. "A way to spend time together. And if you can't be bothered to do that, then the specific thing I want from you is a divorce!"

A dead silence followed her pronouncement. Ira looked completely nonplussed. Dr. Guttman looked like he might want to call his mother. Ruth was more than a little surprised herself.

"You can't be serious," Ira said.

"Mrs. Melnick, you can't possibly want to throw away a half a century of marriage? Why don't we . . ." the doctor began again.

"No," she said, unwilling to take anything back. No amount of talking, nagging, or counseling had made the slightest bit of difference and wasn't likely to. She wanted tangible proof of Ira's love for her. Surely that wasn't too much to ask. "If my husband can't find the time to take an occasional dance class with me, then I don't want to be married to him anymore."

She turned to look Ira in the eye. For the first time she didn't see the man she'd fallen in love with over brisket at his mother's house, or the father of her children, or the years working side by side with him to build the bagel business that had taken him away from her.

Ruth stood on unsteady legs and hated that she had to wait several moments for her body to finish straightening. Ira might want to believe he was middle-aged, but she knew just how old they were.

She looked down at Ira, who was still sitting on the sofa looking like someone had just landed an unexpected punch.

"I've never been more serious in my life," she said. "We take some dance classes together or I file for divorce. Betty Weinman's son is a big-time divorce lawyer. I'm sure I won't have any trouble getting an appointment with him."

"Ruth, come on," Ira said. "You've had your little joke. Sit down, let's talk about this."

"No," she snapped. "I'm finished talking. And this is no joke." She walked toward the door.

"Mrs. Melnick," Dr. Guttman said. "This is no way to settle things. Come back and sit down. We still have ten minutes left."

But Ruth wasn't interested in settling. She was going

to have a real marriage again. Or she was going to have a divorce.

"Ira can stay and make sure he gets every penny out of the session," she said as she swept herself up to her full five feet two. "I'm not wasting any more of my time on a husband who doesn't appreciate my worth."

7

THE DRIVE FROM inside the perimeter of Highway 285 to the suburbs that sprawled around it like the spokes of a wheel took about twenty-five minutes at this time of day. By three thirty P.M. when rush hour began in earnest, the drive to the northern suburbs could stretch into what might pass for eternity.

The drive up Interstate 75 passed largely in silence. Melanie concentrated on the zooming cars and trucks that wove around them. Vivien watched exit signs flash by and studied the occupants of the cars as they passed. Almost everyone drove with a cell phone pressed to one ear. In some frightening cases they also texted or checked email while piloting their multiton vehicles.

When they reached her exit, Melanie slowed. A series of turns took them onto the four-laned Marietta Highway, which was also called Upper Roswell Road or simply 120. In the Atlanta area and its environs, it had apparently been decided that there was no reason to settle for one street name when you could use two or three. If the name had the word "Peachtree" in it, so much the better.

Here, despite a recent gas crisis and an alleged fear of dependency on foreign oil, vans and SUVs of all shapes and sizes dominated. A large percentage had at least one car seat in the back, most of them occupied. Those who'd already been there and done that displayed college bumper stickers on their rear windows; in many cases more than one. And almost every vehicle bore multiple decorative magnets that proclaimed the occupants' activities, possessions, and affiliations.

Reading them as they flew by, Vivien knew what schools their children attended, how many sports they played, where they vacationed, what diseases they wanted to wipe out, and who they'd voted for as well as where they worshipped and exactly how proud they were to be an American.

"Why does everybody have so much personal information plastered all over their SUVS?" she asked.

"Hmmm?" Melanie asked, her gaze following Vivi's finger to the Ford Expedition in front of them. It sported a cutout family that included a mother, a father, two children, and a dog. Beneath these figures were spheres for an elementary and middle school, the logo for a youth baseball team and a cheerleading megaphone as well as an "I'd rather be playing golf" bumper sticker, a Girl Scout trefoil, and an Atlanta Lawn Tennis Association magnet.

Melanie shrugged, seeing nothing out of the ordinary. But Vivien was already playing with the opening hook of a possible column. *In the suburbs people don't wear their hearts on their sleeves; they put them on the backs of their minivans.* She smiled as she fiddled with the wording, relieved. She'd thought it might take a couple of days to come up with a first topic, but they weren't even at Melanie's and she already had a solid idea.

The fall foliage might have faded, but despite a recent drought, plenty of shades of green dotted the landscape.

The man-made landscape wasn't quite so impressive. Banks, gas stations, and drugstores dominated the busiest corners. Big-box retailers like the Home Depot, Target, and Wal-Mart edged up to half-empty strip centers each with its own nail salon, dry cleaner, fitness center, or cell phone store. Fast-food chains had apparently mated and reproduced.

There was plenty of everything a family might need. But nothing was as plentiful as the subdivisions they lived in. The newest of these, especially those still under construction, were fronted by signs announcing the price range of the homes inside.

"Why do they tell everybody how much the houses cost?" Vivien wondered aloud. "Do you have to show a financial statement to look at one?"

Melanie shrugged again, clearly unperturbed by the idea that everyone would know what you could afford or chose to spend. "I don't know," she said. "But when you meet someone around here one of the first things you ask is what subdivision they live in. When they answer, you know right away where they . . . fit."

"Fit?"

Melanie nodded. "Think about how it is in New York," she said. "If I live on the Upper West Side like you do, who am I?"

"Well." Vivien didn't have to really think about this one. "You're probably upper middle class and a liberal Democrat."

Melanie nodded. "And in the East Village?"

"You're more likely to be gay, artistic, and apolitical except for gender issues."

"Long Island?"

"If you live in the right neighborhood, you're Republican, wealthy, and well educated and your husband spends a lot of time on the LIRR." Vivien smiled.

"Well, here in the suburbs we have country club and swim/tennis communities. Gated or not gated. Under a million dollars or over. Pemberton school district or Kilborn. If you put all the details together, you have a clear idea of a family's income and standing, sometimes even their religious affiliation."

"So you don't really need all the extra clues on the back of their cars?" Vivien asked.

Melanie laughed. "Maybe that's just sort of a cheat sheet for the out-of-towners. Actually, you can tell most of those things just by what vehicle somebody drives."

"They're all SUVs, Mel. What's the difference?"

"I'm surprised at you, Vivi," Melanie teased. "You're an investigative reporter. You're not using your powers of observation. Take that for instance." She nodded toward a shiny black vehicle passing on their left.

Vivien squinted to see the emblem on the hood; she'd barely driven since moving to New York. Cars were not something she spent any time thinking about. "It's a Mercedes."

"Right," Melanie said in the tone of a teacher leading a student. "But is it C- or E-Class? An older model or brand-new? And what about that one?" She pointed to a silver vehicle that also had a Mercedes emblem coming up on their right. "Is that the forty-five-thousand-dollar ML350 or the sixty-thousand-plus crossover?"

Vivien shrugged. "Why do they spend so much on . . . transportation?"

"Because here you spend a ridiculous amount of time in your car. And because what you drive says almost as much about who you *are*, as how much you have. A two-seater Mercedes convertible and you're probably a divorced father or a trophy wife. Or my incredibly annoying neighbor Catherine Dennison, whose divorce settlement has enabled her to live in a style far beyond that to which she was accustomed. A Volvo sedan or SUV? You're late thirties, early forties, fairly conservative with at least one child in private school."

As Melanie warmed to her topic, Vivien wished she could whip out a tape recorder. "That woman over there driving the Porsche Cayenne? She hasn't really accepted who she's become. Or the fact that all of her driving will take place in a three-to-five-mile triangle between school, the grocery store, and the dry cleaner. And her husband doesn't want her to.

"It's suburban Morse code; you just have to know how to decipher it."

Pleased with all the valuable information she'd already gleaned, Vivien vowed to stick with her interpreter as much as humanly possible. But as Melanie turned the van into her neighborhood, Garrett Farms, an all-too-familiar tidal wave of exhaustion swamped Vivien. In the garage her sister parked the minivan next to a gold-colored Toyota SUV.

"I sold J.J.'s BMW and bought the RAV4 used for Shelby," Melanie said when she saw Vivi looking at it.

"She doesn't drive it to school?" Vivien asked, stifling a yawn.

"Not since I found out she wasn't actually going to school, when she was going to school."

"Oh."

Melanie looked like she was about to say more but then apparently thought better of it. Vivien suspected her sister was just waiting for her to ask, but the exhaustion was a living thing now, weighting her limbs and dogging her steps. They entered through the eat-in part of the large, cheery kitchen with its dappled granite counters and deep maple cabinets. The family room, which extended from it, had floor-to-ceiling windows overlooking a heavily wooded backyard and French doors that opened onto a bricked patio. A big-screen television hung above the fireplace. The back stairs angled upward on their right.

Vivien felt the last bit of her energy drain out of her. "I hate to be a poor guest," she said. "But would you mind if I took a little nap?"

Melanie looked at her more closely. "You do look really tired. Do you think you're coming down with something?" She put the back of her experienced mother's hand to Vivien's forehead.

Just a baby. Vivien sincerely hoped this couldn't be gleaned from a hand on a forehead. Another yawn escaped.

"You're in the guest room at the top of the stairs." Melanie reached out. "Here, give me your bag."

"No, no," Vivien protested. "I've got it." She grasped the handle of her suitcase more tightly.

"There're fresh towels in your bathroom," Melanie said. "The kids won't be back for another hour and a half or so. Dinner'll be around six thirty."

"If I'm not up, will you wake me then?" Vivien asked.

"Sure." Melanie looked away, a sure sign that she was disappointed.

But Vivien didn't have the energy to apologize or suggest some sisterly gabfest. If she didn't get into a bed soon, she was going to be horizontal right here on the floor. Squaring her shoulders, she began to heft her suitcase and laptop up the stairs, grateful she hadn't had more expandable clothing; what she'd packed was much too heavy already.

⊙

A SHARP KNOCK on the door woke her from a deep sleep. Groggy, Vivien rubbed the sleep from her eyes and managed to pull herself up on her elbows. "Come in!"

The door creaked open and a shaft of light from the

hallway sliced into the darkened room. Shelby stood in the center of it spotlighted like a performer on a stage. "Mom told me to tell you that dinner's ready."

There was no welcoming smile, no launching into her aunt's arms like Shelby used to do as a little girl when the amount of enthusiasm had nothing to do with how often Vivien appeared. Or how long she stayed.

Vivien took in the skintight jeans that perched low on her hips, the equally tight layered Ts that molded to the curves of her body and drew attention to the fully developed breasts. It had been almost a year since Vivien had seen her niece and the difference was startling; as a sixteen-year-old, Shelby had been all arms and legs, awkward as a Great Dane puppy trying to find her feet. At seventeen, she looked like she'd slunk out of a music video, the kind where the female object seethes with barely suppressed sexuality. Her shiny dark hair was board straight and hung well below her shoulders. Dark lashes framed heavily made-up eyes that were the same clear green as J.J.'s. Her full lips carried the bright sheen of gloss; they seemed intentionally pursed, as if showing any hint of teeth might somehow be construed as a sign of welcome. Or weakness.

"Thanks." Vivien sat up all the way and swung her legs over the side of the bed, gingerly checking for her old friend, nausea, pathetically grateful to discover it still absent. She yawned and shot a glance at the bedside clock, surprised to discover she'd slept for almost four hours. Her once-crisp blouse and pants attested to how deeply she'd slept.

Shelby still stood in the doorway watching her in the same way one might watch an unusual specimen at the zoo. Vivien straightened slowly, trying to regain her equilibrium, then walked toward the doorway. Any last thought of a hug fled as Shelby shrank back into the hallway. Careful not to react, Vivien stepped into the hall, pulling the door shut behind her. Shelby's perfume hit her full force, something too heavy and too musky for a girl her age, and Vivien regretted how sensitive her nose had become. When she moved toward the stair, her nose encountered a whole new aroma. She sniffed carefully, waiting for the smell of food to trigger the nausea, but miracle of miracles, for the first time in ages, the response triggered was hunger. She sniffed again, this time appreciatively. Her stomach rumbled loudly in response.

"We're finally having real food now that you're here." Shelby sniffed, not in appreciation of the smells that were now making Vivien's mouth water, but with palpable resentment.

Vivien, who had subsisted on saltines and 7UP for longer than she cared to remember, was unable to feel even a twinge of sympathy. "Is that lasagna?" She tried not to salivate as she turned to her niece for confirmation.

"From scratch." The words were a condemnation.

"Then what are we waiting for?" Suddenly ravenous, Vivien started down the back stairs, not pausing to see whether Shelby followed or not.

"Oh, my God," she said as she reached the bottom step. "Have I died and gone to heaven?"

Melanie looked up from the salad she was mixing. A basket of garlic bread slices sat on the counter. "You were sleeping like the dead when I checked on you a while ago. If you hadn't been snoring, I would have called nine-one-one."

Vivien ran a hand through her hair and ignored the snoring comment. It was impossible to feel this hungry and insulted at the same time.

"Want a glass of wine?" Melanie held up a wineglass and swirled the deep red liquid in the bottom. Vivien salivated again. She'd always been an indifferent drinker, enjoying a glass or two socially. Now that she couldn't have alcohol, it had become much more attractive. "Um, no. Thanks." She averted her eyes so that Melanie wouldn't see the lie in them. "I'm afraid it might put me right back to sleep. Maybe I am coming down with something . . ."

A very tall, broad-shouldered person walked into the kitchen and reached for a piece of the bread in the basket. Melanie gave his hand a halfhearted slap.

Vivien craned her neck upward to look at the young man who used to be her nephew. "What did you do, put him on the rack and stretch him?"

"If only," Shelby said.

"Is that really you, Trip?" Vivien ignored Trip's grimace. Going up on her toes to reach it, she gave his downy cheek a quick peck. "You must have grown a whole foot in the last year. I didn't think that was possible."

"Only for mutants," Shelby, an apparently equal-opportunity offender, pointed out from behind her.

Melanie ignored her daughter's comment. "He did grow almost eight inches last year. He's already taller than J.J. was and the doctor claims he's still growing. Too bad his game isn't basketball instead of baseball."

"Like he even plays baseball anymore." Shelby was like a rain cloud intent on sprinkling her displeasure all over everybody's parade.

Trip flushed but didn't speak. Munching on a second piece of garlic bread, he turned and went into the family room. The TV flared to life. A moment later a cartoon character began to shout at the top of his lungs.

Melanie gave her daughter an irritated look and pushed the salad bowl and the basket of bread toward Shelby. "Since you've gotten rid of your brother, you can finish setting the table."

Shelby's sigh was drawn out and put-upon. Vivien thanked God that setting her straight wasn't her responsibility. She was preparing to hurry everybody to the table while she could still keep herself from falling on the food and wolfing it down with her hands when the doorbell rang. She was the only one who registered surprise.

"Trip?" Melanie called. "Turn off the TV and get the door, please!"

Trip didn't answer, but the TV snapped off and her nephew brushed by on his way to the front door.

"Hey, man." The voice in the foyer was male and upbeat. It sounded familiar, but Vivien couldn't quite place it. "How're you doing?"

If Trip responded, he did so too quietly to reach them, though she saw Melanie straining, just as she was, to hear. The front door closed and two sets of footsteps sounded on the wood floor of the foyer.

Vivien froze when she recognized the man whose arm was slung so casually across Trip's shoulders and who sauntered into the kitchen as if it were his own. It was Clay Alexander, J.J.'s longtime friend and campaign manager; the only other person at the hunting lodge where Jordan Jackson Jr. had died.

Their gazes locked as he removed his arm from Trip's shoulder and accepted a kiss on the cheek from Melanie. "Welcome, Vivi," he said. "It's good to have you back in town. I know Mel's been looking forward to spending time with you."

Clay Alexander was tall, though not quite so tall as Trip, with the lean build of a long-distance runner. His hair was a dark brown bordering on black and his gray eyes were wide set under well-arched brows. He'd obviously come straight from work and wore a European-cut black suit with a white-on-white striped shirt and a red tie with a bold diagonal stripe. The words 'male model' flitted through Vivi's brain. He could have stepped off the cover or out of the pages of a glossy men's magazine, but his gray eyes were far from vacuous; they gleamed with intelligence and other things she couldn't quite identify.

Vivien hadn't seen him since J.J.'s funeral, but it was clear the same could not be said for the Jackson family. Even the up-to-now-surly Shelby allowed him to ruffle her hair in greeting as if she were a child.

Clearly at home, he removed his jacket and slung it over the back of the nearest barstool then pinched a handful of peanuts from a bowl on the counter.

"Mel told me you were coming to . . . recuperate." He neatly sidestepped the details of her injury and his tone was casually friendly, matter-of-fact. But there was something about the way he used her sister's nickname that made Vivi think of a dog who'd already marked his territory and wanted to make sure the other dogs knew it.

"What a pleasant surprise to see you," Vivi said and saw a blush bloom on Melanie's cheeks.

"Clay took us out for dinner last week and I figured since I was cooking in your honor it would be a good time to reciprocate," Melanie said.

Clay reached for the open bottle of wine. "Vivi?"

"No, thanks." She watched him pour a glass for himself, then top off Melanie's without asking.

During dinner Clayton Alexander presided over his former best friend's table like it was his, asking the kids about school, trying to draw Trip out, for which Melanie kept shooting him grateful looks. He did this from J.J.'s former seat at the end opposite Melanie, which no one but Vivien seemed to find significant.

It all looked very Oedipal to Vivien, but then she made her living tapping into undercurrents beneath the surface, examining relationships and words for hidden meanings and unspoken intentions.

It wasn't as easy as usual to do this what with the hunger that she couldn't seem to satisfy no matter how many helpings of lasagna she consumed. She caught the others watching her surreptitiously, but was far too busy eating to try to make excuses. In truth, it was hard to actually lift one's head from one's plate to assess anything when one was completely preoccupied with the act of eating.

Still, there was something about the careful way Clay watched her that made Vivien's investigative antennae jangle. Once when she reached for the basket of garlic bread she accidentally caught his eyes and thought she saw a flash of guilt in them. But guilt about what?

Vivi thought back to the first news reports about J.J.'s death. The press had raced to the hunting lodge in the north Georgia Mountains hot on the heels of the local sheriff and the team he'd called in from the Georgia Bureau of Investigation. The death had been ruled accidental and no one but the seediest tabloids had claimed that the investigation was anything but thorough. At the time it hadn't occurred to Vivi to question the findings. She'd been in the middle of an investigative report of her own, one that had consumed her for close to six months, and everything had seemed clear-cut.

But Clay Alexander had been the only one there with J.J. He'd found the body and called the sheriff. And now he seemed an integral part of his dead friend's family.

Vivien thought about the guilty look she'd intercepted. And felt like a bull who'd just had a red flag waved in its face.

8

ANGELA RICHMAN STARED into the lens of the camera, trying to feel bridal.

"Do you think you could work up a smile, luv?" Brian Jennings, her partner in Photo Ops, stepped out from behind the camera, big and rangy and relentlessly upbeat. "You are getting married to a perfectly lovely chap who seems to worship the ground you tread on. And the gown's not bad, either." He stepped closer to pull the white satin train of the Norma Kamali strapless gown into a semicircle at her feet, then rearranged the veil behind her shoulder.

"Sorry." Angela willed her shoulders to relax and tried to resist licking her overly made-up lips. "I just can't get used to being on this end. It's way too weird. Can't you just squeeze off a couple shots so we can go have a glass of wine?"

He didn't dignify the suggestion with a response, but he did bring a glass of water from a nearby table, held it up for her, and positioned the straw between her lips.

Angela had been photographing others since high school when the Nikon she received for her fifteenth

birthday had become her entrée to the things that other
students seemed to do so easily: the football and basketball games, cheerleading tryouts, student council elections, prom. No one but her parents had ever thought to
photograph her; perhaps they didn't have lenses that were
wide enough. More likely they figured, quite rightly, that
she wouldn't want a reminder of how overweight she was,
how completely outside the realm of attractiveness she
had fallen with her carrot red hair and her full moon of a
freckled face.

"Come on," he said, setting the water back on the
table. "You're going to be a Wesley," he reminded her.
"We want a photo that screams, 'I'm all that.'"

Angela straightened, turning her body so that she
could throw out her chest and angle her shoulders, creating a more flattering line, just as she had instructed so
many of her subjects. But the dress felt too fitted, too
close to her body; there was not enough material to hide
anything. And she was certain her bare arms were jiggling. "You're going to have to shave some off my upper
arms when you do the touch-up," she said. "I don't know
why I ever chose a strapless dress."

It didn't matter that the scale now read one-thirty
instead of two hundred five; that she'd actually managed
to shed seventy-five unwanted pounds and keep them
off for more than three years. That she'd had a breast lift
and a tummy tuck and all kinds of other procedures to
help clean up the unsightly result. That she exercised like
a fiend six days a week and knew she could never stop.
None of those things, not even the reality of the reflection
that now stared back at her from a mirror, could banish
the fat person, the one her classmates had called "Fangie,"
short for "Fat Angie," who still lived inside.

"You chose it because it's perfect on you and because
you have fantastic shoulders," he said as he repositioned

the tripod, studied her through the viewfinder, then
stepped from behind the camera to adjust her key light.
"Because all of you is now completely gorgeous—*SI*
swimsuit edition gorgeous."

"And you are completely full of shit, Brian," she said,
wishing she could believe him, that for just a few minutes
she could be thin on the inside, too. "But don't stop telling me, okay?"

"Never, luv." He'd known her at her heaviest. Only he
and her childhood friend, Susan, continued to treat her
as they always had. Behind the camera he crouched down
and considered her through the viewfinder again. "Now
tilt your chin just a bit to the left and give me that smile
James Wesley fell in love with."

Angela curved her lips upward and widened her eyes
intriguingly. She even managed to add a semblance of a
happy twinkle into their green depths.

But she felt like a complete and utter fraud.

They said that you should be careful what you wished
for because you might get it. And *they* were right.

Angela Richman had spent more than half her life wishing to be thin, wanting to be someone different, hoping to
one day find a special man who would love her. Somehow,
against all odds, all of these things had happened.

But no matter how hard she tried, she couldn't really
believe it. Or figure out how to enjoy it.

☺

VIVIEN WOKE IN the predawn darkness to a silence that
simply didn't exist in New York City. There were no cars,
no horns, no footsteps on the street below. Cocooned in
her blankets, cushioned in quiet, she lay there listening
intently. But the only sounds that emerged were the occasional snore from Trip's nearby bedroom and the steady
tick of the grandfather clock in the foyer.

After a quick bathroom run, she scurried back to bed. Her bladder was now blissfully empty, but her mind was too full for sleep. It called up Melanie's determined optimism, Shelby's belligerence, Trip's stinginess with words. The way J.J.'s absence felt so . . . present. How strange it had felt to see Clay Alexander sitting in J.J.'s seat at the table, presiding over J.J.'s family.

Though she spent much of her waking hours trying not to dwell on her pregnancy, it was always at the core of her thoughts. She'd believed she knew her mind and her body. But now both had become alien and unfathomable. Her body taunted her with each change it went through; it seemed that as soon as she got used to some new indignity another took its place. Worse, her mind seemed stripped of its free will. Not to mention the ability to think.

In a few hours the household would be awake. The kids would head off to school. Melanie would—she realized with some surprise that although she knew Melanie owned and ran a ballroom dance studio, she actually had no idea what Melanie did all day and hadn't thought to ask.

But it was part of her job as a suburban columnist to find out. Which meant she'd have to get up and dress in the morning so that she could accompany Melanie wherever it was that she went. Vivi set the alarm clock beside the bed for six thirty, just in case she lucked out and fell back asleep. But although she closed her eyes again and tried to concentrate on nothingness for a good thirty minutes, she finally gave up and flipped on the bedside light.

There was a novel in her carry-on, but she'd barely finished a page on the plane and she didn't feel like reading it now. What Vivi really wanted to do was talk to Stone, but she was afraid that if she actually reached him and heard his voice, she'd immediately spill all. Clamping down on her neediness, she booted up her laptop and brought up a blank page on the screen. After a few moments of thought, she typed the opening line that had come to her the day before.

I have been observing the denizens of this pocket of suburbia in which I find myself for less than twenty-four hours and have already learned one important thing: here people don't wear their hearts on their sleeves; they put them on the backs of their minivans.

For a few minutes she just sat and thought about what she'd seen on the drive from the airport to Melanie's, replaying her sister's comments in her mind.

As they pass you, and believe me they will, you'll know everything there is to know about them. Because who they are, what they care about, and where they "belong" has been reduced to decorative magnets that have been stuck all over the backs of their SUVs.

These magnetized spheres and shapes will also tell you where they worship and where they vacation, what illnesses they've dealt with or would like to see eradicated, who they voted for in the last election and who they plan to vote for in the next.

She was careful not to quote Melanie too closely in case her sister, who had never been a major newspaper devotee, ever happened across the column. But as Vivien typed, the words began to flow from her mind and through her fingertips in that wonderful way that she didn't understand and tried not to question. Slowly, she began to relax, her body unclenching bit by bit as the words formed in her mind, then found their way onto the page.

All of the schools their children attend from preschool to college are there like some public scrapbook. There are magnets and bumper stickers that inform you if their child made the honor roll or was once named the student of the month. Bottom line, if they or one of their children has ever done it or even thought about it, they've got the magnet to prove it. And every magnet deserves to be displayed on the back of the family chariot.

She added a few jabs about what might drive people to reveal so much, then did some cutting and pasting until she had her observations in an order that belied the amount of editing she'd done and, instead, felt like a natural progression. And then she concluded, *As it turns out, these clues aren't even necessary because your entire personality is revealed by your choice of vehicle. Apparently you are not only your magnets; you are also what you drive. Just a quick look at the color, make, and model you're driving and your fellow suburbanites will know everything about you from how much money you make to how often you have sex.*

She played with the car thing for a while, paraphrasing Melanie's comments in a shocked, yet slightly snide tone that gave it an edge.

She did feel a tiny fissure of guilt for putting her sister's world under such a judgmental microscope, but she pushed it aside; like the pseudonym she'd borrowed for her byline, she'd think about that "tomorrow."

After getting in as many zingers as she could under the guise of "reporting," she closed with a breezy, *I feel like a scientist transported to a newly charted planet that is absolutely teeming with alien life-forms. So stay tuned. I'll have more observations for you next week!* She signed it, *Your stranger in an even stranger land, Scarlett Leigh.*

Then she attached the document to an email to John Harcourt and sent her first postcard from suburbia on its way to New York.

Before she could talk herself out of it, Vivi dialed Stone's cell phone and was both equally relieved and nervous when he picked up.

"Hi there," he said. "You're up early."

"It's so quiet," she said, cautioning herself to keep it light. "I'd forgotten the sound of grass growing."

He laughed and she smiled in return. Stone had always been her best audience.

"So what do you have planned today?" he asked. If she closed her eyes, she could pretend he was here in the room with her and not on the other side of the world. "I'm just going to hang around with Mel, see how she spends her days."

"That's good," he said and she let his voice wash over her. "How are she and the kids doing?"

Vivien felt a familiar flush of guilt at how little she'd done for Melanie, Shelby, and Trip over the last two years. Was that why she'd found Clay Alexander's role in her sister's life so jarring?

"They're okay," she said. "Well, not really okay. They're all going through the motions, but I don't know if any of them have really moved on. And . . ." She paused, not sure how to put her reaction to Clay Alexander into words. "His best friend and campaign manager—the one he was with when he died—seems to be very involved in Mel and the kids' lives."

"That's a good thing, isn't it?"

"I guess so." She hesitated. "It's just that now that I'm really thinking about it, the whole idea of J.J. shooting himself while cleaning his hunting rifle seems so absurd. I mean he'd been hunting since he was a child. It's not like he was some novice who'd never used a gun."

Stone sighed, a sound she knew well. "Vivi, you covered the police beat starting out just like I did. I don't remember the statistics, but those kinds of accidents aren't at all unusual." She could practically hear him thinking; she just wished he were doing that thinking here. So that she could tell him about the baby, read his true reaction in his face.

"I mean there was a full investigation, wasn't there?"

Stone asked. "Do you have any reason to believe anything was overlooked?"

She flushed again as she acknowledged she was a bit late in worrying about this now. She knew people at the GBI; a couple of phone calls two years ago wouldn't have been out of line.

"Vivi," Stone asked. "Are you still there?"

"Yes," she said, although the truth was at the moment her thoughts were in a north Georgia mountain cabin two years ago. "I was just thinking that maybe I should call my contact at the bureau and see if I can have a look at the file."

"I know that tone, Vivi. If it weren't so early you'd probably already be dialing the number." She could practically hear him shaking his head and picture the smile tugging at his lips.

"Just take it slow," Stone said as they prepared to hang up. "And remember, this is your family you're talking about. Sometimes even when things seem open and shut, it's possible to find out things that no one really wants to know."

9

MELANIE FINISHED PACKING Trip's lunch, tucking the frozen water bottle into its own plastic bag to prevent leakage while keeping things "refrigerated," then pulled a carton of eggs and a gallon of milk from the refrigerator. Coffee dripped into the carafe of the coffee-maker, the smell of the warm brew almost, but not quite, as potent as that first gulp of caffeine.

Upstairs Trip's alarm buzzed and was followed by the sound of her son clomping to the bathroom. A few moments later water ran in his shower. Trip was like clockwork physically—he got up, showered, and dressed each school morning without prodding, but his brain didn't really kick in until much later. This could not be said of Shelby, who would stay in bed until the last possible moment and then require both prodding and ejecting to remove her from it. When she did get out of bed, she was in a foul mood, which she liked to share with those around her.

Melanie was on her second cup of coffee and had Trip's

bacon and eggs plated and on the table when her son thudded down the stairs.

"Morning, sweetie," she said, wondering as she always did how he managed to shower and dress without actually opening his eyes.

His greeting was garbled and his eyes mere slits as she pulled out the kitchen chair and guided him into it. Without further comment he lifted the glass of orange juice and drained it. In a matter of minutes his plate was empty.

"Morning, Mel."

Melanie looked up in surprise at Vivien's greeting. She was even more surprised to see that her sister was fully dressed.

"Oh, my God," Vivi said. "Is that bacon and eggs I smell?"

Melanie hesitated, unable to believe her sister could have an ounce of vacant space inside her, given the amount of lasagna she'd consumed the night before. "Yes. Do you want some?"

"That would be great." Vivien mussed the top of Trip's head as she passed. "I'm completely ravenous."

Melanie lit the burner under the frying pan without comment. "You want some coffee?"

Vivien looked at the pot longingly but declined. "I think I'll just have some tea." She whipped bags of chamomile from her pants pocket. "I'm trying to lay off the caffeine."

"Okay." Melanie filled the teakettle and put it on to boil. When the frying pan was hot again, she laid strips of bacon in it, then popped four slices of whole wheat bread into the toaster. Upstairs Shelby's alarm clock blared on, the beep sirenlike in its intensity.

How Shelby could tune out the sound, which originated

about six inches from her head, Melanie didn't know. But she did know that somebody needed to go upstairs and pry her out of bed.

Despite his superior size and physical strength, Trip wasn't awake enough to be sent into such hazardous combat. Melanie's own hands were full with breakfast. Removing the now-whistling kettle from the burner, she poured the boiling water into the mug that held Vivien's teabag and realized she had another option.

"I've got breakfast under control," Melanie said casually. "Would you mind getting Shelby up? If she doesn't get in the shower right now, I'll get stuck in the car-pool line from hell."

"Sure."

Melanie felt a brief flash of guilt for sending her sister up unarmed and without a warning. But Vivien was a big girl and had managed to survive in New York for over a decade; she'd even been shot. Surely she could handle one seventeen-year-old girl.

She hid her smile as Vivien climbed the stairs. While she cracked eggs into a bowl, then began to scramble them, Melanie eavesdropped. There was murmuring, Vivien's words crisp and pointed, Shelby's an indecipherable whine. The alarm went off in mid beep. Melanie and Trip exchanged a glance, but studiously avoided placing bets on who would win the skirmish.

Just when it seemed there'd be nothing to hear, there was a yelp. Then another. A loud thud followed as something—or someone—hit the floor.

Melanie flipped the bacon and gave the eggs a final scramble. There was a shout. The stomp of angry feet, though it wasn't clear whose. A door slammed, then was yanked open, then slammed again.

Trip snorted with laughter when the shower in Shelby's bathroom went on. He hummed the theme song from

Rocky as Vivien walked unsteadily down the back stairs into the kitchen.

Her blouse had come untucked and her hair stuck out in strange angles from her head. A grim, but satisfied, smile hovered on her lips. Her eyes still carried the glint of battle.

"You might have warned me," she said.

"Sorry." Melanie dished the food onto their plates and handed one to her sister. "I thought you'd be the perfect person for the job. You never used to be a morning person, either." They carried their plates to the kitchen table and settled in to eat. "I'm a little surprised to see you up and dressed," she said as Vivien tucked into her food. "Do you have somewhere you need to be?"

"Just thought I'd tag along with you today."

For a moment Melanie thought she'd misheard. She finished chewing. Swallowed. "With me? You want to spend the whole day with me?"

Vivien piled some scrambled egg on half a piece of toast and lifted it toward her mouth. "Unless I'll be in the way."

Melanie studied her sister for a long moment. She was wearing nice pants and a crisp white blouse. Her shoes were pointy-toed with three-inch heels. "I'm not actually going anywhere in particular," she pointed out. "I'm going to drop the kids off, run errands, do a volunteer shift, give a private lesson—nothing you'd find particularly interesting."

But Vivien's eyes didn't glaze over as they usually did when Melanie mentioned the mostly mundane details of her life.

"No, I'm really curious to see how you spend your day," Vivien said. "If you don't mind, I want to do all those things with you."

"Why?"

Vivien shrugged. "I've always wondered what you do all day."

Melanie tried to process this as they finished their meal. Part of her felt flattered by Vivien's interest. The larger part of her was already cringing at how boring and trivial her day would seem to her sister. "Do you want to go change?"

Vivien took in Melanie's stretch jeans, cotton twinset, and beat-up Nikes. There was a strange note of defiance in her voice when she said, "I don't own any mommy clothes."

Shelby clomped down the stairs at that moment in a low-cut long-sleeved T-shirt and a tight jean skirt that left her long bare thighs exposed. Her hair was freshly washed, blow-dried, and straightened; her makeup had apparently been applied with a trowel.

Melanie sighed. "That skirt is way too short," she said. "Hurry up and change. And while you're up there you can remove some of that makeup."

Shelby didn't move. "There's nothing wrong with my clothes or my makeup," Shelby said. "Besides, I don't have time for that. I need to be at a help session for History."

Melanie's lips clamped shut. Leave it to Shelby to try to turn this into an either/or situation. "If you'd gotten up when your alarm went off, we wouldn't have to choose between looking acceptable or getting to a morning help session."

"If you hadn't sent such a . . . novice . . . to get me out of bed, I would have been ready earlier." Shelby sent Vivien a taunting look.

"Novice?" Vivien took in Shelby's getup. "You look like a professional in that getup. If you insist on advertising, someone's going to want to take you up on it."

Leave it to Vivien to call a spade a spade, Melanie thought as she stepped between them. She might not be able to force her sister to dress appropriately for her surroundings, her daughter was another story. "Shelby, go tone down your makeup and put on a pair of pants or a longer skirt; that one's indecent. You've got five minutes."

With a groan and an exaggerated roll of the eyes, Shelby stomped upstairs.

"Trip—in the car." Melanie dumped the frying pan, spatula, and dishes in the sink to be dealt with later. "Vivi, are you sure you want to come?" She gave her sister one last chance to back out before heading toward the garage to fire up the minivan.

"Shotgun!" Trip called out, grabbing up his backpack and falling in behind her.

"*I'm* riding shotgun," Vivien said in answer as she followed Trip and the toned-down Shelby. "Age before beauty, kid. And as nice as it is to hear your voice, I wouldn't bother trying to call it again. As long as I'm here I've got permanent dibs on the front seat."

Melanie backed down the drive. In the cul-de-sac, she put the car in drive but spotted trouble up ahead. "It's Catherine. Don't make eye contact!" She and both kids snapped their gazes forward.

"What are you doing?" Vivi asked.

"See the redbrick with the convertible in the driveway up on the left?" Melanie dropped her voice to a whisper, keeping her own gaze straight ahead.

Vivien sneaked a look as they drew closer. A long-legged blonde in skintight jeans and a sprayed on T-shirt was leaning over the passenger side of a silver Mercedes two-seater, her shapely rear end pointed at the street. "Not bad," Vivien said, taking in the perfectly sculpted body and, when she turned, the too-perfect face. "But I don't think much of it's original."

"That's Catherine Dennison. Her ex-husband is a

plastic surgeon. Ongoing work was part of her divorce settlement."

Vivi laughed and took another look as Melanie slowed for the stop sign across from Catherine's house.

"Careful!" Melanie warned. "If you make eye contact, we'll . . . oh, damn. Here she comes!"

Cradling a ball of white fluff in the crook of one arm, Catherine left the Mercedes to flag them down. Mouth arranged into what she hoped would pass for a smile, Melanie pulled to a full stop.

"I just wanted to make sure you got the invitation to Claire's starring performance in the high school production of *South Pacific* next week," Catherine Dennison said when Melanie had rolled the window down. "She's playing Nellie Forbush. And just wait until you hear her solos! Why, she's been tapped for a Who's Who in High School Drama, and the head of the drama department at Pemberton thinks she can get a college scholarship for either acting or music performance."

The blonde paused to draw a breath—something she didn't have to do nearly enough—and noticed Vivien in the passenger seat. "That must be your sister," she said. "You all look like spitting images of each other. Why, I bet . . ."

Knowing there was unlikely to be another breath drawn anytime soon, Melanie dove in. "Catherine, this is my sister, Vivien. Vivi, Catherine."

Vivien nodded. Catherine opened her mouth, but Melanie was afraid to let her get started again.

"We'll be glad to buy some tickets, though I'm not sure if we'll be able to make the performance," Melanie said. "Why don't you just have Claire drop them in our mailbox and then I'll drop off a check?"

Catherine opened her mouth again.

"You know I hate to cut you off," Melanie interrupted

again. "But Shelby's already late for an appointment at school." She would not tell this woman that Shelby needed help with History, among other things. "I'm sure we'll be seeing you soon."

Catherine's mouth was still open when they pulled away.

"Good grief," Vivi said, "what was that all about?"

"Once she gets started, you can spend a good twenty minutes listening to the details of Catherine and Claire's great adventures. It just depresses the hell out of me."

"Was that a *dog* she was holding?" Vivi asked as Melanie drove toward the front of the neighborhood.

"Oh, yes. It's a Havanese named . . ." Melanie pursed her lips to try to give it the same inflection Catherine used. ". . . Pucci. And it's even more . . . precious . . . than her daughter, Claire, who's in Shelby's grade. We avoid all of them whenever possible. Trust me, it's easier that way."

As Melanie zoomed out of the neighborhood and onto Roswell Road toward Pemberton High School, Vivien tried to whip up some enthusiasm for what lay ahead. It was barely seven thirty and she'd already wrestled one teenager out of bed and beat out another for the seat she sat in. And people thought living in New York was tough.

Still, the proper frame of mind was essential. If she was going to glean story ideas from how suburbanites like her sister spent the day, she needed to keep her eyes and mind open, try to let go of her preconceived notions, and see things through fresh eyes.

Perhaps it would help if she envisioned herself as a modern-day Jane Goodall about to observe the social interactions of chimpanzees. So thinking, Vivien stared intently out the window as neighborhoods and businesses flashed by.

Throughout the twelve-minute drive, Shelby, whose

most critical body parts were now covered, alternately pouted and texted. Trip stared silently out his window. The tinny beat from both of their iPods dueled it out in the backseat.

Melanie drove quickly and efficiently. In the car-pool line at the school's entrance, she performed the required maneuvers with a finesse born of experience. It was almost like watching a surgeon operate. Or a prima ballerina gliding through the intricate steps of an oft-performed ballet.

"We're lucky traffic's so light this morning," Melanie observed as they left the residential area and turned back onto Upper Roswell Road.

"You call this . . . light?" Vivien, who'd contemplated gridlock from the back of many an NYC cab, thought Upper Roswell Road could give Broadway a run for its money in terms of congestion.

Melanie shrugged as she wove through the traffic. A few minutes later she turned off the road and into a parking lot. A wooden sign read East Cobb Park.

"What happens here?" Vivien asked. It wasn't even eight A.M.; theirs was one of only three vehicles in the lot.

"Walking," Melanie said as she exited the van. Vivien followed behind her.

The park was small and simply laid out; a figure eight of walking track encircled by trees and in turn encircling grassy areas and a fenced playground. It was pretty here, restful. Vivien wouldn't have minded vegging out at one of the picnic tables, maybe reading the paper stretched out under a tree. But Melanie stepped onto the concrete walking track and began to move smartly. Surprised, Vivien had to jog the first few steps to catch up to her.

"Why are we doing this?" Vivien had to bite the words out as she scurried to match Melanie's pace.

"Exercise." Melanie began to pump her arms. Pronounced heel-toe action followed. "It helps get the heart pumping and the juices flowing."

Vivien bit back a complaint. She wasn't exactly in peak physical condition. Given the way she was having to scramble to keep up, it was far more likely that her heart would race, not pump, and that her "juices" would slosh rather than flow. And she definitely wasn't dressed for a workout. Had she really sneered at Melanie's "mommy clothes"?

"You look like you've put on a couple of pounds. Walking's a really good low-impact calorie burner." Melanie smiled. "So's dancing. Belly dance starts tomorrow night. We'll get rid of that excess before you know it."

Not likely, Vivien thought. As the only member of her family who was completely devoid of rhythm, she'd learned at a very early age to avoid dancing in all its forms.

Pride kept her chin up and her strides in line with Melanie's as they walked briskly—some might say too briskly for the Charles Jourdan pumps Vivien wore—on the concrete path. She eyed each tree-shaded bench and picnic table they passed, wishing she could stop and sit for just a moment. But she refused to be the first to ask and did her best to hide how much effort she was expending to keep up.

They talked—when Vivien wasn't too short of breath to form words—about inconsequential things. What time they were expected at Magnolia Hall for Sunday supper. Who had sublet Vivi's apartment. How long Stone would be on assignment in Afghanistan. The lies Vivien had prepared about why she'd left her job at CIN and the reasons for her weight gain proved unnecessary. At least for the moment, Melanie seemed as eager as Vivien to stay away from anything that delved beneath the surface.

It was a great relief when Melanie finally slowed and then came to a stop. In truth, Vivien was more than ready to go back to the house and curl up for the rest of the morning. But when Melanie offered to drop her there so she could do just that, Vivien refused. So far she'd seen the high school and the businesses that lined Roswell Road. Not exactly enough information on which to base a series of columns.

And so the power walk eased into a marathon. For which Vivien had failed to train.

Strapped into the minivan, they drove from place to place at what felt like the speed of sound. Little more than an hour into Melanie's errands, Vivien felt as if she'd traveled to the ends of the earth, even though they'd only traveled up and down the same three roads and hadn't pushed outside a seven-mile radius.

At the post office they waited in line for twenty-five minutes to return a package to a mail-order catalogue company. This was followed by a drop-off at the alteration lady and a pickup at the dry cleaner. Then they were off to Target for household supplies and then to Office-Max for envelopes and flyers Melanie had had printed for the studio.

At eleven o'clock they drove back to the high school, where Vivien assisted Melanie with her two-hour shift on the "copy crew" where they made thousands of copies of things, then stuffed them—one at a time—into the appropriate mailboxes.

A text message from Shelby sent them to the closest bookstore for a book Shelby was required to read and had forgotten to buy and which they dropped back off at the front desk at the high school; that made their third trip to Pemberton that morning.

At the grocery store, Melanie ordered a deli platter and veggie tray for an upcoming committee meeting and

picked up a few odds and ends. Then they went to Old
Navy where Melanie bought Trip a pair of khakis and a
button-down shirt to wear to supper on Sunday.

Like hamsters on a wheel they raced without stopping
but got nowhere near a finish line.

Before each errand Melanie offered to run Vivien home,
but as much as Vivien wanted to go there, she knew she
had to make it through the day so that she could determine
firsthand which parts of it might lead to a future column.

Lunch was a drive-through meal from Chik-fil-A,
which Vivien, who was once again ravenous, devoured on
the way to the Magnolia Ballroom. There Melanie gave a
warm hug to an older woman with stark white hair and a
penetrating gaze, who was manning Grandmother Gray's
antique writing desk.

"Vivi," Melanie said as she straightened. "This is Ruth
Melnick. She is truly fabulous. I don't know how I'd run
the studio without her."

Ruth beamed at Melanie's praise, then turned to consider Vivien. The wattage of her smile dimmed ever so
slightly. "Nice to finally meet you," she said. "You don't
get down here too often, do you?" The tone said, not often
enough, and Vivien wondered just how much Melanie
had confided in the older woman.

"Ruth is my Jewish mother," Melanie said.

"We have a Jewish mother?" Vivien asked, trying,
unaccountably, to win a smile from Ruth Melnick. "Does
Caroline know?"

Melanie laughed.

Ruth was a tougher audience. "I've met your mother,"
she said. "You have the same air about you."

Melanie giggled again. All of them knew this was not
a compliment.

"And you can tell this just from looking at me?" Vivien
asked, annoyed now.

Ruth shrugged as if she really were related and therefore had the right to say whatever she felt. "I only know
what Melanie's told me."

Melanie blushed. Vivien's chin shot up, taking her nose
with it. She knew because she had to look down it to see
the look on Ruth Melnick's face.

"Oh, yes." Ruth nodded. "You definitely resemble her."

Mother Melnick turned back to Melanie. "The Hendersons are waiting over there." Ruth nodded toward a
couple who appeared to be even older than Ruth. "They
want to start on the Latin dances. They're going on a
cruise over the holidays."

"Let me just go change shoes." Melanie waved to the
couple, signaling that she'd be right with them.

Vivien plunked down at a skirted table. She toed her
shoes off as Melanie walked out onto the dance floor. Her
sister smiled at the couple and introduced herself. Vivien
yawned.

By the time Melanie had her students ready to practice
to music, Vivien was ready to admit defeat and beg to be
put in a cab, despite the fact that she hadn't actually seen
one since they'd left the airport yesterday. A small whim-
per escaped her lips at the lovely thought.

But when Melanie walked past to put on another piece
of music and whispered, "Vivi, you look dead and bored
to boot. Why don't you let me see if Ruth can run you
home?" Vivien knew she couldn't cave. She was not going
to give Ruth Melnick the opportunity to pronounce her
lazy or disinterested. And there was always the chance
she'd find something in the lesson that she might write
about.

When the Hendersons left, Melanie brought over
the flyers and envelopes they'd picked up earlier. Ruth
brought a roll of stamps. "So how long are you planning

to stay this time?" Ruth asked as she and Melanie sat down on either side of Vivi.

"I'm not sure," Vivien said, noting Ruth's protective posture. She had the sense the woman would throw herself in front of Melanie, maybe even take a bullet for her, if necessary. "I'm taking a, um, somewhat open-ended break from work."

Ruth sniffed, but made no other comment. Vivien could just picture the woman's internal bullshit-o-meter clanging loudly.

In the near-empty ballroom they prepared the mailing, with Vivien stuffing the newly printed flyers into the envelopes, Melanie affixing the address label and postage on each, then passing it on to Ruth, who glued the envelopes shut. On the way home, Melanie and Vivien would stop back at the post office to mail them.

Home. The word practically made Vivien tremble with relief.

And speaking of relief, once again, Vivien's stomach rumbled. "Melanie, is there anything to eat here?" Vivien asked.

"You're hungry?" Melanie checked her watch as if time had anything to do with the yawning pit in Vivien's stomach. "We just ate two hours ago."

"And your point is?" Vivien asked as her stomach rumbled again, or maybe that was just an echo in the emptiness.

"I think we have some cookies from the last practice party," Melanie said. "And maybe some chips, too."

"Bless you!" Vivien followed directions down the lone hallway to the kitchen, where she poked through the cabinets. The chips hadn't been opened, but she found two different bags of cookies and wolfed down one oatmeal and one chocolate chip right there before filling a plate to take back to Melanie and Ruth. When they both refused them, Vivien settled the plate in front of her. Although she tried to slow her rate of consumption to near-normal levels, the look Melanie and Ruth tried to share over her head told her no one was fooled.

Vivien munched and stuffed envelopes, perking up with each cookie she consumed, until she felt almost revived. There were several private lessons going on now out on the dance floor, little pockets of activity in various corners of the long, rectangular space, and she watched for a while, unable to miss how focused the students looked as they tried to master the steps and how happy they appeared when things started to come together. The music changed regularly, each instructor taking a turn selecting what would play so that his or her students could practice what they were learning.

"We've got six registered for the Wednesday night belly-dancing class, including me and the bride-to-be," Ruth said to Melanie as she affixed the final mailing labels.

"You can add Vivi and me to the list," Melanie said. "Vivi's not so keen about dancing, but belly dancing is great exercise and there's no partner to maim." She grinned. "Um, worry about."

Ruth made no comment, but Vivi had no doubt that the woman would enjoy watching Vivien humiliate herself. Which was all the more reason not to let it happen. Now that her sugar high had begun to wear off, the only thing Vivien was interested in was getting back to Melanie's and crawling into bed. Well, okay maybe that was two things, but they were very closely intertwined.

As she followed Melanie to the minivan and climbed slowly into the passenger seat, she wondered how Melanie could look so . . . awake. They still had to go back to the post office to mail out the envelopes they'd just stuffed and addressed. And then, according to Melanie, there was dinner to be fixed. Homework to be supervised. Children to be spoken to.

Vivien yawned, her lids impossibly heavy.

Her chin nodded down to her chest as Melanie pulled the van out into traffic. As her head ultimately came to rest against the window her last semi-coherent thought was that triathletes had nothing on her sister and the other women she'd seen racing in and out of the establishments in east Cobb today. She was too sleepy to worry about a lead-in sentence, but somewhere in her subconscious she knew she had the subject for her second column.

She was asleep before they got to the post office and only roused when they got back to Melanie's. Later as she hugged the pillow and curled on her side, Vivien knew there was something she'd meant to tell Melanie. Some thing about not dancing. Ever. She yawned, trying to hold on to the thought even as she dove more deeply down into the welcoming abyss of sleep.

First thing tomorrow morning just as soon as she woke up and tossed Shelby out of bed, she'd make sure that Melanie understood. You could lead a klutz to a ballroom, but that didn't mean you could make her dance.

10

"I'M HERE," VIVIEN said from between clenched teeth. "But as I've told you about a thousand times now, I'd rather just watch."

Vivien and Melanie stood in front of the mirrors at the far end of the Magnolia Ballroom dance floor. The six other members of the Wednesday night beginning belly-dance class, as well as their instructor, stood in a ragged line about five feet away from them, trying to act as if they weren't watching or listening.

"Vivi, this could be your opportunity to learn how to dance once and for all. Mother was practically a prima ballerina; I started dancing before I could walk. Even Daddy and Ham can pick out the rhythm of a song and are able to lead. There is no way someone from our gene pool could be as utterly helpless on a dance floor as you pretend to be."

"I am not pretending." Vivien removed her arm from her sister's grasp, but was careful to keep her voice low. Vivi sneaked a peek over her shoulder at the assembled

students. The kindest adjective she could think of for
them was "eclectic."

Ruth Melnick, who was both short and barrel-chested,
was the oldest. She wore black knit pants and a matching
top and had tied the chiffon hip scarf that Naranya had
brought for each student low on her hip—or at least the
place where her hips should have been. It was bright red.

Diana and Delores Shipley were in their midthirties.
Vivien had automatically christened them Tweedle Di
and Tweedle Dee, due to the glaring disparity in their
sizes. Tweedle Diana was tall and leggy while Tweedle
Delores was much shorter and markedly rounder. They
had blondish-brown hair and were attractive in a girl-
next-door kind of way. Individually they wouldn't have
drawn a second look; viewed as a pair it was impossible
not to puzzle over the vagaries of heredity and the ran-
domness of nature.

Angela Richman fell between the Shipley sisters
height-wise and appeared to be the youngest member of
the class. Her deep red hair had golden highlights and
she wore it in a short layered style that drew attention
to her heart-shaped face and deep green eyes. The wrists
that poked out from her long-sleeved black T-shirt were
downright knobby and her ankles and bare feet were nar-
row and trim, but the black yoga pants and T flopped
loosely around her, at least a full size too big.

Vivien, who had squeezed into the only pair of black
pants that still buttoned and tried to hide her burgeoning
breasts and expanding waistline beneath a stretchy black
camisole and black-and-white-striped overblouse, envied
her the extra room.

Sally Hailstock, a fortysomething English teacher at
Pemberton, had had a good bit of trouble stretching the
chiffon hip scarf all the way across her broad hips, but she

had a hearty laugh and a lot of enthusiasm. Beside her, Lourdes Gonzales's body in black leggings and matching jogging bra appeared quite small and curvy. She tied the lime green hip scarf at a jaunty angle and gave her hips a good shake to make the scarf coins jangle.

Vivien did not want to wear a scarf that jangled or learn how to isolate any body parts, which was apparently what the first lessons were all about. She seriously doubted that she could control her stomach muscles at this point—not that she'd ever possessed abs of steel—and she didn't want to draw attention to that fact. She drew a deep breath in a vain attempt to regain her composure and to find the upper hand. "I'd really rather sit this first one out. And maybe start next week."

"No." That was it. No negotiating, no conversation. Somehow, when Vivien wasn't looking, her little sister had begun to grow a backbone. "This will be a lot easier than couples' dancing and it doesn't really matter how good you are; only that you do it." She took Vivi by the elbow, placed her beside Sally, and tied a neon pink scarf with gold coin-shaped jangles around her hips.

"Naranya's a really good teacher," Melanie said as she tied a scarf around her own hips and stepped into line on Vivi's other side. "I'm sure you'll do fine."

But as Naranya punched a key on a laptop computer and the plaintive strains of Middle Eastern music wailed out of the speakers, Vivi suspected her sister's assurances belonged with the better-known and equally untrue "the check is in the mail" and "I'll still respect you in the morning."

"I am Naranya de Costa," their instructor began. "I am from Brazil. Een my country there are many Egyptian and Lebanese and belly dancing is very big. Wherever you go, depending on the country, the version that ees danced is unique to that part of the world. You weel be getting a mixture of Brazilian, Middle Eastern, and American. But we all begin in the same way. With the stretching."

A group tango lesson was underway in an opposite corner of the studio, and a middle-aged couple was being tutored near them, everyone with their patch of mirror. Angela kept her gaze fixed on the golden-skinned darkhaired Naranya, and occasionally on the other members of the class; too often when she glanced in a mirror it was Fangle who appeared.

All chatter ceased as Naranya raised her arms above her head and clasped her hands together, stretching upward. The class followed. Carefully, Naranya led them through a series of stretches, demonstrating each thoroughly. Once her intro was completed, Naranya was not a big talker, but moved slowly and carefully, sometimes moving or turning in a different direction so that everyone could see the subtleties of each movement.

Angela had been exercising relentlessly for three years and had tried all kinds of classes, so the stretching was both familiar and comfortable. Next came the isolation exercises, which were a bit more challenging. Angela kept her gaze on their instructor and the mirrored wall behind her intentionally out of focus. Occasionally, she closed her eyes in an effort to feel the roll of her shoulder, the sway of an arm, the shift of her rib cage. After a lifetime of trying to ignore her body, it was the oddest thing to tune in so carefully to its individual components.

"Now for the basic dance position, we turn to the side with our legs in a . . ." Naranya paused, looking for the right word and tossed a hank of heavy dark hair back over one shoulder. "Our legs they are parallel. Now we pretend to walk a step, we don't do eet, we just pretend. And we put all of our weight onto the back leg."

They "assumed the position" as best they could, all of their gazes trained on Naranya.

"Yes, yes," the instructor said. "That ees it. Point your tailbone to the floor."

She waited for them to adjust themselves. Some, Angela noted, did this more successfully than others. "Hold your arms out away from your body. Your chest, eet must be held high."

There were giggles and more than a few groans as Naranya moved from student to student checking their positions and making slight adjustments. The hip lift and drop was slightly more challenging.

"Pretend that you have a string tied to your right hip bone and somebody is pulling up on it," Naranya said to the taller Shipley sister as everyone's hips went up and down.

"I hate to break it to you," Vivien huffed nearby, "but my hips don't actually seem to work independently."

"Mine don't, either." This from the English teacher who looked like what Angela still felt: too big, over-stuffed, hopelessly jiggly.

Ruth snorted and Angela stole a glance at the white-haired woman. Even though Ruth's body was shaped more like a block of wood than an hourglass, she'd been able to turn the hip lift and drop into the "bounce" it was meant to be.

"Eees good, Ruth," Naranya said, smiling as they all watched Ruth's hip go up and down.

Lourdes was doing pretty well, too. She'd started smiling the minute the music started and hadn't stopped since.

Melanie's arms curved gracefully out to either side and her hip moved fluidly up and down in short controlled movements. She moved in front of Vivien to demonstrate.

"You've got to *feel* your hip, Vivi. Shut out all the . . . stuff . . . and feel it. You've got to get the hip bounce before you can move on to the half-moon."

The hour went by in a blur of calculated moves and laughter. They ended as they had begun, with a series of stretches. "You must practice this week," Naranya said as she collected the hip scarves. "And next week we weel add on to our movements. I weel bring tapes of practice music for next time for anyone who wants eet."

"So what did you think?" Melanie asked after they'd waved good-bye to the Shipley sisters and then Lourdes and Sally.

"It was fun," Angela said. "I like the dance aspect, and it's kinder and gentler than Pilates."

Melanie smiled.

"And if there's even a tiny chance of developing stomach muscles like Naranya's, I'm sold." Maybe she and James should take some ballroom lessons to get ready for their first dance together as husband and wife, like her matron of honor, Susan, had. "How many lessons would we need to get ready for the wedding?"

"We have packages of either seven or twelve that include parents and other important family members," Melanie replied. "It just depends on how much work you feel you need to put in. And how choreographed you'd like the dance to be."

"We're not getting married until April." Angela's voice broke on the word "married." "We wouldn't need to do anything right away, would we?"

"No, of course not." Melanie hurried to reassure.

Angela felt Ruth's considering gaze. Vivien hid a yawn behind her hand.

"But you could bring him to a practice party one Friday or Saturday night just to see how you both feel about it," Melanie said. "It's mostly social, but the admission includes an hour dance lesson before the DJ starts. There's food and drink, too."

But by the time they said their good-byes, Angela was no longer thinking about dancing. She was thinking that April was nowhere near as comfortably far off as it used to be.

11

ON SUNDAY MORNING at eight A.M. a Bagel Baron delivery truck pulled into the Melnicks' driveway like it did every week. It would make several private deliveries after this one: to their son and daughter-in-law's house a couple of neighborhoods away; to Temple Judea for the youth group to sell for fund-raising; and the last to Melanie Jackson's, though the Jackson order wouldn't include the usual portion of lox. Ruth had long ago discovered that while many non-Jews had embraced the bagel, they often mucked it up with toppings like grape jelly and sometimes even ham.

By the time the driver knocked on the kitchen door and handed over their standing order, Ruth had already been up for hours; it was one of life's great ironies that now when she could have slept all day if she wanted to, her eyes snapped open at six A.M. sharp no matter what time she went to bed or how many times she was up during the night.

Ira, too, was an early riser and had already been locked in his study with the Sunday papers—both the *Atlanta*

Journal-Constitution and the *New York Times*—even before Ruth got up.

"Bagels!" she called from the kitchen as she opened the brown paper bag and pulled out two still-warm bagels: an onion sesame for Ira, a poppy seed for her. In the center of the round glass-topped table, she set out a block of cream cheese, a small plate of lox, and another of tomato and red onion slices—everything the bagel purist required.

On the counter, a fresh pot of coffee dripped into the carafe, infusing the kitchen with a warm, homey smell. It was the one day of the week they made a point of eating breakfast together, supposedly keeping them in touch with each other and, as Ira liked to say, "the product from which they lived."

Sports section in hand, Ira entered the kitchen eagerly, only hesitating when she didn't greet him. Ruth wondered if he'd even noticed how little they'd spoken since she'd thrown down the gauntlet at their session with Dr. Guttman. They'd communicated when necessary: "Could you pass the salt?" "What time are we expected at the kids' house?" "The white shirt is at the cleaners; wear the blue." Not exactly deep or meaningful conversation, but apparently enough for Ira.

Ruth sighed as she bit into her bagel and chewed slowly. She had never been a big fan of the silent treatment, though she'd seen other women wield it effectively. When part of your problem was that your husband didn't talk to you *enough*, shutting off all communication seemed completely counterproductive. Not saying all the things she wanted to say to Ira, now, that was hard.

Ira layered his bagel with cream cheese, lox, and slices of onion and tomato. Munching contentedly, too contentedly as far as Ruth was concerned, he ate and read. Soon he'd be done with both the sports and the bagel. He was already dressed for golf and after a couple of hours at the office he'd head out to the country club to play nine holes. If they didn't talk now, when would they?

"You could at least come try a practice party at the Magnolia Ballroom with me. It's an hour lesson and some dancing after. How big a thing is that?" She said this bluntly despite the fact that even Miriam Youngblood had suggested that a more subtle approach might yield better results.

Ira looked up at her in surprise. "I don't know why you're making such a big deal about this. I haven't been a dancer for fifty years, and now all of a sudden you want me to be Fred Astaire." Ira wasn't exactly a sugarcoater, either.

Ruth wanted to wipe the look of righteous indignation from her husband's face. Could a man so aware of the nuances of business really be so oblivious of his wife's feelings?

"I want you to share something that means something to me," Ruth said calmly. Or at least as calmly as she could. "To have some time together that's our own. Why is that so difficult for you to understand?"

Ira lay what was left of his bagel on the plate. It stared up accusingly at her, as did Ira. Inexplicably, Ruth felt the press of tears beneath her eyelids. Unwilling to cry in front of him, Ruth stood, picked up her plate, and carried it to the sink. Flipping on the faucet, she smashed the uneaten portion of her bagel down the disposal, then turned it on for good measure.

There was an exaggerated sigh and Ira's chair scraped back from the table. He came up behind her and she closed her eyes, embarrassed. Both of them were more comfortable with her anger than her tears.

"Ruthie." He put his hands on her shoulders. "What's going on with you? What's with all this *meshugas*?" He used the Yiddish word for craziness. Turning her to face him, he said, "You want me to work less. You want me to dance. You want a divorce. I can hardly keep up with all the things you want from me lately."

He kept his hands on her shoulders. For a big man his touch had always been surprisingly gentle. She'd been much too angry at him for too long now to seek out his touch. Or to be receptive to it when it was offered. Ruth had a brief flash of the scene from *Fiddler on the Roof* when Golde asks Tevye if he loves her. What would Ira say if she asked him that question? She realized she was no longer sure of his answer.

She sniffed back her tears and looked her husband in the eye. She didn't know why after all these years she needed proof of his affection for her. She only knew that she did. But it would mean nothing if she had to beg for it.

What did she gain if he gave her attention so grudgingly? If she had to force him to spend time with her, had to threaten him to get him to come to class, what *was* the point?

"Never mind," she said as he watched her like she was some time bomb that might go off at any moment. "It doesn't matter. If you can't understand why I want you to come to class with me, I don't want you there."

Ruth eased out of Ira's grasp and stepped away from him. For once she made no move to put away the food on the table or double-check his plans for the day. He could go and do whatever he wanted. The lox and cream cheese could spoil. The bagels could turn stale and hard. It wasn't like there weren't a million more where those had come from.

"I'm going to go lie down," she said, not even bothering to look and see how he was reacting to his reprieve. "I guess I'll see you later."

And with that she left the Bagel Baron standing alone near the sink staring dumbly after her. But she didn't think he had any idea that the bomb he'd been worried about had just been detonated. And she wasn't sure what was supposed to happen next.

☙

THE SOUND OF the doorbell barely registered in Vivien's consciousness. She was asleep, blissfully asleep. Subliminally somewhere she heard someone open, then shut the front door. Heard steps on the stairs; heard what could only be someone, probably Melanie, extracting Shelby from bed.

Melanie and Clay and the kids were going to church this morning, but Vivi had chosen getting sleep over being saved. For a time she drifted in a lovely fog, not quite as asleep as she had been but still mercifully not awake. The ringing of her cell phone pushed her unhappily back into the real world. She tried to ignore it, but the ringing continued.

With a groan, she reached for her phone and managed to get it up to her ear. "Ummphh?" she asked, her eyes still closed.

"Viv?" Vivien's eyes flew open as Stone's voice penetrated her fog.

"Mmmmm, I mean, yes." She sat up against the pillows, her mind scrambling into consciousness.

"It's not like you to sleep so late. Did I wake you up?"

"I guess I was a little tired from the week."

There was a moment of silence while he registered what she'd said. "Are you sure you're all right? Marty said the wound was pretty superficial but . . ." He stopped, realizing he'd admitted to checking on her behind her back. Normally Vivien would have given him some shit for acting as if she couldn't take care of herself. But right now, especially, she was grateful that he cared enough about her to be devious.

Vivien drew a deep breath, wishing with every part of her that Stone was here right now so that she could tell him, face-to-face, all the things that he should know. So that he could, what? Give up chasing stories at the heart of the War on Terror so that he could come home and take care of her? Escort her to Tuesday's ob-gyn appointment? Tell her everything would be all right? That he wanted to marry her? Have their child? Live happily ever after?

She didn't even know if she wanted that.

"I had no idea how rough the suburbs were. I think Melanie deserves a medal. I'd pin it on her myself if she hadn't forced me to take a belly-dancing class."

"Belly dancing?"

She could hear him smiling and her own lips tilted upward. "Suffice it to say isolating and controlling individual muscle groups is even harder than it sounds."

"I wouldn't mind watching you try."

"Yeah, well, don't get too excited about the idea. As far as I'm concerned it was a one-time experience. I think my time would be better spent confirming that J.J.'s death really was an accident." And researching her columns. Not to mention coming to terms with all the changes taking place in her body.

"What's going on with that?"

"I finally got hold of Blaine Stewart. He's still in the Atlanta regional office of the GBI, but he's out in the field more than he's in the office. The case is closed, and I'm a family member so there shouldn't be a problem with him talking to me and showing me whatever I ask for, but it's not exactly at the top of his to-do list."

"Well, keep me posted," Stone said. "I'm getting ready to head out toward the Pakistani border. I think

I've finally found the right contact to get me a shot at the interviews I've been angling for. But communication may be sporadic for a while."

She could hear the barely concealed excitement in his voice, knew he could hardly wait to be off, chasing the story, hunting down the sources he sought wherever they might be hiding. However murderous they might be. Vivien was awake now, uncomfortably so.

"Wow," she said. "That's great." She was careful not to sound anything but thrilled for him. This was who he was. This was what he did. As an expert on terrorism, Stone was at the top of the network news food chain. His live reports were featured regularly in prime time, and *TV Guide* had recently begun referring to him as the Afghanistan Adonis. If Vivien had even been considering telling him the truth, and that was a big "if," it was now out of the question. The last thing she wanted was for him to be worrying about what was going on at home.

"Yeah," he said, and she could hear the satisfaction in his voice. "The only downside is not being with you. I miss you, Vivi. A lot."

"Me, too."

"Hey," he said. "Maybe we could meet up in Europe for a few days next month. Hell, if I get the footage I'm hoping for, I might even be able to take a week. I was kind of picturing us back at that little villa we rented last spring in Tuscany." His voice turned low and intimate and Vivi could picture it, too. Mornings in bed. Long walks through the lush countryside. Late dinners on the villa's ancient balcony.

His excitement built as he presented his plan. Everything was coming together for him now. For her, not so much. In fact, pretty much nothing in her life at the moment was of her planning. And a month from now? She'd be well into her fifth month. At which point, according to her trusty copy of *What to Expect When You're Expecting*, she'd probably be showing.

"Oh, I don't know." Vivi began trying to think of some excuse that would sound reasonable. "I, um, don't think I can do that."

"Why not?" he asked, clearly puzzled.

Because by then her stomach and bulging breasts would be the first thing off the plane. Because she should have told him when she found out she was pregnant instead of waiting for the "right" moment, which was clearly never going to materialize. Because the time for decision making was long past. She was having their baby in April and he might still be traipsing through caves in Afghanistan then. Or on his way to cover some new war or natural disaster on the other end of the earth.

When he came back to the States he could decide whether he wanted to be a part of that. Telling him now would do nothing but make her feel better—assuming he reacted positively.

"I may have to be in New York then." She didn't know where that had come from. "I may have some new job interviews lined up." Another big lie, though nowhere near as big as the thing she'd omitted. She just hoped that when everything came out, he would forgive her. It would be way too unfair to lose her career *and* Stone. It didn't even bear thinking about.

"That's great." Stone's happiness for her was so genuine it hurt. He'd always been her greatest supporter. He didn't understand why she'd quit CIN or why she'd gone to Atlanta. Nor did he know how many jobs she'd already interviewed for. "Do you want me to make some calls for you? I might be able to get you in to talk to some people at CBD; Randy Langford owes me. In fact, maybe I could get back to New York at the same time. Even a quick in and out would be better than not seeing you."

Vivien's gut clenched at his eagerness. "No, um, no," Vivien said. "I mean, the appointments aren't totally firmed up. I wouldn't want you planning a whole trip around my schedule when it's so . . . uncertain."

"Vivi," Stone said. "I know you. You need to be working. I could help."

Vivien could hardly believe how hard it was to have this conversation, to offer lie after lie to the one person she'd always told the truth to. "I guess getting shot threw me a little more than I realized. I just need to take it easy a while longer," she said. "I want to hang out with my family."

There was another silence. Even she couldn't believe she'd just said that.

"We're actually going to my parents for dinner a little later," she added. "When Melanie and the kids get back from church."

"That's great," Stone said. "Be sure to give everybody my best."

His tone telegraphed his hurt and surprise at her refusal to meet him. And who could blame him? If she were her usual proactive self she would meet him either in New York or Europe and explain everything face-to-face, being sure to let him know that he was under no obligation whatsoever. But between her whacked-out hormones, her inability to come to terms with her impending motherhood, and her loss of the career that had so defined her, she was about as far from herself as it was possible to be. And she couldn't face the possibility that by telling him the truth she might lose him. Or worse, bind him to her for the wrong reasons.

She, who had always sought the truth regardless of how deeply it was hidden and with little regard for the possible repercussions, was now afraid of it.

"Yeah. I will," she said, hating how things had been

left but unable to say the things that would fix it. "I'll be watching for your reports. I know you'll get the story you're going after. You always do."

"Things will work out for you, too, Vivi," he said, making her feel even worse about deceiving him. "You're way too talented and experienced not to find something even better than what you left. Dan was an imbecile to let you go."

"Yeah," she said. Dan was an imbecile not to ignore her rantings and ravings. A moron for listening to consultants who'd told him she needed to be replaced.

As she and Stone said their good-byes Vivien knew exactly who the real imbecile was, and it wasn't her ex-boss, Dan Kramer. It was the middle-aged pregnant woman presently cowering in her sister's guest room bed, staring forlornly into the dresser mirror.

12

THE DRIVE TO Magnolia Hall was not an especially cheerful or talkative one. Vivien rode silently beside Melanie, her gaze on the traffic, her thoughts her own. In the backseat Shelby's thumbs flew over her cell phone keyboard in constant communication with . . . someone. Trip listened to his iPod, his eyes closed, his head nodding to the tinny beat.

Melanie, who with Clay's help had wrestled both children out of bed and then threatened them into continued wakefulness through what even to her had felt like a never-ending church service, was already exhausted. Finding her sister still lolling around in bed when they returned at noon hadn't helped her mood one bit.

Driving south on Highway 400, she struggled to tamp down her irritation; going to her parents already agitated was like taking coals to Newcastle. As she wove in and out of traffic, she noticed a spanking-new sign declaring 400 the Hospitality Highway, but none of the other drivers looked any more hospitable than she felt.

At the Lenox Road/Buckhead exit she merged off of

400 and turned eastward, taking Piedmont across Roswell
Road. They were now in the heart of Buckhead's residential neighborhoods, which the same people who'd tried
to make the Atlanta interstate system kinder and gentler
liked to refer to as the "Beverly Hills of the South."

On wooded multiacre lots mansions in the making
sprang from gaping gashes in the red earth, their massive
footprints declaring their owners' wealth and aspirations.
There were European and Mediterranean villas next to
the latest version of Tara, shiny new and trying to look
historic. But there were also original Greek Revival and
southern Colonials built by Atlanta's leading architects.
Of these, Magnolia Hall, barely visible from its gated
entrance on Tuxedo Road, was one of the best known.

Four breaths were drawn in a silent girding of the
loins as Melanie punched in the security code and waited
silently for the massive iron gates to swing open.

Inside they crossed a wooden bridge that spanned the
small creek that ran along the front of the property. From
there, the drive wound gently upward through a stand of
trees and up the swell of a hill.

Once this had been virgin forest belonging to the Creek
Indians. After the United States government wrested
it from its original owners, it held a lottery. And in the
early 1820s a Gray widow by the name of Matilda won
fifty-five acres, on which she and her young sons built a
farm. During the Civil War Federal troops closing in on
Atlanta camped in fields around the area, including those
belonging to the widow Gray.

Melanie smiled as she remembered her grandmother's
telling of her ancestors' harrowing story. The widow Gray
was buried on the land she'd won; her descendants sold
off parcels of it to fund a lavish lifestyle and to under-
write their social and political ambitions. In the early
1900s, when the increasing popularity of the automobile

turned the still-rural area into a year-round residential suburb, the current crop of Grays retained Neel Reid, one of Atlanta's most prominent architects, to draw up plans for a magnificent Greek Revival–style mansion. He positioned this masterpiece at the top of a hill in the very center of Widow Gray's remaining six and a half acres. They named it Magnolia Hall.

Melanie had often been uncertain about her role as a Gray and her relationship with her parents. But she'd never questioned her love for the home in which she'd grown up, or the pull she felt each time she passed beneath the allée of massive oaks that led her to it.

Pulling to a stop in the circular drive, Melanie nudged Vivi, who'd fallen asleep, her chin digging into her chest, her breathing slow and even. If sleeping were an Olympic sport, Vivien would have more medals than Michael Phelps. "Wake up," Melanie said. "We're here."

Vivien's return to consciousness was slow; Shelby and Trip's less so. By the time Melanie had gotten Vivien out of the car, the kids were already up the front sweep of steps, past the initial phalanx of Doric columns and halfway across the sprawling porch. Evangeline, Magnolia Hall's longtime housekeeper, stood in the opened front doorway, a huge smile on her elegant ebony face. Her arms were open. One foot tapped impatiently.

Evangeline, who was approaching her eighth decade, stood tall and regal as befitted the descendant of Nubian royalty she claimed to be. She had come to Magnolia Hall while Warren Gray was a teenager and had never left. After a brief power struggle with Warren's bride, the two women had ultimately created a working relationship both could live with; Caroline told Evangeline what to do and Evangeline sometimes pretended to do it.

"Why, I swear you two are lookin' mighty fine," Evangeline said to Shelby and Trip as she took them up in a

bone-crushing hug and then released them to the basement rec room, where they would hang with their older
cousins.

Melanie noted Evangeline's impression of Mammy
from *Gone with the Wind*, a delivery she used to irritate
Caroline. She could tell from Vivien's grin that she had
caught it, too.

"Now you two." The housekeeper sniffed at Melanie
and Vivien. Her dark eyes glinted with affection. "You two
look a might too much like something the cat drug in."

Melanie ignored the jibe, which she suspected was all
too true, and instead focused on the accompanying hug,
an embrace she knew would not be duplicated by their
mother.

"Darlings," Caroline drawled as she descended the central staircase. "How wonderful that you could come." If
Evangeline sometimes channeled Mammy, Caroline Baxter Gray did a mean Ellen Robillard O'Hara, with the
tiniest touch of Zsa Zsa Gabor.

As a child, Melanie had taken the two women's dueling
impressions for granted. As a teenager, she had wondered
whether Caroline and Evangeline needed an audience
to perform these roles or if they did so for their own
amusement.

Evangeline was now busy squeezing the life out of
Vivien, who hadn't arrived with a whole lot of life in
her to start with. When the hug was completed to her
satisfaction, Evangeline took Vivi by the shoulders and
held her at arms' length so that she could study her more
closely. An odd look passed over her face.

"If you're finished here, Evangeline, you may go see if
Mr. Gray needs more ice for the bar," Caroline said.

Melanie perked up at the mention of alcohol. Her
father was undoubtedly already mixing martinis, which

he and their older brother, Hamilton, would have already sampled.

"Why, yes'm," Evangeline said as Caroline air-kissed Vivien and Melanie's cheeks. Both sisters watched surreptitiously to see if Evangeline would throw in the bob or curtsy that she sometimes tacked on to her servant routine, but she managed to refrain, then headed for the kitchen. Whether she was planning to retrieve ice while she was there was anybody's guess. More likely she'd pass some time arguing with Cook, who'd been at Magnolia Hall almost as long as Evangeline. Or harass the two other live-ins—Yolanda and her husband, Ben, who served as maid and man of all work. The couple had only been with the Grays for a decade; Evangeline had been heard referring to them as "fresh meat."

In the study Hamilton and their father talked politics while Ham's wife, Judy, sipped, somewhat desperately, Melanie thought, at her martini. J.J. had once commented on how important alcohol was in smoothing out the rough edges of this family's extended relationships, and Melanie had been forced to agree. A well-stocked bar had gotten them through countless elections and more than a few scandals, including the one that had launched Vivien's investigative career as well as Melanie's shocking marriage to a Republican.

"Thirsty?" Their father, who was freer with affection if not approval, hugged them both and then held up the pitcher of martinis.

Vivien, in the process of greeting Ham and Judy, declined. Melanie accepted the proffered drink gratefully. Caroline, too, was quick to accept.

They made small talk for a time. Here that meant politics, particularly Democratic politics and Hamilton's plans to run for governor in 2012. Evangeline stepped into the study and retrieved the martini pitcher off the sideboard, which was the signal that drinks were over and supper was served.

In the formal dining room they took their accustomed places around the Regency table without discussion, sitting in family groupings and, although no one acknowledged it, in order of age and rank.

This meant that Warren Emerson Gray sat at the head of the table as had his forebears, with Caroline on his right. Ham, as the eldest son and the only one who had not only married acceptably but gone into the family business of politics, sat at the opposite end. Judy sat on his right with their children seated in descending birth order beside her.

Vivien sat to Caroline's right, where she had been placed when they were children. Melanie sat next to her with Shelby and Trip following. Idly Melanie wondered whether the relative gravity of their "sins" might warrant a reversal; she had only married a Republican whose shocking accidental death had made unwelcome headlines. Her parents had barely mentioned J.J. in the last year.

Vivien had destroyed a political ally, lived in Yankeeland for a decade and a half, and been shot in the butt in front of a national audience.

Then again, Melanie wasn't sure she wanted a seat upgrade; getting closer to Caroline didn't necessarily belong in the "win" column.

The table was already set with big platters of Cook's fried chicken and bowls of homemade coleslaw and potato salad. A basket of warm biscuits and pats of butter with an elegant G impressed into each sat at both ends. Their father bowed his head and led them all in a brief prayer of thanks. Before it had ended, Trip and Ham Jr. were reaching for fried chicken. Soon there was a universal chowing down accompanied by desultory conversation.

Vivien picked up an oversized chicken leg and devoured it. She did this without looking up from her plate and with an economy of motion that would have done a competitive eater proud. Caroline's eyebrows jerked upward in surprise. Soon Vivien was the center of attention; even the boys appeared fascinated by the thoroughness with which she consumed her food.

"I don't have the first idea whom you've been eating around, but Grays do not eat like truck drivers." Caroline had dropped the cultivated southern accent and even her inner Zsa Zsa. She sounded now like the queen of England.

"Sorry." Vivien's fingers were halfway to her lips. She lowered them to her lap and wiped the grease on her linen napkin. "I was just so hungry. I . . ."

"Is there no food in Melanie's home?" their mother asked.

Vivien swallowed.

"If you're eating like this every time you have the opportunity, it's no wonder you've put on weight," Caroline commented.

Vivien clamped her lips together, though whether it was to stop what might come out or prevent herself from stuffing more in was unclear.

"Who will put you on the air if you get too heavy? And what will Stone think when he returns?" Caroline paused. "That is assuming you two are still together?"

Evangeline, who'd just delivered another platter of fried chicken to the table, shot a look at Vivien. Actually, everyone was looking at her now, waiting to see the reaction. But for the first time in Melanie's memory, Vivien didn't lower her head and charge.

"Don't worry yourself about it, Mama," Vivien said in the slower cadence Melanie had watched her eradicate years ago. The use of the word "mama" was downright shocking. It was what they'd called Caroline as children, before Caroline had announced her preference for a more formal form of address. "Melanie's already vowed to whip me back into shape. Why, she has me hauling Shelby out of bed in the mornings and racing around east Cobb at a pace that would put a born New Yorker to shame."

Caroline's mouth pursed in disapproval. Still Vivien had managed to disagree without declaring war; Melanie had never seen her exercise this degree of restraint. And if anyone knew how hard it was not to engage with their mother, it was Melanie.

"Melanie?"

"I'm sorry?" She realized with a start that her sister-in-law, Judy, was speaking to her.

"I said Ham, Rebecca, and Rosalee will be graduating before Shelby even gets to UGA. It's a shame she won't have her cousins there to show her the ropes, like you had Vivien."

Grays had been attending the University of Georgia since its founding in 1785. Even Vivi, who had been accepted at Michigan and Northwestern's journalism schools, had ended up there, though not exactly by choice.

"Think you'll be all right there on your own, Shelby?" Judy asked, still trying to turn the conversation.

Melanie dragged her thoughts from her sister to her daughter, who seemed as surprised as Melanie that she was now the center of attention. *Please, God*, Melanie prayed. *Do not let Shelby choose now to mouth off.*

Shelby opened her mouth, closed it. Melanie had bribed her daughter with a trip to Abercrombie and then closely supervised her dress and makeup today, so she looked like a well-mannered seventeen-year-old. *Please, God, let her act like one.*

But it was Vivien who saved Shelby from having to

answer. "Well, good grief," she said. "Has there ever been a Gray female who couldn't have that entire university just eating her up with a spoon?" She smiled like her namesake playing Scarlett O'Hara, then batted her eyelashes, something Melanie was willing to bet she hadn't done since moving to New York. Apparently, batting lashes was like riding a bicycle; you just never forgot how.

"What do you say, Mellie?" Vivien drawled. "Do you think Shelby will have any trouble positively ruling that campus?"

"Hell, no!" Melanie replied.

"Mama?" Vivi asked. "What do you think? Do you think your youngest granddaughter will need any help at UGA?"

"No way in hell!" Caroline said, laying it on thick. Their father pretended to look shocked.

"Rebecca and Rosalee." Vivien turned to Judy's daughters with a cocky grin. "Did you all need your big brother to . . . paaaavve"—she intentionally stretched the word out to a full three syllables—"the way for you?"

The twins flashed identical smiles; their eyes shone with their delight at speaking out at their grandparents' table, something anyone under thirty was rarely encouraged to do. "H-e-double-l, no!" They practically shouted.

"I thought not," Vivien said with a wink for all the assembled women. "Well, I'm here to tell you that I have no doubt whatsoever that Shelby is a Gray through and through. She will be superbly fine all on her own. I would lay a million dollars on it!"

Melanie noticed that her sister didn't say a thing about Shelby actually applying to or attending UGA, but everyone was so fired up by then that no one else seemed to notice.

Shelby shot her aunt a look of such intense gratitude that Melanie practically melted right there. Every time she got ready to write her sister off, Vivien managed to demonstrate a redeeming quality. Anyone that would step up and protect a child couldn't be all bad.

❧

ANGELA RICHMAN SPENT that Sunday afternoon in bed, but she didn't spend it sleeping.

In fact there'd been precious little sleeping the night before and only a few hours of it earlier that morning. She shivered now at the memory even though the warmth of James's bare skin heated up every inch of her own. She closed her eyes to block out what looked like afternoon sun, hardly able to believe how fabulous he'd made her feel. Or how many times.

She'd been a virgin when they met two years ago; actually at the ripe old age of twenty-eight she'd barely been kissed.

"Hey, beautiful." James used the arm slung across her waist to pull her closer so that her bottom spooned even more tightly into him and she had to remind herself that he meant it. That it was okay to be naked because her body was no longer something to be ashamed of, but something that James loved.

His warm breath tickled the back of her neck. Just thinking about the things they'd done together made Angela want to do them all over again.

"Hey, yourself," she whispered, feeling languorous and sexy; adjectives she never would have thought, let alone applied to herself before she met James.

Incredibly, he'd fallen in love with her work first. Had actually walked up to her at the Hartwell Gallery where her first one-woman show, On the Outside Looking In, had been mounted and told her how moved he was by her photographs. He'd bought two of her favorites and then invited her out for dinner so that they could talk about her work.

Who would have believed that James Wesley, son of former legendary Atlanta Braves pitcher Cole Wesley, could have ever felt like an outsider? That the good-looking six-footer had felt completely lost in his father's shadow and had only mastered a crippling stutter in his early twenties. The difference was that he'd shared these things with her, while she'd kept Fangie to herself.

James's finger brushed across her nipple, then trailed languidly—she could get attached to that adjective—down her stomach, which she had to remind herself yet again, no longer needed to be sucked in or camouflaged, and came to a halt between her thighs. Before she could protest, not that she was of a mind to, he'd used that finger to bring her to a gasping release.

"Good God," she said when she was able to form actual words. Turning to face him, they lay in each other's arms while her breathing slowed to match his.

James smiled and kissed the tip of her nose. Angela brushed a lock of blond hair off his forehead and kissed him back. But in her heart she felt a fissure of unease. He'd been honest from the beginning; she knew who he'd been, what he'd overcome, who he was now. He deserved to know those things about the woman he intended to marry.

"Tell him," Fangie taunted. "Go ahead. Show him that picture you keep buried in your purse. And see how much he loves you then."

Instead, Angela showered and dressed, then let him walk her out to her car, sighing when he kissed her good-bye. She'd been doing her best to tune Fangie out for the last three years. Was there really any reason to listen to her now?

◎

LATE THAT NIGHT in her room at Melanie's, Vivien propped
herself up in bed and opened her laptop to write her column. With her fingers poised above the keyboard, she
thought about all she'd seen in the last week; all the running, and doing, and juggling that had filled Melanie's
days.

Vivien typed, *Greetings from suburbia, where I have discovered that the suburban housewife has more in common with
the triathlete than I would have believed before I landed here.
Both race from activity to activity with an eye on the clock and
often push themselves past the point of exhaustion in order to
compete in their chosen events.*

*Of course, triathletes run and bike and swim while the women
here tend to run errands, drive car pools, and volunteer. Athletes
rely on their finely honed bodies, which they clothe in aerodynam-
ically designed spandex. The suburbanite often has saddlebags
and wears mom jeans and depends on an SUV, which has been
surgically attached to her behind.*

*Both are born competitors; the athlete is determined to prove
physical prowess, the suburbanite is too often bent on one-upping
the neighbors. Or convincing others what a great mother she is.*

*If all of this energy were applied to ending global warming
or curing cancer, the world might already be a better place. But
many of these women spend their days in an endless loop of minutiae. Like Sisyphus rolling his boulder up a hill only to have it
roll down again just before it reaches the top, they are doomed to
repeat their days of frantic activity. Over and over. Week after
week. Year after year.*

Vivien paused, feeling a twinge of conscience at the
light in which she was portraying women like her sister.
Her fingers itched to backspace over the last paragraph,
but it was, she reminded herself, all true. And no one,
including Melanie, would ever know she'd written it.

They are on intimate terms with their children's schools, their dry cleaners, their grocery stores, their pediatrician's offices, their bank drive-throughs, and their post offices. They make and serve meal after meal, do load after load of laundry, expend large parts of their days and nights trying to make their families' lives better.

And yet despite occasional grumblings, they seem proud of their unpaid positions. And completely unaware that an alien landing in their midst as I have would assume them to be indentured servants or serfs of some kind. The Emancipation Proclamation freed the slaves from forced servitude. Amazingly enough, the majority of suburban housewives and mothers have entered into this "bondage" of their own free will. And they would not appreciate the efforts of anyone bent on "freeing" them.

Vivien looked back over what she'd written and felt another twinge of conscience. It was a rant, pure and simple, and barely skimmed the surface of what she'd seen so far. Vivien had made no effort to delve beneath that surface to her subjects' feelings or motivations. Melanie, of course, did these things out of necessity, but Vivien chose not to think about that, either. Deciding that Scarlett Leigh was entitled to her opinion and the *Weekly Encounter* was entitled to print it, she concluded, *Perhaps one day the skills needed to survive and compete here will find their way into competitive sports or even become an event in the Olympics. Who knows, maybe while I'm here I'll pitch the IOC on downhill SUVing or cross-country lawn mowing.* She smiled and typed, *Then again, maybe not.*

Adding her signature, *Your stranger in an even stranger land, Scarlett Leigh*, Vivi saved the column, attached it to an email, which she addressed to John Harcourt, and sent it on its way.

13

O N TUESDAY MORNING, Vivien silenced her alarm and
opened her eyes. Yawning, she threw off the covers
and staggered to the bathroom. She took a quick shower,
dropped her wet towels in the hamper, and hurriedly
dressed before retrieving the pot and pan she now kept
carefully hidden. Despite the blare of the alarm clock
six inches away from Shelby's head, her niece was deeply
asleep. Without makeup, she looked like the seventeen-
year-old girl she was, her skin young and unwrinkled,
a natural flush on her high cheekbones. Her dark hair,
not yet relentlessly straightened by the flat iron, swirled
across her pillow, a frame for the lovely face.

But Vivien knew better than to be sucked in by the
innocent, even malleable expression. The attack had to
be swift and relentless, the chance of remaining asleep
nonexistent.

"Up and at 'em," Vivien shouted as she flipped on the
overhead light. "Time to get going!" She grasped hold of
the covers tucked up under Shelby's chin and ripped them
away, revealing her niece's pink flannel pajamas and fuzzy

pink socks, which were much more appropriate than the clothing she would soon pull from her closet.

Shelby's eyes remained firmly shut, but Vivien knew from her niece's lowered brows and tightly set mouth that she was no longer sleeping.

Vivien banged the wooden spoon against the bottom of the aluminum pan inches from Shelby's ear.

"Stop it! Leave me alone!" Shelby's eyes remained closed. "You're a freakin' nightmare!"

"Then open your eyes and make me disappear!" Vivien shouted back even as she smiled to herself. Ripping Shelby from bed every morning had become one of the day's most satisfying moments. She banged the pot again for emphasis, taking up a really annoying cadence with which she'd had success before.

Shelby's eyes and lips squinched more tightly together. Her flannel-clad arms stole around her middle. "I am not getting up. There is nothing you can do to . . ."

Vivien set the pan and spoon down with a clatter, and Shelby's lips spread into a triumphant smile. Vivien rubbed her hands together in anticipation. When she saw Shelby's body relax slightly, she reached down and snatched both socks off of Shelby's feet.

"No!" Shelby shrieked, but it was too late. "Stop it!"

Vivien laughed maniacally as she tickled the exposed bottoms.

"Oh, my God!" Shelby shrieked as she tore her feet away. She sat up and tucked them underneath her.

It was Vivien's turn to smile triumphantly.

"Shit!" Shelby got out of bed in a huff. "You are sick and twisted! Why can't you just leave me alone?!" Turning her back on Vivien, she flounced into her bathroom and slammed the door. Through the wood she shouted, "Why don't you go back to New York and find some innocent people there to torture?"

Satisfied that someone else was more miserable to be awake than she was, Vivien stashed the pan and spoon under Shelby's bed and raised her arms, fists clenched in victory. Humming the theme song from *Rocky*, she did a victory dance down the back stairs.

"You are the champ," Melanie said from behind the kitchen counter. "Undisputed. It's barely over a week and you've already beat my ejection time by almost five minutes."

Vivien smiled. "I haven't even had to get devious yet. Just loud. And persistent."

"Tea?" Melanie asked, slipping into what had become their morning routine. Melanie was embarrassingly grateful anytime Vivien did anything remotely helpful.

"Yeah, that'd be great." Vivien walked past the kitchen table where Trip was eating breakfast, his eyes still half closed. "How does he do that?" she asked as the spoonfuls of cereal slipped cleanly between his lips.

"Heredity, I guess." Melanie placed the kettle on a burner as Vivien slid onto a barstool and took a banana from the fruit bowl. Her prenatal vitamins remained hidden in the bottom of her purse. "J.J. could brew coffee, consume a major breakfast, and carry on a fairly complex conversation almost in a dead sleep." She sighed and changed the subject. "I'm having lunch with Clay today. You're welcome to come along if you like."

Vivien watched her sister pour the boiling water into an oversized mug that had become Vivien's and wondered, again, about Clay Alexander's role in Melanie's life. Was he really just a friend? A mentor to the kids? He seemed such a constant part of their lives that Vivi couldn't help thinking he was angling to take J.J.'s place permanently. She watched Mel dunk the tea bag several times until it was the way Vivien liked it. But she wasn't sure how to ask.

"No, I have an appointment a little later." Vivien poured and stirred milk and sugar into her steaming mug as she considered how much to say about her morning plans. She added another couple of spoonfuls of sugar, trying to get the real thing somewhere near the sweetness level of the artificial sweeteners she'd given up.

She raised the cup to her lips, wishing she could mention that she was seeing the ob-gyn her doctor in New York had referred her to. Which would allow her to talk to another human being who had actually lived through pregnancy and come out the other side.

Instead she asked only for the thing she really needed. "Could I borrow the Toyota?"

Shelby chose that moment to huff down the stairs. "You're not going to let her take my car, are you?" She shot a withering look at Vivien. "I bet she doesn't even know how to drive."

"I was driving way before you were born, honey chil'," Vivien said. "I could drive circles around you. And I actually stop where I'm headed unlike some people I've heard about."

The jibe was automatic; something about Shelby's constant pout pulled Vivien right back into adolescence herself. She chose to blame this on the pregnancy hormones coursing through her veins.

Melanie shook her head. "It is way too early for arguments."

"But not for physical assaults!" Shelby turned to Vivien and stuck out her tongue. Vivi returned the favor.

"Children, children," Melanie said. "That's enough." She finished packing Trip's lunch and shoved a breakfast bar toward Shelby. "We've got to get going. Of course, Vivi can use your car." She rummaged through her purse, then tossed Vivien the keys.

"Thanks. I'll try to bring it back in one piece."

Shelby rolled her eyes. Melanie laughed. But the truth was Vivien had barely driven in more than a decade and wasn't completely comfortable with the idea. As she discovered an hour later when she'd finally managed to back out of the driveway and aim the car in the right direction, she was, perhaps, the slightest bit rusty.

"Jesus, lady, what did you think you were doing back there?" The policeman leaned into Vivi's lowered window. His round face was on the way to jowly; caterpillar eyebrows punctuated close-set brown eyes, which said they'd seen it all.

Vivien drew deep breaths into her lungs in an effort to regain control. Her hands, which still grasped the wheel, were shaking. "I, um, was just trying to get out of the neighborhood. Did I do something wrong?"

In the last week Melanie had turned out of Garrett Farms at least a million times without comment or incident. Vivien hadn't realized how tricky it was to maneuver out of the neighborhood and make a left across the four-lane road on which traffic raced in both directions, without the benefit of a light.

"You're joking, right?" He gestured toward the four other cars that had beached themselves on the median and roadside in a frantic effort to get out of her way. It was a miracle no one had actually crashed.

"I, um, thought I had enough time. Things looked clear when I pulled out." She didn't mention that she'd actually been aiming for the brake, not the gas. And that she might have lost hold of the wheel for just a few seconds when she took off by mistake. She should have practiced a little in the neighborhood before venturing out, but she'd been running late and wasn't sure exactly which building the doctor's office was in.

The other drivers got out of their cars. Vivien looked

up at the officer, wondering if he'd protect her if it became necessary.

"License and registration, please."

She handed him her driver's license with a shaking hand then searched the glove compartment for the car's registration.

"This isn't your car," he said.

"No, it's my niece's. Actually, my sister's."

He wrote down all her pertinent information while she watched the other drivers warily. They were conferring among themselves, deciding, she imagined, whether to come over and give her some shit or wait for the policeman to take their statements.

"Hey," he said. "I thought you looked familiar." He smiled. "You're the one who got shot in that parking garage. My kid showed it to me on YouTube." He guffawed. "Maybe they shot you because of your driving!" He laughed, delighted.

"I was on assignment," she said, not amused. "There was no driving involved."

"Couldn't believe you took it in the butt." He was really enjoying himself now. "We had a bet at the station about whether it was staged. Was it?"

Vivien took back her identification. She wanted to get out of there before the other drivers decided to try to take the law into their own hands. "Listen, I hate to rush you," Vivien said. "But could you give me my ticket now? I'm late for a doctor's appointment and it doesn't look like anyone got hurt or had their cars really damaged or anything."

"All right." He glanced over his shoulder at the other drivers and motioned to them to wait just a minute. He leaned farther in her window, smiling, obviously eager to get back to the station and tell the guys who he'd just written a ticket to. "But you be more careful behind the wheel, you hear? I won't be so lenient next time you create this kind of mess."

Grateful, Vivien averted her eyes from the others' glares as she pulled carefully back into traffic. Slowly and with great care she drove the approximately seven miles to the medical building and managed to arrive without causing any further problems, though she still had to think through each move she made. Unlike the batting of eyelashes, there was nothing automatic or instinctual about her driving.

In the waiting room, which was filled with bellies of all sizes, she filled out forms and focused on unclenching. She heard two women talking and noticed that one of them was holding a copy of the *Weekly Encounter*. Neither of them sounded like fans. She sank down in her chair and hunched over the clipboard in her lap as one of them muttered, "Who the hell is Scarlett Leigh?"

❧

DR. GILBERT HAD steel gray hair, a well-worn face, and a direct, reassuring manner that reminded Vivien of Dr. Sorenson. During her checkup he amplified the baby's heartbeat and she listened, fascinated, to its frantic pace. There might have been an out-of-whack metronome ticking away inside her.

"You're about seventeen weeks and the baby is about the size of a small cantaloupe now," he told her in all seriousness as he examined her. "I'd say we're looking at a mid-April delivery." His touch was gentle and experienced and she began to relax.

"I think my uterus may have secretly joined the fruit-of-the-month club," Vivien replied. She felt even more reassured when he smiled. "Last month Dr. Graber compared it to a grapefruit. According to *What to Expect When*

You're Expecting, before that it was the size of a prune, a plum, and then a peach."

"Just a frame of reference," he said, smiling again. "You've got a ways to go, but ultimately it could be the size of a watermelon."

At which point there would be no keeping her pregnancy secret. No way to deny her impending motherhood.

Dressed and with next month's appointment scheduled, Vivien left the office and took the elevator down to the lobby. As she crossed the marble floor toward the main entrance, she heard her name called out.

"Vivien, over here!"

The male voice sounded vaguely familiar and much too close to ignore. Turning, Vivien saw Matt Glazer and had to bite back a groan.

Matt had been in journalism school with her at the University of Georgia. They'd worked together on the *Red and Black*, the student newspaper. They'd gone out once, which had been one time too many for Vivi but apparently not nearly enough for Matt.

During their four years in Athens he'd insinuated himself into every possible situation until she'd resorted to avoiding him in self defense. She'd thought when they graduated and begun to pursue their careers that his interest would die a natural death, but he'd continued to pop up over the years reminiscing about a closeness that they had never actually shared.

"Hi, Matt," Vivien said, careful to smile with enough warmth not to offend but too little to encourage. "How have you been?"

"Good, actually," he said. "I'm at the *Atlanta Journal-Constitution* now." His still-scrawny chest puffed out in pride. "I have my own column."

Vivien tried to hide her surprise. As a reporter, Matt
had always settled for a perfunctory answering of "who,
what, where, when, and why." The last she'd heard he was
with a tiny weekly in Minneapolis covering high school
sports. "That's great. What kind of column?"

"I've got my finger on the pulse of Atlanta. I deal with
all the movers and shakers," he said. "I've done a few
pieces on your family, you know."

"No, I didn't." She took in the puffed-out chest, the
prideful tone. "Shame on them for not telling me."

He smiled. "I write the Just Peachy column. It's the
first thing Atlanta society reads in the morning. Everybody wants me to cover and write up their events."

Like she might during a crucial interview, Vivien kept
her expression neutral, giving nothing away. But in reality she was appalled that even Matt would boast about
writing what was little more than a gossip column. Of
course, what she was writing at the moment wasn't much
better, but at least she wasn't bragging about it. In fact,
she was counting on no one ever knowing. Vivien eyed
the revolving door and began to plot her escape.

"Wow," she said. "That's really . . . something."

"So what are you doing here? Are you seeing somebody
about your wound?" He paused dramatically, as if playing
to a camera. "Were there . . . complications?"

"No," she said firmly as his gaze strayed to the list
of doctors mounted on the wall nearby. "No, I'm just in
town visiting my family and decided to have a routine
checkup."

A skeptical smile tilted his thin lips. "Oh?"

"Yes," she said. "Not that I think that's any of your
business."

"Is that right?" The smile disappeared. So did the
general air of good humor. "Well then, why don't we
stick to your professional life?" His eyes narrowed. "I

heard you were fired from CIN. Would you care to comment on that?"

Vivi knew she should tread carefully. Matt Glazer might not be a journalist in her eyes, but he had instincts. Like a rat sniffing out a piece of cheese, he was trying to figure out what she might be hiding.

"No, I wouldn't care to comment."

"That's what I thought," he smirked. "It's not like we haven't all seen Regina Matthews in your spot."

"As usual you've got your facts wrong." Her smile was cool, her voice frigid. "I wasn't fired. I quit."

"You left CIN of your own free will?"

"Isn't that what I just said?"

"So what are you doing now?"

"I'm taking a break," she said. "Visiting my family and considering other offers."

"Are you still dating Stone Seymour?" he asked.

She hesitated a tad too long. His pointy rat nose quivered. "Ahh," he said. "The plot thickens."

"Oh, sweet Jesus," she said. "Stone and I are still dating. I just don't see how that's any business of yours, either."

He stiffened. "You always thought you were better than the rest of us," he said. "Do you really think you would have ended up at the network without your family connections, Vivien? Where do you think you'd be without the Gray name?"

She could have told him that she'd made it there despite her parents, that in fact, they'd done everything possible to prevent her from exposing a political ally, that her quest for the truth had never been anything but inconvenient and slightly embarrassing to them. But she could see in his little beady eyes that he'd never believe her. He'd rewritten her history in a way that made him feel better; that allowed him to compare his achievements to hers and still find a way to feel they were on even ground. She looked him up and down, taking in the cheap blue blazer, which he'd paired with khaki pants that didn't quite cover his knobby ankles, and all thought of censoring herself evaporated in the heat of her anger. Where would she be without the Gray name behind her? The word that sprang to mind was simply, "free." But he'd never believe that, either.

Once again she ignored the unwritten rules on which she'd been raised and said, quite stupidly, "If I weren't me, I guess I might have ended up slinging crap every day in the *Atlanta Journal-Constitution*. But I sure as hell wouldn't be bragging about it. Especially not to someone who would understand what a pitiful little job it is." Vivien turned her back on him and strode out of the building. For the second time that morning she hummed the theme song from *Rocky* under her breath and lifted her fists in victory toward the late-morning sun.

14

ON WEDNESDAY NIGHT Vivi answered the doorbell to find Clay Alexander standing on the welcome mat, briefcase in hand, beautifully dressed and impeccably groomed as always.

"May I come in?" His practiced smile seemed a bit frayed around the edges and the tiny web of lines at the corner of his eyes cut deeper.

"Is Melanie expecting you?"

"Yes, Vivi," he said when she finally moved out of his way. "I take the kids out once a week. It helps me stay in touch with them and gives Mel a night when she doesn't have to worry about making dinner."

He took in the sweatpants and baggy T-shirt she'd taken to wearing and winced slightly. "I came a few minutes early because I need something from J.J.'s desk." He said this as if he had every right to go through J.J.'s things without asking.

Vivi had been waiting for her opportunity to go through J.J.'s desk, too. Unfortunately, she had no idea what she would be looking for, while Clay obviously did.

Vivi was loitering around the office doorway pretending not to watch him, when Melanie came downstairs. "Is Clay here, Viv?"

Vivien nodded. "He's looking for something of J.J.'s." She watched Melanie's face closely to see if this was unusual or objectionable, but all Melanie said was, "Oh, okay. Can you get the kids up here? Trip's in the basement and I think Shelby's upstairs."

Vivi would have preferred to look over Clay's shoulder and listen in on his and Melanie's conversation, but she did as she'd been asked. After they waved Clay and the kids off, Vivi started up to her room where she intended to hide, er, read until Melanie left for the Magnolia Ballroom.

"Hurry up and change, okay? I'd like to get to the studio a little early."

Vivi turned to face her sister. "Well, actually . . ."

"I need you, Viv. One of the Shipley sisters did something to her ankle. Without you, the class will feel too small. And if anyone else doesn't show up, the students who are there will feel like the studio isn't taking the class seriously."

"Mel, I . . ."

"You said you wanted to help me however you could."

"I meant with the kids. Or the house. Or . . . whatever." Vivian felt, and undoubtedly sounded, like a trapped animal.

"Sincere offers of help don't usually come with exclusions," Melanie said.

Vivien didn't answer, but if she *had* been that trapped animal, she would now be gnawing at her leg in an effort to get out.

"I haven't pressed for the real reason you're here. Or asked why you've been riding all over east Cobb with me, even though I know you must be bored to tears." She held up a hand to stop the objections she saw forming. "I figure if you wanted me to know, you'd tell me."

Vivien stopped imagining her escape. "All right, Mel," she said. "I'll do it. But I don't think I'm destined for the Middle Eastern nightclub circuit."

"Fair enough," Melanie said. "I'll give you fifteen minutes to 'freshen up.'" She glanced pointedly at the sweatpants and baggy T. "I appreciate it," she said, as Vivi went upstairs to change, though she had no idea what she was supposed to change into.

She barely managed to zip up her favorite black pants and the black camisole stretched so precariously over her gargantuan breasts that modesty forced her to wear her black-and-white-striped blouse, which was unbuttonable, over it. Every part of her seemed to be expanding exponentially. Even her feet bulged over the edges of her lowest-heeled pumps. She felt like a sausage ready to split its casing.

In the bathroom Vivien brushed her teeth and gargled with mouthwash in an unsuccessful attempt to rid her mouth of the ever-present metallic taste, then dotted concealer under her eyes and on the blemishes that had sprung up. Her hair lacked luster and felt coarse and springy under her fingers. She'd always heard that pregnant women took on a "glow," but her hormones seemed to have reverted to adolescence. There was no glowing going on here.

Taking a tissue from the counter, she tried yet again to blow her nose clear, but the stuffiness remained. According to *What to Expect When You're Expecting*, nasal congestion and even occasional nosebleeds were not at all unusual. It seemed completely unfair to Vivien that even her ability to breathe had been impacted. Although she didn't look blatantly pregnant yet, there was virtually nothing about her that remained as it had once been.

They arrived at the studio a good fifteen minutes before class was scheduled to start. Ruth Melnick was seated at the sign-in table and seemed surprised to see Vivien, as if she'd somehow assumed that she would have already upped and disappeared. Melanie slipped into her office to take care of some paperwork. Spotting Angela Richman at a table near the dance floor, Vivi walked over to join her.

The young redhead once again wore baggy black workout clothes that swamped her body, but her smile of welcome was bright. So was the diamond, probably about three carats' worth, that sparkled on her finger.

"When's the wedding?" Vivi asked as she sank into a chair.

"April nineteenth."

Just a week after Vivi was due to become a mother, this girl would become a wife. "You say that as if it surprises you."

"Oh, it does," Angela said, her smile rueful. "I feel like I'm starring in some fairy tale. You know, one minute I'm cleaning out the garret and taking abuse from the ugly stepsisters and the next I'm dancing with the handsome prince at the ball." She laughed. "Not a bad thing, of course. Just not what I was expecting."

Vivi thought she'd prefer Angela's surprises to her own: young and about to be married versus old and about to become a single mother. But there was something in the younger woman's tone that reminded her of her own amazement each time Stone said he loved her; how hard it was not to come out and ask him, "Why?"

"So he's not the kind of guy you were used to dating?"

"Hardly," Angela said, her tone wry. "James is . . . not even in a ballpark I thought I'd ever play in." Her smile softened. "On the surface we have almost nothing in common. Sometimes I look at him and I just can't figure out how we ended up together."

"It's funny how things work out, isn't it?" Vivi asked once again, thinking about her own relationship. She and Stone weren't exactly two peas in a pod. They came from very different backgrounds and upbringings—Stone's was decidedly midwestern and middle class; she'd pretty much grown up in a modern rendition of *Gone with the Wind*. Yet both of them had focused almost exclusively on their careers, and both of their careers had been built on their compulsion to discover and share the truth.

As always when she thought the words "truth" and "Stone" together, Vivien cringed inside. Her dishonesty was a burden that she carried with her at all times; no matter how many times she told herself she was keeping her pregnancy secret for Stone's own good, she knew he'd never see it that way.

Pushing the uncomfortable thoughts aside, Vivien turned her gaze to the dance floor where three private lessons and one small group class were in progress, each an island of activity unto itself. Vivien and Angela watched in silence as one obviously advanced couple glided through the intricate steps of a carefully choreographed waltz.

"I love the way they move together," Angela said as Ruth walked over to join them.

"That's the Millers," Ruth said. "Dolly and Bruce. They've been married almost as long as Ira and me."

The Millers danced by, their movements in perfect synch. Ruth turned her head as if she couldn't bear to watch. "My husband prefers business to dancing. Actually, he prefers business to pretty much everything."

"Well, he makes the best bagels I've tasted outside of New York," Vivi said in an attempt to change the subject.

"Yes," Ruth said. But she didn't look at all happy about it. Or much of anything as far as Vivi could tell.

When they'd gathered at the end of the dance floor, with the injured Shipley sister in a chair near her sister, Melanie stepped into position between Vivien and Ruth. "You all ready to get started?" she asked.

"Some of us may be more ready than others," Vivi said.

"Why start a class when you're not planning to stay?" Ruth asked. "What's the point?"

"The point is I asked her to come, and I think this is the perfect opportunity for Vivi to experience dance," Melanie said, tying a scarf around her hips and passing one to Vivi. "I've never seen her fail at anything once she sets her mind to it. Never."

Naranya took her place in front of them. The music swelled to fill their end of the studio, and without fanfare she lifted her arms and began the opening stretches she'd shown them last week.

Ruth sniffed as they all clasped their hands together above their heads. "If you'll excuse me for saying so, ruthlessness isn't a major asset on a dance floor."

"And I suppose rudeness is." Vivien sniffed back.

"No, but determination goes a long way. And Vivi has more of that than anyone I've ever met." Melanie smiled, as always trying to placate as they began their stretches to the side. "You've got quite a bit of determination yourself, Ruth. It isn't automatically a negative characteristic."

"It is when someone runs right over other people to get what they want." She stared past Melanie at Vivien, her gaze accusing. Vivien stared back.

They sniped at each other through the remainder of the stretches and most of the isolation exercises, but fell silent to concentrate on the hip lift and drop and after that the controlled pivot of the half-moon.

"Almost right," Naranya said, demonstrating carefully. "Eet ees a half circle to the front, then the drop.

You see? Then a pivot of the hip to the back, and then the drop." She led them through it over and over in an effort to make the move smooth and continuous.

"This is a lot harder than it looks," Angela said.

"That's for sure." Vivi caught Ruth watching her in the mirror. Mother Melnick's gaze was far from friendly.

Naranya left them to demonstrate in front of Dee and Sally. Melanie dropped back to work with Lourdes. No longer pretending to practice, Vivi turned to Ruth. Their gazes locked. "I can't figure out why you dislike me so much. We've met, what, three times? People usually need to know me longer, or have been interviewed by me, before they hate me."

"You want the truth?" Ruth challenged, fisting her hands on her stocky hips.

Vivien nodded.

"I've been taking lessons here for a long time. I like your sister. I have a lot of respect for her. I care what happens to her and Shelby and Trip. I've watched her trying to get over her husband's death. It hit her really hard. And she hasn't really had anybody rallying around her, you know? I mean your parents were upset about the way he died and the whole media hoopla, but now they seem almost glad he's out of the picture. And nothing personal, but your mother's not the most touchy-feely person in the world. She's got the guilt thing going all right, but she doesn't have the warmth that a Jewish mother usually balances it with."

Vivien couldn't argue with that. She nodded in acknowledgment and waited for Ruth to continue.

"When things were the worst, just after J.J. died, I heard Melanie talk about you coming. And it was like she couldn't wait for you to be there to help her and the kids through. They really needed you."

Vivien would have liked to look away, but Ruth refused to release her.

"You were gone so fast I'm surprised you didn't leave skid marks. And she excused you. Said you had to get back to work, that you had some big interview coming up. That you'd be back as soon as you could."

Vivien drew in a deep breath as the shame spread through her. Ruth's gaze showed no mercy.

"Only you didn't come back, did you? Except for a day or two each year over the holidays to drop off presents and pretend like you were family. Now you're here, but you don't say why. And I've been worrying that you're going to bail out on her again, but all of a sudden you don't look like you're in any hurry to go. Someone not as generous as Melanie would have to ask why. What does she want? How can she have the nerve to show up two years later without an apology or explanation or anything?"

Vivien didn't respond. There was nothing she could say in her own defense. She had behaved horribly. She'd been frightened by her sister and niece and nephew's grief. She had cut and run. And she had never made amends.

"You're not gonna hurt her and the kids again. That's just not gonna happen on my watch."

Naranya came back to the front and clapped her hands for everyone's attention, then signaled them to raise their arms into position.

Ruth Melnick raised her arms. So did Vivien.

"In my world, mothers don't let other people hurt the people they care about, especially not people they think of as being like their own children. Are we clear?" the woman asked before they stepped apart to make room for Melanie. Ruth Melnick might have been Don Corleone addressing a lesser crime boss. Or a mother lioness protecting a newborn cub.

"Crystal," Vivien replied.

In the van on the way home, Melanie took her eyes off

the road to turn to Vivien. "What was going on between you and Ruth? I thought I was going to have to break something up."

Vivien looked out the window. "She gave me some serious shit for bailing out on you after J.J. died. She really does see herself as your surrogate mother. As if dealing with Caroline's version of motherhood weren't enough."

Melanie smiled. "Ruth's pretty protective of the kids and me. I kind of like it. At least her bossiness comes out of love; Mother's is pretty much all about her. Or not embarrassing her. Or making us be more like her."

"You've got that right." Vivien's glance slid back to Melanie then away again. "But Ruth's kind of scary in her own right. I'm kind of afraid I could wake up one morning and find a horse head in my bed or something."

"More likely a bagel with a shmear of lox." Melanie laughed. "Or maybe a few matzoh balls. Which are quite good by the way."

"Well, she has it in for me," Vivien said, forcing herself to turn and face Melanie. "And she's not all wrong."

"It's all right, Vivi. You don't have to . . ."

"No," Vivi said. "It's about time I apologized for taking off like that. I knew it was wrong even while I was doing it. I just didn't know how to handle all that . . . pain. I chickened out. The only thing I could think to do was run."

The flash of streetlight played across Melanie's face. "It's too late to worry about," she said. "Besides, you're here now. And I'm glad. It's good for me and for the kids."

Vivien would have felt even worse, if that were possible. She'd done so little and for all the wrong reasons. "Yeah, I've been a big help."

"Hey," Melanie chided. "Anyone who can pull Shelby

out of bed in under ten minutes is worth having around. And I've kind of gotten used to you tagging along during the day."

Vivien actually hung her head in shame. But Melanie didn't seem to notice.

"I'm glad you're taking the class. I have no doubt you can learn to belly dance."

"You always were the positive one, Mel." Vivi, on the other hand, had always considered herself a realist. But maybe that had just been an excuse to do what she wanted without worrying about how it impacted others.

"I bet you'll pick up some other valuable skills while you're here, too." She smiled. "I'm just not sure what they might be."

Vivien wanted to groan with frustration. Melanie should be telling her off, not letting her off the hook. Ruth Melnick had it right. She knew Vivien had her own reasons for being here. And she suspected, also quite rightly, that they were selfish ones.

15

ON FRIDAY NIGHT just after sundown, Ruth led her family to the table for Shabbat dinner. She was thrilled to have her son Josh and daughter-in-law, Jan, there along with their youngest son, Jonathan, who was home from college for the weekend. Ruth's greatest regret was that her two daughters, who'd gone to universities in the northeast, had married and stayed there as had their children. That left a whole branch of her family much too far away.

She'd invited Evelyn Nadoff from two doors down as well as Bernard Templeton, one of Ira's golf buddies, whose wife was out of town. It was a mitzvah to include those who had no one with whom to share the Sabbath. Ruth wasn't an especially religious woman, but she liked to think she did what was right.

The table was set with her own grandmother's china and crystal. The silver she and Ira had received as wedding gifts, over fifty years ago, framed each place. She'd spent the day in the kitchen, something she rarely had reason to do anymore, and now the whole house smelled just as it should, of matzoh ball soup and brisket of beef warming in the oven. A faint hint of the chicken livers she'd sautéed as the base for the chopped liver appetizer they'd already consumed perfumed the air.

In the center of the table, silver candlesticks, also a wedding gift, held two stubby white Shabbat candles. A challah sat on a silver plate beside them. Ira's father's kiddush cup, which would be used to say the prayer over the wine, had been placed next to his water goblet.

Content, Ruth lit the candles, voicing the prayer that would welcome the Sabbath. She studied her husband as he made the *bruchas* over the wine and then passed pieces of the challah around so that everyone at the table could join him in the blessing over the bread.

Ruth enjoyed the serving and sharing of the meal. And so, she saw, did Ira, though he would probably never think to say so. They'd shared a lifetime together, raised three wonderful, productive children, who'd produced six lovely grandchildren, two of them boys to carry on the Melnick name. It was everything she'd been raised to do and expect. But no one had warned her of what would happen when her "job" was over and no one actually needed her anymore. Or, in the case of her husband, wanted to know her.

"Fabulous meal, Ruth." Bernard groaned and patted his belly. "We'll have to get a cart tomorrow morning. I'm sure I'll still be too full to walk."

Ruth smiled at the compliment but knew Ira's regular foursome would walk no matter how full or how frail any of them became; it was a matter of honor. They'd been playing together every Saturday morning for the last twenty-five years, and they rarely varied their routine. They teed off at nine, played eighteen holes, then stayed for lunch at the club. Ira would be home by two P.M., settled into his club chair in the den with his feet propped up on the ottoman. There he would watch golf on TV for the rest of the afternoon. With his eyes closed.

"It's true," Evelyn added. "The brisket practically melted in my mouth. Delicious!"

Ruth smiled again. Her daughter-in-law, Jan, got up and began to collect the empty dinner plates. "Wait until you taste dessert," she said. "Ruth made apple strudel and Mandelbrot with vanilla ice cream on the side."

Evelyn and Ruth joined Jan in clearing, though Ruth was careful to give the older woman only the smallest plates and serving pieces to carry. The men's conversation turned to business and Ruth listened with pride as Jonathan, who would be receiving his MBA from Vanderbilt in June, was invited to participate.

When the strudel had been duly admired, Ruth cut and plated slices for everyone while Jan added a scoop of ice cream. Evelyn passed the plate of Mandelbrot.

"It's good, Nana," Jon said between bites. "Your best strudel ever."

"You're a good boy," Ruth replied, her heart swelling with love for her children and her children's children. The grandchildren up north were also professionals, or soon would be. Two doctors, two lawyers, one accountant. Three, including Jon, were planning to come into the family bagel business. "And you're such a hard worker."

He grinned and nodded to Ira. "Well, Papa's always been a huge example."

His father feigned hurt. "So what am I, chopped liver?"

They laughed at the ancient lament.

"No," Jonathan said. "But how many people would have passed up this latest offer from Inamatta Foods to keep working?"

Josh shook his head. His tone wasn't quite as admiring. "Not many."

"What offer?" Ruth's hands stilled. She looked at her husband as a hush fell over the table. The only person who didn't seem to notice was Evelyn, who was methodically dunking her piece of Mandelbrot into her coffee and then taking a softened bite.

"What's he talking about, Ira?"

A flush of guilt suffused her husband's cheeks. Josh dabbed at the corners of his mouth with his napkin as if to prevent himself from speaking further. Jan studied her plate while Bernard added sugar to his coffee and stirred intently. It was clear Ruth and Evelyn were the only people at the table who didn't know anything about this.

"What new offer?" Ruth asked again.

They all looked at each other. Only Jonathan didn't seem to fully comprehend the magnitude of the topic he'd raised. "Tell me, Jon. I'm dying to hear." She tried to keep the hurt and anger out of her voice. No point in frightening the child.

"Inamatta offered an obscene amount of money for the business, Nana. I mean, *Lifestyles of the Rich and Famous*, *Pimp My Ride*, the-whole-family-could-be-living-on-their-individual-private-islands-for-the-rest-of-their-lives obscene." He shook his head in wonder. "There aren't many people who could turn down that kind of money for something they built from nothing."

Ruth stood on shaky legs. She wanted to shriek and yell, wanted to demand to know why Ira would do such a thing. If it had been only family, she might have given in to the rage coursing through her. What a relief it would be to throw back her head, open her mouth, and howl. "I'm going to go put on a fresh pot of coffee," she said through clenched teeth.

Jan started to rise, but Ruth motioned her back down. "Thanks. Ira will help me." She looked directly at her husband as she said this. Her voice was the steely one she'd saved for the times the kids needed to be set straight. Josh actually flinched when he heard it. So did Ira.

She turned and headed to the kitchen, not even looking to see if her husband followed. When they were alone with the kitchen door closed behind them, she faced him.

"You turned down that kind of money without even mentioning it to me?" Ruth asked Ira, too upset to worry about who heard what. "After all the begging I've done to get you to slow down, you've rejected an . . . obscene . . . amount of money that could set your entire family free for life so that you can continue to be the . . . Bagel Baron?"

Like he always did when questioned, Ira stuck out his chin and prepared to dig in to defend his position. Normally Ruth worked her way in from some angle and slowly circled in on the point. In this way, she generally got what she wanted. But it was a lot of work and took way too much time. At this moment she didn't possess the patience for subterfuge; she was far too pissed off to pretend.

"I think I deserve to know what kind of money was offered. I helped you build that business. I have shared your life for the last fifty years. You owe me that much."

She could see in his face that he didn't want to tell her. Actually saw him consider offering a lie of some sort. This was what happened when you'd lived with someone for three quarters of your life; you knew their habits and their processes like your own. Not that this had kept him from hiding something big from her.

"You might as well tell me, Ira. I seriously doubt either my son or grandson would refuse to fill me in." She shook her head as if to dislodge some of the disappointment she felt. "Even Jan and Bernie know. I guess *I'm* the chopped liver in this family."

"It wasn't all that much, Ruth. The boy's exaggerating."

"Tell me."

"Sixty-five million." He had the nerve to puff out his chest in pride.

"You turned down sixty-five million dollars." It was a statement, not a question. She stared into his eyes as she processed this.

"Have you taken leave of your senses?" She didn't wait for an answer. "You're almost eighty years old. And yet you intend to spend whatever time we have left running a bagel company? You'd rather do that sixty-seventy hours a week than spend time with the people who love you? I never thought I'd say this, Ira, but you're a fool!"

The shock on his face was nothing compared to the shock she felt. They hadn't always agreed about things; often over the last half century she'd questioned him. They'd had their share of arguments. Most of the time they'd found a way to compromise at least enough to live to argue another day. But deep down she'd never doubted his intentions. She'd always believed he'd do what was right not just for himself but for her and the kids.

But he was like a dinosaur caught in a tar pit of his own making, stuck in the sameness of his life, afraid to evolve, to adapt, to let go of the old and try to embrace something new. "I am not going to spend what's left of my life watching you work yourself like a slave for whatever is left of yours. I want to travel. With you, Ira. Take a class, learn something new. With you. I want to be with you. Not waving good-bye in the morning and then spending the rest of the day trying to fill my time until you come home, eat dinner, and fall asleep in front of the television. Your rut is my rut, and I don't want to spend the rest of my life in it."

"Ruth, I just . . ."

"No," she interrupted. "I can't think of a single legitimate excuse for hanging on to that company. You know what? I take back the word 'fool.' That was the wrong thing to say."

Ira's shoulders relaxed slightly. His chin slipped down a notch. It was clear that he thought she was going to apologize and sweep this whole mess under the rug. He was wrong.

"You're not a fool," she said more calmly. "You're a coward. And I'm not prepared to spend the rest of my days with someone who's afraid."

She left him in the kitchen. And when she walked back into the dining room, no one asked about the coffee she'd supposedly left to make. When Ira came back with a fresh pot, Ruth ignored him. She and Evelyn and Jan cleaned up afterward and mostly Ruth just listened to their chatter. She kissed everyone good-bye when it was time and then she simply went into the master bath, where she creamed and washed her face as she'd done every night of her married life. Then she put on her nightgown, robe, and slippers; took her satin-covered pillow from the bed; and carried it to the guest bedroom. Under more normal circumstances, Ruth might have evicted Ira from their marital bed. But this was not a punishment or even a statement. She simply couldn't sleep next to a man who thought so little of her. She could barely bring herself to stay in the same house.

"ARE YOU SURE you don't want to come to the studio with me?" Melanie asked Vivien as she rooted through the accumulation of stuff on the kitchen counter in search of her keys. "You might enjoy the Friday-night lesson and practice party. It's very social. On a good night we might have sixty-seventy people." She raised her eyes heavenward, apparently offering a little prayer that this would be the case tonight. "Clay's coming and he's a really good

dancer. I'm sure he'd be glad to take you under his wing."
She offered this as if it might be some sort of induce-
ment. Was there any part of Melanie's life that he had not
insinuated himself into?

"Sorry," Vivien said. "Belly dancing's kind of growing
on me, but I think one dance class a week is my limit."

"You do fine when you concentrate, Vivi," Melanie
pointed out. She was opening drawers now, still in search
of the elusive keys.

"Well, it's hard to do too much damage when you
don't have a partner. I think we should leave well enough
alone."

"But what'll you do after you drop the kids at the
game?" Melanie asked, striking pay dirt in the vegetable
bin of the refrigerator. She pulled the key ring out from
between two bags of chopped lettuce and waved them triumphantly. "I hate to think of you sitting at home alone
with nothing to do."

Vivien would actually have enjoyed some time alone;
the last two weeks with Melanie and the kids and the cast
of characters at the dance studio was a lot more "togeth-
erness" than Vivien was used to. "Don't worry about me,
Mel. I could get a bite out or veg in front of the TV. It's
not as if I'm out every night in New York."

In truth, Vivi had already decided to stay at the Pemberton High football game, where she expected to mine
for gold. Or at least material for this week's column.

"All right." Melanie shouted good-bye to the kids and
hurried out to the van.

"Come on, guys," Vivien shouted upstairs to Shelby
and Trip. "Let's go!"

Vivien backed the Toyota down the driveway just a few
minutes after Melanie, though with none of her finesse.
"Maybe I should have let it warm up a little bit longer,"
Vivien said.

Shelby rolled her eyes. "I don't think it's a mechanical problem." Trip made no comment, but as Vivien drove through the neighborhood she could feel both of them judging her and finding her wanting. At the exit onto 120, she waited until there were no cars whizzing by in either direction rather than pulling out between medians; that move hadn't gone so well the other morning.

"Oh, my God," Shelby groaned. "We'll be lucky to get there before the game is *over*!"

"Better safe than sorry," Vivien said like some old fart. Shelby laughed at her. Even Trip grinned.

"Hey," Vivi said to Shelby. "If you behaved responsibly once in a while, you could be driving yourself to the game right now."

Shelby stopped laughing.

"In fact, if you can't do the right thing for yourself, maybe you could take your mother into account. It'd give her one less thing to worry about." Vivien hardly recognized her voice with its lecturing tone.

"You're kidding, right?" Shelby snapped. "Since when did you become the queen of considerate behavior?"

The girl had a point. But then Vivien had never spent two weeks watching her sister run herself ragged trying to take care of a home, a business, and two children before. She'd had no idea at all what Melanie dealt with on a daily basis. And if she had?

"I don't even know what you're doing here," Shelby said. "None of us knows. Why don't you just go back to New York and mind your own effing business?"

Vivien's mouth tightened. No matter how Shelby dressed or liked to think of herself, she was only seventeen. Trying to ignore the insult itself, she focused on Shelby's use of the F-word.

"Vulgarity is a mark of a limited vocabulary." This had been Caroline's response to anything even approximating a curse. Vivien hadn't heard the reprimand in almost twenty years, and yet it tripped off of her tongue without conscious thought and in the same insulting upper-class drawl with which her mother had always delivered it.

The remark got Shelby's attention all right, but not because she took the reprimand to heart. "Oh, my God. You didn't really just say that did you?" She chortled. "What century did that come from? No, I know, I bet it came from Grandmother Caroline's bible—*Gone with the Wind*!"

Vivien had thought the remark asinine when it had been used on her and she was appalled that it had come out of her mouth. Would all of those things she'd rejected as a child become part of her repertoire after she gave birth? Were they even now fighting their way out of her subconscious for use later? Was she, in fact, doomed to be her mother? Once during an argument Caroline had hissed, "I hope you end up with a child just like you!" What if that actually happened? Oh, God, what in the world was she doing?

Lost in her own frightening visions of parenthood, Vivien didn't respond to Shelby's taunt. In the wrong lane when it was time to turn, she reacted without thinking and cut off another driver, who laid on the horn. After that they inched along behind a long stream of cars heading toward the high school.

"Parking's to the left. You can just drop us off at the corner and leave if you go straight." Shelby pointed toward the drop-off spot. "You can pick us up at ten thirty. Or we'll call if we want to come home early."

"I'm not the help," Vivien said, making the left instead. "And I'm planning to stay for the game."

There was a shocked silence.

"Show me where to park," she said.

Trip sat up straighter in the backseat, tuned in now.

Shelby's gaze narrowed. "Trip might be willing to be seen with you. I'm not."

"Um, grown-ups and kids don't, um, hang together at games." Trip shifted uncomfortably behind her. "There's like separate sections and everything." It was a long speech for Trip; apparently even the strong, silent types wanted to evade embarrassment.

"That space is mine!" Vivien said as she zoomed into a vacant parking spot and received more horn from the SUV driver that had been eyeing it. But Vivien didn't care. She was thinking how odd it was that she'd reached an age where her mere presence could be an embarrassment to her niece and nephew. "Well, you all go on ahead then so nobody suspects we arrived together," Vivien said. "I'll just get my cane out of the back and hobble in on my own."

They were out of the car and distancing themselves so fast she was talking to herself, like any senior citizen might.

Vivi paid at the gate and then walked across the track to the Pemberton side. The stands were filling rapidly and even from a distance the separation of teen from adult was apparent; at the far end the marching band filled an entire section; the strains of the school's fight song filled the air and wafted across the field where the Pemberton team warmed up. A steady stream of students paraded from one end of the stands to the other, busy seeing and being seen. An even greater number milled about in amoebalike groups that continually expanded and contracted.

She slowed in front of the concession stand, a cinderblock rectangle, which was knee-deep in teens waiting to buy food from parents working feverishly to serve them.

Vivi scanned the bleachers for a good observation point. Out of the corner of one eye she caught a glimpse of Melanie's neighbor, Catherine Dennison, who waved eagerly and motioned her up.

"You look like you've gone native," the blonde said, taking in Vivien's sweats and sneakers. Vivi had noticed plenty of other parents dressed this way, but Catherine, who wore tight designer jeans and a cropped sweater, wasn't one of them. "What brings you to the game?" She slid over to make room for Vivien on the hard metal bleacher.

"I brought Shelby and Trip and thought I might as well stay and watch," Vivi said. "I feel obligated to embarrass my niece and nephew as much as humanly possible while I'm in town. Not that they're going to get close enough to me to allow that to happen."

Catherine smiled, showing perfectly capped teeth. "Usually the only time you see them is if they run out of money."

"Is your daughter here?" Vivi couldn't remember the girl's name, only that she was a junior like Shelby.

"Of course." Catherine pointed down to the field where a long-legged blonde stood at the very top of a six-person pyramid. "Claire cheers *very* competitively. She's cocaptain of the squad and she's been on the Homecoming Court every year since she started at Pemberton. She's also a member of the National Honor Society and has a GPA of four-point-five."

Claire Dennison did a summersault and a half off the pyramid and made a perfect landing with her arms up in a V. Her mother's artificially endowed chest puffed out in pride.

"Wow," Vivien said, beginning to understand Melanie's reluctance to converse and compare. Still, she'd come looking for someone who would dish, and Catherine might be just self-absorbed enough not to notice that Vivi was more interested in the people who were watching the game than the people who were playing.

A trumpet sounded a cavalry charge and the game

began. Below, the migration of students from one end of the bleachers to the other continued. She saw Trip in the middle of a group of guys, looking oddly alone. Vivien peered more closely, not sure why she'd thought that. Maybe it was how still he was in the midst of everyone else's constant fidgeting and movement. Or the slightly removed look on his face.

Down by the fence Shelby strutted up to a tall broad-shouldered boy lounging carelessly against a fencepost. Like most of the girls, Shelby wore tight jeans slung low on her hips. Despite the mid-November chill, the layered T-shirts she wore were extremely thin and bared the flat of her stomach when she moved, and she moved a lot, not-so-subtle gyrations meant to get and hold the boy's attention.

Catherine had apparently been watching, too. "That's Ty Womack," she said. "All the girls think he's totally hot." She watched the interplay between Shelby and the boy. "But he's got a reputation for being wild. He was suspended from the football team for drinking and for 'unbecoming behavior,' though that could mean almost anything."

The boy, who had the height and broad shoulders of a man, leaned down to whisper something in Shelby's ear. Shelby said something back, and they both laughed.

"My Claire knows to stay away from boys like that. I'm surprised Melanie allows it."

Shelby tossed her dark hair and laid a hand on the boy's arm. Despite the noise and the constant stream of students ebbing and flowing around them, Shelby and the boy were completely focused on each other. A moment later he slipped an arm around her shoulders and they walked off around the back of the bleachers.

Vivien didn't know whether Melanie was even aware of Ty Womack's existence. Nor did she know what, if anything, she could do to protect Shelby from him. If she charged down there and broke up what might be an innocent kiss or conversation, Shelby would never speak to her again and any chance of establishing a relationship would be gone. But it felt wrong not to act.

"I hate to say it," Catherine said. "But ever since J.J. died, Shelby's seemed a bit . . . wild herself."

Vivien's hands knotted into fists. With some surprise, she realized she wanted to tell Catherine to mind her own business. But she'd come seeking information; she knew from experience that you couldn't always control what kind you got.

"J.J. was a good man," Catherine said, her eyes softening. "I know losing their father has been a huge thing for both Shelby and Trip. Claire was devastated when her father and I divorced, and he hasn't disappeared from her life. She still sees him regularly."

It made sense that J.J.'s death would affect Shelby and Trip's behavior. How could it not? But Vivien had no idea what would help other than time.

"Did you know J.J. well?" Vivi asked.

Catherine looked out at the field, her gaze seeking out her daughter. "Oh, about as well as you know any neighbor. After Charles moved out, J.J. used to help me with things around the house when I needed it. I used to be in the neighborhood book club with Melanie."

There was a roar as the Pemberton quarterback sent the ball flying down the field where it was caught handily. The receiver was taken down just a couple of yards from the end zone.

For the rest of the game, Vivi split her attention between her niece and nephew, the parade of students, and Catherine Dennison, who turned out to be a real font of information about Pemberton and the suburbs surrounding it. As long as she was able to get in the occasional boast about Claire, who was apparently not only a prodigy but one of Pemberton's most popular students, Catherine seemed happy to answer any question Vivien raised.

To supplement Catherine's insights, Vivien eavesdropped on the conversations around her. Mostly the parents complained about their children's demanding schedules, which depended on constant chauffeuring and frequent check writing. They complained of feeling overwhelmed, overscheduled, and overextended. But underneath the complaints Vivi heard their pride in all the things their children had undertaken. In how attractive and well rounded they would appear when all those things could be put on those all important college applications.

"What are you doing?" Catherine asked late in the fourth quarter when she caught Vivien leaning perilously close to one of the players' mother who was complaining that the harsh economic climate had forced her and her husband to cut out their personal trainer. "If you lean over any farther, you're going to be sitting in her lap." She frowned slightly, though no corresponding lines appeared on her forehead. "You certainly do ask a ton of questions."

Vivien shrugged and smiled. "Just curious," she said as innocently as she could. "Occupational hazard, I guess."

16

ON SUNDAY NIGHT while Melanie, Clay, and the kids settled in front of the family room television, Vivien went upstairs where she sat on her bed and pulled out her laptop.

Tentatively she began to turn her observations from Friday night's football game into a lead. There were a few false starts, but ultimately she typed, *Greetings from suburbia, where children are the suns around which parents revolve. In truth, children are their parents' reason for being, not to mention their reason for being here.*

Vivien thought about all that she'd seen and heard since she'd arrived: the hockey practices at six A.M. for children barely big enough to hold a hockey stick. Weekday volunteer shifts at school, afternoons, evenings, and weekends crammed full of extracurricular activities. Busy children were a badge of belonging. The overscheduling was something to complain about, only the complaints were a socially acceptable form of bragging.

They are driving before the sun comes up and long after it's gone down, she wrote. *They are fund-raisers, boosters, ticket takers, concessionaires, burger flippers, timekeepers, and pregame meal providers. They fill the stands of every sport known to man and a few I'd never heard of before arriving here. They man the welcome desks, phone switchboards, media centers, and copy machines at their children's schools. They are involved in virtually everything their children do from the cerebral to the physical. On the weekends they are coaches and team moms, and there are teams for everything. Because clearly if an activity exists— it's even better if your child competes in it. They are exhilarated by their children's successes and depressed by their failures, though the word "failure" is rarely used.* Vivien made a note to address this concept in a future column.

Weekends are so jam-packed that fathers and working mothers are relieved to return to the office on Monday morning so that they can slacken the pace. They're exhausted from supporting their children's busy lives. It makes one wonder if this busy life is simply a substitute for "parenting." After all, if everyone is so exhausted all the time, less genuine interaction is required.

Vivien continued with this line of thought for several paragraphs, then reread what she had written. It was, perhaps, a bit harsh; she cringed at the idea of including Melanie, who worked and parented single-handedly, in this blithe condemnation. And it was possible that city dwellers did the same revolution around their offspring. But she left it as it was. There was not a line she'd written that was untrue.

When I was a child, she wrote in conclusion, *children fit into their parents' lives. Today, especially in this suburb in which I've landed, it is clearly the opposite. Because here parents don't have lives of their own. They are much too busy revolving around their sons. And, of course, their daughters.*

As always she signed it, *Your stranger in an even stranger land, Scarlett Leigh.* And then sent it on its way to New York.

But when she turned out the light and hunkered down

under the covers, the murmur of voices from downstairs turned her thoughts from the exhaustion of the locals to her disturbing reaction to Clay Alexander.

She had no idea if he'd been this involved in the Jacksons' life before J.J.'s death; that was yet another detail of Melanie's life that Vivien had failed to tune into. But his continual presence struck her as calculated, and the way he hovered between friend of the family and head of the household left her unsure of what he was trying to achieve. He seemed attached not only to the kids but to Melanie, and yet there was no indication that they were "dating." She'd finally been able to set an appointment with Blaine Stewart for Tuesday. Presumably a look at the file would either confirm or eliminate her suspicions.

The whole thing reminded her of that movie with Richard Gere and Jodie Foster where an imposter comes back from the Civil War and even though the wife knows it's not her husband, she acts like he is. Not that she didn't think Mel and the kids knew the difference between J.J. and Clay. It was just that she had the weirdest feeling that Clay Alexander might be trying to eliminate those differences.

☺

RUTH SPENT MUCH of that Wednesday afternoon at the Magnolia Ballroom working on a holiday mailing for Melanie. When that was done, she tidied the place up a bit, straightening the tables and chairs that bordered the dance floor, polishing the beautiful burled wood of the welcome desk at which she often sat, stacking the CDs and miscellaneous items that accumulated in the DJ area. Mostly she just wanted to keep her hands busy and her body in motion. Her brain was completely occupied with Ira. Or rather her marriage to Ira.

They'd barely spoken since last Friday night's disastrous Shabbat dinner. Ruth had always believed in talking things out and, in fact, often erred on the side of too much talking. But now whenever she even looked at Ira the anger and disappointment rose up to clog her throat, holding her words and thoughts prisoner inside.

Seeing no reason to go home for dinner before class, Ruth ran over to the nearby McDonald's for a burger, then came back to the studio to man the front desk. Smiling and greeting students as they arrived for that night's classes, she could pretend that her world had not crumbled around her.

By eight P.M., they stood in their ragged line at the far end of the dance floor waiting for Naranya to finish setting up the speakers. The Shipley sisters laughed identical trilling laughs as the uninjured one helped the other into a nearby chair. Melanie took up a spot in the back to help two newcomers who'd come for a free first trial lesson. Lourdes and Sally stood together chatting.

Ruth stood between Angela, whose clothes seemed far too big, and Vivien, whose clothes were clearly too small. In fact, Ruth had noticed that Vivien's breasts swelled precariously over the top of the camisole as if they'd grown a whole cup size in the last week. Her face looked fuller, too. The woman was definitely piling on the pounds, but what did she care how much Vivien Gray weighed? Or why? All she cared about was that she hadn't bailed out on Melanie. Yet.

The music wafted out of the speakers, slow and plaintive, matching Ruth's mood. Naranya passed out the hip scarves, then stepped in front of them to begin the opening stretches. Ruth followed, bending to the right and then the left, reaching down to touch each toe before coming back to center. Slowly they rose up onto the balls of their feet and stretched their arms up toward the ceiling. Ruth tried to clear her mind, but it was like trying to part a fog.

They circled their shoulders, then worked with their arms, forming S's, making them slither like snakes, but Ruth could barely force herself through the motions. She caught a glimpse of herself in the mirror, something she'd noticed Vivien and Angela were careful not to do, and saw a solid block of a woman with a puff of white hair at the top; she might as well have been the Q-tip she resembled for all Ira seemed to care.

Naranya drew them into a circle to practice a walking step that looked suspiciously like the Israeli folk dance the hora. Ruth's hands, clasped in Angela and Vivi's, felt slippery with sweat as she thought of the weddings and Bar Mitzvah parties when she'd danced these steps joined with Ira.

"Are you all right?" the redhead asked her, holding tight to her hand. "Can I get you something cold to drink?"

"No, I'm fine." Ruth's response was automatic, though this time she wasn't sure it was true. Her shoulders drooped despite her efforts to hold them up and she was relieved when Naranya led them out of the circle and back into their lines.

"You all look very good today," Naranya said. "I think you have been practicing?"

She heard the others laugh at that and someone shook her hips so that her scarf jangled loudly.

"Thank you, Sally. I heard that. We weel work more with our hips. When your half-moons look good, I will show you the eights." Naranya strode over to the computer to restart the music, and there was an excited buzz.

Ruth just stood there, silent and numb, one thought filling her mind: she'd drawn a line in the sand, and now she was afraid that Ira would refuse to step over it.

Not knowing where to turn, she raised her eyes to the mirror and her gaze met Melanie's.

"I need Ruth to help me with something," Melanie said as she stepped up to Ruth's side and slipped an arm around her shoulders. "Will you excuse us?"

Melanie led Ruth off the floor and into the empty office. Ruth was embarrassed by how much the physical contact meant to her; she was far more used to offering comfort than receiving it. But she felt as if she might weep with gratitude.

"It'll be all right, Ruth," Melanie said as she closed the office door behind them and helped Ruth into a chair. "I know it will. Sometimes it just takes men a little longer to figure things out."

They sat for a while listening to the odd mixture of Naranya's oriental music and the insistent beat of a rhumba. But Ruth couldn't imagine why Ira was having such a hard time figuring this out. Surely even Ira at his most stubborn wouldn't choose divorce over a couple of hours of dancing? Her mind said, of course not, but her heart wasn't so sure.

◎

IN HER ROOM at Melanie's, Vivien picked up her cell phone on the third ring.

"Hello there, stranger." Marty's voice was its usual teasing self. "I thought we were going to talk regularly. I don't think once a month qualifies."

"Sorry. Just haven't had much to report." Vivien carried the phone over to the chaise lounge near the window and lowered herself into it.

"I think I may be going through Gray withdrawal," Marty said. "I don't even hear from your mother anymore. If I hadn't reached you, I might have broken down and called Caroline."

Vivien smiled, realizing as she did just how much she'd missed the irrepressible Marty. "Wouldn't she have loved that?"

There was a pause. And then because she couldn't help herself she asked, "So . . . how's the Barbie doll doing?"

"Okay," he said carefully.

"Are you shooting for her?"

"No, they assigned Drew Haynes to her. I'm working with Terry."

Somehow this made Vivi feel better. Giving her Marty would have been like handing a family member over to the enemy.

"She was a bit of a 'bitchy Barbie' in the beginning. Tried bad-mouthing you at first," Marty said, knowing Vivien well enough to know she'd want the details. "Took potshots at you whenever she could. But she's a relatively brainy Barbie. She finally figured out that nobody wanted to hear it."

Well, that was something. "Thanks."

There was another protracted pause. Vivien didn't want to hang up and break the connection, but this brush with her old life was even more painful than she'd imagined. For the past weeks she'd been able to shove it to a corner of her consciousness and had wrapped it up in a sort of hazy "then" that had allowed her to focus on the all-too-sharp "now."

"Listen," Marty said. "I know this isn't really my business . . ."

Vivi smiled again. This was how Marty had always begun his swan dives into her personal life. "But I think you need to be in better touch with Stone. Assuming you, um, want to continue your, um, relationship with him."

Vivien closed her eyes as another stab of pain pierced her. She wanted to be in touch, actually craved the sound of Stone's voice when she felt overwhelmed, which was far more often than she wanted to admit. But she'd been afraid to talk to him too often, afraid that she'd break down one day and give away her secret.

"He's worried about you," Marty said. "He seems to think you're hiding something."

She winced. "Who, me?"

"I just spoke to him a few minutes ago. He's reachable on the satellite phone for the next few hours." There was a pause. "The guy's out in a war zone worrying about you, Vivi. I think you need to set his mind at rest so he can pay attention to what he's doing."

Her mind raced. Not talking to Stone was hard. Talking to him was even harder.

"Seriously, Vivi. Don't jerk the guy around. Stone deserves better than that."

That was for sure. "I won't."

His message delivered, Marty moved on. "So when are you coming back? Stone seemed to think you were coming up for some interviews?"

Vivi sighed. Lying to Marty felt almost as bad as lying to Stone. "I'm not sure," she said. "I just don't know yet. I'll let you know if I get something firmed up."

Vivien hung up. For a time she simply sat with the phone in her lap trying to figure out what to do; the secrets she was keeping loomed so large she couldn't imagine how she could stop them from slipping out. Before she could chicken out, she placed the call to Stone.

Coward that she was, she almost hoped he wouldn't pick up. But he picked up in the middle of the first ring.

"Greetings from the back of beyond," he said.

Vivien closed her eyes the better to enjoy the sound of his voice. "How are you?" she asked. "Is everything okay?"

"I'm fine," he said. "Things have been a bit quieter here than I expected." He said this with regret, but Vivi was glad. The constant jagged-edged worry for his safety smoothed out ever so slightly. "We've been in villages so small they're not on any of our maps. But once we get a little deeper into the border region things will heat up."

"Just like you like it." She knew better than to admit to the worry; they'd been together too long for that. It was simply part of their relationship, just as danger was part of his job.

There was a brief moment of silence in which she could practically feel him getting ready to question her. Not wanting to be forced to lie outright to anything he might ask, she took charge of the conversation.

"I met with Blaine Stewart and the agent in charge of J.J.'s case yesterday and I wondered if I could run something by you," she said just as she had countless times over the years. She trusted his instincts more than anyone else she knew; Stone had often helped her pick apart and analyze the threads of a story she was trying to piece together.

"Always."

She smiled. It was his stock answer to her request for help. "We went through the file."

"Mmm-hmmm."

She thought about how sure she'd been that she'd find something that had been overlooked. How eager she'd been to make Clay Alexander responsible. But it was hard to argue with the evidence. "There's nothing inconsistent with the finding of accidental death. No cause for suspicion. The wound—well, calling it a wound is a gross understatement—was clearly self-inflicted and consistent with what would have happened if the rifle went off while he was cleaning it."

Stone didn't comment, knowing she'd want to lay it all out for him first, but even she could hear the disappointment in her voice. "When they interviewed him at the scene, Clay Alexander told them that he saw J.J. carrying his rifle over to the couch in the study just before he went outside; he'd told Clay he was going to clean it. Clay was still outside when he heard the gunshot."

There was a silence and then, "And?"

"And he went running back inside and found a lot of J.J.'s head splattered all over the place." She swallowed, glad they'd removed the photos before showing her the case file. Even more glad that Melanie would never see them. "They found bone fragments imbedded in the wall behind the couch where he was sitting. The only fingerprints found on the gun were J.J.'s."

"So that's it then."

"Yeah. I guess so."

"There's that tone again," Stone said. "You don't think it was an accident? Or you don't think he killed himself?"

"I don't know," she admitted. "I don't really know what else could have happened. Something just feels . . . off."

There was another silence while they both processed her answer.

"I have a lot of respect for your instincts, Vivi," Stone said carefully. "But you know cops. They're suspicious folks—rightfully so. And if they didn't see a need to look further, well, it could be because there is no reason."

Vivi knew this; she'd been telling herself this since yesterday. But something niggled. Clay Alexander had been the only one there, and Clay Alexander looked awfully comfortable as acting head of his former best friend's family.

There was another protracted silence. "So what are you planning to do next?" Stone finally asked.

"Who said I was going to do anything?" Vivien asked.

"Vivi," Stone said, "I may be on the other side of the

world, but that doesn't mean I don't still know how your mind works." His tone was gentle, but there was something underneath it that Vivien didn't want to address. As long as he didn't come out and say that he knew she was hiding something from him, she wasn't going to go there. "You certainly have the skills to look into this further. But the findings seem pretty clear. And you have to consider how Melanie would feel about you poking around in this."

Vivien remained silent, but not because she didn't know the answer. It had taken two years, but Melanie seemed to finally be moving on with her life. And Clay Alexander, for all that Vivi couldn't define his role or motivation, was a part of it.

"This is not a work assignment, Vivi," Stone reminded her. "You have a choice."

But did she? Didn't Melanie deserve to know the truth? Didn't everyone?

Vivi had screwed up her chance to be there for Melanie and Shelby and Trip when they needed her most. She was not much of a caregiver, not then and not now. But she was good at hunting down information. She could give them the gift of knowing what had really happened if, in fact, the truth differed in any way from what the GBI investigation indicated. Surely there would have to be some peace of mind in that.

"I could look a little further without saying anything," Vivien said. "Ask a few questions, see if there are any leads that weren't evident at the scene. I don't mean physical evidence necessarily, but maybe looking back at J.J. and Clay's history might turn up something. If I'm barking up the wrong tree, Melanie doesn't ever have to know. I can just satisfy my curiosity and that'll be that."

"I feel compelled to remind you what happened the last time you conducted an investigation that touched your family," Stone said quietly. That was the thing about Stone; he had her thirst for truth, but he was able to weigh the pros and cons much more objectively.

"Good point." She could still remember Harley Jenkins's shock when she'd exposed the longtime senator's illegal use of campaign funds, how much angrier her parents had been at her than at the behavior she had revealed. It had propelled her away from home and family. Relationships that had not been exactly great had become infinitely worse. Was she willing to take that chance again? Should she?

"The truth can only hurt her if I tell her. Which I wouldn't have to do." Vivien sighed. She missed Stone at this moment almost more than she could bear. "There's something about Clay Alexander that makes me think he's not exactly what he seems. At the very least he knows more than he's said. I have this nagging feeling that he's hiding something. I just don't know what."

"Frustrating, isn't it?" Stone asked, reminding her again that it was much more than miles that stood between them. "Sometimes you have to wait for people to tell you things. Even when what you really want to do is wring it out of them."

17

Two days before Thanksgiving, Vivien, unlike Shelby, awoke to the blare of Shelby's alarm clock. Pulling on an old robe of Trip's decorated with cowboy boots and lariats that she'd found in the back of her closet, she pushed her feet into a pair of ancient slippers and rooted around in the back of her closet for the pot and spoon she'd hidden there. Her eyes popped fully open when she realized they were gone.

In Shelby's room, Vivi crossed her arms in front of her chest and considered the sleeping teenager. "Verrry tricky," she said to the tip of Shelby's nose, which was practically all that stuck out from beneath the covers. "But not tricky enough." After a check of both closets, Shelby's laundry basket, and a pile of dirty clothes that Vivien had to hold her own nose to get close to, she was forced to acknowledge that Shelby had done a better job of hiding the ejection device than Vivi had.

Still, there was a mission to accomplish. With a flick, she silenced the alarm clock so that she could think. In the resulting quiet she could hear Shelby breathing, the sound of Trip's shower, and Melanie in the kitchen below. Unwilling to resort to brute force, she scanned the bedroom for a new means of ejection. Her gaze landed on a long discarded New Year's Eve party hat. The feather in its crown drooped beneath a heavy layer of dust. Smiling evilly, Vivien applied it to the tip of Shelby's nose.

"Aaaaaacchhhhhooooo!" The force of the sneeze jack-knifed Shelby's body upward into a sitting position. The second sneeze forced her eyes open.

"Bless you." Vivi hid the feathered hat behind her back. "And good morning! Time to rise and shine!" Knowing just how annoyed Shelby was by perkiness of any kind, Vivien laid it on thick. "Today is the first day of the rest of your life!"

Shelby sneezed in response.

"We're running a little behind this morning, so you might want to get moving." Vivien smiled as she said this, then broke into an ultraperky rendition of "Tomorrow" from *Annie*. She'd barely belted out "The sun'll come out . . . tomorrow. Bet your bottom dollar . . ." when Shelby threw off her covers and climbed out of bed. "How much would it take to get you to go home?" she growled. "I'll get a job to pay for it. Just tell me how much!"

Vivien laughed, but she didn't move. She'd learned the hard way not to leave the room until Shelby did. On Monday Shelby had doubled back, gotten into bed, and fallen back asleep. By the time Melanie got her to school, Shelby had missed her first two classes.

Vivien let herself enjoy today's victory. She was still smiling with satisfaction when she reached the kitchen. The look on Melanie's face wiped the smile from her lips. "What?" she asked, moving toward the kitchen counter where Melanie stood, a section of newspaper clutched in her hands. "What is it?"

"It's not that bad," Melanie said tentatively. "It's just kind of . . . bitchy. Not really damaging or anything."

Vivien held out her hand for the paper.

"It doesn't even mention you by name," Melanie said. "Hardly anybody will know it's about you." She handed Vivien the section of the *Atlanta Journal-Constitution*, which was neatly folded open to Just Peachy, by Matthew Glazer.

The lead sentence jolted Vivien completely and irretrievably awake.

What investigative journalist from Atlanta's uber-connected political family has lost her network gig? she read.

Oh, shit.

It has come to Just Peachy's attention that one of our own is back from her stint with CIN with her tail tucked firmly between her legs. Although the former investigative journalist claims to have quit to pursue other opportunities, this reporter did not just fall off the turnip truck and knows that no sane journalist would willingly give up such a position.

Sources here say she's just home to recuperate from the wound she received when she screwed up her last assignment. But New York folk say differently. Stay tuned for more as Just Peachy investigates.

"Oh, Lord." Vivien dropped the column on the counter and slid onto the barstool. "Glazer thinks he's got some real story here; he won't rest until he makes me the laughingstock of the journalism world." Not that her appearance on YouTube hadn't already achieved this.

Melanie pushed a cup of tea and a croissant toward her. "Don't worry about it, Vivi. No one cares why you left CIN. And I know when you're ready to do something else, you will."

Melanie's faith in her made Vivien feel even guiltier about using her sister's life as fodder for a column she was too embarrassed to put her name on. Not to mention her plans to look into J.J.'s death. "What is the circulation of the *AJC*, anyway?"

"Oh, I don't know," Melanie hedged. "A quarter of a million? Maybe a little more?"

Vivien closed her eyes and covered her face with her hands.

"But probably only about half of those know our family well enough to have any idea who he was talking about."

Vivien was still processing this when Melanie went to the back stairs and shouted up. "Hurry up, guys! You're going to miss the bus and I don't have time to drive you to school."

Trip pounded down the back stairs into the kitchen.

"Just grab a breakfast bar or something," Melanie said to her son. "I can get you to the bus but I can't drive you to school today."

Vivien looked up, noticing for the first time that Melanie was fully dressed and made-up. "Where are you going?"

"I've got an eight A.M. doctor's appointment. I'm going to have to run in a few minutes." Melanie poured Trip a glass of milk, then walked back over to the bottom of the stairs. "Shelby!" she shouted up again. "Get down here!"

Melanie got her things together and began to pace the kitchen floor. "That girl! If I don't leave right this minute, I won't even be able to get Trip to the bus. And I asked for this early appointment because it's the only time you don't end up waiting for an hour to be seen."

Vivien looked more closely at Melanie, who looked ready to hyperventilate. "Go on, Mel," she said. "Drop Trip at the bus stop on your way. I'll get Shelby to school."

"But she'll be late again, she'll have another tardy, she'll lose her incentives, she'll . . ."

"Melanie, stop it!" Vivien grabbed her sister by the

shoulders and forced her to stop pacing. "Trip, go with your mother." He looked up at her surprised by the note of command in her voice. "Now."

The boy picked up his backpack. Rummaging through the piles of stuff on the counter, Vivien located Melanie's keys and placed them in her palm. "Go. Stop worrying. I'll get her there as fast as I can, but she's going to have to learn the consequences of her actions, Mel. If all those things you're worrying about happen, then you'll just have to let Shelby deal with it."

Melanie looked stricken. "But the bell is at eight fifteen and . . ."

"Just go." She closed Melanie's fingers around the keys then located her purse and slung it over Melanie's shoulder. "Really."

Melanie and Trip raced out the door at seven forty-five. Shortly before eight A.M. Shelby strolled down the stairs in a black corduroy skirt that barely covered her rear end and a low-cut sweater that she'd failed to put anything under. She seemed surprised not to see her mother or brother.

"Where's Mom and Trip?"

"Your mother dropped Trip at the bus. She had an early doctor's appointment. But I believe she mentioned that to you."

Shelby shrugged as if it was of no concern to her. "What's for breakfast?"

"Whatever you get for yourself after you go up and change."

"There's no time to change." She took in the cowboy robe and slippers, Vivien's lack of makeup. "How am I supposed to get to school?"

It was Vivien's turn to shrug.

"But I'm going to be late. And I'm hungry."

They glared at each other for a long moment.

"Fine, I'll just drive myself," Shelby declared, storming toward the hook where the spare keys were kept.

As she passed, Vivien held up her hand, from which Shelby's keys dangled. "Not an option," she said.

Shelby stopped. "So how do you suggest I get to school?"

"Personally, I'd like to see you have to walk after the way you blew off your mother."

Shelby's mouth tightened.

"But I'm prepared to take you after you change. You can bring something to eat with you in the car."

"But I'm going to be late." Shelby's nonchalance had been replaced by panic. "Will you write me a note? Say I had an appointment or something?"

"No," Vivien said calmly, though she was relieved that Shelby did, in fact, care about school, however hard she might try to hide it. "You had plenty of time. And if you didn't have to be dragged out of bed every morning and change your clothes before you left every day, you'd have even more time. You're freaking your mother out every morning for no reason. And it's time for you to stop."

Without another word Shelby stomped upstairs. Drawers opened and shut, doors slammed. Five minutes later she was back to take a granola bar from the pantry and a bottled orange juice from the fridge. "What are we waiting for?"

Not bothering to dress, Vivien got into the RAV4 and fired it up. She and Shelby made the twelve-minute trip to school in silence, and while Vivien wouldn't go so far as to say that signaled a truce, she did hope they'd reached some sort of meeting of the minds. Melanie let Shelby get away with things because she was overwhelmed and alone and she was so busy racing from obligation to obligation that she couldn't take the time to dig in her heels and make Shelby toe the line. Well, at the moment Vivien had all the time in the world. If nothing else, she could run a little interference for Melanie.

Vivien was on her way back to Melanie's when the car began to slow of its own accord. By the time she reached LA Fitness, she was barely moving. Not understanding what was happening, Vivien pressed harder on the gas pedal, but the car continued to slow. Virtually at a stop, Vivien tried to pull over to the side of the road but glided to a stop straddling two out of three lanes instead. The Toyota's front bumper edged up to the curb. The only open lane was a left turn only. She looked down and realized she was wearing only a cowboy robe and slippers.

Vivien didn't know what she was supposed to do next. The laying on of horns all around her made it impossible to think, but not to forget that she was practically naked. Before she could decide what to do, a siren screamed above the blare of horns. A flashing blue light raced into view.

The line of cars stuck behind her shifted as best they could to let the police car through. Moments later the siren went silent in midscreech. A car door opened and slammed shut. At least the police car's arrival had silenced the blaring horns. In the quiet she could hear boots thudding across asphalt, crunching on loose gravel. Vivien was thinking small, but it didn't seem to be working any better here in the middle of Roswell Road than it had in the Wall Street parking garage. Through the windshield she watched the Vietnamese couple come out of the dry cleaner to see why traffic had stopped. The barber shop beside it began to empty out. A few drivers managed to make a right turn into the strip center parking lot and circle back in the other direction. Everyone else sat in their cars waiting for her—or the approaching policeman—to do something. The stress and irritation emanating from the crowd hung like a cloud in the chill morning air.

The boots made a final crunch against the grit on the road as they came to a halt. She lowered the window and felt the crisp morning air rush over her. There was a short bark of male laughter. "I should have known," a familiar voice said.

Vivien turned to look at the policeman. It was the same one she'd met on her first outing. "Hello, officer . . ." she said.

"McFarland," he supplied. "License and registration, please."

She handed them over.

"What seems to be the problem?" he asked.

Careful not to look out her passenger or rear window or anywhere else where she might have to see the pissed-off expressions of those around her, she said, "I don't know. It just . . . stopped and I couldn't make it to the side of the road in time."

"Put it in neutral and let's get you out of the way." He commandeered the driver directly behind her to help him push as she steered over to the side, then he had her turn on her emergency flashers. With a wave of his hand, he started traffic flowing again. She thought she saw Catherine Dennison drive by and considered flagging her down, but the blonde's gaze was fixed straight ahead and she had a cell phone pressed to her ear. Pucci gave her a good look though; she had the oddest impression the dog was laughing.

Officer McFarland leaned in through the window. "There's no sign of smoke or overheating. Turn the ignition on and let's look at your gauges."

She glanced down toward the ignition and saw a bare thigh poking out from the robe. With a groan of embarrassment, she pulled the robe closed just as the instrument panel lit up. Vivien was too flustered to register what she was looking at. Officer McFarland wasn't. "You're out of gas, Miss Gray. It's a funny thing, but these vehicles just don't do well without it." His tone was dry.

Vivien closed her eyes and hugged the steering wheel. So far this morning had completely sucked and it was only eight thirty. She would have liked to put her head down on her arms and cry out her frustration and embarrassment, but with her luck someone would whip out a camera phone and put her right back on YouTube. Or in another edition of Just Peachy.

Vivien opened her eyes and forced herself to look into the officer's face, which bore an almost even mixture of irritation and amusement. She sensed he could hardly wait to radio this one in.

"So how do I get some gas?" Vivien had no idea whether Melanie belonged to AAA or any kind of road service, not that she was going to interrupt a doctor's appointment to ask. It was possible if she just sat here long enough Melanie would drive by at some point and rescue her. But, of course, she wasn't wearing clothes. And she didn't think Officer McFarland was going to let her abandon her vehicle here. Or offer her a ride home.

"Well, typically you go to a gas station and buy some. Preferably before the tank is bone-dry," he said. "There's one over on the opposite corner." He pointed toward the far end of the strip center where she could see part of a towering sign and the large shadow it cast over the street. "I'm sure they'll have some sort of container. If you make it quick, I can wait here with the car."

"But I'm not . . . dressed," she said pulling the lapels of her robe closer together and wishing she'd at least put on underclothes beneath the knee-length terry cloth.

"I know." His voice and expression confirmed that amusement had clearly won out over irritation. At least he didn't laugh.

Vivien reached across the seat for her purse and waited for him to step back so that she could open her door. They considered each other there on the side of the road as drivers slowed ever so slightly to check out the policeman talking to the woman in the powder blue cowboy robe. She wondered if this could be considered police brutality.

"But you do have your purse with you."

He bit back a smile as she turned and marched away from him, holding her purse up against her robe in an effort to keep it closed, her slippers slapping against the pavement.

18

It was the Wednesday night before Thanksgiving and the Magnolia Ballroom felt decidedly . . . empty. The other classes were on hiatus until after the holiday and only Ruth, Angela, and the uninjured Shipley sister had shown up for belly dance.

"The holidays are tough," Melanie said to Vivien as they entered to an unnatural quiet that made the space seem even larger than usual. "People are out of town or they're just too busy. I can't really afford to shut down, but we're not likely to add new students now no matter how many specials I offer."

It was the first time Melanie had even alluded to finances; Vivi had assumed J.J.'s insurance had been sufficient, but she realized now she had no idea how much Mel and the kids needed to live or whether she made enough from the studio to come out in the black.

They tied the jangly scarves around their hips and formed a very small line in their usual spot.

"I saw Just Peachy this morning," Ruth said as Vivien

stepped into line. "At least now we know why you haven't rushed back to New York."

Tweedle Di looked at her more closely. "I thought that was you! I told Dee you were the one who got shot in the butt, but she didn't believe me!"

"I saw eet on YouTube," Naranya said. "Oh, my goodness, it looked like it hurt very bad."

Vivien sighed, but didn't comment. Between Matt Glazer's attack and what she'd come to think of as her "semi-naked gas dash" it had been quite a week. At least no one had shot a video of her in Trip's bathrobe; at least not that she knew of.

Angela shot her a sympathetic look. "That was a really nasty piece. He usually fawns all over anyone with a 'name.' He once referred to James's dad as one of the ATL's most treasured resources."

"Vivien probably pissed him off," Ruth observed as they fell into the beginning stretch routine. "She probably looked down her nose at him and gave him the mistress of the plantation routine."

Melanie, the traitor, giggled.

Vivien drew a deep breath and turned her gaze, pointedly, to Naranya, willing her to begin. She sincerely hoped her parents had been too busy to read today's newspaper. But given the way her luck was running, what were the chances of that?

By the next morning Vivien had to concede those chances were slim. It seemed everyone who had ever met Melanie had driven by the stalled Toyota, then felt compelled to call and find out who the pajama-clad driver was. Vivien vowed to never leave the house again unless she was fully clothed and at least partially made-up. A vow that would be much easier to keep if she had any clothes that still fit.

Her black pants were now held together by a large safety
pin, and the black camisole, which had been stretched
well beyond its limits, was not completely hidden by the
black striped shirt she'd put on over it—probably because
it no longer came close to buttoning. A look in the mirror confirmed what she already knew: her waist no longer
existed and her rear end needed its own zip code. The
only good thing about her now gargantuan breasts was
that they blocked her view of her swelling stomach.

Despite her dismay, her nose, which in her pregnant
state would have done a bloodhound proud, detected a
mouthwatering smell. She sniffed again, recognizing the
flaky crust and rich warm spice of a freshly baked pumpkin pie. Vivien followed the scent downstairs intent on
filling her now-rumbling stomach even though she'd
sworn never to eat again. Just as she did after every
calorie-laden meal.

At the kitchen counter Vivien came to "point" in front
of four cooling pies, two pumpkin and two pecan. Melanie had started baking as soon as they got back from class
last night and had still been at it when Vivien went to
bed. Tins Vivien knew were full of spiced and sugared
pecans, decorated sugar cookies, and fudge and rum balls
sat stacked and ready to take to Magnolia Hall for today's
Thanksgiving meal.

"Do you need help?" Vivien felt compelled to ask,
though eating, not baking, was foremost in her mind.

"Not really," Melanie said clearly surprised at Vivien's
offer. "All I have left to make is the sweet potato casserole." Already dressed and ready for the day, she smiled
and said, "Don't you just love Thanksgiving?"

"Apparently not as much as you do," Vivien replied
as she began opening tins and sampling the wares. What
she did love was that Trip and Shelby were still asleep,
which meant she hadn't had to wake up or drive anyone

anywhere. The house was quiet and there was no rush. The
only place they had to get to today was Magnolia Hall.

For so many years Thanksgiving for Vivien had been
about booking flights, flying down, staying long enough
to put in an appearance, but not long enough for Caroline
to really get to her. Stone usually went home, too, but
they'd always come back to the city in time to have a
couple of days together before going back to work. Up till
now, Thanksgiving in Atlanta had been something she
did because she was expected to and she could hardly wait
to get home to her "real life." But now this was home.
And she had no other life to get back to. This was not a
cheering thought.

"Hey, stop that," Melanie removed the tin of fudge
from Vivien's hands and snapped the lid back on. "We're
going to have a feast in about two hours. You know, roast
turkey and dressing, mashed potatoes, cranberry sauce?"

"I just need a little something to tide me over."

Melanie shot her an assessing look but nonetheless
reached under the counter and pulled out a small tin.
From it she selected an assortment of misshapen pieces
of fudge, broken cookies, and a large handful of sugared
pecans, which she arranged on a small paper plate for
Vivien.

Slipping a pecan into her mouth, she savored the sugar
as it dissolved slowly on her tongue, then began to work
her way through the plate of sweets while Melanie poured
the sweet potato mixture into a greased casserole pan. Vivi
had sent a case of wine to her parents as her contribution
to the meal. She tried not to think about the fact that she
wouldn't get to drink any of it. It was one of the great
ironies of pregnancy that things that had only seemed
mildly interesting when she could have them whenever
she felt like it had become incredibly tempting now that
she could not.

The oven beeped to signal it had reached the correct temperature, and Melanie slid the casserole dish in and set the timer. "Tea?"

"Thanks," Vivien said as she watched her sister puttering happily in her kitchen. Since she was contemplating irony, she noted that so many of the things Vivi considered "chores" seemed just the opposite to Melanie.

After her first sip of tea, which she sincerely wished were highly caffeinated coffee, Vivien asked, "So what does Clay Alexander do for Thanksgiving?"

Melanie opened the oven door to peek at her casserole. Apparently satisfied, she carried her cup of tea back to the counter. "Clay goes to his mother in Asheville for the holiday. They're very close; his dad left when he was a toddler and she raised him by herself." She cocked her head to one side to consider Vivien. "Why?"

Vivien kept her tone casual. "Oh, I don't know. He just seems so much a part of the family I wondered . . ." She let her voice trail off as she sometimes did in an interview to camouflage the importance of the question.

Melanie shrugged. "He and J.J. were so close it just seems natural to have him around," she said. "I mean in some ways he probably knew J.J. even better than I did."

"Why is that?"

"Well, they were already friends when I met them during my freshman year at Georgia. You'd already left for your senior year abroad then, remember? They were fraternity brothers and really tight. They both pretty much lived and breathed politics. Just like at home only from the other side of the fence. Clay ran J.J.'s campaign for student body president."

Vivien thought back, trying to pinpoint when she'd first become aware of Clay Alexander. "But he wasn't at your wedding. I don't remember meeting him until Shelby's christening, when you named him and me her

godparents." Vivien felt a quick stab of guilt as she realized how little time and thought she'd given to the hon-
orary position. Could Clay's presence now be a simple
matter of Clay taking this obligation seriously when she,
who was Shelby's blood relative, hadn't?

"They had some big falling-out in the middle of their
senior year," Melanie said, taking another sip of tea. "Clay
dropped out of Sigma Sigma over it and he just sort of
disappeared from our lives. He was still on campus; I'd
spot him occasionally at the student union or at some
activity or other. But they didn't speak, and J.J. never
would talk about it."

"And then one day he was back?" Vivi asked, making
a mental note to find out what had happened between the
two men at UGA.

"In a way. When J.J. decided to run for his first local
office, you remember he ran for a seat on the county commission, he said there was no way he could get where
he was planning to go without the right campaign manager. Clay had already run a couple of campaigns in the
Asheville area by then, and J.J. went there and hired him
away. That was almost eighteen years ago."

"So J.J. never talked about what had happened between
them? Even after Clay moved here to work with J.J.?"

Melanie laughed. "It just wasn't that big a thing, Vivi.
They had a falling-out in college. They made up. And
Clay's been a good friend to all of us ever since. End of
story."

Vivi's gut, and her years of investigative experience,
rejected Melanie's too-easy explanation. Human relationships were never that uncomplicated. "So, what's his current story? Is he divorced? Does he have kids?"

Melanie shot her a look of amusement. "Are you looking to be fixed up? Maybe I should warn Stone that he's
got competition."

"I don't think I'm the one Clay Alexander is interested in," Vivi said, eager to test Melanie's reaction.

Melanie blushed, but Vivi wasn't certain it was with pleasure. She looked down into her mug and then back up at Vivien. "He's just a friend, Vivien, one of my oldest friends. And I, for one, appreciate that friendship."

"Fine. Just answer the question. Was he married? Does he date? I'm just trying to get a sense of things." Trying to keep the questioning casual, Vivien got up to put more water to boil. "More?" She pointed to Melanie's mug and, at her nod, emptied what remained in the sink.

"Clay was married briefly after college. He was in the process of getting divorced when he moved here to work with J.J. He doesn't have any kids, which is really a shame because family is huge to him. I think he'd make a great father."

"Any idea why his marriage ended?"

"Not really," Melanie said.

Vivien continued her tea preparation.

"As to dating," Melanie continued, "I've never seen him at a political function or fund-raiser or even a dinner party without a good-looking woman on his arm. There've always been women, but no one he ever got really serious about. Every once in a while he'd start seeing someone who really seemed perfect for him, and they'd last for a time. But then the woman would be looking for a commitment, you know. And he just never seemed to be able to do that. I think there must have been someone he never got over . . ."

Vivien looked closely at Melanie to see if she noticed how odd that sounded. "So he's over forty now and has never been in a serious relationship since his divorce seventeen-eighteen years ago?"

"Why do you have that weird look on your face?" Melanie asked. "Maybe he just never met the right woman."

She shrugged. "You're forty-one and you've never been married. What difference does it make?"

"No difference," Vivien said. "I'm just curious as usual." She smiled then and changed the subject, but she was even more certain now that something about Clay Alexander simply didn't add up. And more determined than ever to search J.J.'s office for some clue as to why.

❧

EVANGELINE MET THEM on the porch of Magnolia Hall in what might have been a historically correct copy of a Civil War–era house slave's uniform. The gray homespun dress, with its white Peter Pan collar, nipped in at the waist and fell to Evangeline's trim ankles. A white lawn apron was pinned at the shoulders and tied around her waist. A white cotton turban hid her Buckhead salon haircut. She wore black leather dance shoes like the kind Melanie sold at her studio. She was in top reenactment form.

"Oh, Lawsy!" she proclaimed as she kissed and hugged Shelby and Trip with all her might then prepared to do the same to Vivien and Melanie. "Y'all do look fine!"

"Amen, sister," Vivien said as the housekeeper enveloped her in a rib-crunching hug that almost dislodged the tins of goodies in her arms. She flashed Evangeline a smile and a wink, but Evangeline returned neither as she stared at Vivien's bust and bump. A worried look spread over her face. "Oh, Lordy," she said more quietly. "I thought maybe I was imagining things, but you sure enough have a bun in your—"

Vivien freed up a finger and put it to Evangeline's lips and shook her head slightly. She would announce her pregnancy when she absolutely had to and that was definitely not today. Not here in the middle of a Gray family Thanksgiving, with everyone primed and ready to pounce. She spotted Caroline coming down the hall from the kitchen and locked gazes with Evangeline to make sure she'd made herself clear. "We didn't bring any buns or rolls," she said pointedly. "Maybe next time. Not today."

Melanie leaned in for Evangeline's kiss and Vivien shot Evangeline one last warning look; there was no such thing as overkill with Evangeline. Skipping her usual verbal duel, the housekeeper retreated to the kitchen as they greeted Caroline, who wore pencil-straight black pants and a body-hugging cream cashmere sweater. Caroline was a tough act to follow under the best of circumstances; today she made Vivien feel like King Kong lumbering along after Fay Wray.

The kitchen was a hotbed of activity with Cook directing two helpers who'd been brought in for the day as well as Yolanda and Ben, who would plate up and stage the meal and then help Evangeline serve.

In the study, Vivien greeted Ham and Judy, who were already slurping up martinis. Melanie took one from their father and sank down into the overstuffed sofa beside Judy. Vivien, who was completely dreading the Just Peachy conversation and the long meal to come, hesitated beside the drinks cart, eyeing the pitcher of martinis like a diabetic trapped in a candy store. She knew it was off-limits, but could one tiny drink actually do damage?

She was contemplating this question when her father put a drink in her hand. Before she could blink, Evangeline, who'd just arrived with a tray of hors d'oeuvres, removed it.

"Evangeline," Caroline said, "why don't you pass those hors d' oeuvres and . . ."

Evangeline ignored Caroline completely. While this was not unusual, the speed with which she dropped the hors d'oeuvres in Caroline's lap then poured and shoved a Coke into Vivien's hand and a glass bowl of nuts in the other, was.

In the silence that descended, Vivien carried Evangeline's offerings to the sofa and lowered herself into it.

"Evangeline . . ." Caroline began, but Evangeline had already tsked at Vivien and flounced out of the room.

"Now then," Caroline said as the study door closed behind the housekeeper. "What's all this business in Just Peachy?"

Vivien wished desperately for a shot of rum to go in her Coke, but knew that Evangeline would never allow that to happen.

"I heard from people I haven't spoken to in years," her father said. "Were you fired from CIN? I thought you said you resigned."

"Everyone at the club asked me about it. I left bridge early yesterday; no one could talk of anything else." Caroline was not a happy camper. "I thought that Glazer boy was a friend of yours, Vivi. Weren't you in school together?" She downed her martini in one long gulp, then signaled her husband for another.

Resentment and a weary sort of resignation warred within Vivien. She'd told her mother all about Matt Glazer and her attempts to rebuff his attentions in college and after, but Caroline clearly didn't remember a word of it. And there would be no point in reminding her now.

"Matt Glazer is no friend of mine," Vivien said, wishing now for anesthesia in any form.

Did they give out early epidurals? "He writes a gossip column, for God's sake, and thinks he's a journalist. I ran into him the other day and I could hardly believe the personal questions he asked. He was way too nosy."

"Too nosy?" Hamilton laughed. "Isn't that the pot calling the kettle black?"

Vivien saw Judy hide a smile behind her hand.

"Well, there's no benefit to pissing him off," her father pointed out. "The next time you see him, you should at least be polite. Politics is more perception than reality these days. And we have to keep Hamilton's political career in mind."

"Maybe we should invite him over some Sunday, cultivate him a bit," her mother mused. "He may be printing gossip, but people read him. And Hamilton *is* looking seriously at a run for governor."

"You're joking," Vivien said. "He attacked me, questioned my word in print. And you want to curry favor with him? What happened to blood being thicker than water?" Vivien knew she shouldn't be surprised at what she could only see as their betrayal, but it hurt nonetheless.

"And what happened to your understanding of the political process?" her father asked. "Bad enough with all those investigative pieces and the way you destroyed poor Harley. Now you're alienating a member of the press."

"That piece on Harley Jenkins was fifteen years ago," Vivien pointed out. "And Matthew Glazer is not a serious member of the press. He writes a thing called Just Peachy, for cripes sake."

Judy and Ham were following the conversation as if it were a tennis match. Melanie just looked uncomfortable. She seemed to have a much greater talent for becoming smaller than Vivi did.

Caroline turned to her husband as if Vivien hadn't spoken. "What do you think, Warren? Maybe a Sunday afternoon barbecue this spring? Or we could invite him for cocktails at the club one evening if we need to move sooner."

Vivien downed her Coke, chased it with a fistful of nuts, and shot an imploring look at Melanie.

"We could include him in the party we're holding

for Ham's largest political donors," Judy offered. Hamilton nodded sagely, clearly practicing his gubernatorial look.

"Good grief!" Vivien exclaimed. "I'm pretty sure gossip columnists don't offer or print political endorsements."

All eyes were back on Vivi.

"There's no reason why they couldn't, is there?" her mother mused. "Is there some journalistic requirement that they remain neutral?"

"You mean other than the fact that no one with an ounce of intelligence would take them seriously?" Vivien asked, though she could see her sarcasm was lost on them. They were actually considering currying Just Peachy's favor for political purposes.

"Why don't you just try to win over Jonny Quest and George of the Jungle," Vivien snapped. "The Cartoon Network is right here in Atlanta. And I'm sure voters would really appreciate their political insights."

There was a silence during which all eyes hovered on Vivien, who filled her mouth with yet another handful of mixed nuts in order to stop herself from saying anything else.

"Did, um I mention that Cole Wesley's future daughter-in-law is in the, um, Wednesday night belly-dance class at the Magnolia Ballroom?" Melanie said tentatively into the quiet.

As distractions went, this one worked pretty well. Everyone's eyes left Vivien to refocus on Melanie. "They're getting married in April."

"I always loved watching Cole Wesley play," their father remarked. "Didn't the son make it into the minors?"

"Yes." Ham, too, was a huge baseball fan. "He made it to Double A, but he just never had the consistency to go farther. I think he's with the sports marketing firm that manages Turner Field. Boy, I would have given an arm and a leg to meet Cole Wesley when I was a kid. I still would."

The kids arrived in the study, shooed there by Evangeline. "Cole Wesley?" Ham Jr. asked. "Do you know him, Aunt Mellie?"

"No," Melanie said. "Just his future daughter-in-law."

"Well, if you ever get to meet him, shake his hand for me," Ham Jr. said. "And I wouldn't turn down an autograph, either."

Trip didn't say anything, but Vivien saw a look of interest light up his face.

"Are you a Wesley fan, too?" Vivien asked her nephew.

He nodded; his smile was genuine. "Oh, yeah. He's about my favorite pitcher of all time." It was the most animated Vivien had seen him since she'd arrived in Atlanta.

Vivien reached for more nuts, thinking that maybe she could finagle an introduction for Trip. Maybe she could ask Angela Richman to help make it happen. While her hand was still in the bowl, Evangeline removed it. "Drop 'em," the housekeeper said. "You and you-know-who have had enough."

Vivien dropped the nuts as instructed. "Evangeline," she said quietly, glancing around to make sure no one had overheard. "I thought we had an understanding."

"I understand that you're eating for two. But I'm not going to stand by and let you feed that little one junk. Or alcohol. Or anything else that might be bad for it."

Unfortunately, Evangeline was as good as her word.

Yolanda and Ben did the serving and taking away. For everyone that is, but Vivien. Evangeline was her personal server for the holiday meal. While everyone over twenty-one had a different wine with each course, Evangeline filled Vivi's goblet with apple juice, which might have looked like Chardonnay but definitely didn't taste like it.

And while the entire family was served countless helpings of all their holiday favorites, Vivien had approximately four ounces of turkey, a plateful of green beans and carrots, and a serving of Melanie's sweet potato casserole that was so small it might have actually dropped onto Vivien's plate by accident rather than design.

"Sweet potato is a vegetable," she hissed in Evangeline's ear when the housekeeper refused to give her more.

"Not when it's covered with all that butter and brown sugar, it's not," Evangeline replied. "You want some more of those green beans? Or how about some of that tofu dressing the twins made?"

As the meal drew to a close Melanie unbuttoned her pants so that she could breathe. Shelby's eyes appeared glazed, as if she were in some sort of food stupor. Trip was working on his third plate of dessert. When the last plate had been cleared and the rest of her family was clutching their stomachs and groaning how full they were, Vivien's stomach felt cruelly empty. Except, of course, for its tiny occupant. Whom Evangeline, Vivi's own personal food policeman, had sworn to honor and protect.

19

FEELING MORE THAN a little ridiculous, Vivien pulled the floppy hat brim down low over her forehead and slipped on a pair of dark glasses. Fortunately, on this first Wednesday morning in December it was chilly enough to justify the lined trench coat she'd buttoned all the way up to her chin. Even though she was running late for her ob-gyn appointment, she paused outside the entrance of the medical building to study the lobby just in case Matt Glazer had staked out the place.

When she was fairly certain the coast was clear, she scurried across the open space toward the elevators with her chin buried in her chest, her eyes on the marble floor. In Dr. Gilbert's waiting room she kept her gaze cast downward as she walked to the sign-in counter. Though she knew it was overkill, Vivi decided to use an alias just in case Glazer had identified the office and had someone on the "inside." Realizing she should have thought about this before she'd reached the desk, she scribbled the first name that popped into her head, then without removing

her "disguise," she made her way to one of the few open
seats.

It was hard to see through the dark glasses, but not
hard to tell that the other women were stealing glances
at her. The woman beside her got up under the pretext of
looking for a magazine on another end table and didn't
come back.

Vivien removed the sunglasses, but kept her hat and
coat on. After a few minutes passed and she didn't pull
out a gun or make any sudden moves, the women around
her went back to their magazines and their conversations.
Opposite her a woman picked up a copy of the *Weekly
Encounter*. The woman beside her said, "Did you read this
week's Postcards from Suburbia?" and Vivien tensed in
her seat. "Of course, I did. Can you believe the nerve of
that Scarlett Leigh?"

"Everyone at book club last night was incensed. 'Here
parents don't have lives of their own. They're much too
busy revolving around their sons and daughters,'" she
paraphrased in a snide tone that made Vivi sink lower in
her chair. "With that name and the things she's saying,
she must be somewhere in the southeast."

"She better not wander into my suburb, she'll have tire
tracks from a Chevy Suburban on her back," the other
woman said. "I've never read anything so insulting in my
life."

Vivien thanked God that she hadn't used her pseudonym on the sign-in sheet. The door to the inner sanc-
tum opened and a nurse with a clipboard said, "Venus
Williams? Miss Williams?"

There was a stunned silence as the rest of the patients
stopped whatever they'd been doing to scan the room for
the six-foot tennis player. Vivi winced as she slipped her
sunglasses back on and stood. She could feel every eye in

the place on her as she crossed the room. Clearly, she was going to have to do a little better in the alias department if she wanted to remain incognito.

"Have you felt the baby move yet?" Dr. Gilbert's hands were warm and gentle on the taut skin of Vivien's stomach.

She nodded her head as he probed gently; she still started with surprise every time she felt what had to be a kick or a jab.

"Here's the top of your uterus," he said kneading a spot just above her belly button. "The baby's about one and a half pounds now. He's definitely outgrown the fruit references, though your stomach will hit that watermelon stage along the way."

Vivien smiled at his teasing tone.

"Any swelling?" he asked as he pulled the band of her underpants back into place and pulled the gown closed in front.

She shook her head again, figuring the swelling of her stomach went without saying.

"All your vitals look good," he said as he helped her sit up. "How are you feeling?"

"You mean other than the constipation, heartburn, and gas? And the fact that I can't seem to keep a thought in my head for more than five minutes at a time?"

"That's standard operating procedure," he said. "Most of your brain cells will come back after you give birth. Or at least once the baby starts sleeping through the night."

"And how long is that likely to take?" she asked.

"It depends. Every situation, like every baby, is different. But I'd say somewhere between a couple of months and a couple of years."

Vivien blinked. "Years?"

He shrugged. "It's not the norm, but it happens."

"This is one of those small details that I think women should be made aware of *before* they get pregnant."

"If there was full disclosure, I'd be out of business." Dr. Gilbert smiled at her, but he didn't sound too worried. He paused a moment, then nodded toward the chair where her clothes lay folded. "My assistant mentioned that you were, um, hiding behind a trench coat and dark glasses when you arrived. And that you signed in as Venus Williams." He cleared his throat. "Are you in some kind of trouble?"

Vivien blushed. She'd felt like an imbecile sneaking into the office in her "disguise" and, of course, the alias she'd chosen had been ill-advised. But the last thing she needed was for Matt Glazer to figure out which doctor she'd been visiting and why.

"No, I, um. . . ." She closed her eyes for a moment but couldn't come up with a lie that was remotely convincing. "I haven't told anyone about my pregnancy yet, and I just didn't want word to get out until I was ready."

He nodded. "Well, of course that's your business. But I'm not sure how much longer you're going to be able to keep it a secret," he said. "You're carrying small, but your shape is definitely changing. And you're going to get a lot bigger before it's all over."

He smiled and signed off on the paperwork he held in his hands. "I will promise you that my people know better than to give out information about our patients. You can be assured of that."

After the doctor had left, Vivien put on her trench coat and dark glasses and pulled the hat low on her head. Although it was hard to see with her shades on, Vivien managed to pay for the visit and schedule her next checkup as well as an ultrasound at the checkout desk. Then she walked quickly through the waiting room, which was still packed with bellies of all sizes, with her head down and her face averted.

Once again, she felt slightly ridiculous but while she had no doubt that Dr. Gilbert believed in his staff's discretion, she also knew Matt Glazer. His first piece about her had stirred up all kinds of attention. He was unlikely to drop something that had struck that loud a chord.

As it turned out, Dr. Gilbert was right about the difficulty of keeping her pregnancy a secret. That very afternoon Vivien was dressing, or rather trying to figure out what on earth she could squeeze into that would see her through decorating the ballroom as well as tonight's class, when Melanie rapped lightly on her bedroom door and entered, catching Vivi studying herself unhappily in the dresser mirror.

"Looks like I unearthed these just in time." Melanie held up a short stack of clothing, which she placed on the bed.

"I hope they're extra larges," Vivien said as Melanie came to stand beside her, both of them now studying Vivien's reflection in the mirror. The gap in the black pants had stretched well beyond safety pin range and the camisole was so tight that it made her already sensitive breasts hurt. And there was, of course, the fact that she couldn't actually breathe.

"Oh, they are." Melanie smiled as she plopped down on the foot of the bed. "What are you now, around the end of your fifth month?"

Vivien stared at her sister's smiling reflection in the mirror while she tried to think what to say. A denial sprang to her lips.

"Don't bother denying it, Vivi," Melanie said. "I've been pregnant three times and given birth twice. Your stomach hasn't popped all the way, but the signs are pretty hard to miss."

Vivien dropped down onto the bed beside her sister. "How long have you known?"

Melanie shrugged. "Awhile. Honestly, if I hadn't been so blown away by your coming to stay and my life in general, I probably would have known the first time I watched you eat." She laughed. "The boobs are a dead giveaway. And so is the stomach, kiddo."

"And here I thought I had everyone but Evangeline fooled."

"I saw her torturing you on Thanksgiving." Melanie laughed again. "I thought you were going to choke on all those vegetables."

"Worst Thanksgiving ever," Vivien acknowledged. "I didn't even get a piece of pumpkin pie."

"I carried a lot bigger than you when I was pregnant," Melanie said. "I just sort of . . . inflated. I used to envy those women who stayed the same except for a little pouch of a stomach." She smoothed a hand over the stack of clothes. "I kind of liked having boobs, though. I really hated to give those up."

Vivien sighed. "Are you kidding? I feel like they're alive; they've taken over everything."

"Just wait until you start nursing and you feel them fill up with milk." Melanie's sigh was a happy one. "I loved nursing Shelby and Trip. I felt so . . . necessary. In those early months you are absolutely all they need."

"I don't know," Vivien said. "I never pictured myself as a milk dispenser, though I am feeling pretty cowlike." She paused. "Or as a mother, really."

"How does Stone feel about it? It must be so hard for him to be away."

Vivien took the top piece of clothing from the stack Melanie had brought. It was a pair of khaki pants with an elastic waist and stretch fabric at the stomach.

"Is he upset? Unhappy about you being pregnant?"

Vivien refolded the pants and reached for the next item. It was a black knit top with three-quarter sleeves and a generous pleat down the front. There were black knit pants to match.

"Because it takes two people to make a baby, you know. It's not like you got pregnant all by yourself. Why he should . . ."

Vivien kept her gaze on the clothes, trying not to think about Stone and really not wanting to talk about him. There was a pair of jeans and a white long-sleeved oxford shirt that looked tailored but had generous panels on the sides. The last items didn't seem to belong with the others. The first was a low-cut fuchsia halter top in a thin stretchy material meant to tie around the neck and across the back. With it was a matching palazzo style pant designed to ride low on the hips, exposing the midriff. Vivien wasn't sure if it was designed for the bedroom or a nightclub, but it looked vaguely familiar. "Where did this come from?"

"It was a gift," Melanie said. "Someone sent it to me when I was pregnant with Shelby."

"This?" Vivien held the pieces up. Even at eight weeks the outfit would have looked ludicrous. She didn't even want to think about how it would make her look now. "What moron sent this outfit to a pregnant woman?

Melanie raised an eyebrow. There was a strange expression on her face. "You did."

Vivien blinked in shock. If ever there was a symbol of just how far apart she and Melanie had grown, how little she'd understood or cared about the life her sister was living, this outfit was it. Vivien could hardly believe that she'd acknowledged her little sister's pregnancy and impending motherhood with an outfit better suited for an exotic dancer than a mother-to-be.

"Oh, my God," Vivien whispered. "I was such an idiot."

Her sister had called her all excited about her pregnancy and Vivien had sent her lingerie. Had she imagined it would be stretchy and comfortable? Or had she thought that maybe Melanie would like something sexy for after the delivery? "What was I thinking?"

But of course that was the point. The occasion had required a gift and she had sent one. She hadn't really been thinking about Melanie at all.

"Oh, Mel. I am so sorry. I was so out of tune with you. I didn't understand . . . anything. And I didn't try to."

Melanie took the pink strips of fabric from Vivien and laid them out on the bed. "I put it on once for J.J. when I was about nine months pregnant." Her lips quirked upward. "He told me all I needed was a pole and a stage." A giggle escaped as she looked at Vivien and then back at the outfit. "We laughed for a good thirty minutes." Another giggle. "And believe me, when you're that far along, there aren't all that many things that feel even remotely funny."

Melanie slipped the halter over Vivien's head and over the straining blouse. "I'm so glad I saved it for you," Melanie said as she tied the ends behind Vivien's back. Another giggle escaped. "It's perfect!"

They erupted into laughter then, side-splitting, stomach-jiggling, can't-get-your-breath laughter. They laughed so hard that tears started to form.

They stopped trying to talk and just gave in to the laughter. Vivi felt it deep down in her fingers and toes. It suffused her body; she even imagined it twining its way down into the strands of her DNA. She had no doubt that her cantaloupe-sized little one could feel it, too.

They rolled on the bed in their mirth, laughing and giggling. Every time one of them began to get herself under control the other would snicker and they'd be helpless again.

"Oh, my God," Melanie finally got out. "I can't think of the last time I laughed this hard." She lay limp on the bed.

"My life hasn't felt all that funny lately, either," Vivien said. "Embarrassing and humiliating, yes. Funny? No." She, too, lay on her back, staring up at the guest room ceiling.

Without moving, Melanie reached over and grasped the tissue box from the nightstand. She pulled one out and handed it to Vivien then took another for herself. They both dabbed at their eyes and cheeks. Vivien hiccupped sporadically. Other than that neither of them moved.

"You know," Melanie said in the silence. "I'm going to need to say something to the kids about their cousin-to-be. I don't want them surprised in the wrong way or unclear about what's going on."

Vivien nodded.

"Now, tell me how Stone feels about the baby."

Vivien continued to stare up into the ceiling, but there were no answers there. It was an incredible relief not to be shouldering the burden of her secret alone anymore. She'd been dying to talk to Melanie about her pregnancy. She'd begun to feel overwhelmed by the enormity of what lay ahead and was keen to share the experience with someone who had already been through it. But accepting help and support also opened her up to unwanted advice. Melanie considered marriage and motherhood her greatest achievements; she would never understand Vivien's reservations about either.

"He doesn't know," Vivien said so quietly that she almost didn't hear it.

"What did you say?" Melanie sat up on the foot of the bed and waited for Vivien to do the same.

Shoulder to shoulder, they turned to face each other.

"He doesn't know I'm pregnant," Vivien said. "I haven't told him yet."

Melanie's forehead creased in confusion. "I don't understand," she said. "Don't you love him? Are you afraid he won't want to be involved?"

"No," Vivien said, all the laughter gone as if it had never been. She caught a glimpse of the two of them in the dresser mirror. She was fuller and rounder than Melanie; her hair was shorter. Her eyes more uncertain. But at the moment they wore equally earnest expressions.

"Just the opposite," Vivien said. "I'm completely afraid that he will."

☙

Melanie waited in the kitchen while Vivien changed into the black knit maternity top and slacks. No doubt she'd need at least one trip to the potty before they could leave to meet Ruth and Angela, who had offered to come before class to help decorate the ballroom for the holidays.

Melanie closed her eyes and massaged her forehead as she contemplated the Christmas season—their third without J.J.—that lay ahead. Once again they'd have to decorate without him, bake cookies and drink cider without him, wake up Christmas morning and exchange presents without him. Time was supposed to heal all wounds and in many ways the gaping hole in their lives had begun to knit; it just took so little to tear it back open.

Opening her eyes, Melanie turned her attention to the mound of clutter that covered her kitchen counter. Needing to be busy, she pulled the trash can over and began to work her way through it. The circulars and sales pieces went into the trash. The school notices and miscellaneous were stuffed into a cubicle above her kitchen desk where they would most likely sit until the beginning of the next

school year when she would finally feel safe in jettison-
ing them. The most difficult to deal with were the quasi-
personal things like the flood of Christmas letters that
had begun to arrive. Some were from people she hadn't
spoken to in years but who apparently felt the need to fill
her in on every single thing that had happened in the past
twelve months.

Pretty much none of these letters mentioned children
who had ended up in jail, were still living at home because
they refused or were unable to get a job, or whose social
skills were nonexistent. In these letters only the positive
was worth mentioning, and the more positive the better.
Even those couched in humor were designed to make the
recipient feel as if their family didn't quite measure up.
They were exercises in one-upmanship cloaked in holiday
cheer.

Catherine Dennison's, which had been mailed despite
the fact that the woman lived only a few houses away,
was a prime example. *Claire, Pucci, and I wish you the best
of holidays. We will be celebrating with friends in Aspen again
this year and can hardly wait to hit the slopes.* A photo of the
three of them—who knew skis came doggie-sized—was
included. Pucci's ski clothes were the height of doggie
couture, and the small ball of fur looked quite determined
behind his designer ski goggles.

*In the new year, Claire, who has been identified as a potential
merit scholar, will take the SAT. Although we typically travel
to Europe over spring break, this April will be spent touring Ivy
League schools. We will do our best to keep you posted.*

Melanie crumpled the letter and dropped it in the
trash. She couldn't even get Shelby to talk about the
SAT let alone sign up to prepare for it; their relationship
seemed to worsen by the hour.

"Viv!" she shouted up the stairs before heading out to
fire up the van. "Hurry up! We're going to be late."

Despite Melanie's impatience, Vivien stopped in the downstairs guest bathroom to make what seemed like the millionth pit stop of the day. As she washed her hands she noticed that the washbasin didn't exactly sparkle. When she looked up at her reflection in the vanity mirror, it was pockmarked with water spots. Rushing out to the garage, she spied several black streaks on the hardwood floor.

As they pulled out of the neighborhood and onto 120, she said, "You need to have a talk with your cleaning people, Mel. I think they've gotten a bit lazy."

Melanie didn't look at her as she said, "I had to let Amanda go eight months ago. I just couldn't justify the expense."

"Oh," Vivien said, realizing as she spoke that she hadn't actually seen a cleaning person since she'd been at Melanie's. "I thought she came while we were out." She turned to Melanie, who was still looking straight ahead. "But someone's been changing my sheets every week and delivering fresh towels. And . . ." Vivien's voice trailed off as she realized who that someone was. "Good God, Mel, why didn't you say something?"

Melanie shrugged, finally turning to look at her. "What was there to say?"

"Well, I would have at least taken care of my own room and bath." Vivien cringed when she thought of all the work she must have added to Melanie's already over-whelming load; the wet towels she'd dropped in the hamper without a second thought. "I sure as hell hope Shelby and Trip have been helping."

Melanie snorted. "Right. You've seen what it takes to get them to clear the table or do the dishes. It takes a lot more energy to force them to do something than it does to do it myself."

"Have you been doing everyone's laundry?"

Melanie continued to stare out the windshield, her eyes on the road. "I taught both kids how and every year I swear I'm not going to touch their clothes. But Shelby would just wait until she didn't have a single clean thing to wear and then use that as an excuse for not being able to get ready for school. And Trip would keep wearing his dirty clothes until you could barely be in the same city block with him. It just wasn't worth the hassle."

"Well, that's ridiculous. You can't do everything all the time. We need to get them on the stick and I'll certainly help."

"Have you ever mopped a floor or really scrubbed a toilet bowl?"

"Well . . ."

"I never had, either. I mean we always had Evangeline and whoever she was torturing at the time. And after J.J. and I got married he insisted we have someone in every other week for the heavy cleaning. But the economy sucks and I had a lot of the insurance money in stocks and, of course, business at the studio is down." She paused as she slowed for a light. "I just can't see spending money on a cleaning service when I can handle it myself."

"Right," Vivi said as she berated herself for being so dense. Tonight she'd discovered how little attention she'd paid to her sister's pregnancies, but at least she'd had the excuse of distance and work. How could she have been living in her sister's house for over a month and not noticed that her sister was the maid?

20

AT THE MAGNOLIA Ballroom, a low samba played over the speakers. In a far corner a couple practiced a choreographed routine while an instructor looked on. The man was tall and lithe with silver hair and patrician features. The clothes he wore were black and well tailored. His partner looked a good twenty years younger and had a dancer's svelte body. They moved gracefully in each other's arms, each movement of the head and hand intentional and eye-catching. "That's Lawrence Reardon and his partner, Carlotta. They're competing next weekend," Melanie explained. "They've been with Enrique for a long time; he does all their choreography."

Ruth and Angela stood near a group of tables piled high with cardboard boxes marked "Xmas." Ruth held an electric menorah. Angela, who was wearing what Vivi had come to think of as her trademark baggy black, stood next to an artificial Christmas tree roughly her height. She flashed both of them a smile.

Ruth gave Melanie a big hug. Vivien got a nod and

the once-over. Without preamble Ruth asked, "When are you due?"

Nonplussed, Vivien bit back the "None of your business" and "What makes you think I'm pregnant?" that sprang to her lips.

"She didn't think anybody had noticed," Melanie said.

Ruth snorted. "I may be getting old, but I'm not blind. Although at first I did think she was just getting fat."

"Well, I hadn't noticed," Angela said with an odd little grimace at the word "fat." "That's great. Congratulations."

"Yes," Ruth added somewhat grudgingly. "Mazel tov. I didn't realize you were married."

Vivien felt the heat rise in her cheeks. "I'm not, and according to my ob-gyn it's not actually a requirement."

"No. But it's a lot better for the children to have two parents," the older woman replied.

"Yes, well," Melanie said stiffly. "That may be. But it doesn't always work out that way." She slipped an arm around Vivien's waist in a show of solidarity. "For all sorts of reasons."

It was Ruth's turn to flush. She was clearly unused to being at odds in any way with Melanie. "Of course not, but . . ."

"And I don't think any of us need to pass judgment on the other."

"Well, of course not, but . . ."

Melanie didn't let Ruth finish. "Here," she said as she turned to the boxes and began to open them. "Let's put the snowflakes up first. That'll be the biggest job, because I want to cover the whole ceiling except the area immediately around the chandeliers."

The three of them began unpacking the boxes while Melanie went to get the ladder. "She always protects you," Ruth said to Vivien. "No matter what you do. Or don't do."

"I know," Vivien said. "And I know I don't deserve it. But it's kind of amazing, isn't it?"

"I think it's great," Angela said, her hands overflowing with snowflakes, her expression wistful. "Both James and I are only children. I, for one, would love to have a sister or brother to run interference for me. Or at least deflect some of my parents' attention."

Vivien looked at the bride-to-be and wondered, not for the first time, about the mixed signals she sent. She was young and attractive and engaged to the son of a major sports celebrity, yet she hid what appeared to be an above-average figure in clothes at least a size too big and seemed oddly determined not to call attention to herself.

Vivi would have liked to know why, but it wasn't really her business nor did she want to get too personal. She was just passing through. Observing and reporting. She shouldn't get any more involved with the people here than a scientist might get with the earthworm he was dissecting.

Parental distance was apparently an alien concept to Ruth Melnick. "You believe a parent can give too much attention, too much love?"

Vivien looked at Ruth. "Do you really think love and attention are the same thing? We're debating mother love versus mother attention," Vivien said when Melanie returned, curious to see whether Melanie, who was not only Caroline's daughter but a mother in her own right, would feel the same as Ruth. "Ruth thinks they're one and the same. I'm not so sure."

"Well," Melanie said. She'd gotten the ladder positioned and was now giving the question serious thought. "I think everything I direct at Shelby and Trip is out of love and wanting what's best for them, though they probably wouldn't agree. But I know from being our mother's daughter that a lot of things she thought were best for me weren't. And that loving your child doesn't automatically make you right.

"I mean, if I'd listened to Caroline, I never would have married a . . . gasp . . . Republican," Melanie continued. "Or chosen to live in the suburbs. Or sent my children to public school, even one as good as Pemberton." She looked at Vivi. "And if you had paid the slightest bit of attention to her, you certainly wouldn't have become a network-level investigative reporter living in New York City. But I think in her way she loves us. She just loves us best when we're doing what she thinks is right."

Vivien was having a hard enough time coming to grips with the idea of becoming a parent without thinking that she might be the kind of parent Caroline was.

"I'll do the hanging if you want to hand the snowflakes up to me," Angela volunteered.

Still intent on their conversation they formed a chain, sort of like an old-fashioned bucket brigade, but they passed gossamer snowflakes on string instead of pails of water.

"My mother has become someone I hardly recognize," Angela said as she climbed the ladder then reached down for the first snowflake. "My parents have always been so levelheaded and supportive. Now they're obsessed with the details of the wedding. I know part of it's their relief that I'm actually getting married; the other part is their amazement that I'm marrying Cole Wesley's son. That's how my parents say it, 'Our Angela is marrying Cole Wesley's son.' I'm having a hard time believing it myself."

Angela removed the ceiling tile and hung a snowflake at each corner before replacing it. Then she climbed down to reposition the ladder. "I mean it's such a big step."

Melanie offered another snowflake. "Being married to J.J. was the best thing that ever happened to me," she said. "Well, that and having Shelby and Trip. Being a family." Her eyes glistened. "There's nothing better than that.

"Don't you agree, Ruth?" Melanie asked.

On the dance floor the couple glided effortlessly while Enrique watched, but they might have been on another planet. Vivien felt like the four of them were an island unto themselves.

"I would have said the same as Melanie when I was her age," Ruth finally said. "Even a few years ago, I wouldn't have questioned the life I've had with Ira. Or that we would simply go on like we always have. But now . . ." Her voice trailed off as she seemed to struggle to find the right words. "Now, well, things are a lot different than I expected."

They worked until the entire ceiling appeared to shimmer and glow, softening the stark angles of the ballroom.

"I love the snowflakes," Melanie said as she pulled strands of tiny white lights from one of the boxes. "Let's put these around the mirrors."

"Our lives have been so different." Angela picked up their thread of conversation as they began to frame the mirrored walls with strings of the lights. "I'd barely been to a professional sporting event before I knew James. Between his dad and his work, sports are pretty much his life. I can't go to everything; I don't even want to. But I hate for him to feel like I'm not interested."

"What do you think?" Melanie asked once they'd gotten the lights plugged in.

"Festively elegant," Ruth said and all of them agreed as they considered their collective reflection in the mirror. They were different ages and sizes and, Vivi thought, they had little in common but membership in a dance class and their regard for Melanie.

"Well, I'm sure James's feelings for you aren't based on how many games you make it to. Or how you feel about sports." Again, Melanie was all reassurance, a veritable poster child for love and commitment.

"If you ever can't make it to something, I happen to have a nephew who would love to fill in for you," Vivien said. "Don't you think Trip would enjoy going out with James and his father sometime, Mel?"

Melanie blushed and shot Vivi a look. "We wouldn't want to put the Wesleys on the spot, Vivi. I'm sure they . . ."

"No, I'm sure James and Cole would enjoy having him along," Angela said. "I'll check and see what's coming up."

Melanie raised a warning eyebrow at her sister as she thanked Angela. "We need to finish up," she said. "There's Naranya and Lourdes. It's almost time for class."

They began to move more quickly then, doing more decorating and less talking.

"You never did say when you're due," Angela said as they tidied up and prepared to join the others. "And I don't know how to tell by looking."

"Around the twelfth of April." Vivien gulped. Just saying the date aloud made it so much more real.

"That's just a week before the wedding," Angela said, also gulping. Her face did not reflect unadulterated joy. "I guess it's going to be a big month."

Vivien just nodded her head. But what she was really thinking was that her due date was now barely four months away. There was a decisive movement in her belly and as her hand flew to the spot, she had the thought that the baby wasn't any happier about that than she was.

"So I suppose that's actually why you're here. To have your baby," Ruth muttered under her breath as they moved into their places in front of the now-twinkly mirror.

If she'd said it louder, Vivien might have felt compelled to argue with her. But now as she weighed the accusation, Vivi realized that it was true. She'd told herself she was here to research and write her column, pretended—even to herself—that she didn't actually need anything from her sister or her parents. But that was just a great big rationalization. Once again Ruth Melnick was right about her, she thought after the Shipley sisters and Sally arrived and they stretched out into two ragged lines. When Vivien had found herself unemployed and pregnant, she hadn't turned to Stone or drawn strength from her own life; she'd thrown up her hands and come running home to her family.

Her lack of self-awareness might have been comical if it hadn't been so pathetic.

Vivien sighed as they began to stretch. Following Naranya was not as difficult now, so she could actually think even as her body moved. For someone who'd always hunted for and demanded answers, it was amazing how many she'd allowed herself to sidestep. Lying to others was bad. Lying to yourself was infinitely worse.

The kids were already up in their rooms when they got back to Melanie's. Tired and out of sorts, Vivien hugged her sister good night and went up to her room. Logging on to her email account, she spotted an email from Stone and hesitated; just the sight of his name in her inbox dredged up a mixture of guilt and longing that practically paralyzed her. Bracing herself, she clicked it open. The email was short and carried none of the probing questions or recriminations she knew she deserved. Her relief at being let off the hook made her feel even worse.

Now know exactly what the middle of nowhere looks like. In fact, we've got footage of it. Have been on the northern border where the army is focusing its efforts on

*rooting out militant strongholds. The villages we pass
through barely have names and don't appear on maps.
Another aid worker was abducted this morning and I've
got a lead, so we're packing up to head back into the field.
Don't know when I'll be able to be in touch again. Send
me an email and I'll pick it up when I can. Need to know
that you're okay and how investigation is going. Miss
you, Stone.*

She sat for a few long moments wishing Stone were
here and a few more glad that he wasn't. He was exactly
where he was supposed to be, doing exactly what he was
meant to do. He didn't need his thoughts muddied by
news of his impending fatherhood.

The house grew quiet around her. Vivien had been
waiting for an opportunity to search J.J.'s study and when
she felt certain that everyone was either asleep or at least
in their room for the night, she tiptoed downstairs and
went inside, pulling the door closed behind her.

She'd been in the room several times, but never alone.
As before, the mahogany gun cabinet, emptied of all but
dust, dominated the wall opposite the door. A deer head
with an impressive rack and suitably glassy eyes had been
mounted beside it.

The walls were a warm putty color and were covered
with framed photos that spanned J.J.'s political career.
There were shots of J.J. with his tie loosened and shirt-
sleeves rolled up, shaking hands on what must have
been a campaign stop, a shot of him in the county commission chambers where he'd begun his professional
political career, another being sworn in to the Georgia
House of Representatives. On the adjoining wall were
the obligatory photos of J.J. with other political figures;
one with each of the President Bushes, another with
Governor Sonny Perdue. There was even a shot of him

with California governor Arnold Schwarzenegger, the
two of them mugging for the camera and flexing their
muscles.

The rest of the wall was covered with plaques and commendations, including one from Georgia State University.
Easing herself into the executive chair behind the large
and decidedly masculine desk, Vivien began her search.
The first few drawers yielded little more than stray rubber bands and paper clips, a few dried-out pens, notepads
with company names or logos on them. She wondered
what Clay Alexander had been looking for. And whether
he'd found it.

In a bottom drawer she found a large envelope stuffed
with credit card and phone bills. A stack of old day plan-
ners filled another. She leafed through them quickly but
was afraid of getting caught with them, so she tucked
them back into place until she could get back when she
was truly alone.

On the bookshelves that filled one wall of the office,
bestsellers and thrillers sat beside tomes on government
and politics while biographies of famous politicians and
historical figures sat cheek to jowl with those about well-
known dancers and performers. Interspersed between the
books were family photos that began with a wedding shot
of the brand-new Mr. and Mrs. Jordan Jackson Jr. in front
of the church where they'd just been married and continued through the appearance of first Shelby and then
Trip; the Jackson family's life played out in a progression
of photographs from birth to right around the time of
J.J.'s death. There were also numerous shots of J.J. and
Clay in hunting gear with their arms around each others' shoulders, though presumably none from their final
tragic trip.

On the last bookcase she found a photo of J.J., Melanie, and Clay Alexander. She couldn't tell where it had

been taken, but all three of them were dressed formally, the men in tuxes with snowy white shirts and crisp black bowties. Melanie, who was sandwiched between them, her arms around each of their waists, wore a strapless black gown that exposed creamy shoulders and a swell of breast. Her brown eyes shone with good humor and her lips curved upward in an unself-conscious smile. She looked directly into the lens of the camera, her eyes contemplating the photographer from beneath arched brows. Both men were tall and dark and well built, though J.J. was slightly taller and broader than Clay. Both men were looking not at the camera but at Melanie.

Vivien tilted the photo in her hands but the photographer had focused on Melanie and no matter what angle she tried, she couldn't make out the expressions on the men's faces.

Setting the photo back on the shelf, Vivien squatted down so that she could read the titles on the bottom shelves and realized that they were high school and college yearbooks arranged, like the rest of the shelves, in no particular order.

Lowering herself the rest of the way to the floor, Vivien sat cross-legged on the oriental carpet and pulled the copies of the *Pandora*, which were from the University of Georgia, into her lap. She flipped through them quickly at first more out of nostalgia than anything else. But when she opened the copy from what would have been Melanie's freshman year and J.J. and Clay's junior year, she began to read the autographs and inscriptions. In the faculty section, she came to a page whose corner had been turned down. Across the photo of a Professor Sturgess in the political science department there was a message that read, *Congratulations on your successful run for student council president. I trust you will find governing as satisfying as running.* It was signed, Phillip Sturgess.

Not sure why the name seemed familiar, Vivien carried the annual over to the photos and commendations on the wall. She found the professor's name at the bottom of the Georgia State University commendation, which thanked J.J. for his participation in the Georgia Legislative Internship Program. The letter was dated just over two years ago, not long before J.J.'s death. Which meant the professor might still be teaching here in Atlanta.

Excited to have a name to start with, Vivien took the yearbook upstairs and left it open on the bed beside her as she used her laptop to do a search of Georgia State University faculty. She was rewarded with a current photo and contact information for Professor Phillip Sturgess.

Scribbling his number and email address on the pad beside her, Vivien refused to speculate on what she might discover or how it might impact others. But she was very pleased to have a place to begin.

21

IN THE LAST weeks before Christmas, Vivien took Melanie's place setting up for the teachers' holiday buffet,
helped restock the Pemberton spirit shop, and spent an
afternoon at the school's welcome desk to give Melanie
time off to get ready for the holidays. Her sister was at
first unflatteringly stunned and then embarrassingly
grateful, which made Vivien, whose ulterior motive had
been research for her column, feel horribly guilty.

John Harcourt felt none of the guilt Vivi did at her
subterfuge. On the phone, he crowed about the success
of the column and the intensity of reader response. City
dwellers found it funny, suburbanites, especially women,
were increasingly incensed. He hinted that the *Weekly
Encounter* might be able to come up with more money at
the beginning of the new year.

Vivien had been composing her next "postcard" in her
head since the first decorations had appeared in stores
sometime after Halloween. In her room, she booted up
her laptop and worked at turning them into a holiday
column.

After several false starts she opted for, *Christmas in New York City is a vibrant and elegant thing. It begins with the Macy's Thanksgiving Day Parade, which is viewed with envy by the rest of the country, and in terms of excitement and grandeur it goes uphill from there. There's the tree in Times Square. The show at Radio City Music Hall. Skating at Rockefeller Center and in Central Park. The tastefully exciting windows in the shops on Fifth Avenue. Red ribbons on the horses and carriages that drive the tourists, the jangle of bells, the smell of snow.*

There's a lot of holiday spirit here in suburbia, too. But like pretty much everything else here, each person seems to feel compelled to personalize that spirit and then display it for all to see. One of the places they display their homage to the holiday is surprise, surprise—on their cars, with which they are in love. The first time I saw the big green wreath with the bright red bow on the front grille of a Jeep Cherokee, I thought I was imagining things. But such a sighting is quite common here. Just as the magnets on the back of their vehicles tell us what they're into, the wreaths poking out over the asphalt like figureheads on the prow of a ship tell us just how festive they feel. I for one am grateful that no one has figured out how to hook up blinking colored lights around their windshields. But it's probably just a matter of time.

Vivien settled back against her pillow, enjoying the rant.

For those not satisfied with wreaths there are what I can only think of as "car costumes." Like the Mercedes sport coupe that I saw with a red nose on the grille and two brown antlers protruding above the front driver and passenger windows. She was, of course, describing Catherine Dennison's reindeer-ized silver two-seater, which she'd spotted for the first time just yesterday. *A fine example of German engineering rendered ridiculous. And they don't stop with their cars,* she continued. *The most insistently celebratory wear green-and-red holiday T-shirts with pithy holiday greetings on them. And some insist on dressing up their pets for the occasion, too. Like the small white Havanese wearing a big red nose and a plush pair of antlers that I saw strapped into its car seat in that Mercedes. The poor animal was so mortified it didn't even look out the windows. Its face was downcast as I beeped in sympathy, but it was too embarrassed to meet my eye.*

Vivien laughed at the memory of poor Pucci, who seemed to have more sense than her owner. She summed up with a few last licks. *I know there's an energy crisis and house decorations are nowhere near as prevalent as they used to be. But I simply don't believe that cars were meant to be decorated. And I believe dressing up animals against their will qualifies as a form of cruelty. Maybe it's time to get the Humane Society on it. Or PETA. Just somebody to make it stop so the rest of us aren't forced to dodge cars and animals along with the sugarplums already dancing through our holiday dreams.*

Vivi closed this time with, *Happy holidays from your stranger in an even stranger land, Scarlett Leigh.*

◎

ON A CRISP morning in late December, Vivien drove Shelby's car to the Georgia State campus in downtown Atlanta and parked as close as she could get to the Andrew Young School of Policy Studies building, where Professor Sturgess's office was located.

The students were already out for the holidays and so the campus, unlike the city it was tucked into, was unusually quiet. Inside the building, her heels echoed in the empty hallway as she made her way to the professor's office. His was one of the few open doors, and she found him leaning back in his desk chair, his feet propped up on his desk, his hands pillowed behind his head. He was staring out the window.

"Professor Sturgess?" She stood in the doorway and waited for him to acknowledge her.

"Miz Gray," he said in a pronounced southern drawl. "Do come in."

He removed his feet from the desktop and rose to greet her. The professor was six foot three or six foot four and looked to be somewhere in his midfifties, which meant he would have been fairly young when he'd taught at Georgia. His dark hair was streaked with gray, the blue eyes behind stylish tortoiseshell glasses were intelligent and assessing. There was a mutual sizing up as they shook hands. His eyes widened slightly as he noted her obvious pregnancy.

"Thank you for seeing me on such short notice," she said as he motioned for her to sit.

"No problem. I had to be in to take care of some paperwork. The interruption is welcome."

Vivien had debated her approach, not knowing how close the professor had been to either J.J. or Clay or how in touch he'd stayed. She'd also been unsure whether he might recognize her from CIN, so had been reluctant to use an alias.

"As I mentioned, I'm doing some freelance work and I had an idea for a series on the new breed of politicians and their impact on the political process."

He listened intently and if he saw anything strange in her choosing not only a family member but one who was deceased he didn't say so. Still, she thought it important to address the issue. "J.J. wasn't the only one cut down in his prime and I'm toying with using that angle. But I'm just in the early stages." She smiled as if that particular part of the story were neither here nor there. "You don't mind if I record our session, do you?" she asked as she pulled out a portable cassette player. "If I actually do the series, we'll rerecord more formally. This is just so I get it all right."

He nodded his assent and leaned forward, folding his hands on his desk.

"So, tell me, Professor Sturgess," she said as if this were a real interview. "What was J.J. like at the University of Georgia and what do you think propelled him into politics and public service?"

"He was one of my most motivated students from the beginning," the professor said. "And although I'd like to take credit for his commitment to the political process, he was already completely focused on a career as a public servant when he arrived in Athens. He'd held positions in student government all through high school and he had an understanding of what it took to get elected that I suspect he was born with."

She nodded encouragingly, careful not to interrupt the flow of words.

"He was extremely charismatic and he knew how to get others to do what he wanted. Not all that different from your father and brother," he said with a smile. "Though their political points of view were quite different."

Vivien let the reference to her family go by; both she and Melanie had been drawn to magnetic public figures, but she wasn't here to debate whether they'd been looking for versions of Daddy. "So he ran for student government at UGA, too?" she asked.

"Oh, yes. He ran in his freshman and sophomore years and won by a landslide. He was the ultimate candidate: good-looking, personable, but with a drive that very few young people have at that age."

"Did you know Clay Alexander then?"

"Of course. You couldn't know one of them without the other. He and J.J. were the kind of students every teacher hopes for. They loved to debate each other and anyone else that would sit still long enough. They actually ran against each other in their freshman and sophomore years."

"How did that turn out?" Vivien asked.

"Clay always came in second. He was very astute and very tuned in to the nuances of campaigning, but he wasn't the extemporaneous speaker J.J. was. He was always a little more cautious, more of a planner. In many ways he was a more private person all round. And he wasn't as willing to tell people what they wanted to hear."

"I'm surprised losing to J.J. like that didn't impact their friendship," she said. Or maybe it had.

"Didn't seem to. In the spring of their junior years, Clay became J.J.'s campaign manager in a bid for student council president. Did a bang-up job, too. One of the most professionally run campaigns I've ever seen at the student level. I think the backroom position suited Clay best. J.J. had tons of personality and the glibber tongue. But Clay was a long-term thinker. Together they were pretty much unbeatable."

"Interesting," Vivien said, trying to picture it. If she had lost repeatedly to a good friend, would she have been willing to put her whole heart into supporting him? Or would she have been waiting for her opportunity?

"There was some sort of falling-out the following fall as I recall," Professor Sturgess offered. "I remember Clay sort of kept to himself after that. I think he even dropped out of the fraternity he and J.J. belonged to."

"Do you know what it was about?" Vivien held her breath, hoping for some insight, but the professor shook his head.

"Nope, neither of them ever talked to me about it. But when Clay moved here to run J.J.'s first campaign, I figured they must have patched things up. And, of course, I've seen the two of them at functions over the years since I moved to Atlanta. They were both very helpful with our legislative internship program.

"It's a shame about J.J." Professor Sturgess shook his head, then glanced down at his watch and Vivien knew it was time to wrap things up.

"Yes." Vivi put her pad and the recorder into her purse. "And I really appreciate your time and your input," she said as she prepared to leave. "But I have one last question about J.J. and Clay and their, um, approaches. Was there any one fundamental way in which they differed? Anything that stood out in your mind?"

"Well." His gaze shifted from her face to settle somewhere behind her as he thought. When he met her eyes again he said, "If I had to pick one thing I'd say that although J.J. was very into appearances—playing the part, presenting the right image, very driven to achieve his goals, there was a certain volatility that took over on occasion. He could make a decision based solely on his gut and act on it before he'd cooled down enough to think it through. Not hotheaded exactly, but impulsive at times."

"And Clay?" she asked quietly, not wanting to interrupt his train of thought.

"Clay was very controlled and purposeful. I don't think he ever acted without forethought. Even as a college student he was all about doing the 'right thing.' Honoring commitments and obligations regardless of how he might feel."

There was a brief silence as Vivien considered his answer. She would have liked to pursue this line of questioning, but the professor was standing, offering his hand.

As she walked out through the echoing hallways she thought about Professor Sturgess's take on the two men. She didn't know if anything he'd told her had any bearing on how and why J.J. had died, but she'd learned long ago not to discard the smallest bit of information. Sometimes the tiniest key unlocked the biggest door.

❧

THE LAST WEDNESDAY night before Christmas the class was so small they fit into one line.

"This is why we're breaking for the next two weeks," Melanie said as she positioned herself between Vivien and Ruth. Angela and Sally fell in on either side of them. "Everybody's way too busy with the holidays. I just hope we get enough reservations for the New Year's Eve party to make it worthwhile."

Naranya started the music while they tied on their scarves. A month full of "Rudolph, the Red-Nosed Reindeer" and "Jingle Bells" coupled with the Christmas decorations that surrounded them rendered the ancient oriental melodies even more exotic than usual.

"Maybe we should just blow this Popsicle stand and go away for the holidays," Vivien said as she tried to balance on one bent leg while resting the ankle of the other above the knee.

"You should come with me," Naranya said as she reached her arms into the air, watching as they followed. "I am going on thee Princess of the Sea for two weeks. All expenses paid. I teach only one class a day."

"That's what I'm talking about," Vivi said, "The Caribbean. Lounge chairs by the pool. Midnight buffets."

"You *would* be fixated on the food," Melanie said as they went up on their toes and reached toward the snowflake-covered ceiling. "I'm pretty sure there'll be some of that at Magnolia Hall."

"Oh, sure," Vivi said. "If my personal food policeman lets me eat any of it."

"A personal food policeman?" Angela shot Vivi a look. "I could so use one of those right now. I hate how the holidays revolve completely around food."

"Ach," Ruth said. "I baked rugalach for all of you.

Don't let me forget to give you the tins." They stretched to the side, bending low. "Girls today are too thin. In my day curves were a good thing, not something to try to get rid of." She looked at Angela. "Or hide."

"Ruth . . ." Melanie looked at her friend, her tone a warning.

With arms extended they began to roll their right shoulders backward, then forward. At Naranya's signal they repeated the controlled movement with their left.

"I'm only saying that wearing clothes a size too big makes a person look larger, not smaller," Ruth said. "I heard that the other night on *What Not to Wear*."

Angela's cheeks flushed. Melanie, too, had wondered why the redhead wore clothes too big for her body, but only Ruth would come out and say so.

"There's a lot of 'hiding' going on," Ruth continued looking now at Vivien. "This one hid her pregnancy until we called her on it. And now she's hiding out at your house. For someone who has a reputation for digging up the 'truth' she doesn't seem to feel too inclined to share it."

Melanie's chest tightened as it had when Caroline and Vivi went at each other. Dance class was meant to relieve stress, not cause it. "Ruth, really," she began, "I don't think this is the time to . . ."

Perhaps practicing the tact that would be required of her on a holiday cruise ship, Naranya placed herself in front of Sally and rolled up her black stretch pants so that she could demonstrate the movement of her legs. "Watch how my knees control what my hips do," she instructed, leaving them to their conversation.

"So you and Ira have always told each other everything?" Angela asked with an odd sort of urgency as they all touched a toe forward, bent at the knees, and began a series of hip rolls. "You don't keep secrets of any kind?"

Vivi didn't say anything, but she watched with a sharp-edged interest. They turned and touched the other toe, bent at the knees, and rolled the opposite hip in unison just as Naranya was doing with Sally.

"I always thought so. I thought we shared everything," Ruth said. "But I was wrong." Ruth's hips stilled and Melanie reached out to give her arm a squeeze.

"I think complete honesty is necessary in a long-term relationship. If you don't tell the truth or you withhold parts of yourself, well . . ." Melanie closed her eyes as she thought about J.J., the Band-Aid momentarily ripping free. "I don't think a marriage based on anything less has a chance of surviving."

Vivien blew out a breath and stopped moving her hips. She looked distinctly uncomfortable; but then Melanie already knew that her sister had a sliding scale when it came to the truth. One standard for others, especially the subjects of her investigations; another for herself.

"So you'd want to know the truth about your significant other, even if the truth were unpleasant?" Vivi asked her.

"Absolutely," Melanie said.

"What about you, Vivi?" Angela asked. None of them were even pretending to practice anymore. "Do you believe both parties in a relationship should know everything about the other?"

Vivi looked away for a long moment and then back. "The answer's not as black and white as I used to think," she admitted. "Everything becomes a lot more complicated when you care about someone."

They all nodded in agreement, though no one seemed especially happy about it.

"That cruise is looking better and better," Vivi observed as Naranya passed out the zills she had promised and showed them how to slip them onto their fingers.

"Maybe we could sign on as Naranya's assistants and belly dance every night at the midnight buffet."

They chimed their finger cymbals enthusiastically in favor of the idea and laughed at the sounds they made. But Melanie knew there'd be no sailing off into the sunset. At least not anytime soon.

22

MELANIE HAULED VIVIEN out of bed early on Christmas morning, much as she had when they were kids.

"Come on," she said. "I've got hot chocolate ready. Put a robe on. This is the one morning of the year the kids don't have to be dynamited out of bed. We always exchange gifts first thing."

"What time is it?" Vivien mumbled, her eyes still closed.

"Doesn't matter. Santa left presents under the tree. Some of them even have your name on them."

They were expected at Magnolia Hall at one o'clock for the official Gray Christmas. On previous visits Vivi had stayed there in her old room and had typically slept in until it was time to make an appearance. She'd never thought to ask if or how the Jacksons had celebrated.

"Mmmphh." Vivi got one eye open. Melanie wore a bright red robe with white cuffs and collar. Her slippers curled up in an elflike fashion and were striped like candy canes. A Santa hat sat on her head.

"Come on." Melanie grasped her hand and pulled her from bed. "Go pee. I'll wait here."

Still half asleep Vivien did as instructed. Then she splashed water on her face and brushed her teeth. From a hook on the back of the bathroom door she withdrew the cowboy robe and pulled it on.

Downstairs, Trip and Shelby sat on the family room sofa ogling the Christmas tree, which the four of them had wrestled home and decorated two weeks ago. More specifically they were ogling the wrapped packages beneath it. A fire blazed in the fireplace and steaming mugs of hot chocolate sat in front of both kids. A large tin of Christmas cookies, which Melanie and Shelby had baked earlier in the week, sat open on the cocktail table. Clearly, her sister had been up and busy for some time. She looked as excited as her children.

"Don't you just love Christmas?" she asked, much as she had about Thanksgiving.

"Apparently not as much as you do," Vivien replied, though it was difficult not to smile at the happy faces turned in her direction. Despite the early hour, Trip seemed to be fully awake. Well, at least both of his eyes were open.

"I wanted to use the pot and spoon to get you out of bed. Or maybe that feather," Shelby said with an evil smile that was strikingly absent from her tone. "But Mom wouldn't let me."

"It's a good thing," Vivien replied. "I'd hate to do you bodily harm on a holiday."

"As if," Shelby said. But the sarcasm was automatic and decidedly halfhearted. Apparently a Christmas cease-fire was in effect.

"Okay, Trip," Melanie said, removing the Santa hat from her head and depositing it on her son's. "You go first." The hat was much too small and looked ridiculous perched on Trip's head, but nobody commented on it.

Walking to the tree, he bent down and retrieved three clumsily wrapped packages, which he distributed to each of them.

Shelby got Stephenie Meyer's new book and Melanie and Vivien received gift cards to the nearby Borders. Trip was clearly a one-stop shopper. But Vivien was touched that he'd actually gone out and shopped and so was his mother, who gave him a kiss on the cheek, which he didn't wipe off. Shelby plucked the Santa hat off his head and gave him a noogie. Vivien blew him a kiss. He blushed at all the attention and sat back down.

"Shelby?" Melanie nodded at her daughter, and the girl put the Santa cap on her own head. Vivien was stunned by how beautiful her niece was when she ditched the surly expression.

Shelby went to the tree to retrieve the gifts she'd stashed there. Trip loved the new video game and Melanie's eyes dampened when she opened the massage gift certificate her daughter gave her. If Vivien had been Melanie, she would have exchanged the massage for this version of her daughter the other 364 days of the year. Then she scolded herself for the thought, recognizing it as decidedly Caroline.

When Shelby placed a large carefully wrapped present in Vivien's lap, Vivi looked up in surprise.

"This is from Mom and me."

Vivien ducked her head to hide the moisture blurring her own eyes. "Well, at least it's not ticking," she joked, then made a show of shaking it in a search for clues.

"I'd say it's an even better thing there's no glass inside," Melanie quipped.

The white clothing box bore the stamp From Here to

Maternity and had an Atlanta address. Inside the pink-and-blue tissue paper lay two maternity outfits, one casual, the other slightly dressier. Vivien looked from her sister to her niece.

"Mom told us," Shelby replied to Vivi's unasked question. "While she was explaining the importance of birth control no matter what your age is."

"Shelby!" Melanie said.

Shelby just shrugged. "Well, she's awful old for something like this to happen. Shouldn't her eggs be all dried up by now?"

"Sick," Trip said, but Vivien wasn't sure if he was referring to the state of her eggs or the video game box he was reading.

"And this came for you last week." Melanie went to the tree and retrieved a small box wrapped in distinctly foreign gift wrap. "It came addressed to me with instructions not to let you open it until Christmas Day."

Vivien sniffed back tears as she undid the ribbon with clumsy fingers. Nestled in a bed of cotton was a necklace of what looked like ancient stones in shades of blue. An intricately carved silver amulet hung in its center. "Oh," she breathed as the tears spilled over. A tiny card written in Stone's loopy handwriting said simply, *To protect you and keep you safe. With all my love.*

Melanie reached over to take it from Vivien's trembling hands. "It's beautiful. I think that's lapis lazuli." She pointed to a bright blue stone. "I'm not sure what the others are." She fingered one edge of the amulet. "It looks like this opens." She smiled. "Maybe you should put a picture of you and Stone in it."

Vivien's vision blurred as Melanie fastened the clasp around her neck. The stones were rough and warm on her skin, the amulet smooth and cool. She batted her eyelashes frantically to hold back the waterworks as she contemplated how very far away Stone was. And of all she hadn't told him.

"You're not gonna get all mushy, are you?" Trip asked in horror.

"Here, have a cookie." Shelby shoved the tin toward Vivien.

"Okay, my turn," Melanie said, taking the hat from Shelby's head and placing it on her own. She handed similarly wrapped packages to Shelby and Trip, both of whom yelped happily when they saw the iPod boxes. "Thanks, Mom!" they said in unison as Shelby held up her pink iPod and Trip held up a silver.

Vivien unwrapped the flat rectangular box that Melanie handed her. "But you already gave me the clothes!"

Melanie shrugged. "This is just a little something extra."

Inside the box Vivien found a wooden plaque with a wire hanger looped through it. It said *Vivi's Room*. Her eyes teared up again. She felt decidedly faucetlike.

Melanie leaned over and hugged Vivien. "Just wanted you to know that the room is yours and the baby's as long as you want it."

Vivien gave in to her tears then because she simply couldn't help it. Trip and Shelby looked away, embarrassed. Melanie gave Vivien's shoulder a squeeze. "I'm really glad you're here." This produced more waterworks. And guilt.

The kids stood. "We're gonna go download some apps from iTunes," Trip mumbled.

"I'll make us some more hot chocolate." Melanie rose from the couch and reached for Vivien's mug.

Obviously they assumed the gift exchange was over.

"Hey, wait a minute," Vivien said, sniffing back the last of her tears, not at all flattered by the assumption. "Don't I get my turn to give gifts? Give me that stupid hat," she said, plucking it from Melanie's head and plunking it down on her own.

While they watched, she went to the coat closet and retrieved two boxes and an envelope, which she brought back to the family room.

She handed the bigger box to Shelby. "This is for you." She sat back down. "I hope you like it."

Carefully, as if it might in fact contain a bomb, Shelby removed the bow and wrapping paper. A little glimmer of surprise lit her eyes as she noted the designer logo on the box. "Oh, my God," Shelby shrieked when she'd opened it. "A Coach bag! Look, Mom, it's real Coach!" She tried it on over her forearm then slipped the strap over one shoulder and struck a pose. "Oh, my gosh, I just can't believe it!" She swooped down to throw her arms around Vivien. Vivien hugged her back.

Smiling, Vivien beckoned Trip over. "This is for you," she said, watching him closely, eager to see his reaction.

He examined the box she handed him, a smile still on his face. She could almost see his determination to act happy whatever lame thing she gave him. "I hope it's not a purse."

"It's definitely not a purse," she promised as he shook the box. "In fact, I suggest you open it because you're never going to guess."

Trip focused on unwrapping then, first the large box she'd started with then the two smaller ones she'd wrapped and tucked inside it to prolong the suspense.

"Finally!" he said as he held up the long envelope. "Well, at least it isn't some girly thing."

"No." Vivi smiled. "It definitely is not."

They all waited as he ripped the envelope open and read the sheet of paper inside, Shelby and Melanie as in the dark as Trip.

"Oh, wow!" he shouted, looking at Vivien, his mouth open. "Is this for real?"

Vivien nodded happily, more than pleased with his delight.

"What is it?" Melanie asked.

"Read it to us!" Shelby demanded.

Trip was still blinking back his surprise. "This entitles Jordan Jackson the third, or Triple, also known as Trip, to accompany James and Cole Wesley to the January Hawks versus Celtics game at Philips Arena."

His mouth hung open. As did Melanie's and Shelby's.

"You're not messing with my head, are you?" He checked the paper again.

Vivien shook her head, no, sending the top of the Santa cap flopping. She couldn't stop smiling, so pleased was she with her surprise. "Angela couldn't go and James and Cole—that's his father the pitcher"—she said as if everyone in the room didn't already know that—"thought it would be fun to have another guy along. You're the guy."

"I'm going to a basketball game with Cole Wesley? Me? Really?" He simply couldn't seem to absorb it. This was by far the most words she'd heard come out of his mouth, cumulatively, since she'd arrived. "Wait till I tell the guys!"

He rushed off, pulling his phone out of his pocket as he went.

"That is so cool!" This was high praise from Shelby. "I think I need to tell a few people myself." She already had her phone to her ear before she'd gotten to the stairs.

Melanie and Vivien exchanged glances.

"Wow!" Melanie said. "You are formidable when you apply yourself, Vivi. Even I'm impressed."

"Why, thank you." Vivien smiled. "But I'm not completely finished. Here." She handed the large envelope to her sister. "This is for you. With thanks." Her smile faltered a bit. "And apologies."

Melanie slipped a fingernail under the flap and pulled it open. Slowly she removed the handwritten card. *This entitles the bearer, that's you, Mel, to the services of Wilda and Carlos, cleaners extraordinaire, every week for the next six months. Date and time to be determined.*

Melanie dropped the card into her lap. "Oh, no, Vivi, that's too much. I can't accept . . ."

"You cannot refuse a gift. That would be too awful," Vivi said. "Especially not after everything I've taken from you."

"But . . ."

She held up a hand to silence Melanie's protests. "And especially not after I humbled myself by calling Ruth and begging for a referral. She wasn't even going to give me a name until I told her it was for you."

Vivien smiled. "Otherwise you're going to have me mopping and swabbing, and we both know just how unsatisfactory that would be."

The rest of the morning was completely satisfactory from Vivien's point of view. She and Melanie spent it sipping hot chocolate and munching on cookies in front of the fire while they watched first *Miracle on 34th Street* and then *National Lampoon's Christmas Vacation.*

Before they knew it, it was time to shower and dress and clamber into the van for the drive to Magnolia Hall. They backed over the still-rolled-up newspaper at the foot of the driveway, having never even thought about bringing it in, let alone reading it. Which was why they arrived at Magnolia Hall happily festive and unreasonably optimistic. Which turned out to be a rather strategic mistake.

23

THERE WAS A warm glow in Melanie's chest as she drove the minivan to Magnolia Hall. The morning had been wonderful. Not as wonderful as it would have been if J.J. had been with them, of course, but Vivien's presence and unexpected enthusiasm had allowed the three of them to celebrate without being consumed by J.J.'s absence.

Beside her, Vivien stared out the window lost in thoughts of her own. She wore one of her new maternity outfits, but Melanie suspected this was out of necessity rather than an intentional gambit for opening discussion of her pregnancy. Though it was cowardly and somewhat selfish of her, she hoped Caroline was too distracted to notice Vivi's rounding shape. Or to question the flimsy reasons Vivi had given for the length of her stay. Melanie had spent the last year forging a tentative truce with her mother. She hadn't forgiven Caroline for her disapproval of J.J., and she had repeatedly refused the help that would have never been offered when he was alive, but she'd managed to avoid engaging in any major battles. She was already far too stressed to be at war with her mother.

A glance in the rearview mirror confirmed that the kids had their new iPods plugged into their ears, but today that didn't leave Melanie feeling intentionally excluded. This morning had gone a long way toward smoothing out the jagged edges of their loss, and she wanted desperately to believe that it marked a turning point for all of them. That although life would never be the same without J.J., it might one day be all right.

In the open doorway of Magnolia Hall, Evangeline waited. Dressed in her everyday uniform, she wasted no time on affectations or "Mammyisms." "Merry Christmas, y'all," she said as she hugged them each in turn, careful not to smash the gaily wrapped gifts they carried. She held Vivien the longest and when she took the gifts into her own arms so that she could look her up and down more thoroughly, she sighed. "Oh, Lordy. I hope to hell you're prepared because your mama . . ."

Whatever warning Evangeline had intended was swallowed up in Caroline's arrival. "Darlings!" she said, scooping Shelby and Trip into delicate hugs that wouldn't damage the gifts or mess up her hair or makeup.

Evangeline's eyes went very wide as if she were trying to communicate something silently, not exactly her forte. She handed the stack of gifts back to Vivien, positioning them directly in front of her stomach and chest.

"Santa left a ton of things for you two under the tree," Caroline went on. "I swear we'll have to rent a U-Haul to get all that loot back to your house.

"Isn't that right, Evangeline?" Caroline said much too sweetly.

"Oh, yes'm," Evangeline replied with an exaggerated curtsy and bob of her head even while she tried to send yet another wide-eyed warning. "Santa came all right. And so did the morning newspaper." Again, she widened her eyes and shot them a look.

Melanie glanced at Vivien to see if she'd gotten the
intended message, but she shrugged back, equally baffled.
If she ever had to choose up sides for charades, Evangeline
was going to be her very last pick.

"Why don't we go ahead into the library?" Caroline
asked, though as usual it was more of a command than
a request. "Please tell Cook we'll be ready to eat at two,
Evangeline."

Evangeline stood rooted in the doorway, uncharac-
teristically uncertain. The fact that she wasn't perform-
ing or trading barbs with Caroline was a surer sign of
trouble than any of her attempted communicative looks,
but Melanie still had no idea what she was trying to tell
them. Evangeline finally took herself off to the kitchen,
muttering to herself.

"Now then." Caroline took the gifts out of Vivien's
arms and gave her a slow once-over that made them both
squirm. "I see you have on a new outfit," she said pleas-
antly, though her expression was pained. "And you've
got such a . . . rosy glow about you." An eyebrow arched
upward. "The holidays certainly seem to be agreeing
with you."

Melanie braced herself for the dawning of understanding to wash across their mother's perfectly made-up face.
For Vivien to come out and tell her she was going to be
a grandmother again. For Caroline to gasp in horror as
she confronted the fact that her unmarried daughter was
going to have a baby. But Caroline simply handed the
gifts back to Vivien, turned on her heel, and led them
back to the library.

Melanie and Vivien exchanged glances. "That was
really weird," Vivien said.

"Yeah, in a really scary way. I'm not having a good
feeling," Melanie said, trying to still the flutter of unease.
"But if she's not in complete denial and the subject of

your pregnancy should come up, this would be the perfect day to plead immaculate conception."

For a while the pandemonium of their arrival and the gift exchanging covered the odd undercurrent. There were, in fact, a ton of gifts for both Trip and Shelby and everyone else present. A lack of material generosity had never been an issue in the Gray household, and there was a good deal of smiling and laughing during the allotted hour.

But when they moved en masse into the dining room, the veneer of frivolity disappeared. Granted it was difficult to be completely carefree and unguarded in this most formal of rooms under the best of circumstances, but as they took their seats Melanie felt a distinct change in the atmosphere. And as they ate she saw the same change reflected in Caroline's face.

Melanie had come prepared to make sure Vivien's Christmas dinner wasn't a vegetarian affair; she'd promised that she'd even slip her food from her own plate if necessary. But Evangeline continued to be distracted and off her game, barely bothering to censor what Vivien ate. It didn't take a rocket scientist to figure out that Evangeline's food policing was nothing compared to whatever was brewing with their mother. Caroline's face flushed as she watched her eldest daughter eat, and Melanie didn't think it was a result of the amount of wine Caroline consumed or the quantity of food that Vivi inhaled.

The main course had been cleared and coffee poured when Caroline clanged a spoon against her water goblet and called for their attention. The skin on the back of Melanie's neck prickled as her mother stood at her place. The table grew quiet as everyone watched Caroline, but Caroline's gaze never left Vivien.

"I'd like to propose a toast to our daughter Vivien," Caroline said, her jaw set and her tone hard. "Who has once again found a way to embarrass and humiliate this family."

She paused dramatically as everyone else froze. Out of the corner of her eye Melanie watched Vivien's face drain of color, but other than the chalky whiteness of her skin and her complete stillness she gave no other outward sign of distress.

"When are you due, sweetheart?" The endearment was both chiding and chilling. "And did you really have to piss off Matthew Glazer to the extent that he had to expose your unmarried pregnancy in his column on Christmas morning?"

"It was in the paper?" Vivi asked through lips that had gone as white as her face. "He actually wrote that?"

"And ran a picture, too. Perhaps you should start wearing the hat and dark glasses on your stomach!"

Caroline removed a folded section of newspaper from the pocket of her sweater. In the silence that had descended, the rustle of the paper might have been a thunderclap. She read, "What former investigative reporter from a prominent and politically connected Atlanta family is apparently pregnant despite the lengths she's gone to to try to hide it? This shot of Vivien Armstrong Gray was snapped as she snuck out of a recent ob-gyn appointment. Ms. Gray, of Magnolia Hall in Buckhead and more recently of New York City, seems a bit long in the tooth to be having a baby. The big question would be who and where is the baby's father?" Caroline paused and drew a deep breath. "He then goes on about some column in the *Weekly Encounter* that has suburban soccer moms all in a twitter, but you were his lead story. And this picture . . . honestly!" She grimaced as she wadded the paper into a ball and dropped it on the table.

"I guess Christmas *is* the slowest news day of the year," was Vivien's only comment. She took a bite of food and

chewed nonchalantly, but her body was rigid as if the
fierceness with which she'd clamped down on her emotions precluded any movement at all.

Their father harrumphed. Hamilton and Judy looked
away, making it clear they'd already known. Ham's kids
were watching the proceedings with real interest, no
doubt eager for a story worth repeating to their friends.
Only Shelby and Trip looked as uncomfortable as Melanie
felt; she hated seeing the easy comfort of the morning
and what should have been the true focus of the holiday
snatched so meanly away. Her anger built; there was no
reason on earth for her mother to bring this up in front
of the children.

"This is no joking matter," Caroline said, her tone
knifelike and deadly. "Wasn't it bad enough that you
ended Harley Jenkins's career, then spent your life lifting up rocks to see what crawled out from under them?
What kind of woman has a job that allows her to get shot
in the butt while the country watches? And what kind of
daughter gets herself pregnant and then doesn't even have
the common courtesy to warn her family?"

"Now, Caro," their father said. "She hardly got herself pregnant. Why don't we just discuss this calmly in
private? I'm sure if pressure were brought to bear, Stone
would do the right thing." He looked at Vivien. "It is
Stone's baby, isn't it?"

"This is why New Yorkers think that southerners live
in the Dark Ages," Vivien bit out. "What are you sug-
gesting, Daddy? That you'll get out your shotgun and
run on over to Afghanistan so you can march Stone down
the aisle?" Vivi laughed, and it was a bitter, ugly thing.
"You could live with that, I suppose. It certainly wouldn't
be the first shotgun wedding in this family."

Judy blanched, though Melanie was certain the taunt
wasn't aimed at her. Melanie had the bizarre urge to tell

her children to cover their ears. She wanted to sweep them out of here and never bring them back. More than anything she wanted the arguing to stop. Conflict made her stomach churn and her heart pound, a result, according to some long-ago therapist, of a childhood spent as witness to her sister and mother's constant combat. At the moment she was not actually conflicted, but she was angry. She wanted to shout at her mother to just shut the hell up. The urge was shocking in its intensity.

"What if it's not Stone's?" Vivien taunted. "What if it came out of a test tube? What if I have no idea whose baby it is? What if I've been sleeping with half of New York and . . ." Her words were sharp and cutting, forged with the same heat as Caroline's. But Melanie saw the way her sister's hands shook, the way Vivi clutched them into fists in her lap in an effort to hold them still.

The kids' eyes were wide, much wider than Evangeline had managed earlier. Evangeline stood in the corner of the room, slightly behind Vivien. Melanie had the sense that she was waiting to see whether her services would be needed.

"Vivi." Melanie reached out a hand and laid it on her sister's shoulder. "Don't. It's not worth . . ."

Vivi shook her off without even looking at her, her gaze still locked with Caroline's. "Don't what? Don't defend myself? Don't talk back? Don't tell her what a self-centered, manipulating bitch she is?"

Caroline's gasp of outrage sliced across the room. "How dare you? How dare you come back here to sully our reputation and then talk to me like I have no right to call you on it? I'm your mother! You will not speak to me that way!"

Melanie's stomach churned away. Bile actually rose in her throat. She wished with all her heart that J.J. were there with his gentle, calming air.

"A cat is a better mother than you!" Vivien stood, still trembling at her place at the table. "I believe your hero Rhett Butler said that to your idol Scarlett O'Hara and the line certainly applies. I pray to God I'll be a better mother than you are because in all my forty-one years I have never actually seen you put any one of your children before yourself. Not once!" She turned to Melanie. "Mellie is a real mother to her children. I don't know how in the world she figured out how to do that given the example she had to follow, but she did. I have to believe I can do it, too."

Melanie would have liked to disappear beneath the table; she wished desperately that they had never come. Her legs trembled, but somehow she managed to rise and stand on them. She moved so that she stood next to her sister, so close that their shoulders brushed. She could feel Vivien drawing breath into her lungs.

Melanie didn't know what was supposed to happen next. She would never have chosen this time or this place to confront her mother. Nor would she have chosen to do it in front of her children. But she was sick to death of pretending that she was any less angry and disappointed than Vivien; she could no longer bear that every choice that either of them had made, every action they'd taken over the years, had been evaluated through the prism of what reflected best on Caroline. And all too often those choices and actions had been found wanting. As had Vivien and Melanie.

"Melanie, are you going to let your sister talk to me that way?" Caroline asked.

Vivien turned to her and there was nothing in her eyes but understanding. "It's not your fight," she said quietly. "Just give me your keys and let me go. Ham or Daddy will drive you all home."

Melanie took Vivien's hand and squeezed it. She looked

briefly to Shelby and Trip to make sure they were hanging in there and was relieved to see that although they appeared understandably shaken, neither of them looked as if they were in danger of falling apart. Underneath all the teenaged angst and the devastating loss, they were strong. The thought pleased her.

She looked at her father, who generally meant well but who ceded almost all family issues to Caroline. He was studying the alignments at the table, possibly trying to determine whether all the dynamite had been detonated or if there were more shock waves to come.

Because she could see no other course, Melanie looked her mother in the eye. Words she'd never thought to utter began to spill out. "Vivien's not the only one who's tired of your judgments and disapproval, Mama. You say you love us; I even think you believe you do. But it's all so . . . conditional. And we never really know when you're going to snatch it back. Or come up with new hoops we need to jump through to earn your affection."

She nodded to Shelby and Trip. "Go get your things, please. We're leaving." She watched for a moment while her children stood and then did as she'd asked. Evangeline went with them and she heard them in the library, Evangeline insisting they take their gifts with them when it was clear they preferred to leave them behind.

"So, you choose your sister over me."

"It should never be a choice, Mama. But if you mean, am I leaving with Vivi right now or staying with you, then, yes, I choose her."

The room was perfectly quiet. Only the hushed conversation between Evangeline and the kids and the occasional clank of dishware in the kitchen broke the silence.

"So," Melanie said, knowing that the time had come to make her stand. "When and if you're ready to support us rather than judge and dictate to us. When you're ready to try to make things between us different, you know where to find us." She waited several long moments, her mouth unbearably dry, her heart pounding, hoping that Caroline would respond, but her mother's gaze was unwavering; she didn't move or speak.

Ham and Judy refused to meet her eye. Her father's gaze expressed regret, but he, too, remained silent.

"Fine," Melanie said, commanding her still-trembling limbs to move. "We'll show ourselves out." And then she walked carefully out of the dining room with her sister, her shoulders squared and her chin up. As if every part of her wasn't wobbling like Jell-O.

⌒

THAT NIGHT VIVIEN watched Stone's six P.M. live report from "a cave somewhere on the border between Pakistan and Afghanistan" where the abducted aid worker had been found, his head separated from his body. She heard his somber recounting of what the dead man had apparently been put through, and her heart went out to the man's family. As she had when she and Melanie had huddled together to conduct a postmortem of their Christmas dinner at Magnolia Hall, Vivien reminded herself that in comparison to so many others, she was incredibly lucky.

She smoothed out the edges of the Just Peachy article she'd cut from the paper and studied the horribly unflattering and obviously rounded side view of her leaving Dr. Gilbert's building. She'd been holding it in her lap since they'd gotten home.

So now Matt Glazer's readers knew she was pregnant; she'd just have to hope his readership didn't extend beyond Atlanta. So she and Melanie were now personae non gratae at their parents' home and, presumably, in their lives, something she regretted more for Melanie, whose defense of her had been so surprising, than for herself. So, she had no job she was prepared to admit to and a ton of suspicions about the man her sister considered, at the very least, a valued friend.

Fingering the silver amulet of the necklace Stone had given her, Vivien felt his absence so keenly she imagined her heart pulsing not with blood but with emptiness. She wanted to curl up in a ball and hide under the covers until he came home. Even more than that, she wanted to talk to him, to hear his voice, to tell him everything and hope like hell that he would understand.

Knowing how unlikely it was that she would reach him, she nonetheless dialed his cell phone, holding her breath while it rang alien-toned rings that were just one more reminder of how far away he was.

When she was about to give up, his voice sounded in her ear and the flood of relief nearly swamped her. She'd already opened her mouth to speak when his "Hi," was followed by the "Sorry I can't answer" of a recorded message.

Vivien closed her eyes as a potent mixture of regret and despair washed over her. At the beep, she searched deep inside herself for a suitably upbeat tone with which she said, "Hey. Just calling to wish you a Merry Christmas and to thank you for the beautiful necklace. I love it." She swallowed. "And you." She swallowed. "I hope you got the package I sent."

She touched one of the stones as she worried her lip between her teeth. "I saw your report tonight, and I, um, hope you're okay. I can't tell you how much I wish you were here." Oh, God, she was getting maudlin. She needed to hang up before she dissolved into tears or announced his impending fatherhood via voice mail. "So." She swallowed again, appalled by the quiver in her voice, then cleared her throat for good measure, as if she'd simply had something other than her heart lodged in it. "Call me when you can, okay? I'd, um, really like to talk to you."

For a long time after she hung up, Vivien simply sat there, struggling to get herself and her emotions under control. This whacked-out neediness was as foreign as it was unnerving. She'd always been proud of her independence and self-reliance; they were the qualities she prized most in herself. And she knew Stone did, too.

As she readied herself for bed, she told herself she should be glad she hadn't reached him, glad she hadn't been able to dump her ill-defined worries and fears all over him. Stone was in a foreign and dangerous place, reporting on people who would just as soon slice off his head as talk to him. He did not need to be worrying about her. Or wrestling with what to do about a child he'd never intended to conceive.

24

"WHAT'S WRONG, LUV? Didn't expect to see you here till after the holidays."

Angela looked up from the computer screen she'd been staring into and conjured a smile for Brian. She'd pulled up the photos she was considering for her next gallery show but had ended up poring over the images from her original outsider series instead; the stark image of a lone child watching a group of others at play, a television screen filled with the images of bathing-suit-clad beauty contestants shot over the shadowed shoulder of a lumpy teenage girl on a couch, twentysomethings on the dance floor of a nightclub watched by a lone female figure who stands on its edge. Dark and dramatically lit, the images were both beautiful and painful. In each, she had focused on the figure left out. All of them, in their own way, were her.

It was only when she'd allowed them to be hung and shared that she had discovered that all but the most relentlessly confident could relate. They had been meant to put her past behind her. But no matter what front she presented to the world and to James, she hadn't been able to let go of who she'd been. She couldn't get rid of Fangie; nor could she bring herself to introduce her to the man she loved.

Angela shook her head, mute, afraid if she tried to speak, she'd end up crying.

Brian sat beside her and slung an arm over her shoulders, pulling her close. "Tell Uncle Brian what's wrong. If that fiancé of yours is acting up, I'll . . . call him out. Challenge him to a duel."

Angela buried her head in the crook of his shoulder. Her partner was more Monty Python than Sir Galahad, but he always had her best interests at heart.

"Really, you know I'd do anything for you, Ang. Except let you blow your nose on my shirt." He reached for the tissue box on the worktable. "Here. Blow. And tell Uncle Brian all."

Embarrassed to wallow so blatantly when she had so much, she blew her nose loudly and added an extra honk for effect.

"Very ladylike," he teased. "I'd try not to do that when you're with your future in-laws in the Braves Clubhouse." He gave her a moment to compose herself. "Tell me."

Wadding the tissue into a ball, she dabbed at her eyes. "James's parents tried to give me a Lexus convertible from one of their dealerships for Christmas."

"No!" he said in horror. "Oh, you poor thing!"

"And all through the Christmas parties and the open houses, James just kept looking at me in this really sappy way and telling everybody how much he couldn't wait to marry me." The tears squeezed out of the corner of her eyes and dampened her cheeks.

"Shame." He shook his head. "How bloody awful!" Brian tut-tutted—he was one of the only people she'd ever met who actually knew how.

Angela dabbed at her cheeks, trying her best to ignore his cheerful sarcasm.

"James gave me these earrings." She pulled her hair away from her ears so that he could see the diamond studs that he'd fastened onto her earlobes Christmas morning.

"Far too sparkly," he said. "And much too large. I don't know how you manage to keep your head up."

She fought back a smile along with the urge to completely unburden herself.

"Ang," he said quietly, his eyes, as always, warm and accepting. "I'm not seeing the problem. Most of the female population and a large percentage of males would trade places with you in a heartbeat." He took her by the shoulders and set her back a bit so he could look down into her eyes. "What's wrong? Why are you so upset?"

She met his gaze. "Because I don't deserve any of it. And I definitely don't deserve James. He's been so honest with me." She looked down into her lap at the wadded-up tissue crumpled in her hands. "And I haven't been at all honest with him. He has no idea what I used to look like or who I really am."

"Then tell him, Ang," Brian spoke quietly, all trace of humor gone. "Tell him what you did, all the weight you lost, all that you achieved. I *watched* you do it and I could hardly believe the magnitude of it. And I don't just mean the pounds. You were beautiful before and you're beautiful now. But what you did—how strong you are—that's all part of you, too. A good part; a part you should be proud of."

In her head, she knew he was right. But in her heart . . . "I'm just so afraid of losing him. I should have told him right away, but I just couldn't do it. And now I can't bear to give up the 'me' I see in his eyes."

She looked away, her gaze landing briefly on the image of the lumpy girl on the couch that filled the screen.

"You're not on the outside anymore, Ang. You hauled yourself inside by sheer force of will. I think James would respect and understand that and love you even more." He put a finger under her chin and tilted her face up. "I wouldn't think you'd want to marry anyone who couldn't."

⊙

VIVIEN SAT ALONE in Melanie's family room on New Year's Eve watching the big-screen TV and waiting for the ball to drop in Times Square. In her previous life she might have been there. In fact, Stone had talked her into it their first New Year's together, promising her as they'd pulled on countless layers of clothing, then walked through driving snow to stand shoulder to shoulder with thousands of other people, that it would be worth it. And at midnight when he'd kissed her in what had felt like the very epicenter of the universe at the very instant of the New Year, she'd admitted that he was right.

Tonight she couldn't have made it out of the front door, let alone to Times Square. They'd all spent the day scrubbing the house for tomorrow's brunch, and Vivien had the sore back and chapped hands to prove it. Vivien had tried to talk Mellie into letting Wilda and Carlos clean, but Melanie had already scheduled them to start "in the new year" and had refused to budge.

It was late afternoon by the time Melanie pronounced the house acceptable and told Vivien she could stop whining. Trip had departed to spend the night at a friend's house. Shelby and Melanie had sprinted upstairs to shower and dress: Shelby for the New Year's Eve party her mother would drop her off at, Melanie for the New Year's Eve shindig at the Magnolia Ballroom.

"Are you sure you won't come, Vivi?" Melanie had

asked on the way out. "The DJ's first-rate, there'll be tons of food, and it's a complete sellout, thank God!"

"I am not moving." Vivi clutched the big bowl of buttered popcorn cradled in what was left of her lap. "Ever." She snuggled deeper into the chair. "I don't even care if I make it to midnight."

"You old slug," Melanie said, leaning over to kiss Vivi's cheek. "Don't forget to keep an ear out for Shelby." She gave her daughter a stern look. "One of her friends is bringing her home, but she's required to be here no later than twelve thirty."

"It's so humiliating," Shelby complained. "No one else has a curfew on New Year's Eve. And there's nothing I could do after twelve thirty that I couldn't do before."

"I really wish you hadn't said that," Melanie replied "And there's no reason in the world to be out later than that. If you can't observe your curfew, you can't go. Period."

"Uuggghhh!" Shelby flounced out in front of her mother, her short silver party dress swirling around her thighs. If it had been possible to stomp in the strappy high heels she wore, Vivien was certain she would have. "I am so not going to torture my daughter this way," Shelby huffed as she rushed out to the garage. "These rules of yours are like from the Stone Age."

For a while after they left Vivien munched popcorn and changed channels, flipping between the buildup of performances in Times Square and anything else that grabbed her attention, letting the quiet of the house and the idea of tomorrow's implied "fresh start" soothe her.

Around ten she decided to do a last read through of her New Year's column, which she had promised to send tonight even though it wouldn't run until the paper came out on Monday. She felt slightly guilty as she carried the empty popcorn bowl to the kitchen, washed her hands in the sink, then settled back into the club chair with her laptop. Now that she was paying more attention to the details of her sister's life and had even taken over a few of her volunteer shifts in the interests of research, it had become more difficult to write Scarlett Leigh's derisive tirades. Because instead of railing at or making fun of nameless, faceless women, she now saw not only Melanie but Melanie's co-volunteers and friends when she began to rant.

The column began innocently enough with, *Happy New Year from suburbia, where I'm sure the residents have made all kinds of resolutions for the coming year. Lots of them will vow to lose weight, stop smoking, and not only join a gym but use it. Even those who are resolving to let a plastic surgeon take care of the changes they wish to make are, at least, looking to improve in some way.*

But I have to tell you there's something even more important that the adults here should consider. And it's not complicated or expensive. Any one of them could do it if only they could find the willpower.

Vivien paused to rework the next sentences, finally typing, *The parental population here needs to promise to stop hovering over their children like helicopters. Now. This minute. In other words, they need to*—here Vivien hit the Caps Lock button for emphasis—*GET A LIFE!* After another moment of thought, she added, *OF THEIR OWN!*

Oddly enough, she continued, *the problem is not rooted in a lack of education or good intentions. The biggest offenders are, in fact, grossly overeducated for their roles as parents. Did Ozzie or Harriet have a PhD? Did June Cleaver need an MBA?*

Unfortunately, this suburb, like many others, is filled with overachievers who were once highly successful in their chosen professions. Now that they have decided to become full-time mothers and over-involved fathers, they are applying their formidable brain power, energy, and competitive spirit to things that don't require any of those attributes. Like their eight-year-old's science project. Their ten-year-old's batting average. Or their sixteen-year-old's plans for the prom.

They text their children throughout the day, despite the fact that their children are not supposed to turn on their cell phones during class. Because THEY DON'T HAVE ANYTHING OF THEIR OWN TO THINK ABOUT.

They will tell you that they're much too busy taking care of their children to do anything for themselves. They are focusing on their seventeen-year-old's course assignments, SAT scores, and college applications. The act of getting a child into college can consume a good year and a half and require sedatives and sleeping aids.

And once they get their children into college their over-involvement and micromanagement continue. Because they cannot stop hovering and do not know how to land their helicopters.

Some of them actually admit to reading their children's college textbooks to help their children prepare for tests, calling up their children's guidance counselors or professors to question individual grades, and a score of other activities and actions our parents, for all their faults, would never have dreamed of engaging in.

After college they communicate with potential employers on their children's behalf. Sometimes they even go on job interviews with their children, negotiate their contracts directly with the employer, then call later to complain if their children are not promoted quickly enough.

In my heart I believe these parents mean well. They love their children and will tell you that all they want is for them to be happy. But they don't believe their children have the ability to do this on their own. Nor can they bear to allow their children to suffer from a mistake or poor choice.

And of course, if they stopped managing their children's lives, stopped competing and living vicariously through their children's achievements, what would they do all day? How would they fill their time?

Vivien winced slightly at the strident tone, but reminded herself that this was Scarlett Leigh talking and not Vivien Gray. Which, of course, was the very kind of self-deception that these hovering, helicoptering parents employed.

Once again, she read back over what she'd written, cleaned up the language, and tightened where she could. And then she concluded, *I'm not really sure how those who are honest enough to see themselves in this unflattering light might actually stop this behavior. Is there a twelve-step program? A chapter somewhere of Helicopter Parents Anonymous? Maybe we could experiment with shock therapy and provide a collar that would zap the wearer each time he or she tried to live their child's life for her. Make her decisions. Speak up inappropriately on her behalf.*

I can see that it's not easy to pull back and even harder to cease and desist. But I highly recommend it. Because this hovering business is not good for anyone. It deprives the child of the opportunity to live their own life, learn from their mistakes, and realize their potential. And for those who are doing the hovering, well, I think we all know that flying in neutral doesn't get anybody anywhere.

After signing and saving the column, Vivien sent it to John Harcourt with best wishes for a happy New Year. She still hadn't heard back from Stone after her Christmas Day message and so she sent him a quick email saying that she'd try to reach him again tomorrow and that she was thinking of him. And then she shut down her computer.

She dozed. At midnight, the shouted countdown from the television woke her, and she turned bleary eyes on the television as the ball descended the last few inches and horns blew and shouts and confetti filled the air. She roused a little as they showed couple after couple kissing in the frigid night air, and the love on the couples' faces made her want to cry.

But she must have fallen asleep instead because the next thing she heard was the slamming of the front door followed by a giggle and a very loud, though decidedly feminine belch. The clock on the cable box said one A.M.

"Hi, Vivi," Shelby cooed as she tiptoed through the kitchen and into the family room to stand, or rather sway, in front of Vivien. "Happy Yew Near," she over-enunciated, giggling when she registered her mistake. "I mean nappy Hew Year."

This was apparently even funnier, because Shelby laughed hysterically when she heard what she'd said. "Oh, shit." She dropped down onto the couch and giggled some more. "You mow what I nean."

Vivien looked at her niece and didn't feel at all good about what she saw. Her eye makeup had smeared, leaving her with a raccoonlike ring around her dark eyes, and her lipstick had been rubbed well beyond the scope of her lips in the way of a clown. The silver dress was in one piece but looked decidedly rumpled. One shoulder strap hung down over a bare arm, and there was a dark smudge just under the bust line. One of the biggest hickeys Vivien had ever seen colored the side of her slim neck.

She stood and moved closer to Shelby. "You're late and you're drunk," she observed.

Shelby opened her mouth into a great big red O of shock and surprise. "How san cou yay that?" she asked, far too gone to sound indignant.

Vivien leaned over her and sniffed. "And it smells like rum and Coke." She shook her head. "I guess some things never change."

"'S okay," Shelby murmured. "The Coke was diet." She was swaying in her seat, or at least the top half of her body was, and Vivien realized that if she let her pass out here, she might never get her upstairs. She really had no idea what to do in this situation, but she did know that she didn't want Melanie to see her daughter like this. That was not the way Melanie needed to start her new year.

Vivien didn't waste her breath berating Shelby for her behavior; there was no way anything she said right now was going to register anyway. She'd take this up with her niece in the morning; right now she had one simple goal: to get Shelby into bed before Melanie got home.

"Come on." Vivien reached down and grasped Shelby's hand, which had all the substance of a limp dish rag. The girl's head lolled back against the sofa cushions as Vivien tugged firmly, barely managing to pull Shelby to her feet. The problem was how to keep her there.

She leaned into Shelby's face, trying not to breathe in the fumes. "Come with me," she said firmly as she tugged. "Come on!" She repeated the command and tugged again. Shelby's eyes rolled back in her head and she swayed precariously. "Oh, no, you don't," Vivien said. "Come on, lean on me. Just one foot at a time."

Somehow she got Shelby to the foot of the back stairs, but it was slow going, kind of like herding fish. There she wrapped an arm around Shelby's waist for leverage and placed Shelby's hand on the handrail. "Hold on to that. I'll hold on to you."

"Hmmmmm."

"Open your eyes, Shelby, and step up." Taking as much of Shelby's weight against herself as she could, Vivien got her niece up one step and then another. "Tomorrow you're going to tell me how you got in this condition and who's been manhandling you."

"Rum and Coke," she sighed, "isss soooo good."

It took an eternity, but finally they were all the way upstairs. Vivi had originally thought to take Shelby into the bathroom and let her use the toilet, maybe even put her under the shower, but she rejected all of those plans now as too difficult and too time-consuming.

"To bed with you," she huffed as she wrangled the girl into her room, propped her against the wall while she swept the debris off the girl's bed and skimmed the comforter back. Then she got her across the room, sat her down on her bed, and pulled the dress up over her head, leaving her in her thong. Out of breath, Vivien plucked off the silver high heels, managed to slide a nightgown over her head then pushed Shelby back onto her pillows and pulled the covers up to Shelby's chin. For the briefest of moments she considered getting some aspirin and shoving them down her throat, but thought better of it. She hoped this was the girl's first brush with alcohol and she wanted the negatives, as in the hangover she was bound to have when she woke up, to be memorable. Shelby was already snoring lightly by the time Vivien had picked the dress up off the floor and laid it on the chair.

In the hallway, Vivi felt the garage door open beneath her, the loud noise and vibration impossible to miss. Unless one had had too many rum and Diet Cokes.

Because she didn't want to look her sister in the eye and lie outright, and because she wanted to read Shelby the riot act herself before deciding what to say to Melanie, Vivien tiptoed to her own room, turned out the light, and gently closed the door.

25

R UTH WOKE UP early on New Year's Day. Beside her, Ira slept peacefully, his breathing regular and a half smile on his face. Like everything that her husband did lately, this really pissed her off.

They'd gone to the Kaminskis' last night as they had pretty much every New Year's Eve since they'd moved to Atlanta, and Ruth had enjoyed the excuse to get dressed up, put on a little jewelry, and spend the evening schmoozing with old friends. What she hadn't enjoyed was pretending that she and Ira were fine when everything about their marriage was as not fine as it was possible to get.

The thing was that Ruth, who had always prided herself on making decisions and acting on them quickly, just couldn't figure out what to do. She simply couldn't accept his refusal to even entertain the offer for Bagel Baron that would have freed them financially. Nor could she believe he hadn't so much as attended a single ballroom dance class. But neither could she bring herself to leave him as she'd threatened. Because no matter how brightly her anger burned, she couldn't imagine her life without him.

Worst of all, she felt as if she'd lost her best friend, the person with whom she'd shared both good and bad, with whom she'd discussed everything from the lump their daughter had found in her breast to how often they really wanted the Chemlawn people to come.

In a way, though she was careful not to say this to anyone, she felt as if Ira had died. Or at least the Ira she had always known and loved and thought she understood. And she mourned what she now realized she'd taken for granted. Because whatever happened now, even if they somehow found a way to deal with everything and go on, their lives and their relationship would never again be the same. And neither, she was afraid, would her feelings for him.

Ruth got out of bed careful not to wake him, not so much out of courtesy but because she didn't want to speak to him. After the first week she'd spent in the guest room she'd moved back into their bed because if she wasn't leaving, what was the point? The most intelligent thing Ira had done since she'd moved back was to not touch her. She didn't see how she could deal with that.

In the master bathroom, she showered and put on her favorite robe, one Ira and the kids had given her one long ago Mother's Day. The colors had faded over the years and the fabric had pilled, but it was what her marriage had once been—warm and cozy and molded to her shape.

It was too early to dress, so she brushed out her hair and applied her makeup, then went into the kitchen to put on a pot of coffee.

An hour later she had read the paper and assembled a blintz soufflé to take to Melanie's. The two dozen bagels she'd had delivered sat, still warm, in the large brown paper bags that carried the Bagel Baron logo.

She heard Ira get up and braced herself for his company; she had to work on schooling her reactions now,

smooth down the anger, try not to snap. But instead of
coming into the kitchen to share coffee and the newspaper as he once automatically would have, he went into his
home office and closed the door.

"Hmmph!" The soufflé went into the oven with a little more force than necessary. As she set the timer and
tidied the kitchen, she told herself it was just as well, that
she didn't really want to talk with the old fool anyway.
Nonetheless, she couldn't quite bring herself to ignore
the insult completely. And so on her way back to the bedroom, she stopped in front of his office door and rapped
loudly.

She saw the flare of irritation in his eyes when she
stepped inside uninvited and imagined her gaze telegraphed the same. It took real effort to keep the affront
she felt out of her voice. "We're expected at the Jacksons' at eleven o'clock. I'll set out your khakis and blue
blazer."

He nodded and she knew he considered her "dis-
missed." His gaze strayed to the iPhone he held in one
hand. Unlike other men his age, Ira had embraced new
technology, which now connected him to work like an
electronic umbilical cord. She'd grown to hate the thing
and had thought up all sorts of inventive ways to make
it disappear.

Perversely, she walked all the way in and stopped
directly in front of his desk, standing there until his
thumb stopped scrolling and he raised his gaze from the
screen. He, too, wore a robe and his face was unshaven.
His reading glasses sat on top of a stack of papers.

"What?" he asked.

She folded her arms in front of her and said, "I'd like to
leave by ten forty-five."

He nodded and glanced back down at the iPhone
screen.

"And I expect you to put forth some effort while we're there. No going outside to make or take phone calls. No texting. No checking email while people are talking to you. No looking bored. Please at least pretend like you're enjoying yourself."

"I do enjoy Melanie and the kids," Ira said. "I'd never be rude to them."

It was Ruth's turn to raise an eyebrow. She had lost track of how often his gaze strayed to that blasted phone in any given five-minute period. She did not want Melanie insulted.

"I'm glad to hear it," she said. "Because if I catch you doing any of those things, I'm going to find a sledgehammer and smash that stupid phone to smithereens."

℩

MELANIE FLITTED AROUND the house adjusting furniture, fluffing pillows, and wiping down surfaces that were already clean. Normally, New Year's Day brunch would have included the whole family as well as Evangeline, who would cook greens for health and black-eyed peas for luck, both of which were served with her justifiably famous cornbread. But her parents weren't invited and therefore Evangeline wasn't available. In an apparent effort to remain neutral, Ham and Judy and their kids had accepted an invitation from Judy's parents in Macon.

Because they were a small group—just her and the kids, Vivi, Clay, and the Melnicks—she'd decided that they might as well sit together at the dining room table and had gladly accepted Ruth's offer of bagels and a blintz soufflé. If ever a year demanded to be different, it was this one.

Checking her watch, Melanie got out pans for the cheese eggs she planned to make and preheated the oven for the sausage casserole she'd already prepared. Not exactly a kosher meal, she thought with a smile, but Ruth had assured her it didn't matter.

Occasionally she glanced up the back stairs or paused to listen for sounds from above. Vivien had gone up to wake Shelby, who'd already been asleep when Melanie got home last night. But Vivi had been in Shelby's room for some time now and there'd been no clanging of pots and pans. In fact it was weirdly quiet, and neither of them had come out.

Melanie pondered this as she put the coffee on, added fresh water to the teakettle, and took out a selection of tea bags. The front door opened and Trip appeared back from his sleepover; he was wearing the clothes he'd left in yesterday, there was stubble on his fifteen-year-old jaw and cheeks, and his eyes were only partially open.

"Happy New Year, sweetie," Melanie said, having to reach up to give her baby a peck on the cheek, a fact that never ceased to surprise her. "Why don't you jump in the shower and wake up the rest of the way? I put out khakis and a polo shirt for you. Clay and the Melnicks will be here in about twenty minutes."

He yawned and nodded and went upstairs. A few moments later she heard his shower come on. But there was still that strange silence up in Shelby's room.

Walking upstairs, she hesitated in front of Shelby's closed bedroom door and pressed her ear against the wood. She could hear Vivien's voice, quite emphatic, but not what was said. Curious and unsure whether there was cause for concern, she was taken by surprise when the door against which she was leaning opened inward.

"I was just getting ready to knock," she stammered, stealing a look at her daughter, who was still huddled under her blankets though clearly awake. She turned to Vivi. "Is everything all right?"

Shelby gave a half moan and curled up on her side.

"What's wrong? Is she sick?" Melanie started to rush into the room and over to the bed, but Vivien stopped her.

"She's just overtired from staying up so late last night. And I think she has a bit of a headache. I gave her a couple of aspirin. She's fine."

Melanie glanced at her daughter.

"I don't feel good," Shelby said, looking at a spot somewhere between Vivien and her mother. "I don't think I can—"

"Don't worry about a thing," Vivien interrupted, taking Melanie by the shoulders, turning her around, and pushing her gently out of the room. "I'm going to help Shelby get dressed. Really, I think a nice cold shower is all she needs."

Shelby's groan was louder this time.

Vivien smiled a Machiavellian smile that Melanie remembered from their childhood. Good things had not always come of it.

"Really, Mel, go ahead and take care of whatever you need to. Shelby and I will be down in fifteen minutes."

Melanie looked at her sister and then at her daughter. It was clear something was up, but Vivien shook her head slightly and mouthed, "trust me." And oddly enough, she did.

It hadn't been easy, but fifteen minutes later Vivien did, in fact, guide Shelby down the stairs and into the kitchen where Ruth and Melanie were fussing with the food and Clay Alexander was mixing a pitcher of mimosas.

At Vivi's nudge, Shelby smiled wanly and hugged Clay, Ruth, and Ira hello before slumping onto a barstool between Trip and Ira.

"Are you all right?" Both Ruth and Melanie asked in a motherly chorus. Melanie leaned across the counter to put

the back of her hand to Shelby's forehead. "You don't feel
like you've got a temperature."

"Do you need to go back to bed, Shel?" Clay asked as
he poured a mimosa into a champagne glass for Melanie.

Vivien bristled. She was rumpled and water stained
from her tussle with Shelby while he was perfectly turned
out in chinos and an open-collared shirt with a trim alli-
gator belt at his waist. She took exception to how comfortable he looked in Melanie's kitchen and how easily he
assumed the father-figure role. She'd read Shelby the riot
act and risked life and limb to get her down here; she was
not about to allow Clay Alexander to let her off the hook.

"She's fine," Vivien said. "Nothing to worry about."

"Duly noted." Clay's smile was both amused and superior. As they carried their plates into the dining room, he
claimed the head of the table and throughout the meal,
he played genial host, pulling Ira and Trip into a debate
about that day's bowl games and praising Ruth's blintz
dish. "They're delicious," he said smoothly. "And unbe-
lievably light."

Ruth blushed with pleasure. And regardless of what
Melanie said, her sister did not seem immune, either.
Irritated, Vivi kept an eye on Shelby, ready to provide
another "come to Jesus" meeting if necessary, but as the
meal progressed Shelby's eyes became less glassy and she
began to join in the conversation. When Melanie stopped
eyeing her daughter with concern, Vivi figured the aspirin and glasses of orange juice must have kicked in.

A cell phone rang and they all looked up from their
plates. Ira pulled his iPhone out of his pocket and glanced
at the screen. "I'm sorry, but I have to take this," he said
as he left the table.

"Aaach." Ruth's face flushed as she placed her fork on
her plate. Vivien didn't understand why Ira taking a call

was such a big deal, but then what she didn't know about Ira and Ruth Melnick could fill a couple of libraries.

"How was the party last night?" Melanie asked Shelby.

Shelby stopped chewing. With all eyes now on her she swallowed. "Good. It was, um, good." She nodded her head for emphasis.

"You must have been pretty wiped out. You were already asleep when I got back from the studio."

Shelby blinked rapidly and ran a finger underneath the rim of her turtleneck. "Yeah. I was . . . tired."

Ruth looked between the two of them. So did Clay.

Vivien piped in. "You didn't say how the party at Magnolia was, Mel. Did you have a good crowd?"

"Yes, thank goodness." Successfully distracted, Melanie smiled. "We had one hundred fifty people, even more than had RSVP'd. I'd been so worried we wouldn't break even, but it was a great way to end the year."

"What did you and Josh do last night?" Clay asked Trip, who'd been plowing his way through the mounds of food on his plate.

"Ordered pizza. Played *Call of Duty*." The question answered, Trip turned his attention back to his plate. Vivi had counted three trips to the buffet. Vivi was sure of this because she'd been right behind him.

Melanie seemed to realize how vague Shelby's answer had been and circled back to the topic. "Who all was at the party, Shel? What did Mrs. Barrett serve?"

Vivien had to bite back the "You mean, other than the rum and Coke?" that sprang to her lips. But, of course, it was unlikely the mixed drinks had been an official part of the menu. Shelby had refused to tell her who had supplied the alcohol.

Before Shelby could come up with an answer to the first questions, Melanie asked, "Was Ty there?"

Shelby blushed, and Vivien thought, *Bingo!* remembering the boy from the Pemberton football game.

"Yes," Shelby finally responded. "He, um, asked me to the prom."

"That's great, sweetie," Melanie said, apparently unaware of the boy's reputation. "When is it again?"

"The middle of March," Shelby said.

"Perfect," Melanie said, and Vivien wondered if she'd made a mistake in hiding Shelby's transgression. If Melanie knew that Shelby had come home drunk, would she be as pleased about Shelby's date? Would it have made her watch Shelby as carefully as someone apparently needed to? "That leaves lots of time to find a really great dress," Melanie said.

"I thought maybe Clay could take me shopping," Shelby said.

Vivien's head snapped up. She'd been so busy second-guessing herself she'd only been half listening. "What did she say?"

Melanie laughed. "She wants Clay to help her find a dress." Seeing Vivi and Ruth's doubtful looks, she explained, "Clay has the best taste of anyone I've ever known, plus he's dated two or three Miss Georgias and one supermodel. He's helped me choose pretty much every ball gown and all of the campaign wardrobes I've ever bought. He knows all the best boutiques."

Clay smiled; was she just imagining that it was taunting? "You can come with us if you want, Vivi. We could make a few stops at some of the better maternity shops."

"Thanks," she said, the nature of his smile now confirmed. "I may take you up on that." She assumed his fashion prowess was overstated, but spending more time with him might yield answers, assuming she ever figured out the right questions.

Clay clanged a knife against the champagne glass that

held what remained of his mimosa. "Since the new year seems like the right time to share new things, I have an announcement to make."

Everyone at the table fell silent. Clay's gaze sought Melanie's.

"J.J.'s state house seat is coming open," he said. "And I've been asked to run for it."

Clay continued to watch Melanie. "What do you think, Mel? Do you think I should do it?"

Melanie's eye's shone with unshed tears as they often did when J.J.'s name came up. But Vivien had no idea whether they were tears of sadness or of joy. Vivi, who'd been watching Clay usurp more and more of what had been J.J.'s, was pretty creeped out.

"I think J.J. would be pleased," Melanie said finally "He always said no one was more in synch with what drove him politically than you." She smiled softly despite the sheen of tears. "There's a certain symmetry in having his best friend carry on what he began."

Vivien studied Clay Alexander, once again looking for some clue to what drove him. Professor Sturgess claimed Clay was most comfortable in the background, but now that J.J. was gone, he seemed prepared to move front and center. Had he been chomping at the bit while J.J. was alive, angling for an opportunity? Had J.J. been an obstacle to his own ambitions?

"You know, I've been trying to figure out why you left Asheville, where you were already running statewide campaigns, to run J.J.'s first campaign," Vivien said.

He looked at her as if he didn't understand what she was asking.

"I mean it was a step backward, wasn't it?" Vivi asked. "In political terms?"

Clay dabbed at the corner of his mouth with his napkin, and Vivien sensed him regrouping. "J.J. was an old

friend," he finally said. "And I knew he had what it took
to get elected to a lot more than a county commission
seat." He looked over at Melanie, adding, "And, of course,
there were other incentives. I'm sure Mel would confirm
that J.J. was not an easy man to say no to."

Vivien watched Clay carefully. He was so smooth that
anything he said sounded plausible; yet there was always
some sort of subtext underlying his words.

"Truthfully," he said now. "I don't see how that would
be any bigger a step backward than leaving a network
television job in New York to come back to Atlanta and
have a baby."

Melanie's eyes flashed surprise, but Vivien actually
appreciated the lack of subtlety. It was hard to land a
good punch when you were fighting with gloves on.

She didn't get a chance to strike back because Ira chose
that moment to return to the table. "Sorry," he said, running a hand through his gray hair. "There was a mechanical breakdown at the Alpharetta plant, and I had to track
down the head of our maintenance department."

"That's because no one but Ira can handle anything
at his company," Ruth said. "After all, he *is* the Bagel
Baron."

"My wife seems to forget that it's those kinds of efforts
that feed and clothe all of us," Ira said.

"And my husband seems to forget that we already
have more than enough food and clothing. And that if he
would even talk to the people who want to buy his company, we'd have enough food and clothing for the rest of
our lives. Not to mention actual *lives*."

The two glared across the table at each other; everyone
else shifted uncomfortably in their seats.

"More coffee?" Melanie reached for the carafe she'd set
on the table and held it up, but nobody took her up on it.

"I just can't get it through his thick head that there

could be more to life than running that damned company."
Ruth grimaced in an apparent effort to hold back tears.
"I'm so tired of trying to make him 'get' it. I don't even
see the point of being married anymore." She grabbed her
linen napkin and pressed it to one eye, held it there.

"Ruth, you're embarrassing yourself," Ira said. "And
everyone else, too."

Slowly Ruth lowered the napkin. The sheen of tears was
unmistakable, but not a single one was allowed to fall.

"Well, I'd rather be embarrassing than . . ." Ruth
paused, apparently looking for the right word and finally
coming up with "Obtuse!"

It wasn't a word one would expect to hear from Ruth
Melnick, but Vivien thought it was pretty dead-on. She
felt a grudging admiration for this woman who didn't
like her. At least she was speaking out and trying to get
what she wanted.

Ira, who also seemed surprised by Ruth's word choice,
stared at his wife as if he didn't recognize her, his face awash
with confusion. Vivien leaned closer and said, "Obtuse
means simpleminded, thickheaded, dull-witted . . ."

"Vivi!" Melanie shushed her even as she put an arm
around Ruth.

"I know what obtuse means!" Ira snapped. "I just don't
know how I'm supposed to deal with her. She's always
kvetching and complaining these days; she won't let this
thing go."

"Maybe you should try actually listening to what she's
telling you," Vivien suggested. "Maybe she has a valid
point."

Clay, the consummate politician, excused himself
and led Trip and Shelby down to the basement to watch
the game.

Melanie helped Ruth stand and then directed a lot of
head movement and eye action Vivi's way; she was not

any better at it than Evangeline. Vivi shrugged, palms up. "How many syllables? Is it a movie or a book title?"

Melanie gave up on the charades. "Vivi, please take Ruth to the bathroom so that she can freshen up. I'd like to have a word with Ira."

"Oh!" Vivi stood and walked around the table. "Sure." She took Ruth by the shoulders and realized just how distraught Ruth must be when the older woman aimed a grateful look her way. "Come on, Ruth," she murmured as they walked down the hall. "Mellie will set him straight."

When she and Ira were alone at the table and the guest bath door had clicked shut, Melanie pulled out the chair next to Ira and sank into it. He looked at her warily, but there was no fight left in him. As she watched, his normal buoyancy seeped out of him like air escaping a punctured tire. He drew a deep breath and let it out slowly. "You see what I'm dealing with here," he said more quietly than she had ever heard him speak. "I don't know what I'm supposed to do."

"I can't really tell you that, Ira," Melanie said carefully. "But if you love her, you need to really listen to what she's saying to you."

"I know what she's saying. She wants me to sell the business and retire. I understand. But she doesn't. She knows me better than anybody, and she still doesn't understand that if I'm not the Bagel Baron, I'm nobody." He looked away and drew another breath. "I'm just some old altakaka who was somebody once. I'd rather die than be that."

"Ira you're going to die whether you're the Bagel Baron or the incredibly smart businessman who created the Bagel Baron and is now living happily off the proceeds. But the bottom line is either way you're going to die. And I have a little insight about that."

She felt her own eyes well as she let herself think about J.J., something she'd been trying not to do all morning. "You really never know how much time you have left with the people you love. They can be gone in an instant. Losing someone you love is . . . unbearable. But throwing them away? I can't even imagine how horrible that must feel."

She reached out her arms and hugged Ira Melnick and felt whatever air had remained rush out of him. Eyes closed they rocked gently for a moment. When they separated, she left her hand on his arm and looked directly into his eyes. "She's an incredibly good woman. And she's trying to do what she thinks is best for both of you. Don't just blow her off, Ira. It's not that easy to find someone we can really love and who loves us."

Ira nodded and gave her shoulder a fatherly squeeze. "You're a good girl, Melanie. Thank you for the brunch." He stood slowly, straightening his shoulders. "Could you see if Ruth is ready to go?"

○,

"WELL, THAT WAS quite a kickoff to the new year," Vivien observed as they stood on the front walk watching the Melnicks drive off.

"It certainly was," Melanie agreed. "I hope they can work things out."

The day was clear and cold, the sky a gentle blue. The pansies in the matching pots that bracketed the front door provided a welcome pop of color.

"Well, I learned a few things today," Vivien said.

"Oh?"

"I learned that even someone as seemingly transparent as Ruth Melnick is not really what they seem."

"Is that right?"

"Yep," Vivi said with a smile. "To put it in candy terms, I used to think Ruth was just a jawbreaker. Now I know that she's actually a Tootsie Roll Pop. All hard and crunchy on the outside, but with a soft chewy center."

Melanie laughed as they stared out over the sleeping lawn and the naked limbs of the trees. The sun on their faces was weak but welcome. "Well, you're a bit of a Tootsie Roll Pop yourself," Melanie said. "You've got a lot more heart than you like to let on."

"Oh?" Vivien asked as they went back inside, stopping in the dining room to begin to gather up coffee cups and dessert plates.

"Yeah," Melanie said. "And I think you're going to be a great mother, too."

They carried what they could to the kitchen, where Melanie prepared to load the dishwasher while Vivi began to wrap and put away food. "God, I hope you're not just saying that," Vivien said. "Because I'll be happy if I can be even half as good at it as you."

26

IN EARLY JANUARY not long after Wednesday-night belly-dancing classes resumed, two journalists, a reporter and his cameraman, were abducted from a small village to the north of Kabul. The initial report was sketchy and even the networks didn't seem sure whose people were missing for a tense twenty-four hours.

Vivien left messages on Stone's cell phone but couldn't reach him, which only frightened her further. She didn't eat or sleep until the call from Marty came before dawn the following morning. "It's not Stone," were his first words and so great was Vivi's relief that she didn't hear anything that came afterward.

"Wait. Go back and start over," she said shakily. "I wasn't . . . I couldn't listen."

With her eyes closed and her attention now split between Marty's voice and the act of drawing and releasing air from her lungs, she tried to focus on the details, but the only thing really going through her brain was, "Thank God! Thank God! Thank God!" and "It's not him! It's not him! It's not him!"

"Anyway," Marty was saying when she was finally able to process words again, "he was right near the village, but his guide had heard something was up and got him and Jake the hell out of there." As Vivien knew, this was not always the case with the guides the journalists depended upon so heavily. Even the best of them were somewhat conflicted. The journalists' money was important, but sometimes not as important as the guide's family connections or unspoken political affiliations.

"Obviously, he'll be following the story. It was Deke Slater from CCN and his cameraman who were taken. Deke and Stone go way back. Stone asked me to tell you not to worry and that he'll get messages out when he does his live shots, but he's not going to be able to reach you until he's back in Kabul."

Vivi heard Marty stop talking but she was still several beats behind. Because now she was thinking about how she would have felt if she'd not only lost Stone but had allowed him to die without ever knowing he'd fathered their child. Her hand stole to her stomach as it often seemed to now of its own accord. At just over six months, her stomach was well on its way to the watermelon stage, already football shaped and surprisingly firm. The baby seemed to have a trampoline in there with it; right now, with all her juices stirred up, the acrobatics felt of the extreme variety.

"Are you there, Vivi?" She could tell by Marty's tone that she hadn't responded again when it was her turn to speak.

"Yes, sorry. I should be used to this by now, but I've been so worried."

"I know. It's some scary shit," Marty agreed. "A darkened parking garage is about as far out on the line as I'm prepared to go."

Vivien would have liked to acknowledge the joke, but

her sense of humor had deserted her completely when those first confused reports had started to filter out of Afghanistan.

"Stone's worried, too. But not about himself."

This time Vivien's lack of response was intentional.

"He wants me to come check on you. He's convinced something's wrong."

This time Marty waited her out; she'd forgotten that he was almost as good at that as she was. "Well, he's wrong. I'm fine. Couldn't be better. You are not my mother, and you don't need to check on me."

"How is Caroline?" he asked now, and she offered up a little prayer of thanks that he hadn't already spoken to her. "Maybe I should give her a call and make sure that's true."

Vivien gritted her teeth. That was all she needed, Caroline having an audience to pour out her disappointment in Vivien to. Not to mention her pregnancy. "I'm not speaking to my mother at the moment." If she started trying to prevent Marty from making contact it would be the first thing he'd do; just as she would if their positions were reversed. "But feel free to give her a call. I'm sure she'd love to have someone to complain about me to."

There was a pause. "Seriously, Vivi. You know you can call me anytime if you want to talk or need anything." His voice sort of trailed off in embarrassment, but Vivi was touched by his sincerity.

"Thanks, Marty. I know and I appreciate that. I'm going to have to go, but before I do I'd like to hear one story about Regina Matthews looking bad."

"Hmmmmm, I don't know," he teased. "She's looking awfully good. Do you want me to make one up?"

"I'll get back to you on that," she said and as they said good-bye she was surprised to realize she was nowhere near as upset about Regina Matthew's competence as she should have been.

This time when she got through to Stone's voice mail she couldn't hide how worried she'd been. "I'm so sorry about Deke and Jonathan." She hesitated, trying to get her emotions under control, but her voice broke midsentence and she couldn't seem to stop the waver in it. "I know it's selfish, but I've been thanking God it wasn't you." She paused, swallowed. "I'm counting on you to come back to me," she said. "I won't accept anything else."

A few mornings later Vivien dallied over her morning tea in her robe and slippers waiting for Melanie to leave for the Magnolia Ballroom, where she was slated to begin teaching the new cardio/salsa exercise class she'd added to the weekday schedule.

"What are you doing today?" Melanie asked as she searched the counter first for her keys and then once she'd located them, for her cell phone.

"Nothing much. Maybe a few errands. Do you mind if I take the RAV?" She yawned as if it didn't matter either way.

"Of course not." Melanie finally found the phone in the pocket of her jacket. "Any special requests for dinner?"

"No. But I'll take care of it."

"You?" Melanie stopped in her tracks. "You're going to cook?" She didn't look as happy about that as someone who'd been carrying the load single-handedly at meal-time might.

"I can't guarantee cooking," Vivi said. "But I can guarantee food. And if you need me to handle kid pickup or anything, just call me on my cell."

"Wow," Melanie said. "You mean I just come home and walk in the door and food will be on the table?" The note of wonder in her voice made Vivien realize that she should have offered this long ago.

"That's the plan," she said.

"Wow," Melanie said again as she walked out the

kitchen door to the minivan. A large smile was spread across her face.

As the garage door closed behind her sister, Vivien banished her guilt over her deception. Torn between going through J.J.'s phone and credit card bills and getting dressed for her appointment with Grady Hollis, who'd been the president of Sigma Sigma Fraternity when Clay and J.J were at Georgia, she chose a shower and makeup.

Dressed in the most businesslike of her maternity clothes, she made her way downstairs and out to the car, telling herself that if her suspicions about Clay playing some sort of role in or hiding information about J.J.'s death proved true, there'd be nothing to apologize for. If she was wrong, Melanie need never know she'd asked the first question.

By the time she turned south on Highway 400 for the drive to Macon, the morning rush was over. An hour and forty-five minutes later, after only a few wrong turns, she found the law office of Hollis & Hollis in downtown Macon. A receptionist invited her to take a seat, and she'd barely sunk into the cracked leather-backed chair she was shown to when Grady Hollis came out to greet her. The attorney had the bulk of a former athlete who'd run up against the wall of middle age, a receding hairline, and an easy smile. "Good ole boy" could have been stamped in gilt letters on his gleaming forehead just as surely as Hollis & Hollis was stenciled on the front door.

His handshake was firm but not bone crushing and as she followed him back to his office he chatted amiably, though she could feel his curiosity simmering just beneath his jovial surface.

"So you're Melanie's sister? I sure can see the resemblance," he said. "In fact, when I first saw that video on YouTube I thought . . ." His voice trailed off as he realized what he'd said.

"That's all right," Vivi said. "I don't think there's a man, woman, or child in this country who didn't see me take that bullet. It wasn't exactly my proudest moment."

He laughed. "I get that," he said, looking her up and down. "I didn't realize from the video that you were pregnant. I guess it's actually a lucky thing that bullet hit you where it did."

Vivien realized with a start how right he was. Her first thought was always of the embarrassment that went along with the shooting. She hadn't really stopped and thought what might have happened to the baby she hadn't known she was carrying, if the bullet had entered from the front. "Good point. I'll have to remember that next time I'm feeling like a moron for being caught in the wrong place at the wrong time."

Sitting back in his chair, he steepled his beefy hands in his lap and asked, "So how are Melanie and the kids? I haven't seen them since the funeral."

"They're doing as well as can be expected," Vivi said. "It takes a while to bounce back from a loss like that. And, of course, it was so unexpected," she said, making it both a statement and a question.

"Yeah. I couldn't believe it when I heard," Grady said. "J.J. was practically born with a rifle in his hands. He grew up hunting with his uncles." Grady shook his head. "Terrible thing all round."

Vivien nodded her agreement, then allowed a bit of silence in hope that Grady would fill it, but the attorney just looked at her expectantly.

"As I mentioned on the phone, I'm doing a small documentary on up-and-coming politicians cut down in their prime," she said, sticking to a cover story similar to the one she'd used on Professor Sturgess. "It's going to be dedicated to J.J." She noticed that her lies were getting more outrageous, but Grady nodded approval.

"I wondered if you could tell me about J.J. in college. You know, your perspective as the president of his fraternity."

Grady nodded again and sat a little straighter in his chair. "Well," he began, "J.J. was a real classy guy and really motivated. Hell, he knew he wanted a career in politics before the rest of us had the first idea what we wanted to be when we grew up. Well, I mean I knew I was expected to go into law like my daddy, but I can't say I was particularly passionate about it, you know?"

"I spoke with one of J.J's professors, who said the same thing."

"Yeah, the rest of us would be sitting around the dining room talking trash to each other or going on about girls and who got lucky. J.J.'d be talking about the electoral college and the importance of being involved in the political process." He shook his head. "It was like a religion to him. I mean he lived and breathed that stuff."

"Clay Alexander was really into all that, too, wasn't he?"

A tiny flicker of discomfort registered in Grady Hollis's eyes. "Yeah," he said.

Vivien waited for more, but that was it.

"He and Clay pledged Sigma Sigma at the same time, didn't they?"

Grady nodded, but she could feel him treading carefully, like he'd shown up for a beach party and all of the sudden noticed that the sand was strewn with mine fields.

"They were good friends, right?" Vivi tried again. "Clay ran J.J.'s winning campaign for student council president?"

His earlier expansiveness had all but disappeared at the mention of Clay Alexander. "Yes, they were real tight," he finally said. "And Clay did run that campaign." He

paused for a moment and she had the sense of a rat looking for a way off a sinking ship. "It was a real feather
in Sigma's cap to have a brother as president." He drew
a breath and perked up a bit, apparently thinking he'd
sniffed out an escape route. "Yep, J.J.'s win made us real
visible. I remember one time . . ."

His relief at finding a way off the topic she'd introduced was palpable, but Vivien wasn't having it. "They
had some sort of falling-out, didn't they?" Vivien prodded.
"I understand Clay dropped out of Sigma Sigma over it."

"Yes," Grady admitted, not looking at all happy about
it. "It was our senior year," he said. "Not too long after
J.J. took office their friendship was just . . . over." He
looked pointedly down at his watch, and she knew she
was running out of time to get the answers she'd come for.

"That seems odd, doesn't it?" Vivi asked as nonchalantly as she could. "I mean why would J.J. get rid of the
person responsible for helping him get elected?"

"Well, I don't know that it was actually a question of
J.J. getting rid of Clay," he said, and she could feel how
carefully he was considering his words. As if she were a
judge or jury that he had to tiptoe around.

"So you're saying Clay left of his own free will?" Vivien
pondered that for a minute, trying to understand. "That
seems even odder. That Clay would have gone to all that
effort to get J.J. elected and then just . . . bow out." She
looked up, making eye contact and holding his gaze.
"Wouldn't he have wanted to be involved in the admin-
istration? Or reaped some sort of benefit from what he'd
helped make happen?"

For such a big man, Grady Hollis was looking mighty
small. But Vivi didn't care how tiny he got; she was not
leaving without . . . something. "There must have been
some reason why he would disassociate himself from the

best friend whom he'd helped get elected." She held his gaze, refusing to let go. "And I have a feeling you know what that reason was."

For a moment she was afraid that he'd wiggle out of answering, that somehow he'd be able to get a signal to his secretary to buzz him or some such thing. But a bead of sweat popped out on his already shiny forehead. "You can make it off the record, if you'd like." This was an easy promise, since there was no actual record to go on.

He blinked and finally spoke. "Well, it's a little strange saying this to Melanie's sister, but everyone always speculated that there was some kind of . . . triangle going on."

Vivien's surprise must have shown on her face because he quickly added, "No, I don't mean like something kinky sexual or anything. A lot of the guys just thought that J.J. wasn't the only one interested in Melanie."

He paused, and Vivien felt a small glimmer of excitement at having corroboration of at least part of her theory.

"Clay and J.J.'s friendship revolved around this ongoing . . . competition. Everything from who bagged the biggest deer to their grades to how many votes they got in an election. I kind of thought maybe they tussled over Melanie and Clay got pissed off that he lost. Or maybe he just got tired of always coming in second."

Wasn't this what she'd been thinking all along? That Clay coveted J.J.'s life and was secretly in love with Melanie? If he'd been feeling that way since college, which was some twenty-odd years ago, could the day have come when he just had to do something about it? Had Clay Alexander's frustration and jealousy somehow led to J.J.'s death?

"That's interesting," she said, careful not to look shocked or judgmental, two reactions guaranteed to shut an interview subject down. "But if that's true and Clay's jealousy, or whatever we want to call it, led him to break off the friendship and leave the fraternity and all, why would he come to Atlanta to be J.J.'s campaign manager? And why would J.J. want him to?"

"That," Grady said as he looked pointedly this time at his watch, signaling that the interview was over, "is a very good question." And one, Vivien discovered as he summarily ended their appointment, Grady Hollis was either unwilling or unable to answer.

On the way back to Atlanta, Vivi picked up a voice mail from Matt Glazer, who apparently didn't yet realize that he was the last person in the universe she intended to take a call from. "Hi, Vivi." His tone was friendly, conversational as if he had not exposed her to public humiliation and ridicule in print on Christmas Day. "Just wanted you to know how glad I was to hear it wasn't Stone who went missing." There was a pause and then, "You are still seeing Stone, aren't you? I'm assuming he's the father of your child?"

There was a small laugh. "I really wish you'd call and verify that. Along with a few other things. You seem to think I'm not a serious journalist," the message went on. "But I can sniff out a story as well as the next reporter, and you have become really interesting to me."

Vivien gritted her teeth through his next exaggerated pause. He ended his message with, "Your parents seem to understand my influence as well as the size and makeup of my readership." A smile came into his voice. "They've invited me to a small, intimate gathering at their home. Maybe we can catch up with each other there. Or you could go ahead and give me a call now."

Vivien was tempted to call him back and tell him she'd see him in hell before she'd see him at Magnolia Hall, but she managed to restrain herself. She didn't like the idea of him all pumped up about investigating her, but she disliked the idea of sucking up to him as her parents had even more.

For now she'd just try to stay out of his way. If she was lucky, he'd find someone else to torture. Or some social climbers who would be thrilled to see their names in his column.

27

By the middle of January, Vivien could no longer remember when Wednesday night didn't mean the Magnolia Ballroom and belly dance. Though she didn't intend to admit it, she actually looked forward to the hour with Naranya and crew. Afterward she and Ruth and Angela might linger with Melanie until it was time to close up the studio; other times they came early and sipped soft drinks in the kitchen while they dished about whatever was on their minds. She and Ruth weren't exactly BFFs, but they kept the sniping to a minimum.

Of course, there were things she simply couldn't do, given her rapidly expanding stomach and ever-changing center of gravity, but Dr. Gilbert had approved belly dancing as a low-impact form of exercise that could help make her labor easier. Vivi intended to keep at it even after the chiffon hip scarf could no longer be tied.

Tonight they'd brought Trip with them and handed him over to James Wesley in the parking lot for their "guys' night out." Angela's fiancé was every bit as good-looking as his famous father, and he had a low-key charm that set everyone at ease. The looks he shot Angela were adoring; those she sent in return were tinged with an odd sort of hesitancy that the reporter in Vivi wanted to understand.

"Thanks so much for setting this up," Melanie said to Angela as James and Trip drove off. "He rushed home from school to do his homework so he'd be free to go. I haven't seen him this excited about anything for a long time."

"I'm glad someone who wanted to be there got to go," Angela said. "I'm sure they'll all have a blast."

Inside, they fell into a jagged line with Sally, Lourdes, and the Shipley sisters, who were still trading stories about the holidays. Three newbies, here for a free trial class, spread out behind them. Naranya's golden skin was still burnished from her cruise, and her dark hair cascaded down her back. Smiling, she started the music and waited for them to tie on their hip scarves.

"All right, everyone," she said when their eyes were on her. "We begin with the stretching. You old-timers you know what to do. I weel move to the back so the new ones can see me."

They completed the stretches in near silence and then began the series of isolation exercises. Groans and giggles arose from behind them, and Vivi remembered just how foreign these moves had once seemed.

"You must be so relieved Stone's all right," Angela said to Vivien as Naranya moved back up front and began to move her hips. "I don't know how you live with that constant worry."

Melanie and Ruth pulled closer so they could hear; the days of concentrated silence during class had ended long ago.

"I kind of feel like Ira and I are caught in a war zone," Ruth said, her arms out, her hips thrusting in a carefully controlled motion. "Nobody's shooting, but nobody's laid down their weapon, either."

Melanie moved her hips in a smooth figure eight that none of the rest of them came close to matching. Her upper body remained perfectly still. "I was sort of hoping our talk on New Year's might have gotten through to him."

Beside Vivien, Angela made her hip thrusts smaller, then sped them up until she was doing a respectable shimmy. She, too, kept her head and upper body admirably still. All of Vivien's parts tended to want to move in unison.

"Hey, that looks good," Ruth said, stepping her own movements up trying to match Angela's pace. "Ira did say he'd come to the lesson and practice party this Saturday night, so I guess that's something."

"Of course, that's something," Melanie said, kicking her trim hips up into a shimmy. Vivi attempted a much gentler version, careful not to disturb the baby.

"James and I are in, too," Angela said, still shimmying. "That means Vivi has to come." She looked over her shoulder and down at her behind. "Oh, my God, my buttocks are shaking!"

"They're supposed to shake," Ruth said. "That's the whole point."

"Not when you've exercised your guts out to get rid of anything that resembles Jell-O!" Angela sneaked another look. "Can you see it jiggling?"

Vivien, who was closest, aimed her gaze at Angela's rear end. "Well, it's kind of hard to tell through all that black fabric you're wearing. Seriously, Angela, what are you trying to hide in there?"

"Vivi." Melanie gave her a warning look.

"If there'll be any single men, we'll come," Di said as both she and Dee began to shimmy. The sight of the six of them vibrating with such determination made Vivi smile.

Naranya scurried back to the front and clapped her hands in delight. "Good! Good!" she shouted. "You see that," she gestured to the new students. "Soon you will shimmy, too!"

"I may need you Saturday night, Vivi," Melanie said as the music slowed and the shimmying came to a halt. "I always try to keep the number of females to males as even as possible."

"Mel, I've done way better at belly dancing than either of us ever expected," Vivi began. "But it's different with a partner. I think we should leave well enough alone."

Naranya raised her arms above her head and brought her fingertips together to form a triangle. "Now we use our neck to touch our left ear to the inside of our left elbow—don't bend your head to your shoulder!" She demonstrated the highly controlled neck movement and waited for them to follow. "Only the neck moves."

"Oh, God, I never can keep my head from going along," Vivien groaned. "If body parts weren't meant to move together, they wouldn't be so . . . attached."

"Don't try to change the subject," Ruth said. Her neck was thick but clearly more under her control than Vivi's. "I knew you'd try to weasel out."

"There'll be no wiggling out," Melanie said from beneath her steepled arms. She looked so long and elegant next to Vivi's round and lumbering reflection that Vivi had to turn away.

Angela, who pretty much never looked in the mirror as far as Vivi could tell, was quick to back up Melanie. "That's right," she said, touching her right ear to the inside of her right elbow. "We'll expect you here on Saturday night. No excuses."

"Us, too!" chimed Tweedle Dee and Tweedle Di as

Naranya changed the head move to a forward-and-back motion that made Vivi feel, and look, like a pregnant bobblehead doll.

⊙

THE NEXT MORNING after successfully ejecting Shelby from bed, sliding eggs and toast in front of a zombielike Trip, and waving all three of them off to school, Vivi finally got another shot at J.J.'s office.

She lingered over her tea for another fifteen minutes in case Melanie or the kids had forgotten something, then carried her tea into J.J.'s study and sat down at her brother-in-law's desk. Ignoring the buck's reproachful glance, she opened the bottom drawers and pulled out the stack of Day-timers as well as the phone and credit card bills.

Pawing through the Day-timers until she located the last one, Vivi shivered slightly when she flipped to the back and saw the last entry, dated mid-October, which read *Hunting trip with Clay*. The book was blank after that and this struck her as odd, not because nothing had happened afterward, but because nothing had been scheduled to happen. Thinking maybe he'd bought a BlackBerry, or some other sort of PDA to bring him into the twenty-first century, Vivi made a mental note to look for it then began to read through J.J.'s last nine months.

Her brother-in-law's days had been filled to bursting with meetings and events. The weekends were no exception, though she noticed that at least twice a month there'd been blocks set aside that either read *family time* or had a more specific notation regarding a sporting event of Trip's or some performance or event labeled *Shelby*. There were also notations that reflected trips out of town, and she duly noted how often Clay Alexander went along on out-of-town speaking engagements and constituent forums. The months the legislature was in session were blocked out with thick black lines and social/business events notated in the evenings. Jordan Jackson Jr. had maintained a pretty hectic pace even for a young politician on the rise. She wondered that Melanie had never complained about his unavailability or about the frantic schedule her husband had kept. And then she realized that if Melanie had, it would have been just one more thing that had gone in one of Vivien's ears and out the other, yet another insignificant detail of her sister's life.

Hunched over the daily record keeper, she went back to January and worked her way through the months. In early April the capital letter C began to appear each Tuesday with the entire evening blocked out. In May, the C began to appear one weekend a month. Vivien might have written it off as a simple notation of some function that included Clay Alexander except that the campaign manager appeared even more regularly as Clay. If Alexander were the C in question, J.J. would have had no reason to try to hide it. But if it were another woman. . . . Vivi tried the idea on for size, but the only C she'd met that she knew J.J. had had contact with was Catherine Dennison. Could she and J.J. have been involved? And if they had been, could the knowledge that J.J. was cheating have made Clay want to somehow avenge Melanie's honor? Or convince him that J.J. wasn't worthy?

"Oh, good grief!"

Even in her own mind, Vivi could hear what a stretch that was. The fact that she wanted to cast Clay Alexander as the bad guy didn't make him one. The fact that he might have had a thing for Melanie for some twenty years and now seemed intent on filling her dead husband's shoes might be kind of icky, but it wasn't against the law.

There was no evidence to support the idea that J.J. had died by anyone's hand but his own. Which meant there was no crime.

This was not a mystery novel, this was real life.

Despite these admonitions, the feeling in her very large gut refused to go away. Clay Alexander knew things that he wasn't saying. And she, for one, wanted to know what those things were.

❧

As SOON AS they arrived at the Magnolia Ballroom, Vivi knew her reservations about ballroom dancing were well founded. On Wednesdays their belly-dance class was a tiny island of activity surrounded by an ocean of dance floor. Tonight the ballroom crackled with conversation and laughter; light from the chandeliers shone through the snowflakes that still dangled from the ceiling and sparkled off of silks and satins. At the mixing board the DJ, who would run the practice party once the lessons concluded, sorted through CDs and nodded his head to a pulsing Latin beat.

The beginners stepped out onto the floor for the included lesson while the rest of the crowd socialized around the edge of the dance floor. As Melanie led their group into position, Vivien promised God that she would become a better person if he kept her humiliation to a minimum and her clumsiness off the Internet. Angela and James stood as close to each other as possible; Ruth and Ira did not. Clay Alexander and a recently divorced attorney named Todd were paired with the Shipley sisters. Bradley Horton, a retired army colonel in his late sixties, was Vivi's partner having, presumably, drawn the shortest straw.

Vivi stepped up to Melanie's side and made one last attempt to bail out. "I know Clay just came to even things out. If he sits, I can, too." She swallowed. "Then I could put out the food. Or, um, I could clean the ladies' room."

"I'm not going to ask Clay to sit when he was nice enough to come," Melanie said. "Di and Delores are practically salivating over him. Plus, look over there." She nodded toward another class; without exception all of the women were casting sidelong glances their way. "Todd and Clay are attractive, male, and unattached. For that matter, so is the colonel. Once the word gets out, women will be beating a path to the studio door. I should pay both of them for being here."

Clay shot Vivi an amused look as she stepped back into place, the one he seemed to reserve especially for her. Melanie was right; he was tall, dark, classically handsome, and charming. It seemed that she was the only one who thought that charm too practiced and sensed an agenda that hadn't been declared.

"You okay, Viv?" Angela leaned around James to ask. She'd traded her usual baggy black belly-dance ensemble for a stylish but equally unfitted black gauze ankle-length skirt and an oversized tunic top, which were also at least a size too big.

"Sure," Vivi lied as Melanie instructed them to face their partner.

"There are some very basic basics that we need to understand before we do the first step of any kind." Melanie smiled as she surveyed them and her domain. "The first rule is that 'ladies are always right!'"

A few of the women laughed. The men groaned good-naturedly. Ira Melnick said, "I learned that fifty years ago already." Ruth's lips compressed into a thin white line.

"Well, in this case I mean it quite literally," Melanie said. "Ladies start with their right foot, men with their left. But before we move at all we're going to learn the four connection points." Melanie took them through the connection points, moving up and down the line of couples making slight adjustments, clarifying her instructions.

The colonel stood at attention, his body surprisingly strong for a man his age. Vivien hoped he had a high pain threshold, too. "Ladies, you're going to step to the right, then you're going to bring your left foot to meet the right one like this . . . 'tap.'" She demonstrated how to place the ball of the foot, holding her arms up in the same position as the women. Then she turned, put her arms in the man's contact positions then demonstrated their step and tap.

Okay, Vivien told herself. This didn't look all that complicated. Brad Horton's fingers were at her shoulder blade, his left palm pressed against her right palm as instructed; if ever anyone looked equipped and determined to "lead," it was him. A tremor of trepidation rippled through her, but Vivien beat it back. She'd interviewed surly politicians and sly investment bankers. Once she'd taken a former president by surprise. Surely she could handle a simple step and tap.

"Try to relax," her partner said. "I think it's easier if you're not quite so . . . stiff."

Vivien nodded, but her body felt decidedly boardlike. She instructed it to loosen up, but it continued its imitation of a two-by-four.

"Everybody ready?" Melanie asked.

Vivien wanted to shout no, but her lips were clenched too tightly for any words to slip through. She didn't understand how her thoughts could be moving so rapidly and in so many directions when her body felt completely rooted to the floor.

"Five, six, seven, eight . . . step," Melanie instructed.

There was movement all around her. The colonel's fingers bit into her shoulder blade and she sensed his body moving. Panicked at the thought of being left behind, Vivien yanked upward to detach her foot from the floor and felt her knee smash into a part of Brad's body that

Vivien would rather not name. The air rushed out of her partner's mouth in a loud whoosh!

Confused, Vivien took the step she'd begun and landed directly on top of Brad Horton's foot.

"Ow!" Her partner doubled over in pain.

"Oh, my gosh!" Vivien gasped. "Oh, I'm so sorry!" Vivien moved toward him, her hands outstretched in apology. Despite the fact that he was bent in half, he managed to scoot out of her way.

Melanie rushed to the colonel's side as he struggled to regain his composure.

"Are you all right?" Melanie asked. Vivien couldn't help noticing he didn't try to get away from *her*.

Brad nodded his head, but it was not a forceful gesture. Slowly he straightened, his eyes still closed against the pain.

Clay fetched a chair from one of the tables and brought it to Brad.

"Let's let the colonel and Vivi regroup while the rest of us give it another try," Melanie said, once the colonel was able to sit upright. She took the rest of the class through the step-tap business, moving right and then left. Then she showed them how to step-tap backward and then forward in what she called a "rocking step."

When the color returned to Brad's face and his breathing grew more normal, Melanie helped him to his feet. "Okay, time to rotate partners," she said gaily as if her sister had not kneed one of her students cruelly in the groin.

"Vivi," Melanie said. "You dance with Clay. He's got enough experience to dance defensively."

Ignoring Di's look of disappointment, Melanie led Vivien to Clay and positioned her in his arms.

Clay raised one eyebrow, but seemed unworried about his family jewels.

Melanie stood beside them. "Vivien," she said. "This is your right side." She tapped Vivien's right shoulder and her right hand, which was already in Clay's. "Keep your back straight and your shoulder rolled backward so that Clay has a place to apply pressure. All you have to do is slide your foot to the right. Don't lift, just step. He'll lead you through the rest." Melanie walked down the line of couples, checking everybody's positions, and then once again began to count out the steps. Vivien commanded herself to focus, told herself there was no reason in the world why she shouldn't be able to master a few simple movements. But standing in Clay Alexander's arms, all she could think of were the questions she wanted to ask him: How did an experienced hunter like J.J. die that way? Was J.J. seeing another woman before he died? Did Clay covet J.J.'s wife and family? Staying silent was one of the hardest things she'd ever done, but it cost her. When everyone else stepped, she tapped. When they stepped back, she stepped forward. Despite Clay's best attempts—she was certain his fingerprints must be imprinted on her shoulder blade from all the pressure he applied—she clomped on his instep and both his big toes and almost took him down with an inadvertent jab to the knee. It didn't get any better when Melanie put on music for them to practice to.

"If you focused half as closely on the steps as you do on every little thing I say, you might be doing better," Clay said, his gray eyes challenging. "I feel like a specimen under a microscope when I'm around you. Do you do that to everyone? Or just me?"

They'd stopped moving. She could feel the tension pulsing beneath his skin, could feel his efforts to restrain it. Dimly she heard laughter and conversation; Melanie's worried gaze swept over them, and she knew she didn't have long to answer.

"I just find it hard to believe that J.J. killed himself cleaning his gun. And I think you know more about what happened than you've let on."

His eyes widened in surprise; whatever he'd been expecting, it wasn't that. "There was an investigation, Vivi, and it was open and shut. It was horrible for everyone, including me. And I don't remember you showing a whole lot of interest in the details—or even in being here—then." His voice trembled with an emotion she couldn't identify, but he kept it pitched low so that only she could hear. "If you think dredging all of that back up now would be in anyone's best interests, especially Melanie and the kids', you are completely mistaken." He smiled as Melanie rushed up to them, announcing that it was time to rotate partners, but the smile was grim and didn't come close to reaching his eyes.

28

MELANIE DIDN'T KNOW what Clay and Vivi were talking about, but as the mother of two, she knew when it was time to separate warring factions. Without comment, she delivered Clay to a grateful Dee Shipley, asked Ira to partner with Vivi, and directed Ruth toward the colonel.

Relief flashed over Ruth's features as she disentangled herself from Ira and stepped toward Brad Horton, as if the strain of dancing with her husband had been too great. But Ruth had barely settled in her new partner's arms when Ira excused himself from Vivi and walked over to tap the elderly gentleman on the shoulder. "Sorry," he said. "But I need to cut in."

Ruth shot him a look of outrage and disbelief. Her chin stuck out. "You can't do that."

"Who says?" he asked with a little chin action of his own.

"This is the closest to combat I've been since Desert Storm," the colonel said, stepping out of the line of fire.

Those who didn't know Ruth well were smiling, but

Melanie wasn't convinced that whatever was about to happen would be funny.

Ira raised his arms into position and waited for Ruth to step into them, much like a lion tamer might put up a hoop through which he expected the lion to leap.

Ruth didn't look like she intended to step, or leap, anywhere.

"Come here," Ira said to his wife. "I'm old. I can't keep my arms up forever."

"Oh?" Ruth said, eyeing him with suspicion. "You keep telling me you're too young to retire. I'm sure your arms can last a little longer." She did take a step closer but she did not move into those arms, which had begun to tremble slightly. "And if you think you can just snap your fingers and I'm going to forget everything and fall into your arms, you're completely *meshugenah*."

"I am not crazy," Ira said. "And I'm not snapping anything. Please, Ruth." He kept his chin up and his arms, too, although the strain was beginning to show on his face. "Come here."

Ruth turned to Melanie. "He's probably building another bagel factory and is trying to soften me up before he tells me."

"My money's on Ruth," Vivi whispered to Angela. Everyone was watching the couple intently and Melanie began to worry that Ira might collapse from the strain of holding his arms up like that for so long. She was even more afraid that Ruth, in her anger, would reject him so completely that there'd be no fences left to mend. She moved closer to them, anxious not to let that happen.

"What's going on, Ruth?" Ira spoke so quietly that the whole class had to take a silent step closer in order to hear. "You barely talk to me anymore. I came here tonight to learn to dance with you like you asked me to." He took a step toward her and then another. His gaze was locked with hers. His arms remained in the air.

Silently Melanie willed Ruth forward. Her own arms ached in sympathy with Ira's. He could be gruff and he could be difficult, but in his own way she was certain that he loved his wife. Everyone seemed to be holding their breath now, waiting to see what would happen. Even Todd Bateman and the Shipley sisters watched with avid interest and an air of hope.

This is what we all want, Melanie thought, catching the wistful look on Vivi's face and the uncertainty on Angela's. Someone who will love us. And dance with us if we ask them to. Vivi pressed close, and Melanie saw that her sister was watching Clay Alexander. Following her gaze, Melanie was surprised to see a stark sadness in his normally clear gray eyes. Brad Horton and James Wesley stood still as statues, but even they seemed to be silently willing Ruth forward into her husband's arms.

Finally when it looked as if Ira might collapse and the rest of the group might implode from all the vicarious observation, Ruth took two steps forward and raised her own arms. In a matter of seconds Ira had met her halfway.

"I don't forgive you for making such a big decision without talking to me," Ruth said as everyone else breathed a sigh of relief and moved back into place with their partners. "And if you think you can just sweet-talk me into forgetting about it, you've forgotten who you're dealing with."

They stood in dance-ready position in the center of the floor, staring into each other's eyes.

"I'm not ready to sell the company, Ruth," he warned. "I'm just not sure I can do that."

Everyone else got into position while Melanie motioned frantically to the DJ to put on more music.

"But I'm willing to think about it," he said. "And I'm ready to learn how to dance if you still want me to." His tone was gruffer than a woman might like, and the fingers pressed against her shoulder blade trembled slightly while the palm that clasped hers felt slightly clammy.

"Do you still love me, Ira?" she asked too softly for anyone else to hear.

"Yes," he said, his voice still rough and without any flowery phrases or flattering protestations.

"Good," Ruth said as the music swarmed out of the speakers and Melanie called the class back to order. "Because I think I'm willing to give you another chance to prove it."

⌒

THE MISSING JOURNALISTS had still not been found by the end of the month, nor had any group claimed responsibility for taking them hostage. Stone's daily live reports grew grimmer as he covered the story along with the U.S. buildup of troops in Afghanistan. Vivien and Stone's communication was infrequent and brief, a hurried email, the occasional message relayed before and after live shots through friends at CIN. The only time she heard Stone's voice was on television and while this made keeping her secret easier, it made everything else much harder. She missed him with an intensity that would simply swoop in and steal her breath away any time she let down her guard.

Wednesday nights helped. During that hour while they worked on their snake arms and veil moves, Vivien discovered just how many things could be done with a rectangle of chiffon. Or a shoulder. Or a neck. Or a rib cage. The concentration required to do all these things helped block out the worry, while the time spent talking before and after class made Vivi a part of something.

Now that her only real job was filing a column once a week, Vivi had time for things—and people—to a degree and in a way that she never had before. And so she continued to watch Angela for clues to the thing that furrowed her brow and compelled her to wear clothing that didn't fit and began to notice the glimmer of hope hidden beneath Ruth's laments about Ira. Whenever she could, she looked for ways to lighten her sister's load and connect with her niece and nephew—an intentional involvement that had never occurred to her before and brought its own rewards and which she didn't want to admit were meant to assuage her guilt.

On a clear, crisp Thursday morning in early February, Vivien and Melanie dropped the kids off at school, then treated themselves to breakfast at J. Christopher's, an upscale eatery, in a nearby strip mall. Melanie had taken the morning off to go with Vivi to her ob-gyn appointment. Afterward they planned to pick up supplies for the studio at the Costco near the medical building.

In the van on the way to Dr. Gilbert's office, Vivien relaxed in the passenger seat, glad not to be dealing with the morning traffic, which increased steadily as they neared the Perimeter area. "I probably shouldn't have had that omelet and home fries," Vivi said as she rubbed her bulging stomach. "I am going to have to get on a scale when we get there."

Melanie smiled. "I thought the license to eat was one of the best parts of being pregnant," she said. "I gained a ton with both kids."

Yet another thing about her sister Vivi hadn't known. "Well, I guess it runs in the family. I've been eating like a horse and looking like an elephant. At my last appointment Dr. Gilbert threatened to revoke that license, but I just seem to be hungry all the time."

"Like Trip," Melanie said. "The two of you make your own swarm of locusts."

Vivi laughed. "I am giving him a run for his money, but a little healthy competition never hurt anybody. Maybe we should go on the professional eating circuit as a tag team."

"Well, I really appreciate you asking Angela to organize the outing with the Wesleys. He's still walking on air."

"Yeah. Cole apparently told him when he has his regular driver's license he'll give him a good price on a Lexus."

"My sixteen-year-old son will *not* be driving a nicer car than me," Melanie said.

"Do you promise? I was appalled at the cost of some of those cars in the Pemberton parking lot. I mean we didn't exactly grow up poor, but my first car was that old Trailblazer Daddy got for Ham."

"I know," Mellie said. "Because I drove it after you left for school."

"Speaking of driving, your son asked me to take him out to practice now that he has his learner's permit and I said yes," Vivien replied as they neared the medical complex. "Is there anything I should know?"

Melanie laughed and shook her head. "Um, no. But if you weren't pregnant, I'd suggest tranquilizers. I went through that with Shelby. It can be a little . . . nerve-wracking."

"I sense a gross understatement," Vivi said as Melanie entered the right-turn lane.

Melanie didn't respond, which Vivien took as confirmation.

In the parking lot, Melanie pulled the van into a vacant space. "Boy, this brings back memories," she said. "Between both kids and the miscarriage after Trip, I used to feel like I lived here. It's pretty amazing you ended up at the same practice."

Vivien nodded as she pulled the floppy hat low on her head and shrugged into her trench coat. "What are you doing?" Melanie asked as Vivi searched the coat pockets for the oversized sunglasses.

"I'm putting on my disguise."

"But you've already been outed. Matt Glazer told all of Atlanta that you're pregnant."

"I don't care," Vivien said as they walked toward the building. "I'm not giving his photographer a clear shot at me. And I've, um, been checking in for my appointments under an alias. I've got another hat and sunglasses if you're interested."

"Thanks," Melanie said, her tone dry. "I think I'll take my chances."

In the waiting room, Melanie took a seat while Vivien signed in. Nearby two women talked idly until one of them held up a copy of the *Weekly Encounter*. "Oh, my God," she said. "This Scarlett Leigh is really pissing me off."

"Tell me about it," the other one said. "Her rant about helicopter parents needing to get a life was the worst one yet. And that one about mothers being indentured servants went way too far."

"Don't you wonder who's writing that crap?"

"Yes, and if she's local she better be wearing a disguise."

"Speaking of disguises . . ." One of them nodded toward Vivi. "What's with her?"

Melanie and Vivien sank lower in their seats just as the nurse stepped through the door and said, "Venus? Miss Williams?"

Everyone in the waiting area looked up. "What are you doing?" Melanie asked through locked lips as Vivien stood.

"That's me."

"You chose Venus Williams as an alias?" she asked as they walked through the door and followed the nurse back to the scale. "Because it's such a common name?"

"It was the first name that popped into my head," Vivien said as they continued down the carpeted corridor. "And then I was just sort of stuck with it. Not that it seems to have stopped Mr. Just Peachy."

Melanie shook her head as Vivi eyed the scale, only stepping onto it when the nurse gave her no choice.

"Please tell me that number isn't right," Vivien groaned. "I keep waiting for some recorded voice to shriek, 'Get on one at a time.'"

The nurse made her notation on Vivi's chart without comment and led them through to the examination room.

Melanie sat in the extra chair while Vivi got undressed, put on the cotton gown, and lay down on the examining table looking like a beached whale.

"Well, hello, Venus," Dr. Gilbert said as he entered the room. "How are you feeling?"

"Okay." Vivi struggled up on her elbows. "Dr. Gilbert, this is my sister."

"So you must be Serena," he said with a wink "I'd know you anywhere."

The doctor cracked up over that one. "Listen," he said. "I'm really sorry about that Just Peachy thing. I don't really understand how he tracked you here. But I've told my people that anyone who exposes confidential patient information will be out of here on the spot."

"Thanks," Vivi said, though she knew from personal experience that a little thing like office policy was unlikely to stop Matt Glazer any more than it had ever stopped her.

"Now then," Dr. Gilbert said as he consulted his chart

and then her stomach. "You're right around thirty weeks. We shouldn't be too far off of that mid-April due date."

Only a little over two months to go, Vivi thought, still unable to imagine actually giving birth. Or any of what would come afterward. "Where are we fruitwise?" Vivi asked as he palpitated her stomach.

"Zooming in on that watermelon," he teased. "You've got a big'un in here."

"Football player or cheerleader?" Melanie asked.

"Your sister said she wanted to be surprised," Dr. Gilbert said. "I think that was the visit where she likened her uterus to a Cracker Jack box." He chuckled again.

"So," he said as he helped Vivien into a sitting position. "Tell me about your birth plan."

"Birth plan?"

"Yes, what are you planning for the birth of your child?" he asked. "Have you been taking Lamaze classes? Do you have a birth partner? You need to think about whether you want to do this 'naturally' or you're open to drugs. We do everything we can to do things the way you want."

Vivien almost laughed. She'd done pretty much no planning up until now and it seemed a little late to start. "My plan is to show up at the hospital, get an epidural, preferably in the parking lot. And then let you remove the baby from its resting place as quickly and painlessly as possible. I am not leaving pain management up to my ability to breathe.

"As to a birth partner . . ." Her voice trailed off as she looked at Melanie. "I'm sort of hoping Serena here might be willing to help me out."

"Of course I will," Melanie said. "I wouldn't miss it."

"All right then," Dr. Gilbert said. "I'll see you two four weeks from now. After that we'll be in the home stretch and I'll see you every two weeks."

After the doctor left, Vivien got dressed and shrugged into her disguise. Melanie gave her some shit about that as they walked toward the checkout desk.

"Melanie?"

Both of them turned as the male voice reached them. A white-coated stethoscope-wearing doctor approached with a big smile on his handsome face. "I thought that was you. How are you?"

While Melanie blushed at the obvious delight on the doctor's face, Vivien read the name embroidered on the pocket. His name was Dr. Summers, and every bit of his attention was focused on Melanie. "Fine," her sister said as her hand was swallowed up in the doctor's larger one. "Vivi, this is Dr. Summers. He delivered Shelby and Trip."

Vivi extended her hand to the doctor, noting the salt-and-pepper hair and intelligent blue eyes that would have enabled him to play a doctor on television if he weren't already so busy being one. She looked down at their hands as they shook hello and noted the absence of a wedding ring. Not definitive, of course, of marital status, but promising.

"I was so sorry to hear about J.J.," he was saying now to Melanie. "I meant to call but I hated to intrude."

"Thank you," Melanie said. "How are Barbara and the kids?"

"Good." He hesitated. "I mean they are good, but Barb and I aren't married anymore. We got divorced about a year ago."

"Oh, I'm sorry," Melanie said. "That's too bad."

Vivien could tell just how sorry Melanie wasn't.

"Actually, it's better for everybody. It was long overdue."

"Oh. Well, that's good then," Melanie said, leaving the ball squarely in the doctor's court. There was a long pause while Vivien held her breath waiting to see whether Dr. Summers was as interested as he seemed.

"Maybe we should get together and, um, catch up sometime."

Melanie had apparently been rendered speechless, so Vivien took a turn at charades, jabbing Melanie softly in the side to get her attention and then nodding her head up and down as subtly as she could. "Oh!" Melanie said as Vivien's second jab helped her locate her voice. "Oh! That would be, um, great." She nodded her head vigorously. "I'd, um, really like that."

The head nodding continued with both Melanie and the doctor smiling somewhat inanely. When Vivien couldn't take it anymore, she withdrew a slip of paper from her purse, wrote Melanie's home and cell numbers on it, and handed it to the doctor. Then she grasped Melanie by the arm and dragged her sister down the corridor and out of the office, her trench coat flapping out behind her.

29

THERE WAS SOMETHING about being in the final two-month countdown that made the fact of her impending motherhood impossible for Vivi to ignore. Of course, the bulging stomach and gargantuan breasts, along with the swelling hands and feet, were even more unavoidable reminders than the winnowing number of days on the calendar. The fact that the lethargy had returned didn't help, either. Any last vestiges of denial had been brutally ripped away by the unavoidable changes in her body.

In many ways, she wanted this all to be some horrible dream. Wanted to wake up in her apartment in New York with Stone beside her and be able to laugh with him at the horrific nightmare she had conjured: shot in the butt on national television, out of her network job, humiliated on YouTube, pregnant and unmarried at forty-one, writing a rant of a column that she couldn't even admit to. And that didn't even include the cold war with Caroline or the fact that she suspected Clay Alexander of withholding information about J.J.'s death, although she still had no idea in what way. Or why.

Which made it even more difficult to admit just how gifted the man was when it came to fashion. Vivien refused to acknowledge this even to herself until they'd been through three of Atlanta's finest boutiques where the saleswomen had drooled all over him and by extension Shelby, and paraded some of the most delectable clothing she'd ever seen outside of New York or Paris in front of them.

"No," he was saying now to a sophisticated blonde in a form-fitting black dress, "she needs something more tailored and sophisticated. Something Grace Kelly or Audrey Hepburn might have worn. Not Madonna or Britney."

"But . . ." Shelby, who at first had been simply ecstatic at all the attention, the Cokes and snacks, the private showings, was starting to lose patience. "That color is perfect on me," she said, pointing to the red satin gown the saleswoman held out for their inspection. "And you promised I could get something strapless."

Vivien sat back in her chair and folded her arms on top of her bulging stomach, eager to hear Clay wiggle out of that one. But the man was not even slightly deterred.

"That *is* a good color on you," he acknowledged reasonably, "though I think white or black would be even better. But there's strapless, Shelby, and there's strapless. You don't want to be too obvious. Men like to wonder. It's better to leave something to the imagination. Your mother always understood that and knew how to pull it off. And we don't want to forget that you're barely seventeen."

Shelby didn't appreciate the reference to her mother or the reminder of her age, especially since they weren't the first of the afternoon.

The more Vivi observed Clay, the more contradictory he seemed. He held Melanie in extremely high regard and spent a lot of time with her, but didn't actually date her.

Again, she wondered if he were more interested in besting J.J., even posthumously, than winning Mellie. It was as if he were trying out for the role of J.J., but wasn't positive he wanted the part.

They moved on to the designer departments of Saks Fifth Avenue and Neiman Marcus, where, yet again, the saleswomen fawned all over Clay and Shelby and pretty much ignored Vivien for the lump of non-designer-wearing flesh that she'd become. Vivien saw several gowns that she would have put Shelby in in a heartbeat, but she'd promised herself she'd remain an observer. So far all she'd learned about Clay Alexander was that he could have been working in haute couture rather than politics and women of all shapes and sizes seemed unable to resist him. Even Shelby, who alternately flirted with him and huffed at him as if he were her parent, was anything but immune.

"Did you used to dress your wife, too?" Vivi asked Clay as they waited for Shelby to appear in the first of the gowns Clay had selected for her to try on at a small shop not far from Lenox Square mall.

He paused momentarily as if trying to gauge the intent behind the question. "Yes," he said. "Actually I did."

Vivien tried to keep any sign of judgment off her face and out of her voice, but she could tell she hadn't succeeded.

"It's just something I happen to be good at. Do you find that surprising?"

"Don't you?" she countered. "I mean you don't look like you belong on *What Not to Wear* or *Queer Eye for the Straight Guy.*"

He shook his head; for a moment she thought he might roll his eyes. "I'm sure they're making better money than I am. But I was born with an affinity for color and design. I instinctively know what will work and what won't. And

I know which clothing will enhance a woman's physical
assets and camouflage her flaws. I didn't ask for this talent, but I've got it. Just like I've got a natural top spin
on my backhand in tennis and the ability to estimate the
check at a restaurant in my head." He shrugged his broad
shoulders for emphasis. "I enjoy using this talent on my
friends' behalf."

"What did J.J. think of you dressing his wife?" she
asked, darting closer to what interested her most.

He flashed the pearly whites. "J.J.? He asked me to
help Melanie with her wardrobe." He saw the expression
on Vivien's face and hastened to add. "Not because she
didn't have excellent taste, but because she didn't trust her
own judgment. You aren't the only one your mother did a
number on." Both of their lips compressed as they thought
about Caroline. "Melanie's clothing was a legitimate business concern. Having a wife who looked good on his arm
was key for J.J." An expression Vivien couldn't read passed
over Clay's face. "It's hard to get elected even today without an attractive and well-turned-out family around you. It
was just one of the many things I took care of for him."

They were interrupted by a squeal of delight from the
dressing room. "It sounds like we may have a contender,"
Clay said. "Happily, everything she took back with her is
entirely suitable. I'm betting it's the white chiffon with
the dropped waist and the handkerchief-style hem."

Vivien was glad she hadn't argued when Shelby made
her entrance with a long-strided walk of a model on a cat-
walk wearing the very dress Clay had just laid money on.
Even Vivien, who was not inclined to give Clay Alexander an inch more than his due, had to admit the dress was
perfect. The strapless bodice showed off Shelby's creamy
shoulders and clung to her breasts without being too
revealing or too low cut. The fabric nipped in, hugging
her tiny waist and slim hips then flared down in uneven

lengths around her calves. The longest lengths brushed her ankles.

"Oh," Vivien breathed as Shelby twirled in a delighted circle. "It is perfect. And you do look exactly like your mother."

Shelby was too thrilled with her reflection in the mirror and the sparkly high-heeled sandals and jewelry Clay paired with the dress to take exception to the comparison.

Clay just smiled as he added a delicately woven shawl in beige, cream, and white to the ensemble then showed her how to drape it artfully around her shoulders and hold it in place at the elbows. As they watched Shelby primp and twirl in front of the triangle of mirrors Vivien had the sense that Clay was seeing something other than the teenager in front of them. She was contemplating asking him about it when he said, "This dress reminds me of the one Melanie wore to that first Sigma Sigma formal." He looked into Vivien's eyes and there were too many emotions in his for her to catalogue them successfully. "The one I invited her to and where I introduced her to J.J."

⟡

Ruth sat at the kitchen table waiting for the coffee to finish brewing. It was cold outside, a raw February morning with a projected high somewhere in the forties. The Sunday morning paper was spread out in front of her; a bag of still-warm bagels sat on the counter.

"Good morning. Coffee smells good."

Her head jerked up at the unexpected sound of Ira's voice. He was wearing his pajamas and robe, but he'd already washed up and shaved. A faint whiff of the lemony aftershave he favored teased at her nostrils.

"Can I pour you a cup?" he asked as he moved toward the coffeemaker.

She nodded, surprised. "Thanks."

Turning her attention back to the newspaper, Ruth followed his movements from the corner of one eye.

"Bagel?" he asked as he removed two from the brown paper bag with the Bagel Baron logo.

"Sure," she said, although she wasn't. "Thanks."

She gave up pretending to read as he sliced them each a bagel and then made forays into the refrigerator to retrieve cream cheese and lox, then went back for a tomato and red onion. A few minutes later he brought a plate to the table and placed it in front of her. Before she could comment he'd returned with the pot of coffee and refilled her cup. All of a sudden she was in a full-service establishment.

"Thanks," she said, eyeing him with suspicion. Trying to figure out what he was up to, she waited for him to carry his own plate into his office as he'd taken to doing lately. But he brought it to his old spot across the table from her and sat down as if this were just any other Sunday that had taken place during the fifty years of their marriage. Before the commencement of hostilities had begun.

He was after something; she just didn't know what.

"Are you finished with the business section?" he asked politely.

"Sure." She passed it over, but he didn't open it right away.

They ate for a few moments, eyeing each other tentatively.

"So," he finally said. "I was, um, wondering if you might like to go to a movie this afternoon—maybe that new De Niro film. We could go out for dinner after." His gaze flicked over her, then away as if it had just occurred to him that she might say no. "Or we can see something else. Whatever you want."

Her eyes narrowed in surprise at the unexpected invitation. "You're not planning to go into the office? You don't have something you need to work on?" she asked. "Or a golf game?"

"Nope." He took a bite of his bagel and lox and chewed it thoughtfully. "I'm taking the day off." He looked her in the eye. "So I can spend it with my wife."

She blinked and looked at him more closely. "Is there a punch line to this? Because if there is, I'm not laughing."

"No joke." He took another bite of his food.

She watched him chew and swallow. After he wiped his mouth with his napkin, he said, "Seriously, Ruthie. I'm yours for the day." He smiled and his brown eyes twinkled at her, the old goat. "If you want me."

She dropped her gaze for a moment, not wanting him to see the sudden rush of pleasure she felt. Or the uncertainty that followed so fast on its heels. She hadn't realized how completely she'd given up hope until she felt it flutter back to life.

"Okay," she said, afraid to make too much of the gesture. Showing up at dance class and an afternoon out did not a restored marriage make. "I'll get out the movie schedule and see what time it's playing."

"Great," he said, then hesitated for a moment before adding, "and while you're at it, why don't you get out the travel section, too? I was thinking maybe we could take a little cruise." He swallowed as he sought out and held her gaze. "Or fly down to that place in Mexico the kids told us about. You know, just for a long weekend."

For one of the first times in her life Ruth Melnick was completely speechless. She looked at her husband and could see that he was waiting for a response, but she simply couldn't form a coherent thought let alone words and sentences. She waited for the other shoe to drop, for some ulterior motive to show through, but he seemed completely sincere.

"Would you like that, Ruthie? Do you want to go away with me?"

In the end he had to settle for a nod and a smile. Because even after she thought of the words she might say, she couldn't seem to force them out past the lump that seemed to be stuck in her throat.

30

FOR VIVI, THE first half of February disappeared in a blur of unpleasant physical surprises as her body, which she now barely recognized, grew and stretched in its effort to nurture and protect the baby inside of her. Her legs cramped at will, her ankles and feet were more swollen than not, and her breasts had gotten so big that they no longer seemed real to her. Her brain seemed to have abandoned her, and she often walked into a room or began a task and then couldn't remember why she'd gone there or what she intended to do. Plus she was tired all the time, but when she finally made it into bed at night, she couldn't get comfortable enough to sleep. On those occasions when she did fall asleep she had to get up to go to the bathroom so many times that shutting her eyes in between seemed pointless. Even coughing, sneezing, and laughing were now fraught with peril; doing any of these put her bladder to a test that it was no longer able to win.

Her internal debate over what to say to Stone continued, making those few opportunities when they did get to speak without a whole cadre of network people on the line not only stressful but unproductive. She missed and worried about him constantly and then spent the few precious moments they had censoring herself so carefully that she was practically speechless. She heard in his voice that she suspected something was wrong, but the kidnapping had firmed her resolve not to distract or burden him with her pregnancy. Although she couldn't completely control the way she sounded, she did her best to control what she said.

Especially annoying was Matt Glazer, who refused to disappear and who had taken to leaving her weekly messages asking her to call him.

On the bright side, which Vivi kept reminding herself did exist, there was no shortage of topics for Scarlett Leigh to tackle, and John Harcourt and his bosses were not only ecstatic about Postcards from Suburbia, they'd given her a raise. But each column she wrote left her feeling even more disloyal to Melanie. It wasn't that the excesses she wrote about didn't exist, because they did. It was just that once she'd exempted her sister due to her widowhood and working-single-mother status, she'd begun to realize that other denizens of suburbia also had their reasons. Her attacks began to feel more and more mean-spirited.

Nonetheless Scarlett Leigh lobbied for the surgical removal of cell phones from drivers' and shoppers' hands, bemoaned the demise of family dinners, and poked fun at suburban lawn wars, which encompassed secret watering in the near-drought conditions and the equally secret reporting of those who did. She also wrote a column on the buildup to high school proms and the fortune that was spent on them from the expensive gowns and tux rentals to the pricey limo and dinner out, as well as the kinds of behavior she suspected would take place afterward.

She'd never been more grateful that Melanie didn't

have time for newspapers than when she'd filed that particular column plucked from watching Shelby's frantic preparations and the multi-mother conferences that went on in the weeks leading up to the big event.

Now she fingered her computer keyboard in hopes of building a column out of her first harrowing drive with the newly licensed Trip. But it was difficult to write when one's hands were still trembling and one's mind was still in shock. Deep in her heart, Vivi felt grateful to still be alive.

It had begun badly when Trip, who'd acted as if he knew exactly what he was doing, had turned the key in the ignition and failed to realize he was supposed to let go. Backing down the driveway was even more frightening because he executed this maneuver at the speed of sound and without ever actually looking over either shoulder.

Vivi had wanted to get out of the car then, but she hadn't been able to catch her breath to say so before he'd slammed the Toyota into gear and mashed down on the gas so that they squealed away from the front curb.

Her heart raced again as she relived the experience. "The mailboxes!" she'd shrieked as they'd loomed up beside her, so close that she could see the dents in the metal and could have browsed through the catalogues inside them if she'd had a mind to.

"You're too close!" The words had been torn from her throat as he'd driven, in strange surging motions that made the gorge rise in her throat.

"Why are you doing that?" she asked, looking down at his right foot, which was working the gas pedal like a musician might pump the pedal of a piano. "You've got to keep your foot on the gas to maintain a consistent speed."

She'd held her breath until they'd surged their way to

the stop sign at 120, where he'd put on his blinker as if he were going to make a left turn onto the buzzing highway.

"No!" she'd shrieked again. "We're only making right turns today. No left turns! And definitely not here!" She could still remember the cars she'd beached on the median, and she'd been a professional driver in comparison to Trip, who really didn't seem to be able to keep his foot on the gas for any length of time and was still trying to figure out which way to look as traffic whizzed by in both directions.

"Angle the front of the car to the right," she'd said, and he'd surged right, then slammed on the brakes. This was when she'd truly comprehended that she'd put her life—and that of her unborn child—in the hands of a hormonally driven testosterone-charged beginner who didn't know the gas from the brake.

Vivien, who was not a religious person, had prayed almost continuously for the full thirty minutes she'd spent strapped into the passenger seat of the multiton chariot of death. And in those moments when the prayers stuck in her throat and she was too frightened to even shriek directions at her nephew, she'd promised God all kinds of things. If only he'd allow them to get back to Melanie's alive.

At the corner of Timber Ridge Road and 120, where Trip was supposed to make the next-to-the-last right turn of their endless journey, he'd surged past the actual stop sign before managing to get his foot onto the brake. He did this in full view of an idling police car.

"Sorry, Officer," she'd begun before the face of the patrolman had come into view on Trip's side of the car. "He just got his learner's permit and . . ."

"You?" Officer McFarland had asked. "Someone is letting you teach a minor to drive?" His tone was as incredulous as the expression on his face.

It was only by promising that if they were lucky enough to get back to where they'd started in one piece, she would never do this again, that the officer had let them go with just a warning. And then provided a siren-screaming, light-flashing police escort the half mile back to Melanie's. When they got there, Vivien had fumbled her way out of the car, then lowered herself to the ground to kiss the driveway. Officer McFarland was still laughing as he drove out of sight.

Now she sat in front of her laptop hammering out a lead for her column, which she followed with several paragraphs on what bargains parents might be striking with God as they taught their children to drive. When she'd delivered all the insults she could come up with, she took aim at the overindulgence that seemed so pervasive in Melanie's patch of suburbia. *Almost as upsetting as the fact that these "children" are set loose on an unsuspecting populace is the kinds of vehicles in which these kids are set loose,* she wrote. *Because these teenagers are not driving what we used to call "beaters." Far too few of them are driving ancient relics that serve only as transportation and for which the teenager is expected to feel grateful.*

Like most things given to teenagers in this world in which I've landed, their vehicles are both flashy and expensive—a reflection of the position and wealth of the parents who purchase them.

Again, Vivien felt a faint flush of shame for lumping her sister in with everyone else and with such broad strokes. Melanie had not handed over J.J.'s BMW as many parents here might have. She had not bought Shelby a new car, or a fast one. Or passed down a practically brand-new Mercedes because its ashtrays were dirty. Nor did she allow Shelby to drive the car she did have once she'd demonstrated a lack of responsibility.

Vivien tuned out those truths and reiterated her point instead. *To what does a sixteen-year-old who begins at the top*

*of the auto food chain aspire? How will they understand the
satisfaction of earning and purchasing a car they can afford? Or
appreciate the value of something they haven't paid for?*

She went on in this vein for a time before reaching
several condescending conclusions, which she tweaked so
as to give maximum offense. Then she sent the article to
John Harcourt at the *Weekly Encounter*, closed and pass-
word-protected the file, and shut down her laptop.

As she did so she sent one last prayer God's way. A
thank-you for keeping Stone safe so far and for letting her
live through her drive with Trip. She also expressed gratitude that no one suspected that she was the now-reviled
Scarlett Leigh and apologized for making Melanie her
unwitting accomplice. Then she promised herself she'd
be long gone before anyone found out, though she had no
idea where she might go.

☺

THAT WEDNESDAY NIGHT, as she drove to the Magnolia Ballroom, Vivien kept a watchful eye out for Officer McFarland. The last thing she wanted to do right now was call
attention to herself or provide any kind of photo opportunity for Matt Glazer, whose last message had warned that
if she didn't call him back soon, she'd be "sorry."

At the studio Vivi climbed out of the RAV4 and hurried, as best she could, across the parking lot. The "decorating committee" had stayed after class two weeks ago
to replace the holiday snowflakes and lights with Mylar
hearts and mischievous Cupids, which Melanie insisted
would provide an excuse for new classes and a Valentine-
themed dance party.

The class was already lined up at the far end of the
studio by the time Vivi made it onto the dance floor. She
felt huge and unwieldy and was actually out of breath by
the time she reached them. She was tempted to simply

observe rather than participate, but one look from her sister and she kept that thought to herself.

As she followed Naranya through the opening stretches and into the isolation exercises, she studied those around her in the mirror and realized that she no longer saw them through a stranger's eyes.

Ruth looked all fluttery and smiled more in that hour than she had in the whole first month of lessons. Between exercises and moves, she gushed about the trip to Mexico that had been booked and the private dance lessons she and Ira were going to take from Melanie. She flushed like a young girl when she declared that if she didn't stop pinching herself she was going to be completely black and blue. And then she smiled at them all some more.

Melanie smiled more frequently, too, and Vivi sensed a lightness in her sister that hadn't been there when she'd first arrived. Vivi wanted to believe that her being there had something to do with it. The chain of disasters that had brought Vivi here had not been welcome, but the growing closeness to Melanie was.

There was a good deal of laughter as they worked with the large rectangles of chiffon that Naranya passed out. She showed them how to hide behind them and twirl them seductively. Then she began to teach them a choreographed set of moves that involved lots of swirling the multicolored veils to music.

"Eef you learn this dance," Naranya said, "you can come perform it with me at the Brown Camel, where I dance on Friday nights."

"I don't think so," Vivi and Angela said at the exact same instant while everyone else chattered excitedly.

"We seem to be a minority of two," Angela said, twirling the veil like a lasso.

"I have a reason. I'd scare people right out of the place." Vivi considered her massive midsection, then looked at

Angela's trim one. "You'd look good in one of those two-piece harem outfits, and you're the only one of us besides Mellie who can actually *do* a belly roll." They'd celebrated Angela's abdominal achievement just the week before.

"I don't think so," Angela said again, as if Vivi were making fun of her.

"At least I assume you can. If you wore a little less camouflage, it would be easier to tell what parts you were moving."

Angela's heart-shaped face kind of folded in on itself. One minute she looked perfectly normal; the next she looked as if she were searching for the emergency exit.

"What just happened?" Vivi asked. "What . . ."

"Nothing," Angela said, not meeting Vivi's eye. "Here, pass me your veil."

Angela handed the veils to Naranya, but didn't speak again.

"What did you say to her?" Melanie demanded after the veils were collected and the closing stretches began. "I've never seen anyone shut down so quickly."

"No kidding. All I said was that it would be easier to see her moves if she didn't wear so much clothing."

"Vivi!"

"Well, it's true. It's not like Ruth and I haven't commented on the fact that she's wearing the wrong size before."

Hearing her name, Ruth joined the huddle in mid-stretch. "What have you done now?"

"Me?" Vivi asked. "All I said was . . ." Vivi repeated the conversation.

"That poor girl," Ruth said. "What should we do?"

"I'm not sure," Melanie said as class drew to an end. "But we can't let her leave upset."

Angela tried to slip out with Lourdes and the Shipleys,

but Ruth waylaid her near the exit. Melanie slipped an arm through Angela's. Ruth flanked her other side and they escorted her to the kitchen. Vivi brought up the rear.

Quietly Melanie pressed Angela into a seat at the table, then sat beside her. Ruth took a seat opposite. Vivi lowered her bulk into the remaining chair. "Should I get the rubber hose? Maybe a bare lightbulb for the interrogation?"

No one laughed.

"I know Vivi's sorry for what she said," Melanie began. "She didn't mean . . ."

"I can apologize for myself," Vivi said. "Angela, I'm sorry I said what I did. I just haven't been able to figure out what you're so intent on hiding. I mean if I still had a body, I wouldn't be wrapping it . . ."

Melanie shook her head at Vivi. "We don't mean to pry," Mel said. "But none of us wants to see you upset. Is there something we can do to help?"

Angela sat for a long moment. With all three of their gazes on her she might as well have been under the glare of the bare lightbulb. She clutched her purse tightly in her lap. "No, I'm the one who should apologize. I'm just a little sensitive about my weight." She hurried on before they could protest. "And I'm just getting kind of emotional with the wedding so close. And . . ." She hesitated. ". . . I'm worried that James won't . . ." Angela snapped her mouth shut, but Vivi had interviewed enough people to know when someone actually wanted to spill all.

"What is it, Angela?" Melanie asked gently, perhaps sensing the same thing. "Can't you tell us?"

Angela drew a deep breath. Vivi watched her teeter between fear of rejection and the relief of unburdening. Finally, she spoke. "I've been . . . dishonest. There's something I have to tell James before I can marry him. But I'm afraid if I do, if I'm completely honest like you said, Melanie, I'm afraid he won't love me anymore."

They all looked at each other and then at Angela.

"He doesn't even know who I am," Angela said so quietly they had to lean closer to hear. "He has no idea."

"You're going to have to explain that," Vivi said. "Because now I'm thinking that you've decided to wear a burka instead of a wedding dress, but you're afraid it won't match James's tux."

Melanie and Ruth exchanged glances. Angela almost smiled.

"And I'm worried that you're in the Witness Protection Program. Or running from the law for a crime you didn't commit," Ruth said.

"Whatever it is," Melanie said as they all processed that one, "there's nothing you could tell us that would make us think less of you. Nothing. And I'm sure James feels the same way."

Angela closed her eyes briefly. Just when Vivi thought she might just get up and leave, she reached into her purse and pulled out a photograph. Slowly, she held it out for them to see.

The photo was old and faded and had clearly been handled a lot over a long period of time. A large, shapeless body swathed in black dominated the center of the frame. Two flabby white arms were folded against a shelf of a chest and several chins drooped over a linebacker-sized neck. A full moon of a face perched on that neck. The head was topped by a shock of carrot red hair.

"What is that?" Vivi asked.

"It's not a *what*." Angela's face scrunched up in an effort to hold back tears. "That's the problem. That's not a what. That's me!"

◎

Angela dressed extra carefully for her Valentine's dinner with James. With Vivien, Ruth, and Melanie's assurances ringing in her ears, she pulled a black sleeveless cocktail dress out of the back of her closet and slipped it on. She fastened her good string of pearls around her neck and stepped into a pair of black heels. She smoothed her palms down the silk that skimmed over her hips, not as big as usual but not too tight, either.

Tucking the dog-eared photo into her shiny black clutch, she vowed that this was the night she'd tell James everything. But her heart sped up at the sound of the doorbell, and her palms turned sweaty when she went to answer the door.

His gaze was admiring and his kiss warm as he helped her into the car. But she barely heard what he said during the drive to the restaurant, because she spent the whole time trying to remember when food had become her refuge and the reasons why that had happened.

Should she tell him that by middle school when other girls were agonizing over their hair and their clothes, Angela was thinking about her next meal? Or should she simply whip out the photo and show it to him?

Somehow she made conversation through what turned out to be a six-course meal. They talked about his upcoming trip to the West Coast, and she told him something funny Brian had done during that morning's photo shoot. For once she didn't have to worry about portion control or eating slowly enough to allow herself to feel full. She moved her food around a good bit, but could hardly eat a bite. She thanked him for the beautiful jade earrings he gave her but didn't put them on.

"Are you all right?" James asked over the flickering

candle when she failed to raise her wineglass in response to his toast. "You have the strangest look on your face. Is everything okay?"

It was the perfect opening and she told herself it didn't matter where she began the story; it only mattered that she told it. But when she opened her mouth to begin, nothing came out. The black evening clutch sat on the edge of the table. She thought about reaching for it, but James covered her hand with his and gave her fingers a gentle squeeze.

"Ang?" he said quietly. "You know I love you, right?"

She nodded and swallowed, trying to find her voice, still thinking that she could get it together, but all she managed was, "I love you, too.

"James, I . . ." she began, knowing there'd never be a perfect time for what she wanted to say. Knowing how much better she'd feel once she'd told him about Fangie.

Assuming that he reacted the right way.

"James, I was . . . I wanted . . ." she said just as the waiter came over to recite the dessert menu.

"Do you want to share a chocolate mousse or a Death by Chocolate?" James asked after the waiter had described each selection in detail.

For perhaps the first time in her life the promise of chocolate meant absolutely nothing to her. "No, I want to . . ."

"Go?" he said, although that wasn't at all what she'd been about to say.

He winked at her, then waggled his eyebrows. "I have something better in mind for dessert anyway."

Angela took a deep breath in an attempt to steady her nerves. James was so fabulous. He would understand about Fangie. He would. He'd slayed his own dragons and he would respect the fact that she had slayed hers. Brian and Susan and Melanie had urged her to just tell him. But now he was motioning for the check and staring into her eyes while they waited for it.

She couldn't tell him. She just couldn't take the risk. Even if he understood, could she bear to see the vision of herself change in his eyes? Not after she'd worked so hard to *become* that person.

And so she remained silent as James took the receipt and helped her into her coat. On the way home he teased her with the details of what he intended to be her "final" Valentine's Day present. After he'd carried her over the threshold and placed her gently on the bed, he delivered everything that he'd promised. But although Angela sighed more than once with pleasure, she kept her confession to herself.

☺

NOT EVERYONE IN Atlanta got multiple orgasms *and* jewelry for Valentine's Day that year. No one in Melanie Jackson's house got either, though Shelby did receive a candy thong from Ty Womack, her date for the upcoming prom—something Vivien discovered by accident when she reached under her niece's bed looking for the pot and pan that Shelby had stolen out of its last hiding place inside Vivien's suitcase.

Once again she debated what, if anything, to say to Melanie. But she was afraid if she said something to her sister what little rapport she'd established with Shelby would be eliminated. And she felt a growing need to be there for the girl. She worried it over and over throughout the day and still couldn't reach a decision. It was just one of the many things that preyed on her mind.

She and Stone traded emails on Valentine's Day, both of them sending love, Stone promising that he'd be back in Kabul within the next few days and would reach her by phone then. Even his email sounded weary. The journalists

had been found hacked to bits, and Stone had been forced
to report the gruesome details after their remains were
verified.

Vivien cried when she read his email and again when
she watched his live shot from the site. The weekly rants
of Scarlett Leigh seemed small and petty in comparison,
and not for the first time she missed her former life. And
especially the sense of righting wrongs that used to be a
part of her investigative work.

So thinking, she went back through the GBI case file,
J.J.'s Day-timer, and credit card and phone bill receipts,
looking for something she might have missed. Once again
she came up with absolutely nothing.

31

MARCH IN ATLANTA is a meteorologist's nightmare; a time when Mother Nature frequently exercises her prerogative to change her mind. One day might be frigid with temperatures barely above freezing; the next could reach a balmy seventy-five. Sometimes after a run of summerlike days it snowed.

Nonetheless, by the middle of the month the camellias were already drooping on the branch, cherry and apple blossoms were about to burst into full bloom, and the invitation to the wedding of Angela Amelia Richman and James Coleman Wesley, engraved in a swirl of gold leaf on oversized cream cardstock, claimed a place of honor in the very center of the refrigerator door, where Vivien, Melanie, Shelby, and Trip saw it daily.

Vivien noted the date—exactly one week after she was due—as she opened the desk drawer next to the refrigerator in search of the keys for the RAV4 and wondered whether she'd be able to attend along with the other members of the Wednesday-night belly-dance class and their "significant" others. Or whether she would be at home with a newborn.

As always the thought had her counting down the days that remained and confronting the fact that soon, frighteningly soon, she would no longer be a pregnant woman; she would be a mother.

This was not a reassuring thought, and Vivien shoved it aside to focus, at least temporarily, on the intricacies of the high school prom, which turned out to be even more rigorous than Scarlett Leigh had reported. Shelby and her three girlfriends spent most of that Saturday and a fortune of money on late-morning manis and pedis, followed, after a quick bite of lunch, which the salon happily provided, by early-afternoon hair and makeup appointments.

By four P.M. they were ensconced in Shelby's bedroom and adjoining bath, where they spent the next several hours gossiping, giggling, and dressing. Trip steered clear of the entire second floor. Vivien only ventured upstairs when it was absolutely necessary.

Melanie spent the afternoon tidying the house and preparing for the picture party that would kick off the big night; the parents' photo op before the couples took off for dinner and then the prom in the white stretch limo that one of the boys' mothers had reserved.

Clay came early to help, and Vivien, as always, was irritated by his automatic assumption of the role of host. The fact that he knew Melanie's kitchen and home better than she did still rankled, and she watched him and his interaction with Melanie carefully, looking for clues to his feelings and intentions. The man was not exactly an open book, but he was the only one who had been summoned upstairs by the girls for a fashion consultation.

She sidled up beside him as he opened red and white wine for the adults and put bottles of imported beer into a bucket of ice. Liters of soft drinks were lined up nearby.

"You know your way around Melanie's kitchen pretty well," she observed.

"Um-hmm," he replied as he retrieved a bottle opener from a drawer, then went to the extra freezer in the garage for another bag of ice. He'd dressed for the occasion in gray slacks, a crisp white shirt, and a blue blazer, and as always, he looked annoyingly well put together.

A little before the other families were due, Melanie bustled into the kitchen in a short jean skirt and a brightly patterned silk blouse. Her dark hair swirled carelessly around her slim shoulders and her makeup was minimal, most likely applied much earlier in the day and then forgotten. She walked right past Vivien to Clay with the digital camera extended out in front of her. "It says the memory stick is full, but I don't know how to clear it. Can you take a look?"

"Sure." He took the camera and began to examine it. "I brought my camera, too, just in case, so we're covered." Clay fiddled with the camera for a while, then went over to the kitchen desk where Melanie's desktop computer sat. "Let me see if I can download some of these shots and clear the memory."

"Thanks. I'm going to go check on the girls," Melanie said. "The boys and their parents should be here any minute."

They conversed with the ease of long familiarity, but there was something underneath Clay Alexander's easy manners that, once again, made Vivien's investigative antennae quiver. Was he too at home here? Did he have designs on Melanie and her children? Or was Vivi just jealous of his place in their lives?

Trip appeared to filch appetizers and pour himself a Coke. "It smells like a perfume factory up there," he said, pinching his nose. "How are you supposed to breathe?"

Clay laughed, though he didn't turn from the computer.

"You get used to it. Someday you'll look forward to those smells."

Vivien wandered into J.J.'s office, drawn again to the wall of fame and the family photos. Clay Alexander figured prominently in all of them, just as he did in Melanie and the kids' lives. But so what? Weren't Melanie and Trip and Shelby lucky to have had him in their lives after they lost J.J.? Was it possible that she was so conditioned to digging that she simply couldn't accept anything at face value?

The doorbell rang and an upstairs door opened, allowing girlish shrieks and giggles to float down the stairs. Melanie called from the landing, "I'm trying to mend a small tear in Becca's gown. Can somebody get that?"

Vivien headed for the front door. Clay reached it at the same time.

"I've got it," Vivien said as she grasped the knob, pretty much elbowing him out of the way so that she could open it. Two tuxedo-clad boys stood on the front step. Each held a florist's box with a corsage in it. A cluster of adults stood behind them. Vivi had no idea which ones belonged to the boys and which were the parents of Shelby's girlfriends.

She fell back next to Clay as the guests swept into the house. "I'm Vivien, Melanie's sister," she said as all eyes fell on her protruding stomach. "This is Clay Alexander."

The boys shook hands with Clay and nodded to Vivi.

"When are you all expecting?" one of the mothers asked as Clay shut the door.

"Oh, we're not," Vivien began. "I mean, I'm not . . ."

Clay shot her an amused look.

"I'm due in mid-April," Vivien finally said as they moved into the kitchen, where Clay offered drinks.

Melanie came down the stairs in a rush, flushed and excited as she greeted the other parents. "Wait until you see the girls," she said. "They are simply gorgeous!" Moments later they called for Clay to come up.

The last to arrive were Ty Womack and his parents. The father was big and broad-shouldered like his son; the mother was small and birdlike. Vivien bristled as Ty and his father swaggered into the kitchen; Edie Womack trailed behind them.

Vivi hadn't liked the boy from a distance at the football game. She'd liked him even less when Shelby had come home drunk on New Year's Eve and on Valentine's when he'd given Shelby the candy thong. Tonight, she especially disliked the smug look on his handsome face. The other boys looked like insecure teenagers. Ty Womack looked like a mature adult.

She realized she was frowning. Looking up, she caught Clay doing the same.

Trip had disappeared into the bowels of the basement, and the girls' dates were now huddled with each other and ignoring their parents for all they were worth. Vivi tried to shoot Ty a strong look of warning, but he didn't seem the least concerned. The whole silent communication thing was clearly not her family's forte. Deciding she'd make sure to issue one in plain language he'd be sure to understand, she passed around appetizers while Clay poured drinks.

As the appetizers and wine disappeared, Vivien thought about the fact that one day her own child would be going to prom. Of course she'd be so old by then she wouldn't have to worry about a picture party. They'd probably just ask the limo driver to stop off at the old-age home to see her on the way out to dinner.

She went to join Melanie, who was standing alone near

the stairs. "I wish J.J. were here to see her," Melanie whispered. "Or even Mom and Dad." She sniffed and swiped at her cheeks with the back of her hand.

"Well, I have to think J.J. can see her and is probably bursting with pride," Vivien said, slipping an arm across her sister's shoulders. "And Caroline would just be trying to outshine Shelby and her friends and Dad would be grousing about how Republican the suburbs are. Evangeline would have enjoyed it though."

"Are we going to forgive them?" Melanie asked.

"I don't know," Vivien said. "There'd have to be an apology first, and Caroline's a lot better at demanding them than giving them. The last time she admitted being wrong was in the early seventies, and it was only a partial apology with a long list of disclaimers—remember?" Vivien sighed. "I'm not holding my breath on a satisfying reconciliation. And you shouldn't, either. As far as I'm concerned she's Hamas and we're Israel; there'll be no peace talks until she stops lobbing missiles."

Shelby's door opened and her head popped out. "Clay," she hissed. "We're ready."

It didn't seem to bother Melanie that her daughter was turning to Clay rather than her. Melanie took Vivien's arm as the group gathered in the foyer. They assembled themselves in a rough semicircle so as not to block anyone's camera angle. The only people not holding cameras were Vivi and the boys, who were licking dry lips and wiping what were probably sweaty palms on their tuxedo pants. All except Ty Womack, who looked alarmingly calm and whose eyes were lit with a different and more worrisome light.

"Boys," Melanie said with a smile. "Your dates for the evening."

One at a time the girls descended the stairs in regal

splendor to much parental oohing and aahing. Camera flashes went off as they made their way downstairs.

As subtly as she could Vivien stepped up beside Ty Womack and spoke softly but firmly into his ear. "You're responsible for Shelby," she said. "If you do anything to hurt or endanger her, I will personally tear you limb from limb and feed your intestines to the buzzards."

Ty flinched but didn't reply. As Vivi stepped away from him she realized Clay Alexander was on his other side and was also telling him something.

"Jeez," the boy said as he walked away from them to go claim Shelby. "Nothing like getting shit in stereo."

And then there was a frenzy of couple and group shots that left the kids nearly blinded. "Good thing they're not driving," Vivien said as the flashes popped all over the place, only slowing when the limo arrived and everyone finally realized that they were going to have to actually let the kids go.

The other parents left shortly afterward, leaving Vivi, Melanie, and Clay huddled together over what was left of the hors d'oeuvres.

"Do you feel okay about Ty Womack?" Vivi asked.

"Sure, why not?" Melanie responded, stopping up what was left of the wine and gathering crumpled napkins for the trash.

Vivi and Clay looked at each other, and Clay gave a small shake of the head.

"I'll do the rest," Vivien said, shooing Mel away from the counter. "I know you need to get to the studio."

"Be right back," Melanie said. "Just have to grab my other shoes." As she passed the basement door she yelled down to Trip, "Come on up! Clay and I will drop you at Josh's!" And then she was hotfooting it up the stairs to her bedroom.

Vivien and Clay eyed each other uneasily.

"I would have liked to slap a tracking device on that Tyler business," Vivien said.

"Or a restraining order," Clay said. "He was looking at Shelby like she was his own personal hors d'oeuvres."

"But you don't think we should say something to Melanie?"

He hesitated. "I think Shelby can hold her own. And sometimes it's better not to interfere. Exposing everything isn't always in everybody's best interests. Sometimes things are better left alone."

"Is that right?" Vivien asked. "The people who think that are usually the ones who have the most to hide."

"Everyone has something to hide, Vivi," he said so quietly she almost didn't hear him over the sound of Trip clattering up from the basement. "It just isn't always what you might think it is."

"Well, I don't believe in hiding the truth," she said, trying to ignore the hypocrisy of the remark. "I don't believe anyone is served by that."

"That's too bad," he said, and his smile was unutterably sad. "Because sometimes when the truth comes out, the ones who get hurt are the ones who least deserve it."

☺

VIVI WAS DOZING in the club chair in the family room, waiting for Shelby to get home, when her cell phone rang. It took a few rings for her to come all the way awake and another one or two before she located the phone, which had fallen into her lap. "Hello?" she mumbled as she squinted at the cable box in an effort to make out the time. It was just before midnight.

"Vivi?" Stone's voice pulled her the rest of the way awake. "Were you asleep?"

"I must have dozed off," she said, rubbing her eyes and straightening in the chair. "I'm waiting for Shelby to come home from the prom. Melanie's got a late dance party at the studio."

"God, that sounds so attractive compared to what's going on here." The flip tone barely concealed his distress. "I could use a little dose of normal everyday life right about now."

Vivien rubbed the last of the sleep from her eyes and wished he were there so she could put her arms around him and draw him close. They hadn't been able to speak in private for far too long. After they'd found Deke and his cameraman, Stone had laid low during the days and done live hits all night to appear live on the network during the day here.

"I'm so sorry about Deke and his cameraman. That must have been awful to have to keep reporting all the details." She could feel his sadness on the other end of the line, could feel his despair clinging to him.

"I think I'm getting too old for this," Stone said.

"Who, you?" she asked. "The original rolling stone who refuses to gather moss? And you can't be too old for anything—you're only three years older than I am."

She, of course was too old to be pregnant, too old to be a mother for the first time. Far too old to do it all alone. But for Stone to feel too old for the one thing he'd ever wanted to do?

"I feel a hundred, Vivi," he said. "I think I've finally figured out why you don't see a lot of older correspondents reporting from war zones. Cronkite and Brinkley knew when it was time to take a seat behind the anchor desk. I just . . ."

His voice trailed off, and she could picture him running a hand through his hair in that way he had when he was upset. Imagined him unshaven and exhausted, needing something that she could never give him over the phone. "I'm used to being afraid, Viv. I know how to live with the fear. But seeing Deke in little pieces . . ." She could hear the pain in his voice. "There was barely enough of a finger to lift a print."

Vivien couldn't speak. There was no answer to such ugliness. What kind of people cut off heads and hacked uninvolved third parties to bits?

"When are you coming home?" For about a tenth of a second she considered telling him their news, offering it as an incentive to leave where he was, proof that life did renew itself. But now for totally different reasons than the ones she'd been telling herself, this was not the time. She wanted to distract him from his pain, but not with something as large as their impending parenthood. She'd waited much too long, and now she'd wait until she could do it in person.

"I'm going to finish this story. They're hunting down the people responsible, and I'm staying here until they're caught. But after that?" His voice broke on the pain. "You and I are going to take a nice long vacation while I figure that out."

"That sounds fabulous," she said.

There was a silence and she knew it was time for a topic change, to put both of their minds somewhere else. "So do you have a minute to hear where I am with the whole Clay Alexander thing?"

"Always," he said, and though his voice was still ragged, he listened intently as she ran through what she'd gleaned so far, including her interviews with Professor Sturgess and former Sigma Sigma president Grady Hollis. Which made the fact that Clay was considering a run for J.J.'s former seat all the stranger. As she spoke, it was hard to ignore the fact that she had a whole boatload of suspicions she couldn't seem to give up and no basis for supporting them.

"I haven't found a BlackBerry of any kind and I still haven't figured out who the C in J.J.'s Day-timer is. I'm not completely prepared to give up on Catherine Dennison as a possibility, but, honestly, I can't quite picture them together. I even Googled Clay's ex-wife, but other than the fact that she bears a slight resemblance to Melanie there was really nothing there that has any bearing on anything. I just can't get over the sense that he's got some sort of guilty secret. But I don't actually know if it has anything to do with J.J.'s death."

"Vivi," he said after she wound down. "If this were a work assignment, you would have written it off and moved on to something with real substance a long time ago." He paused, and she could tell he was choosing his words with care. "Be careful. Exposing these suspicions, especially when it's mostly conjecture, could blow a lot of people's lives completely out of the water for no real reason. Including your sister's."

"You're the one who needs to be careful," she said. "I'm counting on you to come back to me." She almost added "in one piece," but even the thought of what had happened to Deke made her sick to her stomach. Tears prickled behind her eyelids, and she blinked quickly to try to keep them from forming. "There's someone I want to introduce you to when you get back." She drew in a breath and laid a protective hand on her stomach as the first tears began to fall. Her face contorted in a futile effort to stop them. "Someone I hope you'll be happy to meet."

Her voice broke on the last words and she began to cry in earnest.

"What is it, Vivi? What's wrong?" Stone asked. "Tell me what's going on."

"Oh, it's nothing," she sobbed, wanting desperately to stop. "Just that time of the month, you know?"

It was a completely inadequate answer and they both knew it. But although she managed to halt the flow of tears as they said good-bye, she simply couldn't marshal the brain cells required to come up with anything better.

Vivi was still sitting in the club chair red-eyed and awake when Shelby tiptoed in at twelve thirty. This time the girl wasn't drunk or laughing. Her dark hair had been pulled out of the carefully arranged hairdo and swirled around her bare shoulders in wild disarray. The beautiful wrap was crumpled and dirty as if it had been trampled on the ground. There was a fresh hickey on her neck and what looked like a bruise on her shoulder.

"What happened?" Vivien asked, struggling to her feet, her earlier despair replaced by a hot flash of anger. "What did he do to you?"

"Nothing." Shelby's chin shot up even as her eyes filled with tears. "He didn't do anything to me that I didn't want him to."

"Oh, Shelby, honey." Vivi moved toward her niece already opening her arms, but Shelby shook her head, warning Vivi away.

"You don't need to be with someone who doesn't respect you or treat you like the prize you are," Vivi said. "You don't want . . ."

"At least he acts like a real man," Shelby said. "And he treats me like I'm a real woman." She held the ball of fabric in front of her like a shield. To Vivi she looked like a little girl hiding behind her blankie.

"Shelby, you're playing with things you don't understand. You could end up . . ."

"Like you?" Shelby sneered, aiming a knowing look at Vivien's stomach. "Maybe you should have followed your own advice before you ended up here telling everybody else what to do."

Shelby turned and stormed up the stairs. The last thing Vivien heard was Shelby's bedroom door slamming shut behind her.

32

At WEDNESDAY'S CLASS Melanie, Ruth, and Vivien watched Angela like worried mother hens. For the past three Wednesdays her face had been too pale and her eyes too bright. She seemed both jumpy and distracted, and the only thing she'd say was that she hadn't told James her story yet. Her exercise clothes remained black and baggy.

They chatted normally through the stretches and isolation exercises, sharing tidbits as they went along. Ira had a flare for the Latin dances and was working his way through the rhumba and merengue; James took Trip for a practice drive and came back badly shaken. Caroline had phoned and invited Shelby out to lunch but made no mention of her mother or aunt.

They'd all mastered the veil dance, though only Lourdes and Sally had had the nerve to perform it on stage with Naranya. Now they were working with the zills, the tiny little finger cymbals, and trying to perfect their "snake arms."

When class was over, Operation Big Good-Bye swung into motion.

"Angela," Melanie called as the redhead moved toward the exit, "could you help me with something?"

Angela eyed the door but didn't make a break for it. She followed Melanie down the corridor. Together they stepped into the kitchen.

"Bon voyage!" Ruth shouted, throwing confetti.

"Arrivederci!" Vivi yelled, though she wasn't sure why. A small sheet cake with a picture of a cruise ship surrounded by waves sat on the table. A bouquet of balloons—some with a bridal theme and some proclaiming Bon Voyage! were tied to the back of one of the chairs. Three brightly wrapped gifts sat next to it.

"This is your bridal shower and going-away party," Melanie said, leading Angela to a place at the table. Vivi slid a glass of wine in front of her. Ruth threw the last handful of confetti.

Angela contemplated them from her seat. "This is really sweet of you," she said. "I get the wedding part, but I don't really understand the bon voyage theme. Who's leaving?" She studied the three of them, her gaze focusing on Vivi.

"Nope. Sorry. That's privileged information at the moment." Vivien smiled. "In the meantime, drink this." She placed the glass of wine in Angela's hand while Ruth cut three slices of cake. Melanie passed Angela the first present.

"That one's from me," Vivi said. "And I expect you to wear it next week."

Slowly Angela unwrapped the oblong box. Parting the tissue paper, she lifted out the emerald green belly-dance outfit. The top was a green velvet push-up bra shot through with gold thread and encrusted with gold coins. Angela gave it a jangle.

The harem pants were chiffon with a green velvet yolk encrusted with gold coins.

"Wow. I hardly know what to say." Angela smiled.

Vivi turned to Melanie. "Don't you think it's completely her?"

"Completely." Melanie laughed. "I hope you got one for yourself."

"Here," Ruth said, pushing the other package toward Angela. "This one's from Melanie and me."

Angela pulled off the paper but not before taking a hefty sip of wine. The box yielded clothing, but with a lot less glitter and a whole lot more class.

"Oh, that's beautiful." Angela ran a hand over the cream silk blouse and matching shantung pants. She held the blouse up in front of her. "It's almost the same color cream as my wedding dress." Her smile slipped.

"It's a perfect shade with your hair and your eyes," said Melanie.

Angela looked inside the collar. "But it's only an eight."

Melanie looked at her closely. "Which may be too big."

Angela shook her head in denial. "No, I can't . . ."

Melanie put a finger to Angela's lips to shush her. "This is where the bon voyage part starts."

Vivi refilled Angela's glass and tilted it up to her lips.

"We're sending Fangie on a cruise," Melanie said.

"Permanently," added Ruth.

"It's time to kiss Fat Angie's ass good-bye!"

◎

THE NEXT AFTERNOON Vivien stopped off at the grocery store to pick up ground beef and frozen French fries. She wasn't a particularly great cook and she didn't attempt anything fancier than the burgers and fries she planned for tonight, but the look on Melanie's face when she got home after a day of work and running the kids and found food on the table had proven pretty inspirational.

As she pushed the rapidly filling cart, Vivien thought about last night's bridal shower/bon voyage party and hoped Fangie's departure would prove more than symbolic.

While they all agreed that Angela needed to be rid of Fangie, they didn't all agree about whether Angela should show the picture to James. Melanie had argued in favor of total honesty and insisted that James would not only understand but admire the change she'd wrought in her life. Ruth had come out in favor of the past staying in the past, since, she reasoned, James had fallen in love with the woman Angela was now and it didn't make sense to muddy the waters. It was like telling a potential husband about all the men you'd dated before you met him. Not much was accomplished, but damage could be done.

Vivi sighed as she wheeled the cart toward the checkout lines. Although she'd felt it too hypocritical to say so, she hoped Angela would tell James her secret. She wished she could do the same.

In line, Vivi perused magazine headlines. Next to the *National Enquirer*, with its headline about a minor celebrity who claimed to have been abducted and then returned by aliens and the *Enquirer*'s oversized photo of Brad and Angelina and their brood, was a fresh stack of the *Weekly Encounter*, which carried her recent rant about SAT prep and the parental obsession with their children's scores. The woman in front of her was blatantly reading Scarlett Leigh's column, most likely with no intention of buying. Her lips were pressed together in a tight, unhappy line.

"This Scarlett Leigh is an absolute idiot," she said.

Vivien arranged a look of interest on her face but kept her mouth closed.

The woman nodded toward Vivien's stomach. "Just wait until your child is ready to graduate from high school. It'll probably feel even more like brain surgery by then than it does now. Obviously this Scarlett Leigh doesn't know squat about raising kids or getting them into college."

Vivien smiled in a way that she hoped could be taken for agreement. An aisle over another woman chimed in. "How can they let some woman who has no idea what she's talking about say whatever she feels like? Where are Scarlett Leigh's child-rearing credentials? I bet she's a damned man who knows as much as my damned ex-husband!"

The woman in front of Vivi had paid and was waiting for the last bags to be put in her cart. "Well, I'd like to see that Scarlett person have to tell her child he didn't get into any of what were supposed to be his 'safety' schools," she huffed. "I suppose she thinks we should just let them get whatever they get even if they never have a high enough score to leave home!"

There was a group shudder followed by a short, heavy silence.

Vivien shrank as far as an eight-and-a-half-months-pregnant woman could. Vivien felt even worse than she had when she was writing her apparently incendiary columns and more than a little afraid of what might happen if Scarlett's true identity were ever revealed. She left the store as quickly as her swollen ankles and aching feet would take her, threw the grocery bags into the back of the SUV, and ditched the cart.

She was heaving herself up into the SUV when her cell phone rang. Caller ID said Matt Glazer. Tired of ducking him, she answered.

"Well, hello at last," he said. "What finally made you pick up?"

"Just trying to clean up some loose ends," she said, ignoring the whine in his voice.

"That's all I am, a loose end?"

Not even, she thought. "I assume you had a reason for calling?"

"Well, yes," he admitted. "I thought we might work together on something."

It appeared Matt Glazer was not only whiny and presumptuous, but delusional. She told herself not to get worked up. Which would have been easier if the man weren't such a complete and utter moron.

"Did you come up with that idea before or after the Christmas Day hatchet job you did on me?"

"Oh, that," he said as if he hadn't, in fact, told all of Atlanta that she was pregnant, long in the tooth, and unmarried. "I just hated not to use the information. You know how that is. Once you dig it up you can't exactly put it back."

This was true as she knew all too well, but as she had that first time they'd run into each other, she resented his putting them on the same level. "I'd really appreciate it if you'd stop digging and leave me alone," Vivien said. "We knew each other a little bit a long time ago. I don't think that gives you the right to print whatever you want to about me."

There was a pause during which she assumed he realized that meant "no."

"Well, actually, *Vivi*, my job does give me that right. As long as what I print is true."

His familiarity had her staring out the car window, gritting her teeth. The chances of getting through the conversation without losing it completely were shrinking at an alarming rate.

"I know about the investigation you're conducting into your brother-in-law's death and I want in," he said.

She grasped the steering wheel and gritted her teeth harder. Matt Glazer was bumbling around in things he didn't understand. Hell, what she'd been doing didn't even qualify as an investigation, though she didn't intend to discuss that with him.

"Look," she said, trying to tamp down her rising temper. "There is no investigation into J.J.'s death, no deep dark secrets to search out. And we don't need to be at odds with each other. Let's just call it a day, Matt. Okay?"

She waited, alone in the car, hoping he'd just pick up his marbles and go home.

"Oh, there's an investigation all right," he said, blowing that hope right out of the water. "I know you requested the GBI file. And I don't really need your permission to conduct an investigation of my own." His tone had turned insolent; waving a white flag had made her look vulnerable.

"Matt," she said, still trying to control the anger that was now pounding in her temple and beating a nasty tattoo in her ears. "I'm asking you to back off. I have no intention of or interest in collaborating on anything. Not that there's anything to collaborate on."

"I know you've been talking to people," he said as if she hadn't spoken. He actually seemed to think that if he just explained things in the right way, she'd go along with him. "Well, I've been talking to people, too. About you. And what you've been up to since you came back to Atlanta. If we're not working together, I'm going to feel compelled to use what I know. After all, I have an important column to fill."

"You are way out of line," she said, deciding that self-control was sorely overrated. She'd been the soul of reasonableness and look where it had gotten her. "And if you think you can blackmail me into anything, you are even stupider than I thought."

She pictured his look of surprise. Did he actually think he could threaten her and she'd cave? If she'd had a story, she sure as hell wouldn't be wasting it on a gossip column in a local paper.

"So that's it?" he said and his own voice had a bite to it. "You still think you're too good to write something with me."

Was she really sitting in a supermarket parking lot listening to this crap? Not a moment longer she wasn't.

"I *am* way too good to collaborate with you, Matt, and everyone but you knows it. Your idea of collaborating is trying to horn in on someone else's story, threatening them to try to get a piece of their work. That is not remotely professional, Matt. And neither are you."

There was sputtering on the other end of the line, but she was beyond caring. "In fact, if I were you—and I plan to start thanking God on a regular basis that I'm not—I'd be embarrassed. But I don't think you're smart enough for that."

"You're going to be sorry you turned me down," he said. "And even sorrier that you've talked to me this way. I'm a colleague. A fellow journalist." He was working himself into a bit of a huff, but he had a ways to go to catch up with her. Testosterone was no match for pregnancy hormones.

"Matt, at the moment I'm sorry about more things than you can imagine. But I promise you you're not one of them. You write a gossip column!" Vivien was shouting now and it felt really, really good. "And you're about as close to being a real journalist as a grain of sand is to being the Sahara desert."

She hung up without waiting for an answer and laid

her forehead against the steering wheel for a few long moments while she attempted to regain her composure. That last little tirade had been a mistake, she knew, but at the moment she was unable to regret it.

Her stomach rumbled and she realized how late it was. Still reliving the whole conversation with Matt Glazer, she drove home quickly. The sight of a rental car in Melanie's driveway took her by surprise.

Instead of pressing the garage door opener, Vivien pulled up beside the rental car so that she could peer inside. When she saw who was there, she parked and raced, or rather waddled quickly, around to the driver's side of the rental car and waited for Marty Phelps to get out.

She stopped short as she registered the serious expression on her former cameraman's long, hawk-nosed face; the blood made a loud whooshing noise in her brain. The military sent a formal bearer of bad news; did the network send a cameraman?

"Tell me nothing's happened to Stone," she said as he stood to face her. Her voice was thick with fear.

"Nothing's happened to Stone," he said. "Nothing he can't deal with anyway."

"Oh, God!" Vivien said. "You gave me such a scare." She was so relieved that she threw herself into his arms, stomach first. The expression on his face turned from serious to shocked as her bulging belly cannoned into him.

His gaze dropped to her midsection. "You're pregnant." It was a statement, but one he was clearly just trying out.

"Never could pull anything over on you," she said, stepping back. Her stomach filled the space between them and then some.

"So this is what you've been doing down here," he finally said. "Reproducing." As if she were an amoeba or some other single-celled organism that had achieved this all by herself.

Not sure what to say, she led him to the SUV and popped open the back. "Here, help me with the groceries," she said as she walked around and leaned into the front seat to open the garage door. "Melanie and the kids won't be home until later. I'll explain while I cook dinner."

He took the bulk of the bags, leaving her to close up the car and lead him into the house through the garage.

"You cook," he said, sounding dazed. "You're ready to spit out a kid and you make dinner. I feel like I'm in one of those early episodes of *The Twilight Zone*. Last thing I remember you were getting shot in the butt. Now you're like a . . . Stepford wife. Have they made you register as a Republican yet?" The most important part seemed to sink in. "How did you get so pregnant?"

"I'm pretty sure it happened in the usual way," she said as she poured him a Coke and a glass of juice for herself and got him settled at the counter.

He blushed and his Adam's apple, always Marty's most reliable barometer, bobbed in his throat as she unpacked and put away the groceries. The hamburger got mixed with egg and bread crumbs and barbecue sauce like Melanie had taught her and formed into hamburger patties.

"Whose is it?"

She looked up at him, surprised. "Well, it's Stone's. Of course."

He remained silent for a long moment. "Then how come Stone doesn't know about it?" he asked. Vivi looked away, unable to meet the accusation in his eyes.

"The guy's been going crazy trying to figure out what's going on with you. Then he loses one of his oldest friends to those crazy terrorist assholes. The last time he talked to you, you were in tears, which is not at all like you. Don't you think you might have mentioned that you were having his baby?"

All of the reasons she'd come up with for not telling Stone felt like so much BS when seen from Marty's perspective. "It's not like I wasn't ever going to tell him," she said and was embarrassed by her apologetic tone. "At first I just didn't want to make him feel obligated. And then I didn't want to worry or distract him. And then . . . oh, hell, Marty. I finally figured I'd just tell him when the time felt right."

"When?" he asked. "When the kid was heading off for college? When Stone got back and asked you, 'What's new?' "

His last comment hit a little bit too close to the truth for Vivi. She felt her jaw set and her chin go up. Unfortunately, it was quivering.

"Awww, man," Marty groaned. "Please tell me you're not going to cry."

She shook her head emphatically from side to side in an attempt to reassure him. But that just forced the first hot, salty teardrops out of the corners of her eyes. They stared at each other in horror as a whole slew of them slid in a torrent down her cheeks. Just like Angela, she thought. Here she was boohooing because she couldn't tell the man she loved the truth.

Later, after dinner with Melanie and the kids, Vivien walked Marty to the door. They hesitated in the foyer; the most important part of their conversation, at least from Vivi's point of view, had not yet taken place.

"You can't tell Stone about the baby." Vivien looked straight into Marty's eyes, wanting him to not just hear, but see, how important this was to her.

"Viv, the guy's worried sick. He practically begged me to come here. I can't just . . ."

"Yes," she said. "You can."

Marty slumped against the front door, not yet ready to admit defeat.

"Marty," she said. "Telling him now would only worry him more. It would not be a kindness, just a complication."

"But he deserves to know. He . . ."

"He does," she agreed solemnly. "And I promise you he will. Just not now. Let him get through the rest of this assignment and back in one piece and I'll introduce him to his child the minute he steps off the plane."

"But what if something happens to him? What if . . ." he began, voicing all those fears that whispered in her ear during the night.

"Nothing's going to happen to him." She held on relentlessly to Marty's gaze, willing him to accept what she was saying even as she prayed that this was the truth and not just wishful thinking. "Not to Stone."

Marty was an uncomplicated guy, straightforward and honorable; she had always admired and loved this about him. He'd been a good friend to both of them. But she knew Stone in ways Marty didn't. The cameraman moved away from the door and straightened to his full height, ready to end this conversation and the dilemma it presented.

"I know you just want to do what you think is right," Vivi said as she reached out and laid a hand on Marty's arm. "I haven't necessarily handled this in the best way. But I will handle it. I will make things right with Stone." Again, she prayed that she could do this.

"But the bottom line is this is not your truth to tell, Marty." She swallowed and dropped her hand. "I don't give you permission to tell Stone. I'm counting on you to keep this to yourself."

"But what am I supposed to tell him?"

"Just tell him that you saw me like he asked you to and that I'm fine." She swallowed again, intent on holding back the tears that threatened yet again. "And tell him that I love him and I can't wait to see him."

Finally he nodded in agreement. Careful of her stomach, he hugged her good-bye. But as she stood in the doorway watching him back down the drive, she felt anything but victorious.

33

ANGELA BECAME AWARE of her breathing at the Magnolia Ballroom seventeen days before the wedding. She'd felt okay during belly dance even though most of the class seemed more interested in the details of the wedding than working on the shoulder thrust and bust shimmy that Naranya wanted them to master. Ruth, Melanie, and Vivi, who had slowed down considerably and did little more than wave her arms around, watched her carefully but didn't press for details after she told them she hadn't 'confessed' to James and wasn't sure she was going to.

It was only when the rest of the class left and James and both sets of parents arrived for a private family lesson that Angela began to feel an odd tightness in her chest. She was standing between James and Cole while Melanie thanked them profusely for including Trip in both the Hawks game and the more recent expedition to Turner Field for a tour of the clubhouse when her breathing became noticeable and no longer simply automatic.

The lesson itself went well. Cole and Cassie Wesley were athletic and agile and picked up the steps Melanie showed them with no difficulty. Angela's parents, John and Emily, were so excited to just be there with the wedding so close that they could have floated on air if Melanie had directed them to. Even she and James moved smoothly together. But each time she stepped into James's arms or felt his gaze settle on her, the breathing thing became more pronounced. By the end of the lesson she was completely aware of each breath she drew in and each one she let out.

The day of her final wedding dress fitting, Angela stood on a small dais in the center of the wedding salon's elegantly appointed fitting room, counting out her breaths. In and out was "one." The next set made "two."

Her attendants had already tried on and lined up in their black-and-cream strapless gowns, then been led by Susan, her matron of honor, to wait for Angela and Emily and Cassie at a nearby restaurant where they were throwing a final bridal shower.

Her mother and James's sat in matching white brocade slipper chairs in places of honor on either side of her. All three of them stared into the mirror at Angela's reflection. The gown was glorious. It was just so . . . fitted. And, of course, it bared her arms and shoulders, hugged her breasts, nipped in at her waist, and molded to the flare of her hips before dropping to the ground in gentle swirling folds. She'd loved the dress the moment she'd seen it and had agreed wholeheartedly with her mother and Susan when they'd taken one look at her in it and proclaimed it "the one." But now all she could see was a dress that left no room for one extra ounce; a shimmer of clinging satin that provided no camouflage behind which Fangie could hide. A lie of a dress in which Angela did not belong.

She stood with her shoulders arched slightly backward and her body angled a bit to the side, just as she had for her wedding portrait so that the dress would hang perfectly and the train could be arranged around her satin-slippered feet. The saleswoman had decided it needed to be taken in a bit more and after pinning the back had left to get someone from the alterations department. Fangie had had a good laugh over that.

"It's perfect," Emily said as she dabbed at the corner of one eye with a handkerchief she'd taken to carrying with her. "With the adjustment it fits you like a glove."

"You look beautiful," Cassie agreed. "James is just going to go crazy over you in it."

Angela breathed in and then out. When she lost count, as she sometimes did, she simply started over. The mothers' faces in the mirror were sharp with excitement; their eyes glowed with anticipation. Angela's face reflected neither of these things. Fear and indecision clouded her eyes, turning them a murky green. She acknowledged the beauty of the dress, but she no longer felt beautiful in it. She could see her chest rising and falling with each breath. *One. Two.*

She knew she should be ecstatic. The big day was almost here; soon her real life with James would begin. The last of her dreams was about to come true.

Angela breathed in and breathed out. *One*, she thought. *Two*.

"Are you all right?" her mother asked. "You have such a strange look on your face."

Angela drew in a ragged breath and then another. She counted up to twenty, but she just couldn't seem to get enough air.

"You sound like you're having trouble breathing," Cassie said.

Both mothers got up from their chairs and moved toward her. She felt suddenly surrounded, though she didn't understand how two people could create such a crowd.

"Is your dress too tight?" Emily grasped the zipper, but the pins blocked its track and she couldn't work them out of the fabric.

"Do you want me to call the sales attendant?"

"Yes, could you do that?" Angela asked, still trying to draw in air as Cassie rushed out of the fitting room to look for help, leaving Emily wringing her hands. She drew in another ragged breath and another one after that.

Angela's reflection wavered before her eyes as something heavy settled over her chest and an invisible fist grabbed hold of her airways and squeezed them shut. Her last thought was that she didn't know why breathing had become so complicated, but she was fairly certain it didn't have anything at all to do with the beautiful dress.

☙

ON A BEAUTIFUL evening in early April, Vivien drove Shelby's Toyota to Pemberton to pick up her niece from her two-night-a-week SAT prep class. With the window down to enjoy the spring air, she sat in the car-pool lane, contemplating the stunning display of deep pink and white azalea bushes that bracketed the school's front entrance as other parents arrived and departed. It was after nine P.M. and yet the school building, as well as the gym, the track, and the athletic fields that surrounded it, still pulsed with activity.

Soon, very soon, she would be giving birth. For the past few days Vivien had been trying to come to terms with this one incomprehensible fact. At her last appointment, Dr. Gilbert had smiled and told her that "all systems were go." The baby was in position (sort of like a missile) and soon would be ready to launch itself through the birth canal and into the world. His words had struck fear in her heart and a fire under her feet as she'd rallied her flagging energy to pack a bag for the hospital (gulp), buy a package of newborn diapers (major gulp), and set up Melanie's baby bassinet in her bedroom complete with sheets and bumpers and a clown mobile that had belonged to Trip (not enough saliva left for the size of the gulp required). From Legalzoom.com she'd downloaded and filled out the proper legal documents to acknowledge Stone as her baby's father and willing all her assets to him and their baby in the event anything happened to her in delivery. "If Stone is ever unable to care for our child," she'd said to Melanie afterward, "you're it, you understand?" And Melanie had told her not to be silly; nothing was going to happen to her or Stone, but she'd promised just the same.

Vivien shifted in the driver's seat, unable to get comfortable, nor that she actually remembered what comfortable felt like. Her stomach pressed against the steering wheel, as always in the way. Her joints ached and everything that could swell, had. She was exhausted all the time and could hardly wait to get into bed at night, but once she was there she couldn't sleep. In so many ways she could barely wait not to be pregnant anymore, and in others—not so much.

Shelby came out of the building well after the stream of students Vivi'd recognized from the prep class and moved toward the car reluctantly, her shoulders drooping and her feet dragging. When she climbed into the passenger seat, she gave Vivien a small hello. The look in her eyes was an odd mixture of worry and belligerence; Vivi had seen this same look reflected in her own eyes more than once. It was not a harbinger of good things.

Still she had learned a few things about teenagers in her time here and so other than returning Shelby's greeting, Vivien remained silent.

At the intersection of 120 and Johnson Ferry, Vivi slowed to a stop at the red light. Shelby sat perfectly still;

no earbuds, no texting, her phone not in evidence—which were all great big red flags. As was the way she was clasping her hands.

Finally Shelby said, "I have a problem."

"Oh?" asked Vivi, hoping it might be something small: a forgotten textbook, a poor grade on an assignment, or one of the hundred other things that could go wrong in a teenaged girl's day.

"I think I might be pregnant," Shelby said.

There was the blare of a horn behind them as Vivi sat, unmoving, at the now-green light.

"It's green," Shelby said. "Drive."

Vivien drove, but her attention was focused on Shelby's face as she waited for the evil smile and the "just kidding." But Shelby's face was a study in misery.

There was another blare of horns, but fortunately they were not followed by the crunch of metal. Hands shaking, Vivien turned off the busy road and into a strip center where she pulled into a parking spot and put the car in park.

"What makes you think you're pregnant?"

Shelby gave her a look and Vivien thought back to the drunken New Year's Eve, the rumpled prom dress, the hickeys. As her own gorge rose, Vivien knew she should not have kept these things to herself. Telling Melanie might have upset Shelby, but maybe it would have prevented this moment.

"Tell me," Vivien said.

"I haven't had my period." Shelby's lip quivered. "I'm never this late."

"How did this happen?" Vivien snapped.

"Are you kidding?" Shelby snapped back. "Yours wasn't exactly a planned pregnancy, was it?"

Vivi closed her eyes and sighed.

"And don't tell me how different this is because you're

old and I'm a teenager. I figured if anyone would understand, it would be you."

"Is it that Ty business?" Vivi asked, though she knew
that was the least of their problems. "I'm going to call
that boy and his parents and . . ."

"Forget it," Shelby said and the weariness in her
eyes was far worse than any shouting or screaming. "He
asked Debbie Stanton out. He hasn't even looked at me
since . . ."

"Oh, Shelby," Vivien said. "I knew that guy wasn't
good enough to get within ten feet of you. Hand me your
phone, I'm going to . . ."

"Vivi," Shelby said. "Could we just find out for sure?"

They looked at each other and then they looked up at
the CVS sign in the corner of the strip center.

"I can't go in there and buy a pregnancy test," Shelby
said and now her voice was whisper soft. "Even if I'm not,
everybody will know."

"Okay," Vivi said, already fumbling for her purse on
the floor of the backseat. "I'll be right back."

Vivi waddled into the store and followed the signs to
the pharmacy. From a shelf of early pregnancy tests, she
chose three different brands. With her thoughts on Shelby
and hoping against hope that these kits would come up
with a great big, "Relax, it's a negative," she carried them
up to the cash register and set them on the counter.

The clerk had streaky blonde hair and a large oval face.
Her body beneath the store smock was beefy and so were
the hands she fisted on her ample hips. She considered
the pregnancy tests in front of her and then took a long
look at Vivi. "I think I can save you a little money here,
honey," she said, her gaze halting for a long moment on
Vivi's bulging stomach. "I might not be a doctor, but
you're pregnant."

Vivien raised an eyebrow at the woman, just managing

to hold back the "Ya think?" that sprang to her lips. "They're, um, for a friend."

"Right." The woman was still staring at her stomach, but she went ahead and scanned the boxes. "A friend," she repeated as she dropped them into a plastic bag. "Tell your . . . friend . . . good luck. And let her know that, uh, she can return any of these that aren't opened."

"Thanks." Vivien took the bag without further comment. She could feel the woman watching her as she waddled away.

When they got back to the house, Melanie was still at the studio and Trip was holed up in his room. The final strains of "Dead and Gone" by T.I. snaked out into the hallway.

"Oh, God, I'm afraid to find out," Shelby said as she followed Vivi to her room.

"Here," Vivi said as she scanned the instructions, then handed a box to Shelby and directed her into the bathroom. "Ignorance is not bliss. Basically, you just pee on the stick and then wait for the color to tell you whether you're pregnant or not."

"Okay." Shelby looked and sounded about ten. Her face was scrunched up in an effort to hold back tears.

"Look," Vivien said from the other side of the closed door. "Let's not worry until we know we have a reason to." Not that the fact that Shelby had reason to think she might be pregnant wasn't reason enough. She heard the sound of cardboard and then paper being ripped open. Vivien offered up a few prayers on Shelby's behalf, not that any of the ones she'd sent up for herself had been particularly successful. A few minutes later she heard, "Oh, man!"

"What?" Vivi asked. "What is it?"

"My hand was shaking so bad I dropped the stick in the toilet."

Vivien drew a deep breath and then let it out. It wouldn't help for her to get as agitated as Shelby. "Okay, we've got backups. Throw that one in the trash and I'll get you another one." She opened the bathroom door and saw Shelby sitting on the toilet with her jeans puddled around her ankles. She looked way too young to be worrying about this. And horribly frightened.

"Leave the door open," Shelby said. "I, I just don't want to find this out all by myself."

This Vivien understood completely. The doctor's message on the day she'd left CIN, all the shocks that had followed, came rushing back to her and she knew they wouldn't have felt like such body blows if Stone had been there or she'd had anyone else she felt she could confide in.

She doubted she could have survived all the curveballs that had been slung her way without Melanie on her side, and she would not let Shelby face this alone. But in her heart she knew Melanie wouldn't appreciate Vivien keeping her daughter's worries from her. And how would she feel about the fact that Vivien, as Scarlett Leigh, had spent the last months poking fun at her life and those of her friends? She was too busy ripping open the box and handing the slim wand to Shelby to answer. Like the character from which she'd drawn her pseudonym, she'd think about that "tomorrow."

Vivien waited, heart pounding, while Shelby peed on the stick and then held it in front of her for the required period of time.

"What color was positive?" Shelby finally squeaked. "Blue or pink?"

Vivi retrieved the box from the dresser where she'd dropped it and reread the instructions, barely breathing as she did so. "Blue is positive. Pink is negative."

There was a gasp from the bathroom.

"Shelby?" Vivien asked, bracing for the answer. "Don't fool around here. What color did you get?"

"It's pink!" Shelby shouted. "Thank God, it's . . ." She paused as if double-checking. "It's definitely pink!"

There was another pause during which the frenetic beat of Vivien's heart began to slow and her brain kicked back into gear. "We've got one more test, and I am *not* returning it," Vivi said. She ripped the box open, removed the wrapper, and shoved the wand at Shelby. "Here," she said. "Let's just confirm, okay? To be sure."

"All right," Shelby said, and Vivi noticed that the quiver in her voice was already gone. "But I'm expecting another negative. It better be another negative."

Vivien waited in the bathroom doorway. She collapsed onto her bed in relief when Shelby's whoop of joy rang out in the bathroom. "Pink!" she shouted. "I've got another pink!"

Vivien felt as if she'd run a marathon. Dazed and out of breath, she waited for Shelby to get dressed and wash up. She still couldn't move when Shelby finally came into the bedroom and collapsed beside her. "I can't believe how relieved I am."

"That makes two of us," Vivien said.

They sat on the bed, their shoulders touching, both of them spent.

"Thank you, thank you, thank you," Shelby said, but Vivi wasn't sure whether the gratitude was aimed her way or to a more highly placed recipient. When she was able to get her thoughts together, Vivien broached the subject that she had stashed away for after.

"I'm hugely glad you're not pregnant. But this risky behavior has to stop now, this minute. Or I'm going to have to tell your mother."

Shelby tensed and Vivien knew she had to talk fast

before the gratitude and relief were replaced by Shelby's more usual belligerence.

"In my opinion you're much too young to be having intercourse, but if you're going to, you have got to practice safe sex and birth control."

"Like you did?" Already the sarcasm was sneaking back in.

"I'm an adult and our situations are completely different," Vivien said. "And right now we're talking about you."

Shelby turned away from Vivi to face the mirror. Like the day she and Melanie had discussed her own pregnancy, Vivien was aware of the picture they presented. But no matter how grown-up Shelby looked, she was still a girl in many ways.

"I didn't even think you could get pregnant from oral sex," Shelby said in a rush. "But then I didn't get my period, and I was so freaked out."

Vivien paused as Shelby's words sank in.

"You didn't have intercourse and you thought you were pregnant." Vivien tried the statement on for size. Her own sarcasm flew right over Shelby's head.

"He wanted me to go all the way, but I only gave him a blow job." She looked earnestly at Vivien, and Vivien tried not to wince at the word "only."

"You didn't have intercourse?" Vivien felt the need to double-check.

Shelby shook her head dejectedly. "I said I would but then I just . . . couldn't. That's why he was so pissed off." She looked down at her hands, which were folded in her lap. "I didn't even like putting his . . . thing . . . in my mouth. It was gross."

Vivien reached out an arm and put it around Shelby's shoulders. "Nothing is gross when you're in an adult relationship with someone you love and no one's being forced to do something they don't want to."

Shelby drew a deep breath and buried her head in Vivien's neck. "I was so scared I was going to have a baby. And Ty wouldn't even talk to me about it."

The tears came then and Vivien held her niece close while she cried. When the flow subsided, she wiped her niece's cheeks with the pad of her thumb and stared down at her tear-streaked face. "I hope you learned a lesson here, Shelby. It's your body and no one has the right to make you feel like you owe them any part of it."

Shelby nodded and took a swipe at what was left of the tears. Downstairs the garage door swung up, signaling Melanie's return.

"One last thing," Vivien said as the girl shot a frantic look at the door. "I'd start paying a little more attention in health class if I were you. You've just freaked us both out completely over something that's pretty much anatomically impossible."

Shelby blushed and looked away.

"It's time to get it together, girl," she said as kindly as she could. "And believe me, I'm going to be watching."

34

RUTH HAD BEEN very careful not to get too excited about Ira's efforts to appease her. But as the Sunday-afternoon movie and dinner turned into a regular thing and the weekend in Mexico proved so much more fun than either of them had expected, she'd begun to let down her guard and to actually believe that her dog might, in fact, be learning some new tricks.

He'd definitely managed to learn some new dance steps and hadn't missed a single one of their private lessons so far. She smiled as she parked in her usual spot in front of the Magnolia Ballroom and hurried into the building. Her hair was newly washed and styled and she'd taken to dressing with extra care. When she caught a glimpse of herself in the reflective glass of the front door, she realized that she was smiling.

"Ruth!" Melanie came out of the office when she spotted her and walked over to give her a hug. "Your hair looks great." She took in Ruth's new outfit, a black gabardine pantsuit that she'd paired with a lime green silk blouse. "And I love that color on you." She stepped back to study

Ruth more closely. "Did you have something done? I can't quite put my finger on it, but you look different."

Ruth shook her head but could feel that the smile was still stretched across her face. She suspected the change was simple happiness. Or should she shock Melanie by telling her she thought it was a result of the sex that she and Ira were once again having as often as possible? She felt the smile stretch wider. Who would have ever thought it?

"Nope." She was beaming now, and it felt good. "It's just me."

They walked into the office, and Ruth sat across Melanie's desk from her. Fliers promoting the new spring classes were stacked in one box, and the envelopes, which one of the assistants had labeled earlier in the week, were in another. They started the folding, stuffing, and stamping process as they caught up with each other.

"How're Shelby and Trip?" Ruth asked. "Will they be at Angela and James's wedding?"

"Well, Shelby seems to be coming so that she can say she was there and is insisting on pictures to prove it. And, of course, Trip pretty much worships the ground James and his father walk on, although both James and Vivi have refused to get in a car with him again."

"I guess your sister isn't so bad," Ruth observed, feeling generous even toward Vivien. "She must be pretty close to D-day."

"She's actually due on the twelfth, so she may or may not make it to the wedding. But she finally seems to have accepted the fact that she's going to be a mother; she's been running around like a maniac getting ready. Her overnight bag is sitting right next to the garage door now, and she made me promise if she was too out of it to speak that I'd demand her epidural the minute we arrive at the hospital."

Ruth laughed. "That was a helluva snake arms she did Wednesday night."

"Hey, all I know is she still shows up for class even though she can barely walk. And she really seems to be connecting with the kids. She's been way more involved in our lives than I ever expected." Melanie straightened the growing stack of stuffed envelopes. "Speaking of better than expected, what's going on with Ira?"

Ruth tried to keep her smile in check, but it just kept taking over her face. "It's been great. I just can't believe that on top of everything else, it turns out he likes to dance! He even said something about maybe competing as a team." Even as she said these things, Ruth could hardly believe them. She felt as if she'd asked for a small loan of some kind and been handed a million dollars.

"Wow." Melanie's astonishment equaled Ruth's own. "It's funny how people can surprise you, isn't it?"

"I'll say," Ruth agreed. "Only most surprises aren't such good ones."

They worked in silence for a few minutes before the phone rang. Ruth picked up and thanked the caller for calling the Magnolia Ballroom.

"Yes," the unfamiliar male voice said. "Is Melanie Jackson there? This is Bruce Summers, um, Dr. Bruce Summers."

Ruth covered the mouthpiece and handed the phone to Melanie. "It's Dr. Summers," she said. "Is everything okay?"

Melanie nodded. "I'm fine. It's, um, not a professional call." Her cheeks turned red.

"Oh," Ruth said. "Oh!" The smile was back. "In that case, I'll go check on the, um . . . janitorial supplies." She stood. "To see if we need any."

Melanie raised the receiver to her ear, but she didn't speak until Ruth was out of the office. As she walked by the plate-glass window, Ruth stole a look into the office and saw a smile curving on Melanie's lips and another blush suffusing her cheeks.

It was the same sort of smile that Ruth felt on her own face; it was a bit strange and alien, but it was one she wouldn't mind getting used to.

ᕫ

VIVIEN WOKE BEFORE dawn on the day she was due. In the early morning quiet, she lay without moving beneath the covers and silently took stock. Large protruding stomach. Check. Massive, overly sensitive breasts. Check. Swollen ankles and hands. Check. Aching back. Check. Urgent need to pee. Double check.

But contractions? Not a single one.

All day Vivi stayed close to home eyeing the packed bag she'd placed next to the garage door. Trying not to imagine the actual delivery, and hoping that her rejection of Lamaze class was not going to prove a problem, she focused instead on no longer being pregnant. Over and over she picked up the phone and pulled up Stone's number, but each time she hung up before punching anything in.

She didn't even have a column to write. She'd filed several in advance, including today's, which painted today's lavish weddings as nothing more than a ticket to suburbia, which she'd railed against as little more than an updated version of the white picket fence. To this she added a terse rant about the ways in which women continued to try to live the fairy tale, afraid to present themselves as they really were. The only thing that had enabled her to write such a piece in view of the upcoming Wesley wedding was her anonymity and her refusal to visualize Angela's face as she wrote it. It was the most hypocritical thing she'd ever written.

The one column she hadn't written was the one she'd planned on the suburbanites who'd flocked to ballroom dance studios after watching *Dancing with the Stars*. Even she, who felt as if she'd dissected and used almost every particle of her sister's life, wasn't ready to sink quite that low.

The house phone rang on and off all day, but the only numbers Vivi recognized on the caller ID were Catherine Dennison's and her parents', so she let everything go to voice mail. After a light lunch that she hoped wouldn't interfere with the availability of anesthesia in case she went into labor soon after, she went back over J.J.'s case file one last time, but found nothing new or worth sinking her teeth into. In his old office, she conducted what she acknowledged as a final search, but she found no PDA, and his credit card and cell phone bills provided no new insights. The person J.J. called most after Melanie was Clay Alexander; given the length of their friendship and their business relationship, this was hardly newsworthy. Vivi had never been one to give up on her gut, but it seemed that her pregnancy had caused it to send out faulty signals. The time had come to let go.

The day stretched into eternity as Vivien waited for something to happen. A contraction. The discharge of the mucous plug. A leaking of fluid that would signal that her water had broken. Anything that signaled the onset of labor would have been welcome. But none of these things happened. She was finally forced to accept that she might not give birth today, just as Dr. Gilbert had warned.

When she finally heard the garage door go up late that afternoon, Vivien practically ran downstairs to greet Melanie, so badly did she need someone to talk her down off her emotional ledge. But one look at Melanie's face told her that whatever Melanie was about to say was not going to make her feel better. Something was terribly wrong.

When Melanie rounded on her and slapped a section of the *Atlanta Journal-Constitution* in her hand, Vivien found out what it was.

Matt Glazer's lead read, *How the mighty have fallen*, and continued, *First she lost her network gig, then she got pregnant. Now Vivien Gray is public enemy number one in our northern suburbs where she's been living undercover and writing as the notoriously nasty Scarlett Leigh.*

Ah, you ask, how can that be when Ms. Gray is so very smug about her role as a serious journalist? Well, in addition to the catty articles she's been ashamed or afraid to admit to, Just Peachy has learned that the very pregnant Miss Gray has been busy investigating the presumably accidental death of her former brother-in-law, Republican legislator J.J. Jackson!

Just Peachy hears that no stone has been left unturned. Except for hunky international correspondent Stone Seymour that is, who may or may not be the father of Ms. Gray's child.

Vivien stopped reading and looked up into her sister's face.

"Is this true, Vivi?" Melanie asked. "Is it?"

"Which part?" Vivien asked when she regained her speech.

"You have written all of those vicious articles?"

Vivi nodded again. And winced.

"All those people I introduced you to, the things I shared about my life, you took those things and mocked them in front of a national audience?"

Another nod. Vivi couldn't think of a thing to say, not that Melanie gave her a chance to.

"And you are investigating my husband's death?"

A nod. "Well, it wasn't really a—"

"Not what?" Melanie cut her off. "Not a real investigation? How dare you go around asking questions about J.J.? How dare you pry into our life and the way that he died? Why would you do that? What were you thinking? What gave you the right?"

Vivien didn't know how to answer. All of Stone's warnings came crashing down around her as she faced her sister's hurt and wrath. "I didn't trust Clay. He seemed to be too attached to you and the kids." Her voice trailed off. "I felt he had an ulterior motive and so I decided to look into it."

"You felt he had an ulterior motive?" Melanie asked. "Because he was kind to us? Because he was there for us when you and the rest of my family weren't?"

Melanie's accusations landed like blows; they were weighted with truth and they were perfectly placed.

"Whatever possessed you to do this?"

"I suspected he was in love with you," Vivi said in a rush. "And there's no question that he's hiding something. I think he knows a lot more about J.J.'s death than he's saying. I—"

"J.J.'s death was an accident, and you're trying to turn it into the crime of the century," Melanie cut her off, her hurt and anger as cutting as any blade. "Is this how you investigated things in New York? Did you just come up with ideas willy-nilly and then look for ways to prove them?"

"It wasn't willy-nilly," Vivi said. "I just went over the case file. And interviewed one of J.J. and Clay's former professors and, um, the president of Sigma Sigma when they were at UGA."

Melanie looked at her as if she were completely mad. At the moment Vivi thought she might be.

"And although I didn't come up with hard evidence of a crime, there are lots of things that just feel . . . suspicious."

Melanie stared at her as if she'd grown two heads and sprouted a tail.

"Mel," Vivi said, feeling the need to at least prove she'd had reason to investigate. "It's all so weird. I mean Clay was the only one there when J.J. died and now he's practically head of J.J.'s household and getting ready to run for J.J.'s seat?"

Melanie looked at her, shook her head. "Vivien, this is ridiculous. You know when you went after Harley Jenkins and Mom and Dad got so upset, I defended you. He'd done something wrong, illegal. He'd abused his office and you were right to go after him. But you're investigating Clay because he was there when J.J. died and has remained our friend?" She laughed and there was not an ounce of humor in it. "You are certifiable!"

"I was just looking for the truth. I figured if there was no proof of any wrongdoing on Clay's part, no harm, no foul. But if he was hiding something, you'd want to know."

"And then you could take what you found to the networks, I'll bet. You always like to say it's about the truth, but what it's really about is you. Finding a story that will take you where you want to go."

"No, that's not it. I . . ." Vivien began.

"I don't really care what your reasons were, Vivi. I thought we had learned something about each other. That we would really be there for each other. But I don't know you at all. And you sure as hell don't know me." Melanie's voice was quiet now, resigned.

"Melanie, please. I did this out of love. I didn't . . ."

"You don't know what love is," Melanie said. "Maybe having this baby will teach you something about putting others first. I hope so. But I'll never trust you again. It's always about the story for you, Viv. Using somebody else's pain or problems, what you like to call the truth, to get ahead."

"Come on, Melanie, that's not it. You know that's not right."

"No? Well, you wanna know the truth?" Melanie asked. "I was happier before I let myself care so much about you. It was better when we lived completely different lives and just waved hello at the holidays." She started to leave the room but turned back.

"You're welcome to stay here until the baby is born and for as long as you need to get on your feet after that. Because you're my sister. And your baby will be my flesh and blood. But after that, you're on your own. I'm ashamed of you and your behavior. And the only other person I've ever felt that way about is our mother. You're a lot more like her than you think, Vivi. And as you know, that is *not* a compliment."

Melanie went up to her room and closed the door firmly behind her. Vivien just stood there for a few long, painful moments trying to process what had just taken place. There was a sharp twinge in her stomach and for a brief moment she thought maybe her time had come, sincerely hoped that it had so that she'd have something to distract her from this nightmare.

But once again, nothing happened. And so Vivien took a bottled water out of the refrigerator, climbed the stairs up to her bedroom, and closed the door behind her. She stayed there the rest of the evening and all of the night and only came out in the morning when she could tell that everyone had left.

For the next week, Vivien waited to give birth. It was by far the worst and longest week of her life and not just because she was so tired of being pregnant she thought she might have to rip the baby out herself. But because Melanie and the kids simply stopped speaking to her. There were no more recriminations, no ugly scenes, there

was always extra food in the fridge for her, but she didn't
join them at meals or join in on any of their conversations
because they'd made it quite clear that although she was
present, she was no longer welcome in their lives.

Equally bad was that all of them were taking flack
for her columns as Scarlett Leigh. Trip got detention for
fighting with another student who'd made fun of him
for being related to "that pregnant bitch Scarlett Leigh."
Catherine had called to say she had *not* turned in any of
their neighbors or watered inappropriately and hung up
rather loudly. And one morning they woke up to the
smell of what turned out to be burning poopy diapers,
which had been spread out in a giant SL on the front lawn
and then set ablaze.

The stack of hate mail left in the mailbox and on the
front step continued to grow, and someone, she assumed
Melanie, had taken to leaving it in teetering heaps in
front of her bedroom door. After reading the first few
scathing messages, Vivi had begun stashing them in the
bedroom closet, where they would be out of sight but
unfortunately not out of mind.

On the bright side, which Vivien tried desperately
every morning to dredge up, Shelby seemed to have settled
down after her brush with motherhood and was studying
both for her SATs and her regular classes, and the too-
wild Ty Womack had not been replaced. Trip seemed a
bit more talkative, though not to her, and it seemed that
the relationship with the Wesleys had begun to bring
him out of his shell. Both of the kids and Melanie were
looking forward to Angela and James's wedding, which
was now only a few days away. She knew this from the
conversations she was now blatantly eavesdropping on,
but none of them asked if she planned to attend. Nor did
Melanie offer her a ride to the last Magnolia Wednesday.

The night before the wedding to which she suspected

she was no longer welcome, Vivien wrote what she intended to be Scarlett Leigh's last column. In it she said all of the things Melanie and the kids refused to hear and bid her readers a final farewell. After she'd sent it off to John Harcourt along with her resignation, Vivien washed her face, brushed her teeth, sent an artificially upbeat email to Stone, and climbed heavily into bed.

35

A NGELA RICHMAN'S WEDDING day dawned bright and
sunny, the most perfect of spring days. Angela sleep-
walked through most of the morning; when she was forced
to confront her image in the mirror, she saw the uncertainty and conflicted emotions tucked away inside just as
she had always seen Fangie.

In the bridal dressing room at the Alpharetta Country
Club, strategically located between the small ballroom
where the wedding would take place and the large ballroom where the elaborate luncheon and dancing would
follow, Angela's attendants sipped complimentary champagne and helped each other dress.

Angela did her best to join in. She smiled and nodded and even raised her champagne glass in acknowledgment whenever someone proposed a toast, but she was
careful not to drink. She had the strangest feeling that
she needed to keep her wits about her. And, of course, she
didn't want to forget to breathe.

When the time came to put on her gown, she allowed

the others to dress her and through it all she remembered to smile and look happy. But the entire time she felt as if she might be dragged under by the great waves of panic that threatened to swamp her; she concentrated on drawing plenty of air into her lungs just in case.

Her mother, Emily, zipped the back of the gown with shaking fingers, and Angela knew the trembling was the result of her mother's excitement and happiness. James's mother, Cassie, affixed her veil and smoothed the netting behind her head. Her smile was heartfelt and unclouded by reservation of any kind. Angela fervently wished she could feel the same. Both mothers told her how beautiful she looked and how lucky she and James were to have found each other. They pressed gentle kisses to her cheeks, careful not to disturb her makeup. She felt like a liar and a cheat. Their certainty made her want to cry.

Brian arrived for a long round of picture taking during which Angela moved and smiled and tilted her head, her chin, and her body as directed. She stood between Emily and Cassie and then with her matron of honor, Susan, and each of her four other bridesmaids. She did her best to look reflective and happy and whatever else Brian suggested, but her mind was off in a place of its own, feinting and dodging. Unable to work up the nerve to do what she should have already done.

"So then I'll go make sure the groom's not off looking to make a run for it, luv," Brian teased before he left, trying to get another smile out of her. But Angela knew James was not planning an escape. Nor was he in his dressing room second-guessing his decision. James Wesley was not a flight risk; she wasn't so sure the same could be said for her.

"Here," Susan said, placing a freshly poured flute of champagne in her hand. "You look like you need this."

Angela tried to hand it back, but Susan refused to take it. The alcohol slid down her throat, unlike the air that seemed to have such difficulty getting where it needed to go. Halfway through the glass her insides began to warm and her pulse began to slow.

There was a knock on the door, and one of her bridesmaids ushered Ruth and Melanie inside. "You look so beautiful," Melanie said. "That dress is fabulous on you!"

Melanie and the mothers hugged, and Ruth was introduced. "You two look pretty snazzy yourselves," Angela said, eager to talk about something besides herself and her failure to tell James the truth. "And you look . . . incredibly happy," she said to Ruth, hoping no one heard the envy in her voice.

"I am," the older woman said, her smile lighting up her face. "Ira's agreed to sell the business. Or at least to entertain a serious offer. And he's promised that we'll cruise the Greek Islands this summer." She looked more closely at Angela. "Are you all right?"

Emily brought them both flutes of champagne and replaced Angela's now-empty glass with a full one so that they could toast Ruth's news. Angela thought that maybe if she drank enough she'd be able to convince herself that the numb, removed feeling was the result of the alcohol. Fangie had been oddly silent today. For a moment Angela pictured her on her fictional cruise and imagined her ticket had been one-way. She drained her glass and asked for another, ignoring Ruth and Melanie's looks of concern.

As they talked and drank, Angela's breathing became a little easier—not quite automatic and unnoticeable, but not so ragged, either. Making conversation became less of an effort. She even managed to stop imagining what would happen if she told her mother that she wasn't sure she could go through with the wedding. Confessed that although she loved James, she couldn't marry him until she showed him who she used to be.

She looked up to see Melanie and Ruth staring at her, clearly waiting for a response. "I'm sorry," Angela said. "What did you say?"

"We were just saying how excited the class is to be here. We can't wait to see you and James have your first dance as husband and wife," Ruth said.

The word "wife" hit her then fully and completely. In thirty minutes she and James were going to stand in front of the minister and say their vows. Life as she knew it would be over and her life as Mrs. James Wesley would begin. Her throat closed, trapping the champagne and cutting off the air she so desperately needed. If she didn't tell him about who she'd been now, when would she? On their first anniversary? Their tenth? Or after she gave birth to their first child and couldn't get rid of the extra pounds?

"Are you okay?" Melanie asked, concerned.

Angela nodded and pointed to her throat, trying to act like it was just a mis-swallow and not abject fear that was making her cough and sputter.

"Your face is awfully white," Ruth observed.

"No, no, I'm fine," Angela said with a final cough. "I just couldn't breathe there for a second."

There was another knock on the door, and then Vivien Gray stepped inside. She wore a bright lime-colored linen dress that stretched to the bursting point over the huge mound of her stomach and a matching bolero-style jacket with oversized square buttons. Her dark hair was tucked haphazardly behind her ears. As she waddled into the room, she looked as out of breath as Angela felt.

"What's she doing here?" Ruth hissed in the silence that fell.

Melanie's lips tightened into a grim unhappy line, but she didn't comment on her sister's appearance.

"I can't believe she has the nerve to show her face after those horrible articles," Emily Richman said. "Especially that one about the excesses of today's weddings. And how marriage is nothing more than an expensive ticket to suburbia."

Cassie didn't look too pleased, either. "She looks like she could pop at any minute," she said. "I sure hope she waits until the ceremony's over to have that baby."

Leading with her stomach, Vivien continued straight toward Angela. One by one the others excused themselves, passing Vivien as they exited. Angela stayed where she was, her gaze fixed on Vivien. The column that had so incensed her mother and future mother-in-law had struck a chord with Angela. It had been rudely put and intentionally combative, but much of Scarlett Leigh's rant had struck Angela as nothing short of the truth. And, of course, telling the truth had been its central theme.

"I didn't come to disturb your big day," Vivien said as she drew near. "And I promise I won't stay." She took Angela's hand between both of hers and held it tightly. "I just wanted to apologize to you in person. I took things that were meant to be serious and special and I poked fun at them. I made vows of love and commitment and the importance of choosing the right person to spend your life with appear secondary to finding the right dress and going with the most current color scheme. I took all those small choices and blew them way out of proportion like I did with all the columns." She gave Angela's hand a squeeze. "And I mean look at me. I have absolutely no right to write the things I did. What do I know about love and commitment? Building a life with someone? Telling the truth?

"I haven't even told the father of my child, whom I

love, that we're going to have a baby. And I can't tell you how much I regret it. I'd do it all so differently now if I had the chance." She looked down at her stomach and back up at Angela. "Anyway, I'm sorry. And I just wanted to say so." She let go of Angela's hand and began to turn away.

"No," Angela said, and for the first time that day, maybe in months, her thoughts didn't skitter away from the truth. "You said a lot of things that deserved to be said. Sometimes it takes an outsider to point out that the emperor forgot his clothes. I think a lot of your observations were dead-on. Like how women still change themselves for men, become things they aren't." Or in her case, hide not only who she'd been, but how that had shaped her into who she was now, because she was afraid that James wouldn't love her.

"Oh, no," Vivi said. "I was not dead-on." She shook her head, adamant. "When I started writing Postcards from Suburbia, I was completely ignorant, and making fun was easy. But later, when I saw people's reasons for their actions and knew nothing was as simple as I was trying to paint it, I just ignored the truth so that I could find an angle that would allow me to write what I needed to. I have twisted the truth to serve my own ends. And I've kept it from people I owed it to."

"So you think I should show James the picture and tell him I'll understand if he doesn't want to marry me?" Angela asked as she drew what felt like her first clear unrestricted breath in weeks.

Vivien's face reflected her surprise. "Well, no, not exactly. I mean I didn't say . . ."

Angela considered the woman in front of her, about to give birth without the father of her child by her side. Maybe if Vivien had told Stone the truth, he'd be here right now. "I'm doing the wrong thing, aren't I?"

"What?" Vivien was beginning to look a little worried, but Angela was feeling infinitely better as the fog of uncertainty began to clear.

"I can't believe I've spent so much time agonizing over this." She was nodding her head now, finally grasping what had to be done. "Thank God you came in to talk to me before I did something both James and I might regret for the rest of our lives."

Her thoughts moved nimbly now and she stopped thinking about her breathing and began to think instead about exactly what she wanted to say to James. She'd been an imbecile to think she could marry him without sharing herself completely. And that included Fangie and the fact that she'd spent most of her life fat and unhappy about it. That even now she feared losing control again. Of sliding back down the slope it had taken so much effort to climb.

Angela reached down to grab hold of the train of her dress, folding it over one arm as she'd been shown, then picked up her purse with the other, the dog-eared photo stuffed in its depths. She drew in a deep breath and let it out, and there wasn't an ounce of difficulty in it now that she'd made her decision.

"Where are you going?" Vivien asked as Angela excused herself.

"I'm going to go find James and explain why I can't marry him today; there's so much we need to talk about. And then I guess I'll need to go find my parents." She threw her arms around Vivi as the relief coursed through her. "Thank you so much for helping me figure this out. I'll never forget what you've done for me."

Vivi's mouth dropped open in surprise, and she felt decidedly ill as Angela rushed out of the room. She'd only come here to apologize and somehow she'd inspired

Angela to call off her wedding? Melanie was never going to forgive her.

Ignoring the bridesmaids' startled looks, Vivi took off after Angela, but by the time she'd waddled out of the dressing room, Angela had already covered the lobby and was disappearing around a far corner.

Trying to catch her breath and still the jumble in her stomach, Vivi slowed to a stop. Angela was long gone, but she spotted Shelby up ahead. By the time she reached Shelby in the doorway of the club's cocktail lounge, Vivien was again short of breath.

Shelby was so focused on whatever was taking place in the empty lounge that she didn't seem to notice her aunt's arrival.

Vivi heard male voices. Looking over Shelby's shoulder, she saw Clay Alexander, his back to them, a drink in his hand. Another man, someone Vivi didn't know, stood in front of him. The two were standing close together, talking quietly, almost intimately.

She was still trying to decipher what felt wrong about the scene when Shelby stepped into the room as if to get a closer look.

"Oh, my God!" Shelby's voice rang out as she moved toward Clay. "You're gay, too! I knew my father was gay, and I knew he had a boyfriend." Her voice quivered. "After he died I found a whole box of cards and letters he had wrapped up with a stupid ribbon. And all of them were signed, 'Love, C.' "

Shelby pointed an accusing finger at him. "It was you, wasn't it?" she said, her voice incredulous. "You're C!"

Vivien became aware of someone standing beside her just before she heard Melanie's sharp intake of breath. As they watched, Clay's face crumpled in on itself, the strong, even features blurring and becoming misshapen in grief.

The other man bent toward Clay, resting his hand protectively on Clay's shoulder. Clay shook his head, his gaze never leaving Shelby. The man left.

"You were like my second dad. You always had all those girlfriends." Shelby began to cry. "I never ever thought it could be you."

"This can't be right," Melanie whispered beside her. "This is a mistake."

But of course it wasn't.

"Your dad loved you," Clay said to Shelby. "He loved all of you."

Melanie pushed past Vivien.

"You?" Melanie whispered, shaking her head. "And J.J.? I don't believe it."

Shelby turned on her mother. "Which part, Mom? That your husband was gay? Or that he was in love with Clay?" She spat the words out, infuriated by her mother's ignorance. "What kind of woman doesn't even know she's married to a . . . a *homosexual*?"

"But I don't understand. How did this happen? How long did it go on?"

Clay looked at Melanie, and Vivien thought she'd never felt so much pain in one place. Except possibly in her stomach. Which had seized up so tightly she could hardly breathe.

"We were always attracted to each other," Clay said. "From the time we met in college. But J.J. didn't want to admit it. He wanted a . . . conventional life." His jaw tightened. "And a career in politics." He searched Melanie's face, looking for something, though Vivi couldn't imagine what.

"So you both got married and played it straight," Vivien said. "Until J.J. decided to run for office and you had your opportunity." It was all so clear now. She'd had all the pieces but she'd refused to see how they actually fit together. "Grady Hollis thought you were in love with Melanie. Professor Sturgess said you always came in second. I thought maybe you resented J.J. and were jealous of his life."

He turned to her as if only now noticing that she was there. "You talked to Phil and Grady? Why would you go to all that trouble?" he asked. "What was the point?"

"At first I thought you'd somehow killed J.J. and made it look like an accident, because you coveted his wife and family, because you were tired of coming in second."

Melanie turned terrible eyes on Vivien. "You had to dig into things that were better left alone. You couldn't just mind your own business and let us get on with our lives."

"You didn't kill him, did you?" Shelby asked, her voice trembling.

"Of course not," Clay said. "I loved him." The sheen of tears filled his eyes, turning them a wintry gray. His face contorted in an effort to hold them back.

Melanie stepped forward and slapped Clay Alexander across the face. Shelby buried her face in her hands. Her sobs filled the air as she rushed from the room.

Vivien's stomach roiled again; heat rushed through her body.

"I was married to someone I never even knew," Melanie said. "The great love of my life wasn't even in love with me." Her words were as cutting as her tone. "Because he was in love with you."

"I'm sorry," he said. "I never wanted you to know."

"I can't even look at you," Melanie said, turning away and heading for the door, calling after Shelby.

Vivien studied Clay Alexander's haggard face, the mixture of regret and relief apparent on it.

"How did J.J. really die?" she asked quietly. "He didn't really kill himself cleaning a gun . . . did he?"

Clay was silent for a long moment. "He couldn't live with the guilt of loving me, of living a double life," he finally said. "So he ended it. He killed himself."

He broke eye contact and dropped his head. Vivi waited while he retrieved his wallet from his back pocket and withdrew two tattered pieces of paper from it.

"I'd gone outside, I don't even remember why. I was on my way back in when I heard the gunshot. He'd written a note of apology to Melanie." He gave the scrap of stationery to Vivien. "And he left one for me asking me to look after his family."

Vivien unfolded the paper and read J.J.'s final words to his wife.

I just can't go on living this way. It hurts too much. And it's not fair to you and Shelby and Trip. All of you deserve so much more than I'm able to give. Don't ever question that I love you all. But I can't change who or what I am. Or how I feel about Clay.

"I removed the notes," Clay said. "So the insurance would pay out, so Melanie and the kids would be taken care of." His voice was unbearably sad. "I've done my best to look out for them." He straightened, but there was a hunch to his shoulders that hadn't been there before. "So now you know the truth. That's what you were looking for, wasn't it?"

Vivi reread J.J.'s plea for forgiveness and realized what she now held in her hand. A legislator engaged in a homosexual affair with his campaign manager? A suicide to end it? A stunned family who'd had no idea? Those were the kinds of story elements that any network would pay big bucks for, that any investigative journalist worth her salt would kill for. This story was an automatic ticket back to the top of network news.

Not long ago she wouldn't have hesitated to cash in that ticket.

But she wasn't that person anymore, was she? She tucked J.J.'s suicide note into her purse.

Clay turned and began to walk away. At the doorway he carefully sidestepped the Melnicks, who blustered in with a still-hysterical Shelby and Melanie between them. Ira called after Clay, demanding to know what was going on, but Clay Alexander kept walking.

The opening strains of the Wedding March were audible from the small ballroom but had barely established itself when the music screeched to a halt in midchord. There was some sort of announcement on the sound system and an agitated hum of conversation. It sounded as if Angela might actually have called off the wedding. Or maybe James had.

Could the day *get* any worse? Ira's face was flushed with anger, but he seemed unsure where to direct it. Vivien's stomach actually rippled with the pain that tore through her, and her skin felt clammy as her sister said, "Are you happy now? Now that you've got a nice juicy story?"

"No," Vivi said. "No, I wouldn't . . ." She doubled over to clutch her stomach. "Not now. Not . . ."

"Melanie," Ruth asked. "What happened? Has she done something to you?" She asked this even though Vivien was the one bent in half, trying to halt the pain. "Ira," Ruth said. "Do something!"

Ira turned to Vivien. "What's going on here?" he demanded.

Vivien would have answered, but there was another burst of pain and her knees began to buckle. She looked into Ira Melnick's face and saw that it had turned a pale and ghostly white. A throbbing vein zigzagged starkly against his forehead. The blaze of anger in his eyes turned to confusion and then surprise as he clutched his chest and sank to his knees at Ruth's feet.

"Ira." Ruth gasped. "What are you doing down there? What's wrong?"

Vivien looked up into her sister's drawn face. She looked down at Ira in a heap on the floor. And she felt something inside her rip loose.

Something warm and wet trickled down the inside of Vivi's leg.

"Call nine-one-one!" Vivi cried as she clutched her heaving stomach and stared down at the amniotic fluid seeping out of her. "I think Ira's had a heart attack!"

She swallowed as the fluid pooled at her feet and formed an amoebalike stain on the plush red carpet. "And I think I'm finally going to have this baby."

36

EVERYTHING HAPPENED SO quickly after that that Melanie could hardly absorb what was taking place. The ambulance arrived and the paramedics carried Ira out, racing him to Saint Joseph's Hospital, with Ruth at his side.

Melanie, who felt as if her own guts had been torn out and stuffed down her throat, gathered up Shelby, located Trip, and got them and Vivien into the car for the ride to Northside, where Vivi was apparently going to give birth.

Vivi managed to reach Dr. Gilbert's emergency service between labor pains and passed much of the ride bemoaning the fact that she'd sloughed off Lamaze classes and trying to remember how long it took for an epidural to kick in. When her fingers grew too clumsy to perform, she passed her phone to Shelby and asked her to text Stone that Vivi was on the way to the hospital to give birth to his child.

"You never even told him he was going to have a baby?" Shelby asked in mid text.

Vivi, who was busy huffing unsuccessfully through another contraction, shook her head.

"Could we *be* any more dysfunctional?" Shelby demanded. "Jesus! What's with this family and all the secrets?"

It might have been a great teaching moment or a chance to at least explain things to Trip, but Melanie was far too freaked out to do any of those things. The truth about J.J. kept hammering at her brain while she tried her hardest not to let it in.

But she couldn't forget Shelby's shriek, "What kind of woman doesn't even know she's married to a . . . a *homosexual*?" But she hadn't. J.J. had been kind and gentle. And their lovemaking had been like that, too. Not a blaze of passion but a warm and encompassing thing. Should that have told her what she should have known? Had she simply been too cowardly to face facts that were difficult? Not now, she told herself. Just drive, don't think.

She made it through several stoplights and onto 400 south when thoughts of Ira and Ruth crowded in; was he okay? Was he even still alive? How would Ruth cope? With a shake of her head, she pushed those worries aside, too.

She drove as fast as she dared, tuning out Vivi's panting and the groans that became whimpers. Her anger at her sister was the one thing she could grab hold of—so much of this could be laid at Vivi's feet—and so she stoked it until it became a solid and tangible thing, something she could cling to. She would see her sister through labor as she'd promised, but she could hardly bring herself to look at her.

"Where is my epidural?" Vivi gasped as the nurse helped her into the hospital gown, then walked her to the delivery room bed. "I need that epidural now!" She gasped again when another contraction grabbed on to her and refused to let go. "And a doctor!" Vivi added, frightened. "Where is Dr. Gilbert?"

She looked to Melanie, who didn't meet her eye and who clearly wanted to be anywhere but here. The contractions were growing stronger and coming faster. Vivien felt her eyes glaze over with pain and fear.

"I know you're upset right now," Vivi panted from the bed. "And I totally get it, Mel. But I need you." Another pain grabbed hold of Vivi and held on with all its might. She wished she'd taken the time to learn where and how to breathe. She wished this was already over. She wished Melanie would speak to her, but her sister was glaring at her now. Like it was Vivi's fault that J.J. was gay and that Melanie hadn't known that he'd been in love with Clay Alexander.

"Mel, please," she said, horrified to realize she was begging. "I am completely sorry I ever started looking into J.J.'s death. I'm even sorrier that you found out things you didn't want to know. And that Shelby had to hear it."

Melanie looked at her then, but she didn't speak. And she didn't leave the room to drag someone in with an epidural, either.

"I am also sorry that Ira had a heart attack over it. That I wrote those articles as Scarlett Leigh." She gasped her way through another contraction, then sent Melanie an imploring and, she hoped, contrite enough look to break through the logjam of anger. "Although I only did it because I had no alternative. And I never, ever, thought of you as being like that. You were completely excepted because . . ."

"Oh, shut up!" Melanie said. "You always have an excuse for what you do. Everybody does. But that doesn't make the people they shit all over feel any better!"

"I would shut up, Mel, if you would just get me that epidural. And a doctor. I'd definitely shut up for a doctor.

These labor pains are"—she gasped as another one took hold and shook her from the inside out—"painful!"

"I believe that's why they call them labor pains and not labor 'owies,'" Melanie said. "You're just lucky that Scarlett Leigh didn't poke fun at the act of giving birth or I'd turn all the other laboring women loose on you."

"Mel, please! If I had a white flag, I'd wave it. I can't fight with you and give birth at the same time." She panted. "Oh, God, don't they have surrogates for this? I could really use a stand-in right now."

"All right," Melanie said and moved closer. "But later you'll have a lot to answer for."

"What do we have here?" The voice was male and jovial, but it did not belong to Dr. Gilbert. The doctor who strolled in, not at all in a rush as far as Vivien could see, was Dr. Summers. And he was looking not at Vivi, who lay panting and miserable on the bed, but at Melanie.

"I need an epidural," Vivi said through the useless panting and breathing. "Now!"

"Well, now," he said, barely able to take his eyes off Melanie. "Why don't we take a look and see what's what?"

A nurse appeared to help Vivi into position, and a sheet was drawn up over her knees as Dr. Summers sat down on a stool and slid into place.

"It won't be long now," he said. "You're dilating nicely. You may not even need . . ."

"Doctor," Vivien said through teeth that were clenched against the oncoming locomotive of pain. "I want the epidural. Now. Sooner would be even better."

Melanie moved closer, but which one of them she was approaching was unclear. "Maybe you don't need it, Vivi. Maybe Bruce is right and . . ."

"I want my epidural now!" she repeated and mercifully an anesthesiologist appeared. Careful not to look at the large needle she'd made the mistake of reading about, Vivi let him lean her forward and swab a spot near the base of her spine.

After that the pain went away and left her alone. She could still feel the contractions, could tell something was happening, but it was all happening at an acceptable distance, muted and manageable. Her mind cleared, now that it wasn't running in fear from the onrush of pain, and she actually conversed with the doctor whom her sister kept calling Bruce and who tried, rather unsuccessfully, to act as interested in her and the baby he was delivering as he was in Melanie.

©

VIVI LAY WITH her son cradled against her chest. He was tiny and perfect and he had a wizened face that looked an awful lot like a prune.

"He's beautiful," Melanie said. She and the kids stood next to Vivien's bed, peering down at the two of them. *Her and her son.* She thought the words for the first time and they didn't frighten her as she'd thought they would.

"He looks kind of like a little old man," Trip said. "Or a wrinkly peanut. Why is he making that face and scrunching all up like that?"

"He's going to the bathroom, stupid," Shelby said. She put a finger out, and the baby grasped it instinctually in one of his tiny hands.

Vivien looked up at them. They all appeared as shell-shocked as she felt. In so many ways their lives had caved in today, the bedrock on which their family had been built crumbling all around them. When she looked into her sister's eyes, she saw fresh pain mixed with an old sadness, and she had to look away.

"I called Mom and Dad. I just thought they should

know they had a new grandson," Melanie said, reaching out to cup the baby's head. "And I left another voice mail for Stone. And one for Marty, like you asked me to."

"Has Stone called back?" Vivi asked.

"No. Not yet."

"How's Ira?" Vivi had forgotten in the throes of labor and then she'd been afraid to ask.

"He's in CCU; they're trying to get him stabilized. Ruth couldn't come to the phone, but I spoke to their son. Their daughters are flying in tonight."

"I hope he'll be all right," Vivi said as the nurse came to take the baby back to the nursery. She was so tired she could hardly speak but oddly exhilarated at the same time.

"Me, too," Melanie said and in just two words managed to remind Vivi that she held her personally responsible for Ira's heart attack. "I'll probably stop by there before I come see you tomorrow. Saint Joseph's is just around the corner. And I'd really like to get hold of Angela." The tight-lipped look she shot Vivi made it clear that the canceled wedding had been chalked up to her, too.

"Good night, Mel," Vivien said, too tired to address all that was between them. Her limbs grew heavy and her thoughts slowed. "Have to have a name for him before we leave the hospital," she murmured. "Wanted to wait for Stone, but . . . you guys'll have to help."

Melanie snorted as Vivi's eyes closed. "Only you could go through an entire pregnancy and never even think about what you were going to call your child."

Vivi half smiled at the truth of it. Denial certainly was a bitch, but those days were over. And then she was off and dreaming. But like her life her dreams were a mixed bag of soft baby smells and her sister's pinched face and stark stories from the nightly news that didn't come with guaranteed happy endings.

◯

RUTH SAT IN the tiny room in CCU watching the blip of Ira's heartbeats on the monitor. Her children and three of her grandchildren waited out in the waiting room. In the first few days while they'd waited for Ira to stabilize she'd thought she'd lose her mind. Then there'd been the angioplasty, and after that a coronary artery bypass graft. Ruth could hardly keep up with the medical jargon and was grateful that she had a son-in-law who could.

Through it all Ira had floated in and out of consciousness. He was there, but he was not. And although the doctors talked in purposefully cheerful tones and described what they were doing in what should have been reassuring detail, Ruth had the horrible feeling that everyone was convinced Ira was going to die.

"Don't you dare," she said to him on the morning of the fourth day as she held his hand and watched the blips pulse across the screen. "After all these years, I finally got you to dance. I'm not letting you wiggle out of it now."

There was a slight movement beneath Ira's eyelids and his lips jerked slightly, but even she wouldn't call them more than reflexive movements. No matter how long she held his hand or how hard she prayed, he rarely even opened his eyes.

"Come on, Ma." Josh stood in the doorway, his eyes sliding over his father and then scurrying away. None of them could bear how quiet and still Ira was, how small he looked in the hospital bed. As if his life force had already departed and only the husk of him remained.

She had coffee in the coffee shop, with a daughter on either side of her, and sat in the waiting room with whichever family member or friend happened to be there at the time. But she refused to go home until Ira could go with her. When she was allowed back into his cubicle, she held his hand and watched the monitor, refusing to even consider a life without him. After all these years, surely God would not let that happen. Not now when they'd finally settled their differences, when Ira had promised to sell the business and had declared that he was ready for them to sail off into the sunset together. They had places to go and people to meet. Dance competitions to enter. Ruth decided then and there that she would not let Ira off the hook. She would not let him slip away. She explained this to him in no uncertain terms over the next days.

His eyes only fluttered open on occasion and he gave no indication at all that he could hear her. But Ruth talked to him anyway, pouring out her love and her hopes and when she couldn't help it, all of her fears. The fact that he didn't appear to be listening had never stopped her before; she certainly wasn't going to let it stop her now.

37

FORTY-EIGHT HOURS AFTER her baby was born Vivien brought him home to Melanie's. The drive from the hospital was fraught with silence; the fragile truce that had held during her labor and afterward left no room for conversation or confidences. Vivien sat beside the car seat in the back of Melanie's van and fixed her attention on the baby the entire drive, unsure what she'd do if he fussed or cried and unable to meet Melanie's accusing gaze in the rearview mirror. He slept the whole time, not even waking when Melanie showed her how to detach the carrier so that she could carry him inside.

Vivien was as tired as he was, and she was also afraid. In the hospital there'd been nurses who brought the baby to and from her and helped her try to nurse; she'd known that in an emergency there were people who'd know what to do. Now she was responsible for another human being in every possible way, and the thought of everything she didn't know how to do, from breastfeeding to changing a diaper, felt infinitely mysterious and frightening. The opportunities for screwing up seemed unlimited. And now when she needed it most, she didn't know if she could count on Melanie's help.

The smell of food greeted them when they stepped inside. They found Evangeline humming happily as she cooked in Melanie's kitchen. Her face broke into a smile when she saw them and she put out her arms immediately for the baby. "Isn't he precious?" she said, cuddling him to her chest and tucking his head under her chin. "He sure is a beautiful boy. And long. Between you and Stone, he's gonna be a baseketball player for sure!"

She kept the baby tucked up against her and still managed to fuss over Vivi at the same time. This was multitasking at its best.

"Is Caroline with you?" Melanie's voice was stiff as she and Vivien looked into the family room for their mother. Both of them let out sighs of relief when there was no sign of her.

"Nope," Evangeline answered. "But she did disinvite that Matt Glazer bozo from the party she's planning and I heard your daddy on the phone with the paper getting him fired. They sent me here to you for two weeks." She shrugged as she gently repositioned the baby in the crook of her arm. "That's about as close to an apology as your mama is likely to get."

Vivien and Melanie exchanged glances. One less thing to be dealt with for now.

"Now come on and have a bite and then I'll take Vivi and her little one upstairs so they can nurse. And then I'm putting them both to bed for a nice long nap."

Evangeline handed the baby to Melanie so that she could fill their plates with heaping mounds of meat loaf and mashed potatoes and set them out on the kitchen table. Fresh-cut flowers sat on the counter and a small dresser with a changing pad on its top had been set up in an empty corner of the family room. Vivien sank into the chair with a sigh of relief. Now she had two people who knew what they were doing, and at least one of them was excited about helping. She tried not to worry about when she would hear from Stone. Who hadn't called. Or texted. Or emailed.

Or whether her sister would ever stop looking at Vivi as if she had single-handedly ruined all of their lives.

⊙

AS OFTEN AS she could Melanie held her new nephew. His powdery baby smell and great big blue eyes soothed and comforted her; the weight of him in her arms carried her back to her own first days with Shelby and Trip and the wonderful sense of completion that she'd felt. As she helped rock him to sleep or took a turn walking with him when he fussed, Melanie's mind wandered back to those days when everything had seemed so perfect.

Like a mountain climber clinging to bare rock, she held the filter through which she'd always viewed her relationship with J.J. in place and used her anger at Vivi and her sense of betrayal to keep it there. If Vivi hadn't started her "investigation," all of them would still be blissfully ignorant. Her sister had so much to answer for.

In her arms, the baby looked up at her and blinked sleepily.

"You are so wonderful," Melanie whispered to him. 'But I really, really want to strangle your mother."

As if he understood completely, he blinked once more and went to sleep.

One day Melanie lost her grip and the filter slipped, allowing reality to poke through. At first this was much too painful, like opening the front door of a home you'd lived in all your life and discovering it was actually a completely unfamiliar vacation rental that belonged to someone else.

Her husband's gentle sweetness took on a new dimension now that she could no longer avoid the truth. She had considered J.J. her best friend, and when his sexual interest in her had waned more quickly than she'd expected, she'd attributed it to the stress of his political career, the extent of his travel, her focus on the kids' needs and then their activities. She'd had a long list of excuses for why their relationship was more comfortable than passionate. And she'd considered it a fair trade-off. She'd been willing to settle for J.J.'s affection and friendship, which had often seemed missing from other people's marriages.

But how real was that friendship based as it was on such a huge lie? And how could she not feel cheated now that she knew all of J.J.'s passion had been showered on Clay Alexander?

She wasn't the only one of her family struggling with the ramifications of their newfound knowledge. For a while Melanie was afraid that Shelby's sense of outrage and betrayal would demolish the strides she'd made, tank the SAT and ACT prep, turn her sullen and angry all over again. There was moodiness and the occasional outburst, but there was something about having things out in the open that prevented them from retreating into their corners and only coming out to fight.

Having Evangeline around didn't hurt, either. If she was aware of the tension between Melanie and Vivien, she made no comment. Between the food and attention Evangeline lavished on them and the baby they all found themselves fussing over, they began to examine the revelations about J.J. in a way that Melanie hoped would one day allow them to heal.

They were sitting in the family room one night stuffed to the gills with Evangeline's fried chicken and okra, which had been washed down with what felt like gallons of sweet tea, when Trip brought up his father's homosexuality.

"I feel like he was a whole other person I didn't know. Was everything just an act?" Trip asked. "How did he get to be . . . gay?" His tone added, Is it contagious?

Melanie's heart broke for what felt like the hundredth time as she contemplated her son. Her emotions were so raw she didn't trust herself to speak. She stole a look at Vivien, who sat silently in a corner of the sofa, holding the baby who'd become her entrée to the family circle. None of them had been able to forgive her for destroying their memories of J.J.; neither had they been able to completely write her off.

But Vivien, who had grown increasingly silent and tentative in their midst, didn't shy away from the subject. She looked Trip straight in the eye and said, "Some people believe that homosexuality is a choice. Other people call it a sin. But I've always thought it was just something that is and that most people know that about themselves fairly early." She looked down at the baby and then back at Trip. "For what it's worth, I don't think you just wake up one day as an adult and discover you like men instead of women. Or vice versa. It's something you'd know by now."

"But can't you make it go away if you really want to?" Trip asked.

Melanie held her breath as Vivien considered her answer. She saw the flash of pain that crossed Shelby's face, but her daughter didn't look away.

"I don't know, Trip, but I don't think so," Vivi said. "I'm sure lots of people would choose an easier path if they could." She looked over at Shelby and Melanie, who were listening intently. Evangeline, who was cleaning up the kitchen, had a quiet smile on her face.

"I think your dad tried to live a more conventional life because of how much he loved you and Shelby and your mom, but he couldn't. I know this is all hurtful and confusing, and I know you've got a ton to think about. But I just don't believe his love for you is one of the things you need to question."

Vivien spoke with a complete certainty that Melanie wished she could feel. Her sister seemed different, softer somehow. And while she wasn't exactly adept at the intricacies of new motherhood, she didn't complain or shirk her responsibilities to her son. The knot of anger in Melanie's stomach loosened slightly and she let out a bit of the breath she always seemed to be holding. But she couldn't seem to dislodge it completely; every time she thought of Scarlett Leigh, or the look on Clay's face at Angela's defunct wedding, the anger reared again, landing squarely in Viv's lap.

Ruth and Angela came to visit about a week after the wedding that didn't happen. They brought gifts and took turns holding the baby until Evangeline carried him up for his nap.

Vivi was glad to see them, but she couldn't help wondering about the secretive smile that pulled at Angela's lips or the way she kept fiddling with something in the pocket of the body-hugging cream silk outfit they'd given her at Fangie's going-away party.

The smile that had been splitting Ruth's face in two was absent. She looked even more tired than Vivien felt since Little Stone, as she'd begun to think of him, had come fully awake in the days following his delivery and turned her days and nights upside down.

Melanie had been to the hospital and kept in regular touch, but the news had not been overly reassuring. Ira had taken one step forward and then several back for a good part of the week.

They moved into the family room with cups of coffee and plates of Evangeline's apple cobbler.

"How's Ira?" Melanie asked once they'd consumed and exclaimed over their first few bites. "What do the doctors say?"

Ruth set down her plate and it was apparent that while she had survived the ordeal so far, her appetite had not. She'd shed too many pounds too quickly, and the shadows under her eyes were dark and deep. "They say all kinds of things, but they never really seem to be saying anything. At least nothing I want to hear."

Melanie reached out to squeeze Ruth's hand as they waited for her to go on.

"But this morning he was more aware, closer to himself than he has been since his surgery." Her eyes moistened. "And when I asked him what he was doing hanging around in bed so much, he told me he'd just been resting up so he'd be ready to take me dancing." A broken smile formed on her lips. "He said he hadn't spent all that time and money learning how to dance for nothing."

The tears slid unheeded down her cheeks. "The doctors say it'll be a long recovery and he'll have to make some significant changes, but he's going to be okay."

Dabbing at her eyes and cheeks with the corner of her napkin, Ruth turned to Angela. "Your turn," she said.

"I don't know what you could mean." Angela smiled.

"I expected you to be completely pitiful, but you look like the cat that swallowed the canary." As always Ruth stated what the others had been thinking. "And you finally stopped dressing like an Italian widow from the old country."

"Yeah," Vivi said. "Spill it. Or I'll sick Evangeline on you. Nobody holds out on her for long."

Without further prodding, Angela said, "I decided to get married after all."

There was a stunned silence as they all took this in.

"Was it to anyone we know?" Melanie asked carefully.

Ruth was nowhere near as gentle. "Unbelievable. You called the whole thing off, told everybody to leave, and then married someone else?"

"Not exactly," Angela hedged.

"Exactly how was it?" Vivi asked. "And you can start with what happened after we made our spectacular exit."

"Well," Angela said as the three of them leaned forward expectantly. "After you all left for your assorted hospitals, it was pretty grim. Worse than grim actually," Angela said. "But I had to call it off. Seeing what not telling the truth was doing to Vivi's life finally pushed me to tell James everything."

"Good grief!" Melanie said.

Vivien cringed.

"When you came into the dressing room, it just all hit me. I realized I was so caught up in marrying James, in having this fairy tale 'happily ever after' that you talked about that I was willing to keep the very thing that had defined me for most of my life a secret from him rather than trust him with the truth. Even though it was eating me up."

"Way to go, Vivien," Melanie said. "You were like a one-woman demolition crew that day."

"When I first rushed in and showed James that old picture of me, he looked so shocked and horrified that, well, I didn't really give him much of a chance to absorb anything. I was babbling about Fangie and how the person he was in love with didn't really exist. I mean, all the things I should have been sharing with him over the last year and a half just came pouring out of me in this horrible, uncontrollable rush." She dropped her gaze, remembering how he'd stuttered in surprise, unable to understand. "And then when he didn't immediately say, 'I don't care how much you weighed, or that you didn't trust my love for you enough to tell me this, I love you more than life itself,' I called the wedding off."

A wry smile pulled at her lips. "My parents thought I'd lost my mind. Brian said telling him was good, but that my timing sucked. Susan told me I was a moron."

Ruth opened her mouth as if to concur, but Melanie gave a gentle shake of her head.

"And then I kind of holed up in my house. I couldn't eat or sleep for about forty-eight hours. I started worrying that I'd made this horrible mistake. Because James is so fabulous." Her voice broke. "And I really do love him."

Vivi, Melanie, and Ruth didn't interrupt as Angela poured out her story. Pots and pans clanged in the kitchen, but Vivien knew Evangeline was most likely also hanging on every word.

"I just kept telling myself I'd done the right thing even if I did it at the wrong time, that I couldn't marry anyone I didn't trust with the real me. Me, Angela. The one who was fat for most of her life. Who managed to lose seventy-five pounds, but who worries every single day that she'll gain it back." Her voice dropped to a whisper. "Who looks in the mirror and still sees Fangie. No matter how many going-away parties you give her or how many layers of black clothing I try to bury her in." Angela took a sip of coffee that had to be long cold.

"I just couldn't believe that I deserved someone as incredible as James. I couldn't believe he would still love me if he knew all the crap I was carrying around inside." She smiled as if the story were over.

"And?" they chorused.

"And on the third day when I realized I *was* a moron and that I'd completely screwed everything up, James showed up on my doorstep. And he told me that he loved me. Completely. And that he wanted to spend the rest of his life with me."

She swallowed and they could hear the wonder in her voice. "He said he didn't care how much I weighed when I was twelve or what I'd weigh when I was fifty. That he didn't love me because of what I looked like, although he did want to know if I owned any clothing that wasn't black and too big." She smiled tentatively. "Then he said he'd fallen in love with me the first time he saw my work and that there was so much fabulous stuff inside me he didn't see how there could be room for Fangie or anyone else in there.

"Then he got down on one knee and asked me if I'd go to city hall with him." She pulled a wedding band that cradled her engagement ring from her pocket and slid the set onto her finger so they could see it. "And I did."

There were murmurs of surprise, a few high fives, and plenty of questions. Evangeline brought the coffee in and refilled their cups as they teased Angela about giving everyone the slip. Obviously eager to change the subject, she pulled a copy of the *Weekly Encounter* from her purse.

"I was a little surprised to see that Scarlett Leigh has resigned," she said. "And apologized."

Vivien popped the last crumbs of cobbler into her mouth and considered excusing herself.

"I'd like to see that," Melanie said. "Don't move, Vivi," she said when Vivi reached for her empty plate. "I think we should all hear what Scarlett had to say *this* time."

Angela handed the paper to Melanie, who aimed a raised eyebrow at Vivien and then began to read. *"For the last six months I've described what I've seen in the strange and alien world of suburbia. I've disparaged and poked fun at all kinds of things from doggie couture to secret lawn watering to parental helicoptering. I said that the parents I met needed to stop living vicariously through their children and begged them to 'get a life.'*

"But today I am writing not only to resign—there will be

no more harangues from suburbia, at least not from me—but to apologize. Because my research was faulty. I was too smug and too lazy. I failed to do my job. If I had bothered to look beneath the surface, I would have also written that it's not just competition and self-interest that fuel this involvement. In most cases, it's driven by love. And it is a love so strong that it leads those who feel it to put their families before themselves. It turns women not into doormats, as I sneered, but into the backbone that supports their families, their homes, and their communities. I am humbled by many of the women I've met here, amazed by how much of themselves they give to others. How willing they are to spend their time and energy creating an environment in which others may thrive.

"I was dead wrong. These suburbanites already have a life and it's far richer and fuller and more meaningful than one would ever guess at first glance."

Melanie stopped reading aloud as her eyes skimmed down to the last sentences. Vivien tensed as Melanie looked up at her and then lowered her gaze again. She read more slowly, her voice betraying her emotion. An answering lump formed in Vivien's throat.

"My younger sister, who is a single mother and an incredible individual, taught me a lot of these things. I hope to learn more now that I'm a mother myself. If I'm lucky, I'll end up just like her when I grow up." Melanie paused and swallowed. "It's signed, Vivien Armstrong Gray."

38

LATE THAT NIGHT, Vivi fed the baby in the old rocking chair that Evangeline and Melanie had hauled up to her room from the basement. She peered down into the baby's face, studying it in the dim light, as he suckled intently. Sometimes she thought she saw the beginnings of Stone's nose, the familiar plane of his cheek. And when he opened his almost navy eyes and stared up at her, she stared back struck with awe at what she and Stone had created.

Vivi had spent the first half of her pregnancy in panic and denial and the last half simply holding on with all her might. But in all that time she had never really stopped and thought about what holding her own child would feel like. She'd had no conception at all of how instant and all-consuming the connection between them would be.

It was little wonder that she'd never understood Melanie or her life; she couldn't believe that now when she was finally in a position to forge a stronger relationship, she'd so completely destroyed the opportunity. And left them both living in an odd sort of limbo.

Melanie came in then and took a seat on the empty bed.

"Did we wake you?" Vivi asked. It had taken her a few minutes to quiet the baby down enough to get him to her breast.

"No," Melanie said. "I just can't seem to get all the way to sleep. Every time I start to nod off I find myself thinking about J.J. and Clay. And how completely out of touch with my own life I must have been."

"Not out of touch. Maybe living a little bit in the land of denial," Vivi said. She looked down at the baby and back at her sister. "It can be a mighty cozy place. I just hope I didn't drive Stone completely away with my stupidity."

Melanie pulled her knees up to her chest and rested her chin on them. "I feel pretty stupid myself."

"I meant what I said to the kids," Vivien replied. "I really believe J.J. loved you all more than anything." Her glance strayed to the bottom drawer of her dresser where she'd hidden J.J.'s note to Melanie.

"Not enough to give up Clay. Or to admit to what he was." Melanie closed her eyes and opened them, drawing in a deep breath as if to steady herself.

But enough to kill himself over, Vivi thought but didn't say.

"I feel like I lost him all over again," Melanie said with such sadness that Vivi didn't think she could bear it. "And you . . . I just feel so betrayed. I don't know how I'm supposed to ever trust you again."

Vivien wondered if the words hurt as much to say as they did to hear. Her gaze strayed to the drawer again then back to her sister's face. Why had she kept J.J.'s note? Why hadn't she simply ripped it to shreds when Clay gave it to her? Had she been keeping her own options open even then? How could she have even considered it?

"You're going to have to let go of him at some point,

Mel. Too many things, and way too many people, don't turn out to be what we thought they were, or even what we hoped they'd be. Like J.J. Like Caroline." She looked into her sister's eyes and added, "Like me."

The baby stretched sleepily in her arms as she sought the right words. "But ultimately we have to find a way to move forward. To build something new as best we can. And I . . ." In that moment Vivien knew exactly what she needed to do; the only thing she could do. ". . . I promise I'll never breathe a word about J.J. Not ever, not for any reason. I've sworn off investigating family and friends. No matter what they do. So you can feel free to go out and commit murder, vote Democrat, become a secret superhero. Whatever.

"I know now that the truth, or what I thought of as the truth, just isn't as important as the people you love. Or the lives it can destroy."

"That sounds good," Melanie said. "And I hope to God you mean it. Because you're my sister, my flesh and blood. And I guess I don't have a choice but to let you prove it."

Vivi thought about the truth that she'd kept from Stone; the fact that she'd denied him the right to know that he had helped create the incredible new person that was bits and pieces of both of them. The baby's mouth grew slack as he fell back to sleep, but his tiny fist rested against her breast. She watched his face as his breathing grew slow and regular.

As if reading her thoughts, Melanie said, "Are you sure Stone got your message?"

Vivien slid gently to her feet and walked over to the bassinet to lay the baby down, then tucked a blanket in around him. "Yeah. I, um, spoke to Marty yesterday and he said he did get through to Stone. But he, um, wouldn't say more than that." She looked at Melanie as the love, the doubt, and the fear surged through her. Was it possible he was simply too angry to call her? That her actions had made him assume she didn't want him involved in his son's life?

"I've really screwed this thing up," she said and then as she did over even the littlest thing these days, she cried. Stupidly. Piteously. Copiously. Until Melanie came over and put her arms around her and shushed her like she did the baby.

"Don't worry, Vivi," she said. "It'll be all right. Stone will come."

When Vivi's tears finally stopped, Melanie gave her a final hug and turned to leave. In the doorway she paused and speared Vivi with a look. "I do love you, Vivi. And I want you—need you—in my life." She shook her head gently. "But you can't let me down again. Because I'm afraid that would be the end of us."

After Melanie left, Vivien went to the bottom drawer and removed J.J.'s suicide note from its hiding place. She read it one last time, tracing over the pain-filled letters with one finger. Then she carefully refolded it, tore it into tiny pieces too small to ever be put back together, and flushed them methodically down the toilet. She felt not an ounce of regret.

Vivien greatly regretted the way she'd excluded Stone from the birth of his child. As the days passed, she faced each one with a heaviness that she couldn't seem to shrug off. Now she sat in the kitchen with the baby in her arms while Shelby and Trip ate their breakfasts and prepared to leave for school. Evangeline had found the pots and pans Vivi had used for her niece's morning wakeups in the back of the linen closet and returned them to the kitchen. Then she'd simply plugged in an alarm clock on the nightstand next to Shelby's bed. And that was that.

Even better, Shelby had toned down her clothing

choices and remembered to stop when she reached the
high school parking lot and so had won back her right
to drive. Trip, too, seemed to be regaining his sense of
self. Not that he was a human chatterbox or anything,
but he did seem more interested in life in general and
was looking forward to his next outing with the Wesleys.
Even Melanie appeared to be coming out of her two years
of mourning; as awful as the revelations about Clay and
J.J. had been, they had also provided permission to finally
move on.

Vivi was sincerely happy that these things had happened for those she loved and if she'd had any confidence
that Stone would forgive her—or even show up and tell
her why he wouldn't—she might have felt better about
all that lay ahead. But her worry clung to her like a second
skin and she could tell that the baby felt it, too. He fussed
and fretted right along with her, and Vivi wondered if
he'd drunk it in with her milk. Or if the tension simply
zinged between their bodies like electrical impulses from
switch to bulb.

When she'd finally gotten him down for a nap, Vivi
checked email yet again, but the only one she'd received
was from John Harcourt, begging her to reconsider her
resignation. The response to her last column had been
overwhelmingly positive and the *Weekly Encounter* would
let her write the column however she saw fit and under
any name she might choose. He promised to more than
double her salary and asked her not to say no until they
had a chance to talk. She'd also gotten an offer from *Good
Housekeeping* to write features about new motherhood,
which Mel had said would serve her right.

She'd just finished the baby's after-nap feeding when
she heard a car drive up out front. Melanie was back from
teaching her morning class, so she didn't hurry downstairs. After fastening her nursing bra and smoothing

down her shirt, she put a clean diaper on the baby and snapped him into a fresh onesie just as the doorbell rang.

"Vivi," Melanie called upstairs. "I'm in the middle of something. Can you get the front door?"

Settling the baby up against her shoulder in hopes of a burp, she walked down the front stairs and pulled the door open one-handed. Stone stood on the doorstep, his blue eyes tired and angry, his face covered in stubble, his clothes a mass of wrinkles. He studied her face, then let his gaze travel down to the baby in her arms. "It's true," he said. "I thought maybe it was some sort of bizarre joke. But it's true." The anger didn't exactly disappear, but it was replaced with a look of awe and wonder as she turned the baby to cradle him in the crook of her arm so that father and son could see each other.

The baby blinked still-sleepy eyes. Stone stared back.

This made her want to cry again, though she didn't know whether it was from stress and panic or the gut wrench of emotion she felt as they solemnly regarded each other. "This is your daddy," she said to the infant in her arms. "Stone, this is your son." She paused and waited for his reaction. Despite all the times she'd seen him on TV, she'd forgotten how physically compelling he was. And how completely he'd always been able to read her. "His name is Pebbles," she admitted. "I was sort of waiting for you to help me come up with a better one."

"Is that right?" His voice was deep and quiet, but the rational tone didn't fool her. Under his obvious jet lag and the vise he'd apparently clamped down on his emotions, he was angrier than she'd ever seen him. And rightfully so.

"Do you want to come in?" she asked, stepping back so that he could enter.

"Of course I want to come in, Vivi. It took three days for your text to reach me. Another three to get back to

Kabul and clear things up and hand things over so that I could leave. And another two after that to get here. And the only thing I could think the whole time was, How in the hell did this happen? How could she go through an entire pregnancy without telling me?"

"Yes," she said, falling back a step. "That would be a good question."

And then she felt Melanie behind her. "Vivi, what's . . . Oh." She stepped around Vivien to open the door wider. "Hi," she said as she ushered Stone in. "Congratulations on the birth of your son." She said this as if it were the most normal thing in the world. "Look at the way he's staring at you. Don't you just have the weirdest sense he knows exactly who you are?"

They moved into the kitchen, and Vivi sat on a barstool, the baby still in her arms. Stone took the stool next to them while Melanie took out a pitcher of tea, keeping up a steady stream of chatter. The baby was still watching Stone, as was Vivi, who was practically vibrating with the intensity of her conflicting emotions. She wanted to throw her arms around him and bury her face in his neck almost as much as she wanted to run upstairs and hide from the hurt and anger radiating from him. She only hoped he intended to forgive her. She could take anything he had to say as long as it ended that way.

"I would have been here sooner," Stone said, his tone wry. "If I'd had any idea that I had a child on the way." He turned to Melanie. "Don't you think I was entitled to that piece of information? Your sister and I have been together for three years. I've told her that I love her more times than I can count. Can you think of a good reason why she wouldn't tell me that she was pregnant until the actual moment that she was about to give birth?"

"Yes, well, er . . ." It was clear that Melanie was not any more prepared to defend the indefensible than Vivi.

Which was kind of amazing when she considered how long she'd had to come up with . . . something.

He turned to Vivien and once again his eyes traveled down to his son, who stared right back at him. Stone's gaze softened and he stretched out a long finger to trace the curve of the baby's cheek.

Vivien squirmed in her seat as the two communed. The baby yawned and stretched and Stone smiled down at him before turning a much-less-smitten look on her. "Go on, Viv. I've been looking forward to hearing this."

He and the baby yawned at the same time, and Vivien decided to go with the abbreviated version. "I admit I handled this badly."

A sandy eyebrow went up.

"Make that incredibly badly."

He nodded. The baby yawned.

"At first I was just too freaked out to absorb the whole thing. And then I thought I should wait until I hit the three-month mark and knew for sure. And then I didn't want to make you feel responsible or like you had to marry me or settle down or anything when you might not want to."

The other eyebrow joined the first.

"Well, it's not like we didn't always joke about you being a rolling stone that gathered no moss."

"That was a joke, Vivi," he said. "Not a battle cry."

"Well, I know how hard you've worked to get where you are. And senior international correspondents with a specialty in terrorism don't stay home a lot. I didn't want you to feel trapped."

He sighed and ran a hand through his hair, which was already sticking up in more directions than it was designed to. The exhaustion that he'd held off until now began to settle over him.

"And then when things were such a mess there, I didn't

want to distract you," Vivi concluded. "There just never seemed like a good time. So, I just . . . didn't."

Stone sighed and it turned into a yawn, but he didn't hedge his words. "I'm incredibly offended that you assumed so many things about me and that none of them were particularly flattering," he said. "I wouldn't have felt trapped by the fact that the woman I loved was having my baby. Nor would I have been overwhelmed by or unhappy about marrying you and sharing the responsibility of raising our son. And being a correspondent? Frankly, I'm beat. And I think it might be time to explore some other opportunities."

He yawned again and reached out his hands. It took her a minute to realize that he wanted her to hand over the baby. He grasped the baby at the waist and behind the neck and pulled him up against his broad chest with a surprising lack of awkwardness. Father and son yawned identical yawns as he cuddled the baby close.

"I'm way too jet-lagged to argue properly with you right now," Stone said. "If you point me to your room, the little pebble and I will go take a quick nap." He put a hand up to cradle the back of the baby's head, then stood as Melanie directed him to the first room at the top of the stairs. "I'm sure I'll have the strength I need to set you straight once I get a little shut-eye."

With that he marched up the stairs, carrying the already-sleeping baby with him.

"I don't think he's going to disappear on you," Melanie said to Vivi as they watched Stone climb the stairs with his tiny load. "He's going to give you the shit you so richly deserve, but he doesn't look like he's planning to bow out of either of your lives."

"You've got that right," Stone called as he stopped to peer down at them from the landing. He looked like someone who'd been traveling days to get here, and the exhaustion in his eyes was clear. But there was love in them, too, and not a single sign of doubt. Vivi's heart constricted almost painfully in her chest as she took in the sight of him cradling their child so gently.

Before Vivien or Melanie could think of an answer, man and baby retreated from view. A moment later the bedroom door clicked shut, leaving the sisters standing together smiling at each other in the silence.

READERS GUIDE TO
Magnolia Wednesdays

DISCUSSION QUESTIONS

1. How did you feel about Vivien at the beginning of the story? Did your opinion of her change as the story progressed? Discuss her motivations and mistakes.

2. Discuss the relationship between sisters Vivien and Melanie. In what ways did they help and support each other, and how did their past get in the way?

3. Why do you think it was so important for Vivien to investigate J.J.'s death? Should she have let it go, or was she justified?

4. On multiple occasions, Vivien wrestles with whether to expose her niece Shelby's dating life to Melanie. Do you think that Vivien handles these situations

wisely? Discuss the struggle that comes along with
wanting to be loyal to two people you care about on
opposite sides of an issue.

5. On pages 236–237, Melanie, Vivien, Ruth, and Angela
discuss how secrets should be kept out of relationships,
yet secrets seem to be at the center of each of their lives.
Discuss the secrets that exist in each of their relationships. Do you believe that some secrets are better left
untold?

6. Do you think that Vivien's reasons for keeping her
pregnancy hidden from Stone are valid? Was Stone's
reaction surprising? How would the story have been
different if she had told Stone the truth right away?

7. Do you agree with Angela's belief that Vivien's columns tell important truths that no one is willing to
face on his or her own? Discuss your own reaction
to *Postcards from Suburbia* and what Vivien ultimately
learned by observing her family and new neighbors.

8. Vivien and Melanie were brought up to fear, above
everything else, bringing shame upon their family
name. Do you believe this upbringing has anything
to do with the sisters' inability to recognize certain
problems in their own lives? Discuss instances where
Vivien and Melanie are able to point out each other's
flaws but can't recognize similar flaws in themselves.

9. What will you take away from this novel regarding
both the positive and negative power of secrets, family, and/or friendships?

10. Discuss the ending of the novel and the closure that each character finds. Do you think Ruth, Angela, Melanie, and Vivien's stories would have had different outcomes if they had not met each other?

Now Available from Jove Books

TEN BEACH ROAD

by Wendy Wax

Madeline, Avery, and Nikki are strangers to each other, but they have one thing in common. They each wake up one morning to discover that their life savings have vanished, along with their trusted financial manager . . . leaving them with nothing but co-ownership of a ramshackle beachfront house.

Madeline Singer is a homemaker coping with emptynest syndrome and an unemployed husband. Avery Lawford is an architect—or was, until she somehow became the sidekick on her ex-husband's TV show. And professional matchmaker Nikki Grant is trying to recover from her biggest mistake . . .

No one is going to save them but themselves. Determined to fight back, they throw their lots in together and take on the challenge of restoring the historic beach house to its former glory. But just as they begin to reinvent themselves and discover the power of friendship, their secrets threaten to tear down their trust, and destroy their lives a second time . . .

New from Wendy Wax

꒰ *Ocean Beach* ꒱

Renovating one dilapidated beach house got Madeline, Avery, Nicole, and Kyra a television show. Renovating their second one may make them bona fide stars—or reality has-beens. A once-grand historic house on Miami's South Beach has seen better days, which makes it the perfect project for their new show, *Do Over*. But restoring the house to its former glory poses new challenges—both professional and personal.

With a decades-old mystery—and the hurricane season—looming, the four friends are left to wonder just how they'll weather life's storms . . .

facebook.com/AuthorWendyWax
authorwendywax.com
penguin.com

Life doesn't stop. Not even for writer's block.

THE
ACCIDENTAL
BESTSELLER

by

Wendy Wax

Mallory, Tanya, Faye, and Kendall are best friends—and veterans of the cutthroat world of New York book publishing. So when Kendall gets writer's block, they all collaborate on her new novel, using their own lives as fodder. But soon they'll realize what a bestseller the truth makes.

∽◦◦

"A definite 'must' for any beach bag this summer."
—*Sacramento Book Review*

"A warm, triumphant tale of female friendship and the lessons learned when life doesn't turn out as planned."
—*Library Journal*

"Here's a funny novel that fellow writers will especially love."
—*Blogcritics*

facebook.com/AuthorWendyWax
authorwendywax.com
penguin.com

M1020T1211